**Mills & Boon is proud to present
three super novels in one collection
by an author we know you love
and have made an
international bestseller**

Enjoy these three books by rising star

Jennie
LUCAS

For One Night Only

Contains

Reckless Night in Rio
To Love, Honour and Betray
A Night of Living Dangerously

May 2014

June 2014

July 2014

August 2014

Jennie
LUCAS
For One Night Only

Published in Great Britain 2014
by Mills & Boon, an imprint of Harlequin (UK) Limited,
Eton House, 18-24 Paradise Road, Richmond, Surrey, TW9 1SR

FOR ONE NIGHT ONLY © 2014 Harlequin Books S.A.

Reckless Night in Rio © 2011 Jennie Lucas
To Love, Honour and Betray © 2012 Jennie Lucas
A Night of Living Dangerously © 2012 Jennie Lucas

ISBN: 978 0 263 24656 8

024-0514

Harlequin (UK) Limited's policy is to use papers that are natural, renewable and recyclable products and made from wood grown in sustainable forests. The logging and manufacturing processes conform to the legal environmental regulations of the country of origin.

Printed and bound in Spain
by

Jennie Lucas grew up dreaming about faraway lands. At fifteen, hungry for experience beyond the borders of her small Idaho city, she went to a Connecticut boarding school on a scholarship. She took her first solo trip to Europe at sixteen, then put off college and travelled around the US, supporting herself with jobs as diverse as gas station cashier and newspaper advertising assistant.

At twenty-two she met the man who would be her husband. After their marriage she graduated from Kent State with a degree in English. Seven years after she started writing she got the magical call from London that turned her into a published author.

Since then life has been hectic, with a new writing career, a sexy husband and two small children, but she's having a wonderful (albeit sleepless) time. She loves immersing herself in dramatic, glamorous, passionate stories. Maybe she can't physically travel to Morocco or Spain right now, but for a few hours a day, while her children are sleeping, she can be there in her books.

Jennie loves to hear from her readers. You can visit her website at www.jennielucas.com, or drop her a note at jennie@jennielucas.com.

Reckless Night in Rio

JENNIE LUCAS

To Pete

CHAPTER ONE

"WHO is the father of your baby, Laura?"

Holding her six-month-old baby on her hip, Laura Parker had been smiling with pride and pleasure across her family's two-hundred-year-old farmhouse, lit with swaying lights and filled with neighbors and friends for her sister's evening wedding reception. Now, pushing up her black-rimmed glasses, Laura faced her younger sister with a sinking feeling in her heart.

Who is the father of your baby?

People rarely asked that question anymore, since Laura always refused to answer. She'd started to hope the scandal might be over.

"Will you ever tell?" Becky's face was unhappy beneath her veil. At nineteen, her sister was an idealistic new bride with romantic dreams of right and wrong. "Robby deserves a father."

Trying to control the anguish in her heart, Laura kissed her son's dark hair, so soft, and smelling of baby shampoo. She said in a low voice, "We've talked about this."

"Who is he?" her sister cried. "Are you ashamed of him? Why won't you tell?"

"Becky!" Laura glanced uneasily at the reception

guests around them. "I told you… I don't…" She took a deep breath. "I don't know who he is."

Her sister stared at her tearfully. "You're lying. There's no way you'd sleep around like that. You're the one who convinced me to wait for true love!"

The people closest to them had stopped pretending to talk, and were now openly eavesdropping. Family and friends were packed into the farmhouse's warren of rooms, walking across creaking floors, having conversations beneath the low ceilings. Neighbors sat on folding chairs along the walls, holding paper plates of food in their laps. And probably listening. Laura held her baby closer. "Becky, please," she whispered.

"He deserted you. And it's not fair!"

"Becky," their mother said suddenly from behind them, "I don't think you've met your great-aunt Gertrude. She's traveled all the way from England. Won't you come and greet her?" Smiling, Ruth Parker reached for her grandson in Laura's arms. "She'll want to meet Robby, too."

"Thank you," Laura whispered soundlessly to her mother. Ruth answered with a loving smile and a wink, then drew her younger daughter and baby grandson away. Laura watched them go, love choking her. Ruth was wearing her nicest Sunday dress and bright coral lipstick, but her hair had grown gray and her body slightly stooped. The past year had left even her strong mother more frail.

The lump in Laura's throat felt razor-sharp as she stood alone in the crowded room. She'd thought she'd put the scandal of her pregnancy behind her, after she'd returned to her northern New Hampshire village pregnant, with no job and no answers. But would her family ever get over it? Would she?

Three weeks after she'd left Rio de Janeiro, she'd been shocked to discover she was pregnant. Her burly, overprotective father had demanded to know the name of the man. Laura had been afraid he might go after Gabriel Santos with an ultimatum—or worse, a shotgun. So she'd lied and said she had no idea who her baby's father might be. She'd described her time in Rio as one gigantic shagfest, when the truth was that she'd had only one lover her whole life. And even that had been for a single night.

One precious night…

I need you, Laura. She still felt the violence of her boss's embrace as he'd pushed her back against his desk, sweeping aside paperwork and crashing the computer to the floor. After more than a year, she could still feel the heat of his body against hers, the feel of his lips against her neck, his hot brutal kisses against her skin. The memory of the way Gabriel Santos had ruthlessly taken her virginity still invaded her dreams every night.

And the memory of the aftermath still left a shotgun blast in her heart. The morning after he'd seduced her, she'd tearfully told him she felt she had no choice but to quit her job. He'd just shrugged. "Good luck," he said. "I hope you find what you're looking for."

That was all he gave her, after five years of her love and devoted service.

She'd loved her playboy boss, stupidly and without hope. It had been fifteen months since she'd last seen Gabriel's face, but she could not forget it, no matter how hard she tried. How could she, when every day she saw those same dark eyes in her child's face?

Her tears in the little white clapboard church an hour ago hadn't just been from happiness for Becky. Laura had once loved a man with all her heart, but he hadn't loved her back. And as the cold February wind whipped through their northern valley, there were still times she imagined she could hear his dark, deep voice speaking to her, only to her.

"Laura."

Like now. The memory of his low, accented voice seemed so real. The sound ripped through her body, through her heart, as if he were right beside her, whispering against her skin.

"Laura."

His voice felt really close that time.

Really close.

Laura's hands shook as she set down her glass of cheap champagne. Lack of sleep and a surfeit of dreams were causing her to hallucinate. Had to be. It couldn't be...

With a deep breath, she turned.

Gabriel Santos stood before her. In the middle of her family's crowded living room, he towered over other men in every way, even more darkly handsome than she remembered. But it wasn't just his chiseled jawline or his expensive Italian suit that made him stand out. It wasn't just his height or the strength of his broad shoulders.

It was the ruthless intensity of his black eyes. A tremble went through her.

"Gabriel...?" she whispered.

His sensual lips curved. "Hello, Laura."

She swallowed, pressing her nails into her palms, willing herself to wake up from this nightmare—

from this incredible dream. "You can't be here," she whispered. "As in *here*."

"And yet I am," he said. "Laura."

She shivered at the sound of her name on his lips. It didn't seem right that he could be here, in her family's living room, surrounded by friends and family eating potluck.

At thirty-eight, Gabriel Santos owned a vast international conglomerate that bought and shipped steel and timber across the world. His life was filled with one passionate, single-minded pursuit after another. Business. Adrenaline-tinged sports. Beautiful women. Laura's lips turned downward. Beautiful women most of all.

So what was he doing here? What could he possibly have come for unless…unless…

Out of the corner of her eye, she saw her mother disappearing down the hall with her baby.

Trying to stop her hands from shaking, Laura folded her arms around the waist of her hand-sewn bridesmaid's dress. So Gabriel had come to Greenhill Farm. It didn't exactly require a crack team unit to find her here. Parkers had lived here for two hundred years. It didn't mean he knew about Robby. It didn't. He couldn't.

Could he?

Gabriel lifted a dark eyebrow. "Are you glad to see me?"

"Of course I'm not glad." She bit out the words. "If you recall, I'm no longer your secretary. So if you've come five thousand miles because you need me to go back to Rio and sew a button or make your coffee—"

"No." His eyes glittered at her. "That's not why I've come." He slowly looked around the house, which was decorated with strings of pink lights and red paper hearts along the walls, and candles above the fire in the old stone fireplace. "What's going on here?"

"A wedding reception."

He blinked, then came closer to her, the wooden boards creaking beneath his feet. Laura's eyes widened as the shadows of firelight shifted across the hard angles of his face. He was so handsome, she thought in bewildered wonder. She'd forgotten how handsome. Her dreams hadn't done him justice. She could see why so many women chased after him all over the world…and why he was the despair of them all.

"And just who—" his black eyes narrowed into a glower "—is the bride?"

She was bewildered at the sudden harshness of his tone. "My little sister. Becky."

"Ah." His shoulders relaxed imperceptibly. Then he frowned. "Becky? She's not much more than a child."

"Tell me about it." Laura looked down at her bridesmaid's dress. In the gleam of the fire and pink lights swaying above, the pale pink gown appeared almost white. She looked up suddenly. "Did you think it was me?"

Their eyes locked in the crowded room.

"*É claro*," Gabriel said quietly. "Of course I thought it was you."

The idea of her having the time or the interest to date, let alone marry, some other man made her choke back a laugh. She smoothed her bridesmaid's gown with trembling hands. "No."

"So there is no one important in your life right now?" he asked, in a casual tone belied by way he held his body in absolute stillness.

There *was* someone important in her life. She just had

to get Gabriel out of here before he saw Robby. "You have no right to ask."

"*Sim*." He paused. "But you're not wearing a ring."

"Fine." Laura's voice was painfully quiet as she looked down at her feet. "I'm not married."

She didn't have to ask if Gabriel was married. She already knew the answer. How many times had he told her he would never, ever take a wife?

I'm not made for love, querida. *I'll never have a little housewife cooking my dinner in a snug house every night as I read books to our children.*

Gabriel moved closer, almost touching her. She was dimly aware of people whispering around them, wondering who this handsome, well-dressed stranger might be. She knew she should tell him to leave, but she was caught in the power of his body so close to hers. Her gaze fell on his thick wrists beneath sharply tailored shirt cuffs, and she trembled. She remembered the feel of that strong body on hers, the stroke of his fingertips....

"Laura."

Against her will, her eyes lifted, tracing up his muscular body, past his broad shoulders and wide neck to his brutally handsome face. In the flickering shadows, she saw the dark scruff along his jaw, the scar across his temple from a childhood car accident. She saw the man she'd wanted forever and had never stopped wanting.

His eyes burned into her, and memories poured through her. She felt vulnerable, almost powerless beneath the dark fire of his glance.

"It's good to see you again," he said in a low voice. He smiled, and the masculine beauty of his face took her breath away. Their fifteen months apart had made him only more handsome. While she…

She hadn't seen the inside of a beauty salon for a year. Her hair hadn't been cut for ages, and her only makeup was lipstick in an unflattering pink shade that she'd worn at Becky's insistence. Her dowdy dishwater-blonde hair had been hurriedly pulled back in a French knot before the ceremony, but now fell about her shoulders in messy tendrils, pulled out by Robby's chubby fists.

Even as a girl Laura had always tended to put herself last, but since she became the single mother of a baby, she wasn't even on the list. Taking a shower and shoving her hair back into a ponytail was all she could manage most days. And she still hadn't managed to take off all the extra weight from her pregnancy. Nervously, she pushed up her black-framed glasses. "Why are you staring at me?"

"You're even more beautiful than I remembered."

Her cheeks went hot beneath his gaze. "Now I know you're lying."

"It's true." His dark eyes seared her. He wasn't looking at her as if he thought she were plain. In fact, he was looking down at her as if he…

As if he…

He turned away, and she exhaled.

"So this is Becky's wedding reception?" He glanced around the room with something like disapproval on his face.

Laura thought their home looked nice, even romantic for a country-style winter wedding. They'd scrubbed it scrupulously clean, tidied away all the usual clutter, and decorated their hearts out. But as she followed his gaze, she suddenly saw how shabby it all was.

Laura had been proud of how much she'd been able to accomplish for her sister on almost no budget. Flowers had been too expensive because of Valentine's Day, so Laura had gone to the nearest craft store and cut out large hearts of red tissue paper, festooning them on their walls with red and pink balloons and streamers. She'd decorated the house in the middle of the night, as she'd waited for the cake to cool. For the reception dinner, their mother had made her famous roast chickens and their friends and neighbors had brought casseroles and salads for a buffet-style potluck. Laura had made her sister's wedding cake herself, using instructions from an old 1930s family cookbook.

She'd been tired but so happy when she'd fallen into bed at dawn. But now, beneath Gabriel's eyes, the decorations no longer seemed beautiful. She saw how flimsy it all was, how shabby a send-off for her second-youngest sister. Becky had seemed delighted when she saw the decorations and slightly tilted wedding cake that morning. But what else could she have done, knowing how hard her family had tried to give her a nice wedding when there was never a dime to spare?

As if he could read her mind, Gabriel looked at her. "Do you need money, Laura?"

Laura's cheeks went hot. "No," she lied. "We're fine."

He looked around the room again, at the paper plates with the potluck dinner, at her homemade gown, clearly not believing her. He set his jaw. "I'm just surprised your father couldn't do better for Becky. Even if money is tight."

Laura folded her arms, feeling ice in her heart. "He

couldn't," she whispered. "My father died four months ago."

She heard Gabriel's intake of breath. "What?"

"He had a heart attack during harvest. We didn't find him on his tractor until later. When he didn't come home for dinner."

"Oh, Laura." Gabriel took her hand in his own. "I'm sorry."

She felt his sympathy, felt his concern. And she felt the rough warmth of his palm against her own—the touch she'd craved for the past year and all the five years before. Her fingers curled over his as longing blistered her soul.

With an intake of breath she ripped her hand away.

"Thank you," she said, blinking back tears. She'd thought she was done grieving for her father, but she'd spent most of the day with a lump in her throat, watching her uncle walk Becky down the aisle, seeing her mother alone in the pew with tears streaking her powdered face. Laura's father should have been here. "It's been a long winter. Everything fell apart without him. We're just a small farm and always run so lean, one year to the next. With my dad gone, the bank tried to refuse to extend the loan or give us anything more for spring planting."

Gabriel's eyes narrowed. "What?"

She lifted her chin. "We're fine now." Although they were just surviving on fumes, trying to hold on another week until they'd get the next loan. Then they'd pray next year would be better. She folded her arms. "Becky's husband, Tom, will live at the house and farm the land now. Mom will be able to stay in her home and be well looked after."

"And you?" Gabriel asked quietly.

Laura pressed her lips together. Starting tonight, she and Robby were moving into her mother's bedroom. The three-bedroom farmhouse was now full, since Laura and her baby could no longer share a bedroom with Becky, and her other sisters, Hattie and Margaret, shared the other. Ruth had loyally said she'd be delighted to share her large master bedroom with her grandson, but Ruth was a very light sleeper. It was not an ideal situation.

Laura needed a job, an apartment of her own. She was the oldest daughter—twenty-seven years old. She should be helping her family, not the other way around. She'd been looking for a job for months, but there were none to be had. Not even at a fraction of the salary she'd earned when she worked for Gabriel.

But there was no way she was going to tell him that. "You still haven't explained what you're doing here. You obviously didn't know about the wedding. Do you have some kind of business deal? Is it the old Talfax mine that's for sale?"

He shook his head. "I'm still trying to close the Açoazul deal in Brazil." His jaw tightened. "I came because I had no choice."

Over the noisy conversation nearby, Laura heard a guitar and flute play the opening notes of an old English folk song from somewhere in the house. She heard a baby's bright laugh over the music and a chilling fear whipped through her. "What do you mean?"

His dark eyes narrowed. "Can't you guess?"

Laura sucked in her breath. All her worst nightmares were about to come true.

Gabriel had come for her baby.

After all the times he'd said he never wanted a child, after everything he'd done to make sure he'd never be burdened with one, somehow he'd found out Laura's deepest secret and he'd come to take Robby. And he wouldn't even take their son out of love, oh no. He'd do it out of duty. Cold, resentful duty.

"I don't want you here, Gabriel," Laura whispered, trembling. "I want you to leave."

He set his jaw grimly. "I can't."

Ice water flooded her veins as she stood near the fireplace in the warm parlor. "What brought you? Was it some rumor—or…" She licked her lips and suddenly could no longer bear the strain. "For God's sake. Stop toying with me and tell me what you want!"

His dark eyes looked down at her, searing straight through her soul.

"You, Laura," he said in a low voice. "I came for you."

CHAPTER TWO

I CAME for you.

Stricken, Laura stared up at him with her lips parted.

Gabriel's dark eyes were hot and deep with need. Exactly as he'd looked at her the night he'd taken her virginity. The night she'd conceived their child.

I came for you.

How many times had she dreamed of Gabriel finding her and speaking those words?

She'd missed him constantly over the last fifteen months, as she'd given birth to their baby alone, woken up in the night alone and raised their child without a father. She'd yearned for his strong, protective arms constantly. Especially during the bad times, such as the moment she'd told her family she was pregnant. Or the day of her father's funeral, when her mother and three younger sisters had clung to her, sobbing, expecting her to be the strong one. Or the endless frustrating weeks when Laura had gone to the bank with her baby in tow, day after day, to convince them to extend the loan that would let their farm continue to operate.

But there had been happy times as well, and then she'd missed Gabriel even more. Such as the day halfway into her pregnancy, when she'd been washing dishes in the tiny kitchen and she'd suddenly clutched her curved belly and laughed aloud in wonder as she felt—this time for sure—their baby's first kick inside her. Or the sunny, bright August day when Robby had been born, when she'd held his tiny body against her chest and he'd blinked up at her, yawning sleepily, with dark eyes exactly like his father's.

For over a year, Laura had missed Gabriel like water or sun or air. She'd craved him day and night. She'd missed the sound of his laugh. Their friendship and camaraderie.

And now, he'd finally come for her?

"You came for me?" she whispered. Was it possible he'd thought of her even a fraction of the times her heart had yearned for him? "What do you mean?"

"Just what I said," Gabriel said quietly. "I need you."

She swallowed. "Why?"

His dark eyes glittered in the flickering firelight. "Every other woman has been a pale shadow of you in every way."

If her heart had been fluttering before, now it was frantically rattling against her ribs. Had she been wrong to leave him, fifteen months ago? Had she been wrong to keep Robby a secret? What if Gabriel's feelings had changed, and all this time he'd cared for her? What if—

He leaned forward as his lips curved into a smile. "I need you to come work for me."

Laura's heart stopped, then resumed a slow, sickly beat.

Of course. *Of course* that was all he would want. He'd

likely forgotten their one-night affair long ago, while she would remember it forever—in her passionate dreams, in the eyes of their son. Laura stared up at Gabriel's dark, brutally handsome face. She saw the tension of his jawline, the taut muscles of his folded arms beneath his suit jacket.

"You must want it badly," she said slowly.

He gave her a tight smile. "I do."

Out of the corner of her eye, she saw her mother coming back down the hall, holding Robby in one arm and a slice of wedding cake in her other hand. Laura sucked in her breath.

Robby. How could she have allowed herself to forget, even for an instant, that her son was counting on her to keep him safe?

Grabbing Gabriel's hand, she pulled him out of the room, dragging him out of the house, away from prying eyes and into the freezing February air.

Outside in the wintry night, cars and trucks were wedged everywhere along the gravel driveway between their old house and the barn, strewn along the country road in front of their farm. Across the old stone walls that lined the road, white rolling hills stretched out into the great north woods, disappearing now into the falling purple twilight.

Behind them, next to the old barn, she could see the frozen water of their pond, gleaming like a silver mirror under the lowering gray clouds. Her father had taught all his daughters to swim there during the summers of their childhood, and even though Laura was now grown, whenever she felt upset, she would go for a swim in the pond. Swimming made her think of her father's protective arms. It always made her feel better.

She wished she could swim in the pond now.

Laura looked down at her breath in the chilly air and saw the white smoke of Gabriel's mingle with hers. She realized she was still holding his hand and looked down at his large fingers enfolding her own. The warmth of them suddenly burned her skin, sizzling nerve endings the length of her body.

She dropped his hand. Folding her arms, she glared up at him. "I'm sorry you've come all this way for nothing. I'm not going to work for you."

"You don't even want to hear about the job first? For instance—" he paused "—how much it pays?"

Laura bit her lip, thinking of her bank account, which held exactly thirteen dollars—barely enough for a week's supply of diapers, let alone groceries. But they'd get by. And she couldn't risk Robby's custody—not for something so unimportant as money! She lifted her chin fiercely. "No amount of money could tempt me."

His lips quirked. "I know I wasn't always the easiest man to live with—"

"Easy?" she interjected. "You were a nightmare."

His eyes crinkled in a smile. "Now that's the diplomatic Miss Parker I remember."

She glared at him. "Find another secretary."

"I'm not asking you to be my secretary."

"You said…"

He looked down at her. His voice was dark and deep, his eyes burning though her with intensity. "I want you to spend a night with me in Rio. As my mistress."

His mistress? Laura's mouth fell open.

Gabriel continued to stare down at her with his inscrutable dark eyes, his hands in his pockets. She licked her lips.

"I'm…I'm not for sale," she whispered. "You think just because you are rich and handsome you can have whatever you want, that you can pay me to fall into your bed—and go away the next morning with a check?"

"A charming idea." A humorless smile traced his sensual mouth. "But I don't wish to pay you for sex."

"Oh." Her cheeks went hot. "Then what?"

"I want you—" he moved closer, his hard-edged face impossibly handsome "—to pretend to love me."

She swallowed. Then she tilted her head, blinking up at him in the fading light. "But thousands of girls could do that," she said. "Why come all the way up here, when you could have twenty girls at your penthouse in Rio in four minutes? Are you insane?"

He raked his dark hair back with his hand.

"Yes," he said heavily. "I am going slowly insane. Every moment my father's company is in the hands of another man, every moment I know I lost my family's legacy through my own stupidity, I feel I am losing my mind. I've endured it for almost twenty years. And I'm close now, so close to getting it back."

She should have known it had something to do with regaining Açoazul. "But how can I possibly help you?"

He looked down at her, his jaw clenched. "Play the part of my devoted mistress for twenty-four hours. Until I close the deal."

"How on earth would that help you close the deal?" she asked, bewildered.

He set his jaw. "I've hit a snag in the negotiations. A six-foot-tall, bikini-wearing snag."

"What?"

Gabriel ground his teeth. "Felipe Oliveira found out I used to date his fiancée."

"You did?" Laura said in surprise, then gave a bitter laugh. "Of course you did."

"Now he doesn't want me within a thousand miles of Rio. He thinks if he doesn't sell me the company after all, I'll go back to New York." Gabriel looked at her. "I need to make him understand I'm not interested in his woman."

"That doesn't explain why you'd need *me*. Thousands of women would be happy to pretend to be in love with you. For free." She took a deep breath, clenching her hands at her sides. "Some of them wouldn't even have to pretend!"

He set his jaw. "They won't work."

She exhaled with a flare of her nostrils. "Why?"

"Oliveira's fiancée…is Adriana da Costa."

"Adriana da…" Laura's voice trailed off, her eyes wide.

Adriana da Costa.

Laura could still see those cold, reptilian eyes, that skinny, lanky body. Gabriel had dated the Brazilian supermodel briefly in New York several years ago, while Laura was his live-in personal assistant. She could still hear Adriana's pouting voice. *Why do you keep calling here? Stop calling.*

Find the whiskey, you stupid cow. Gabriel always gets thirsty after sex.

Laura cleared her throat. "Adriana da Costa, the bikini model."

"Yes."

"The one *Celebrity Star* magazine just called the sexiest woman alive."

"She's a selfish narcissist," he said sharply. "And for the short time we were together, she was always insecure. Only one woman has ever made her feel so threatened. You."

"Me?" Laura gasped. "You're out of your mind! She would never feel threatened by me!"

Gabriel's dark eyes gleamed. "She complained to me constantly. Why did I always take your calls, but not hers? Why did I always have time for you, day or night? Why would I leave her bed at 2:00 A.M. in order to go home to you? And most of all, why did I allow you to live in my apartment, only you and no one else?"

Laura's mouth fell open.

"She never understood our relationship," Gabriel said. "How we could be so close without being lovers. Which we weren't." He paused. "Not until...Rio."

The huskiness of his deep voice whipped through Laura, causing a sizzle to spread down her body.

"Adriana has made it clear she wants me back," he said in a low voice. "She'd leave Felipe Oliveira in an instant for me, and he knows it. Only one thing will convince them both I am not interested in her."

Laura stared at him.

"Me?" she whispered.

He looked right at her. "You are the only woman that Adriana would believe I could love."

A roar of shared memories left unspoken between them washed over Laura like a wave, and her heart twisted in her chest. She'd been only twenty-one when, on her second day in New York City, the employment office had sent her to Santos Enterprises to interview in the accounting office. Instead, she'd been sent up to the top floor to meet with the CEO himself.

"Perfeito," the fearsome, sleek Brazilian tycoon had said, looking at her résumé. Then he'd looked at her. "Young enough so you will not be planning to immediately quit to have a baby. At least ten or twenty years before you'll think of that. *Perfeito.*"

Now, Gabriel looked at her with dark eyes. She felt a cold winter wind sweep in from the north and shivered.

"Be my pretend mistress in Rio," he said. "And I will pay you a hundred thousand dollars for that one night."

Her lips parted as she breathed, "A hundred thousand!"

She almost said yes on the spot. Then she remembered her baby, and her heart rose to her throat. She shook her head. "Sorry," she choked out. "Get someone else."

His brow furrowed in disbelief. "Why? You clearly need the money."

She licked her lips. "That's none of your business."

"I deserve an answer."

She set her jaw. He didn't know what kind of trouble he'd made for her by coming here. *Didn't know and didn't care.* He couldn't see how Laura had changed through the anguish of the past year. Who would be the first neighbor to gossip that her ex-boss bore an uncanny resemblance to her son?

She exhaled, clenching her hands. He still thought all he had to do was tell her to jump, and she'd ask how high. But she wasn't his obedient little secretary anymore.

With a deep breath, she closed her eyes. It was time to let it all go.

Let go the sound of Gabriel's warm, deep voice for the last five years as his executive assistant. *Miss Parker, there's no one as capable as you.*

Let go the brightness of his delight when he came home at 6:00 A.M. to find her silently waiting with freshly made coffee and a pressed suit for his early meeting. *Miss Parker, what would I do without you?*

Let go the memory of their time in bed, when his dark eyes, so vulnerable and warm, had caressed her face with unspoken words of love. Let go the memory of his lips hot against her skin. Let go the feel of him inside her. *Laura, I need you.*

She opened her eyes.

"I'm sorry," she said, her voice shaking. "You don't deserve an explanation. My answer is just no."

Around them, the dusting of snow reflected light into the white-gray lowering clouds, in a breathless hush of muffled silence. He blinked, looking bewildered.

"Did it end so badly, Laura?" he said softly. "Between us?"

She pressed her fingernails into her palms to keep from crying. Robby. She had to think of Robby. "You shouldn't have come here." Her cheeks felt inflamed in the winter air, her body burning up and yet cold as ice. "I want you to leave. Now."

He took a step closer, looking down at her. A sliver of moonlight pierced through the clouds to illuminate his face. She noticed the dark shadow on his hard jawline, saw the hollows beneath his eyes. She wondered when he'd last slept.

Her heart twisted in her chest. No. She couldn't let

herself care. She couldn't! Choking back tears, she edged away. "If you won't leave, I will."

He grabbed her wrist. He looked down at her, and his eyes glittered. "I can't let you go."

For a moment, she heard only the panting of their breath. Then a door banged open, and she heard a baby's whine. A chill went down her spine and she whirled around with a gasp.

Too late!

"Where have you been, Laura?" her mother called irritably, holding a squirming Robby in her arms. "It took me ages to find you. What on earth are you doing out here in the cold?"

Ripping her arm from Gabriel's grasp, Laura gave her mother a hard, desperate stare. "I'm sorry, Mom. Just go back inside. Go back. I'll be right there!"

But her mother wasn't looking at her. "Is that—is that Mr. Santos?" she said tremulously.

"Hello, Mrs. Parker," Gabriel said, smiling as he stepped towards her and held out his hand. "Congratulations on Becky's wedding. You must be very proud of your daughter."

"I'm proud of all my daughters." She came closer to shake his hand. "It's nice to see you again."

Laura stared at them, her heart in her throat. Her mother had always liked Gabriel, ever since he'd paid for the family to take a vacation to Florida four years ago, one they wouldn't otherwise have been able to afford. The Parkers had traveled in his private jet and stayed at a villa on the beach. It had been a lavish second honeymoon for Laura's parents, a big change from their first at a cheap motel in Niagara Falls. Pictures of that Florida vacation still lined the walls, images of their family smiling beneath palm trees, building sand castles on the beach, splashing in the surf together. With that one gift, Gabriel had won her mother's loyalty forever.

"I'm glad someone had the sense to invite you to Becky's wedding," Ruth said, smiling.

He smiled back with gentle courtesy. "I've always asked you to call me Gabriel."

"Oh no, I couldn't," she said. "Not with you being Laura's employer and all. It just wouldn't be right."

"But I'm not her employer anymore." He flashed Laura a dark look before leaning toward her mother to confidentially whisper, "And I wasn't invited to the wedding. I crashed. I came to offer her a job."

"Oh!" Ruth practically cried tears of joy. "A job! You have no idea how happy that makes me. Things have been so tight lately and you should see some of the ridiculous jobs she's applied for, as far away as Exeter—"

"Mom," Laura cried. "Please take Robby inside!"

"So she's looking for a job, is she?" he purred.

"Oh, yes. She's totally broke," Ruth confided, then her cheeks turned red. "But then, we all are. Ever since... since..." She turned away.

Gabriel put his hands into his pockets. "I was sorry to hear about your husband. He was a good man."

"Thank you," Ruth whispered. Amid the lightly falling snow, silence fell. Gabriel suddenly looked at Robby.

"What a charming baby," he murmured, changing the subject. "Is he related to you, Mrs. Parker?"

Her mother looked at him as if he was stupid. "He's my grandson."

Gabriel looked surprised. "Is one of your other daughters married, as well?"

"Mom," Laura breathed with tears in her eyes, terrified, "just go! Right now!"

But it was too late. "This is Robby," her mother said, holding him up proudly. "Laura's baby."

CHAPTER THREE

As her mother turned to place Robby into her arms, Laura's heart fell to the snowy, frozen ground. The six-month-old's whine faded, turning to hiccups as he clung to Laura. Ruth leaned forward to hug her.

"Take the job," her mother whispered in her ear, then turned to Gabriel and said brightly, "I hope to see you again soon, Mr. Santos!"

Laura heard the dull thunk of the door as her mother went back inside. Then she was alone with Gabriel; their baby in her arms.

Gabriel's dark eyes went to the child, then back to her. The sound of his tightly coiled voice reverberated in the cold air. "This is your son?"

She held her baby close, loving the solid, chubby feel of him in her arms. Tears stung her eyes as she looked down at Robby. "Yes."

"How old is he?"

"Six months," she said in a small voice.

Gabriel's eyes narrowed. "So tell me." His voice was deadly and still as a winter's night. "Who is the father of your baby?"

She'd wished so many times to be able to tell Gabriel the truth, dreamed of giving her son his father. With their baby squirming in her arms between them, the truth rose unbidden to her lips. "The father of my baby is..."

You. You're Robby's father. Robby is your son. But the words stuck in her throat. Gabriel didn't want to be tied down with a child. If she told him her secret, nothing good would come of it. He might feel he had no choice but to sue for custody out of duty, resenting Robby, resenting her for forcing him into it. He might try to take their child to Brazil, away from her, to be given into the arms of some young, sexy nanny.

Laura would gain nothing by telling him. And risk everything.

"Well?" he demanded.

She flashed her eyes at him. "The identity of my baby's father is none of your business."

His own eyes narrowed. "You must have gotten pregnant immediately after you left Rio."

"Yes," she said unwillingly. She shivered, looking from father to son. Would he notice the resemblance?

But Gabriel turned on her, his dark eyes full of accusation. "You were a virgin when I seduced you. You said you wanted a home and family of your own. How could you be so careless, to forget protection, to let yourself get pregnant by a one-night stand?"

Gabriel had used protection, but somehow she'd gotten pregnant anyway. She said over the lump in her throat, "Accidents happen."

"Accidents *don't* happen," he corrected. "Only mistakes."

She set her jaw. "My baby is not a *mistake.*"

"You mean it was planned?" He lifted a sardonic eyebrow. "Who is the father? Some good-looking farmer?

Some boy you knew back in high school?" He glanced around. "Where is this paragon? Why hasn't he proposed? Why aren't you his wife?"

Robby was starting to snuffle. Even in his long-sleeved shirt, he was getting cold, and so was she. Holding him close to her warmth, she shifted his weight on her hip. "I told you, it's none of your business."

"Is he here?"

"No!"

"So he deserted you."

"I didn't give him the chance," she said. "I left him first."

"Ah." Gabriel's shoulders seemed to relax slightly. "So you don't love him. Will he cause any trouble when you take the child to Rio?"

"No."

"Good."

"I mean—I'm not taking Robby there. I'm not going." Her baby started to whimper as she turned away. "Goodbye, Gabriel."

"Wait."

The raw emotion in his voice made her hesitate. Against her better judgment she turned back. He stepped toward her, and she saw something in his expression she'd never seen before.

Vulnerability.

"Don't leave," he said in a low voice. "I need you."

I need you.

She'd once loved him. She'd served him night and day, existed only to please him. She had to fight that habit, that yearning, with every bit of willpower she possessed.

"Is a hundred thousand dollars not enough?" He

came closer, his dark eyes bright in the moonlight, the white smoke of his breath drifting around them in the chilly night air. "Let's make it a cool million. A million dollars, Laura. For a single night."

She gasped. *A million…?*

Reaching out, he stroked her cheek. "Think what that money could mean for you. For your family." His fingers moved slowly against her cold skin, the lightest touch of a caress, warming her. "If you don't care what it would mean for me, think what it could do for you. And all you need to do," he said huskily, "is smile for a few hours. Drink champagne. Wear a fancy ball gown. And pretend to love me."

Pretend. Blinking up at him, she swallowed the lump in her throat. *Pretend* to love him.

"Although I know it might not be easy," he said dryly. Then he shook his head. "But you are not so selfish as to refuse."

With an intake of breath, Laura clenched her hands into fists. "Maybe I am. Now."

His sensual mouth curved. "The Laura I knew always put the needs of the people she loved above herself. I know that hasn't changed." His dark eyebrow lifted. "You probably stayed up all night making your sister's wedding cake."

Her lips twisted with a dark emotion. "I really hate you."

"Hate me if you will. But if you do not come with me to Rio tonight…" He clawed his black hair back with his hand, then exhaled. His dark eyes seemed fathomless and deep, echoing with pain. "I will lose my father's legacy. Forever."

Shivering in the cold night, cradling her whimpering baby in the warmth of her arms, Laura looked up into Gabriel's handsome, haggard face. She knew better than anyone what the Açoazul company meant to Gabriel. For years, she'd watched him scheme and plot to regain control of it. He hungered for it. *His legacy.*

Living in the house her great-great-great-great-grandfather had built with his own two hands, on the land her family had farmed for two centuries, Laura could understand the feeling. She looked at his face. It was a shock to see raw vulnerability in his dark eyes. It was an expression she'd never seen there before, not in all the years she'd worked for him. She could feel herself weakening.

One million dollars. For a single night of luxury in Rio, a night of beauty and pleasure. She looked down at her baby. What could that money do for her son? For her family?

But oh, the risk. Could she be strong enough to resist telling Gabriel the truth? For twenty-four hours, could she lie to his face? Could she pretend to love him, without falling in love with him again for real?

On the country road in front of their property, Laura saw a parked black sedan turn on its headlights, as if on cue. She heard the smooth purr of the engine as it slowly drove up the driveway. Over Gabriel's head, moonlight laced the ridges of the dark clouds with silver.

She closed her eyes. "You will never come back looking for me after this?" she said in a low voice. "You will leave us in peace?"

Gabriel's own voice was harsh. "Yes."

Looking at him, Laura took a deep breath and spoke

words that felt like a knife between her shoulder blades. The only words he'd left for her to say.

"One night," she whispered.

An hour later they arrived at the small private airport, where his jet waited outside the hangar. As they crossed the tarmac, Gabriel felt his blood rush in his ears as he stared down at her.

Laura was even more beautiful than he remembered. In the moonlight, her hair looked like dark honey. The frosty winter air gave her cheeks a soft pink glow, and as she bit her lower lip, her heart-shaped mouth looked red and inviting. For a single instant, when he'd first seen her at the farmhouse, he'd had the insane desire to kiss her.

He took a deep breath. He was tired, flying straight from Rio on his private jet. Even more than that, he was exhausted from the months of negotiations to buy back his father's old company in Rio, to gain back the business that had been his birthright before he'd stupidly thrown it away as a grief-stricken nineteen-year-old.

He wouldn't fail. Not this time. Gabriel glanced down grimly at his expensive platinum watch. They were still on schedule. *Just.*

As they climbed the steps to the jet, Laura paused, looking behind her. Shifting the baby carrier on her arm, she pulled her diaper bag up higher on her other shoulder and bit her lip. "I think we should go back to the house for a few more things—"

"You have enough for the flight?" he said shortly.

"Yes, but I didn't pack clothes. Pajamas—"

"Everything you need will be waiting for you in Rio. It will be arranged."

"All right." With one last, troubled glance, she followed him up the steps.

Inside the cabin, Gabriel sat down in the white leather seat. A flight attendant offered him a glass of champagne, which he accepted. It had been harder than he'd expected to convince Laura to come. She sat across from him, suddenly glaring at him beneath her dark lashes.

Was she angry at him for some reason? God knew why. He was the one who should be angry. She'd left him in the lurch a year ago. In an act of pure charity, he'd allowed her to quit her job. It had been the act of a saint. He'd barely managed to patch up the hole she'd left in his office.

"You'd better have a very trustworthy babysitter in Rio," she growled, refusing the offer of champagne.

He finished off the crystal flute. "Maria Silva."

She blinked. "Your housekeeper?"

"She was my nanny when I was young."

"You were young?" Laura said sardonically.

Gabriel's throat closed. Against his will, memories of his happy childhood washed over him, of playing with his older brother, of the wrestling and fighting, of his nanny's voice soothing them. Only a year apart in age, Gabriel had competed with Guilherme constantly, always seeking to best him in their parents' eyes. He'd started some stupid battles. Leading up to the night of the accident…

Turning away, he finished harshly, "I'd trust Maria with my life."

Laura no longer looked angry. Now she looked bemused, staring at him with her large, limpid turquoise eyes. She started to ask a question, then was distracted when the flight attendant suggested she buckle in the baby's carrier before takeoff.

Gabriel watched her smiling down at her son, murmuring soft words of love as she tucked a baby blanket into his pudgy hand. The little one yawned again.

A strange feeling went through Gabriel.

He'd won. He'd convinced her. They would make it back to Rio in time. His plan would work. He should be feeling triumphant.

Instead, he felt...on edge.

Why? It couldn't be the money he'd promised her. A million dollars was nothing. He would have paid ten times that to win back his father's company. He would have given every penny he possessed, every share of stock in Santos Enterprises, the contracts, the office building in Manhattan, the ships in Rotterdam. Everything down to the last stick of furniture.

So it wasn't the money. But as the jet took off, leaving New Hampshire behind, he looked out the window. Something bothered him, and he didn't know what it was. Was it that he'd let Laura see his desperation?

No, he thought, setting his jaw. She knew how much his father's company meant to him. And anyway, allowing his vulnerability to show had helped achieve his goal.

It was something else. His gaze settled on the drowsing baby's dark hair, his plump cheeks.

It was the baby. The baby unsettled him.

Gabriel's jaw set as he realized what the edgy feeling was. What it had to be.

Anger.

He couldn't believe that Laura had fallen into another man's bed so swiftly. When she'd quit her job and walked out of his life last year, he'd let her go for one reason only—for her own good. He'd come to care for her. And he knew he couldn't give her what she wanted. A husband. Children. A job that didn't consume her every waking hour. When, the morning after he'd seduced her, she'd suddenly said she was quitting and going back to her family, he'd given Laura her chance at happiness. He'd let her go.

But instead of following her dreams, she'd apparently jumped into a brief, meaningless affair with some man she didn't even care about. She'd settled for poverty and the life of a single mother. She'd allowed her child to be born without a father. Without a name.

Cold rage slowly built inside him.

He'd let her go for nothing.

Gabriel looked at her, now leaning back in her white leather seat with her eyes closed, one hand still on her baby in the seat beside her. She was even more beautiful than he remembered. Even in that unflattering, pale pink satin dress, with that horrible hot pink lipstick, her natural beauty shone through. With all its deceptive innocence.

Against his will, his eyes traced the generous curves beneath her gown. Her breasts were bigger since she'd become a mother, her hips wider. And suddenly he couldn't stop wondering what her body would look like beneath that dress. *What it would feel like against him in bed.*

Erotic memories flashed through him of the first time he'd kissed her, when he'd swept his laptop to the floor in his ruthless need to have her. Taking her against his desk, he'd lost data that had cost thousands of dollars.

He hadn't cared. It had been worth it.

He'd wanted Laura Parker from the moment she'd walked into his office, looking uncertain in her country clothes and wearing big, ugly glasses. He'd seen at once that she had a kind, innocent heart, coupled with the fearless bluntness he needed in an executive assistant. He'd wanted her, but for five years, he'd held himself in check. He needed her too badly in his office, needed her expertise to keep Santos Enterprises—and his life— running like a well-oiled machine. And he knew an old-fashioned woman like Laura Parker would never settle for what a man like Gabriel could offer—money, glamour, an emotionless affair. So he hadn't allowed himself to touch her. Not even to flirt with her.

Until...

Last year, during a helicopter flight from Açoazul's steel factory to the north of the city, Gabriel had looked up from a report to discover his pilot had flown them right over the sharp stretch of road where his family had died nearly twenty years before.

Gabriel had said nothing to the pilot. He'd told himself he felt nothing. Then he'd gone back to the office. It was late, and all his other employees were gone. He'd seen Laura Parker alone at his desk, filing papers in her prim collared shirt and tweed skirt, and something inside him had snapped. Five years of frustrated need had exploded and he'd seized her. Her blue eyes had widened behind her sleek, black-framed glasses as, without a word, he'd ruthlessly kissed her.

That night, he'd discovered two things that shocked him.

First: Miss Parker was a virgin.

Second: beneath her demure exterior, she'd burned him to ashes with her passionate fire.

He'd made love to her roughly against the desk. He'd been more gentle the second time, after they'd taken the elevator up to his penthouse and he'd kissed her for hours, lying across his big bed. The night had been... amazing. More than amazing. It had been the most incredible sexual experience of his life.

Now, looking at her, a cold knot tightened in Gabriel's chest. He'd given that up, and she'd just thrown herself away. She'd let some unworthy man touch her. Get her pregnant with his child.

Gabriel's hands tightened into fists. Perhaps it was hypocritical to feel so betrayed, since he'd enjoyed many women the past year since she'd deserted him. But *enjoy* was not the right word. All Gabriel had done was prove to himself, over and over, that no other woman could satisfy him as Laura had.

Turning away, he set his jaw. He'd get control of Açoazul SA and then send Laura and her baby back to New Hampshire. He'd thought he might ask her to stay in Rio after the deal was done, but now that was impossible. As much as he missed her in the office—as much as he missed her in his bed—he couldn't take her back now. Not now that she had a child.

He couldn't let himself feel, not even for a moment, as if he were part of a family.

"You look tired," he heard Laura say quietly.

He turned to her, and their eyes locked in the semi-darkness of the jet. "I'm fine."

"You don't seem fine."

"A lot has changed." He looked from her to the sleeping baby. He wanted to ask her again who the baby's father was. He wanted to ask how long she'd waited before she'd jumped into bed with a stranger. A week?

A day? What had the man done to seduce her? Bought her some cheap flowers and wine? Given her cheap promises?

What had it taken for the man to convince Laura to surrender the life she'd yearned for, and accept instead just the crumbs of her childhood dreams?

"Gabriel?"

He looked up to find her anxious eyes watching him. "What?"

"What will happen after we arrive in Rio?"

He leaned back in his seat, folding his arms. "Oliveira is hosting an afternoon pool party at his beachside mansion on the Costa do Sul. Adriana will be there."

Laura bit her lip, looking nervous. "Pool party? Like with a swimsuit?"

"And after that," he continued ruthlessly, "you will attend the Fantasy Ball with me."

"Fantasy, huh?" Her full lips twisted. "I hope Brazilian shopping malls sell magic fairy dust, 'cause that's the only thing that will convince anyone I can compete with Adriana da Costa."

"The first person you must convince is yourself," he said harshly. "Your lack of confidence is not attractive. No one will believe I'd be in love with a woman who disappears in the background like a wallflower."

He had the hollow satisfaction of seeing the light in her beautiful face fade. "I just meant…"

"We made a deal. I am paying you well. For the next twenty-four hours, Laura, you will be the woman I need you to be. You belong to me."

Her eyes narrowed with anger and resentment, and as she turned away, some part of him was glad he'd hurt her. He heard the soft snuffle of the baby's breath, and it was like a razor against his throat.

He'd once been comforted by the thought of Laura back at home with her family, following her dreams. Now she'd taken that from him. She'd betrayed him.

And he hated her for that.

CHAPTER FOUR

As they descended through the clouds toward Rio de Janeiro, Laura stared out the porthole window at the city shining like a jewel on the sea. She folded her arms with a huff of breath, still furious.

You belong to me.

Her hands gripped her seat belt. Looking past Robby's baby seat, where he was thankfully sleeping again after a fairly rough night, Laura glanced at Gabriel on the opposite side of the jet. She allowed herself a grim smile.

Poor Robby had been crying half the flight. Gabriel must have been gnashing his teeth to be trapped in his private jet with a baby. Karma, she thought with a degree of satisfaction. Folding her arms, she turned back to the window to see the beautiful, exotic city as they descended through the clouds.

It had been difficult for her to leave her mother and sisters in the middle of Becky's reception. But instead of being angry, her mother and sisters had seemed pleased. They'd hugged her goodbye for the quick weekend trip. "You were so happy working for him once," her mother had whispered. "This will be a new start for you and Robby. I can feel it. It's fate."

Fate.

Laura had barely gotten on this jet before he'd insulted her. Now, he glared at her as if she were a stranger. No, worse than a stranger. He stared at her as if she were scum beneath his feet.

As the jet finally landed at the private airport, her hands gripped the leather armrest. She would never again feel guilty about keeping their baby a secret from Gabriel. After this, she would never let herself feel *anything* for him. She would do her job, pretend to be his adoring mistress—ha!—then collect the check and forget his existence. She *would.*

As the door of the private jet opened, Robby woke up with one of his adorable baby smiles. His toothless grin and happy cooing were worth any amount of sleepless nights, she thought.

"We're just here for one night, Robby," she told her baby, kissing his forehead as she unbuckled his seat. "Just a quick night here and we'll go straight back home."

"Did he sleep well?" Gabriel said sardonically behind her.

She gave him a pleasant answering smile. "Did you?"

As they stepped out of the jet, Rio's sultry heat hit her at once. She went down the steps, blinking in the blinding sunlight and breathing in the scents of tropical flowers, exotic spice and tangy salt from the sea. Lush, white-hot Brazil was the other side of the world from the frigid February weather she'd left behind her.

Looking across the tarmac, Laura saw a waiting white limousine and snorted. The other side of the world? This was a different world entirely!

"Bom dia, Miss Parker," the driver said, tipping his hat as he opened the door. "I am glad to see you again. And what's this?" He tickled beneath Robby's chin. "We have a new passenger!"

"Obrigada, Carlos," Laura said, smiling. "This is my son, Robby."

"Is the penthouse ready?" Gabriel growled behind them.

The driver nodded. *"Sim, senhor.* Maria, she has organized everything."

"Good."

Laura climbed into the backseat and tucked Robby into the waiting baby seat, ignoring Gabriel climbing in beside him. Carlos started the engine and pulled the limo off the tarmac, going south.

As they traveled through the city, now crowded with tourists for the celebration of *Carnaval*, Laura stared out bleakly at the festive decorations. Gabriel didn't speak and neither did she. The silence seemed like agony as the car inched through the traffic. As they finally approached the back of Gabriel's building, Laura heard loud thumping music, drums, people singing and cheering.

"This is as close as I can get, *senhor*," Carlos said apologetically. "The *avenida* is closed to cars today."

"Está bom." Setting his jaw, Gabriel opened the door himself and got out of the limo.

Laura looked out her window in awe. Ahead of them, she saw the street blocked and people gathering on Ipanema Beach for one of the largest, wildest street festivals in Rio. She looked up at Gabriel's tall building above them. He had bought it two years ago, as a foothold in Rio while he wrestled his father's company back from Felipe Oliveira. The ground floors held restaurants and retail space. The middle floors held the South American offices of Santos Enterprises, still officially headquartered in New York. The top two floors of the building were apartments for his bodyguards, household staff and Maria. The penthouse was, of course, for Gabriel—and, the last time she'd been here, for Laura. She swallowed. She'd never thought she'd be back here.

Especially not with a secret. *A baby.*

The car door wrenched open. She looked up, expecting Carlos, but it was Gabriel. To her shock, the expression on his handsome face was suddenly tender and adoring. His eyes shone with passion and desire.

"At last you are home, *querida*," Gabriel murmured. He held out his hand. "Home where you belong. It nearly killed me when you left. I never stopped loving you, Laura."

She gasped.

Suddenly she could no longer feel the hot sun blazing overhead or the fresh breeze off the sea. Loud music, horns and drumming and singing from Ipanema Beach all faded into the background. Her heart thrummed wildly in her throat.

Gabriel's black eyes sizzled as he looked down at her, catching up her soul, collecting her like a butterfly in a net.

Then he dropped his hand with a sardonic laugh. "Just practicing."

Setting her jaw, she glared at him. "A million dollars is almost not enough to deal with this," she muttered.

His lip twisted. "Too late to renegotiate."

"Go to hell."

"Is that any way to speak in front of your baby?"

Turning back into the car, Laura unbuckled Robby. Her son cooed happily, reaching up his chubby arms for her embrace, and she was happy she had one person in Brazil who actually loved her. Leaving the baby carrier in the limo, she scooped him out of his seat. He giggled, clinging to her wrinkled satin bridesmaid's dress.

Laura felt tired, grungy, dirty. After her poor night's sleep on the jet, after traveling halfway around the world, and most of all, after the constant friction of having Gabriel near her, Laura's emotions were too close to the surface. The flash of his dark eyes, the slightest touch of his hand, the merest word of kindness from his sensual lips, still made her tremble and melt.

He was poison for her, she thought grimly. Poison wrapped in honeyed words and hot desire.

She held her baby close and walked around Gabriel with as much dignity as she possessed, her shoulders straight. Her pink high heels—picked out from a thrift shop by Becky for five dollars—clattered against the marble floor as Laura walked through the back entrance and past the security guards toward the private elevator.

Gabriel followed her without a word. The elevator doors closed behind them, and she breathed in his scent. She felt his warmth beside her. She didn't look at him. His tall, powerful body was so close and she felt every inch.

The last time they'd been together in this elevator, they'd been on the way to the penthouse, after they'd just made love downstairs on the desk in his office. It had been her first time. He'd been shocked she was a virgin, even apologetic. He'd kissed her so tenderly in this very elevator, taking her back up to the penthouse with whispered promises that this time would be different, that he'd make it good for her, that he'd make her weep with joy.

And he had.

The elevator dinged at the same instant Robby struggled in her arms with a plaintive whine. Looking down, Laura saw he was peeking behind her at Gabriel, reaching out his plump arms. Gabriel didn't move to take the baby, or even smile. Of course he wouldn't. Why would he take the slightest interest in his own child? She knew she was being unreasonable, but she still felt angry. Exhaling, Laura walked into the penthouse.

His modern, masculine, clutter-free apartment had two bedrooms, a study, a dining room and main room off the kitchen. The whole place had clean lines, white walls and high ceilings, and a stark decor. A wall of windows two stories high showcased the breathtaking view of the pool and terrace, with Ipanema Beach and the Atlantic visible beyond.

"I'm so glad to see you again, Senhora Laura." Maria Silva, Gabriel's housekeeper and former nanny, was waiting for them. Her gaze moved to Robby. "This must be your sweet baby."

"*Senhora*?" Laura repeated, confused at how she'd just gotten promoted to a married woman.

The plump-cheeked, white-haired woman blushed. "You're a mother. You deserve respect," she said, then held out her hands to the baby. Robby gave a gleeful cackle, and Maria took him happily in her arms.

Frowning, Laura slowly looked around her. The penthouse seemed the same, but it had changed somehow. She saw to her surprise that all the electric plugs and sharp edges had been covered. Peeking into the dining room, she saw it was entirely filled with toys.

Laura turned to Gabriel in wonder. "All this?" she said. "For one night?"

He shrugged. "Don't thank me. Maria did it."

Laura's heart, which had been rising, fell back to her shoes.

"We'll have a wonderful time this afternoon, won't we?" Maria said to Robby, whirling the baby around to make him giggle. "If you need us, Mrs. Laura, we'll be making lunch."

Laura turned to follow them into the kitchen, but Gabriel stopped her. "They'll be fine. Go freshen up."

She scowled at him. "Stop barking orders at me. You weren't this bad when I worked for you."

"Do you want a shower or not?"

From the kitchen, Laura dimly heard Maria getting out pots and pans as she sang a song to the baby in Portuguese. Robby started banging the pans with a wooden spoon, keeping the beat. They seemed fine. Laura set her jaw, then grudgingly admitted, "I do want a shower."

"You have ten minutes." When she didn't move, he lifted a sardonic eyebrow. "Need help?"

She saw his lips curve as he turned away, walking down the hallway. Pulling off his shirt, he dropped it to the floor as he stopped in the doorway of his bedroom. He looked back at her with heavy-lidded eyes. "Go. Right now. Or I will assist you."

"I'm going!" With a gulp, Laura ran for the safety of her old bedroom.

Her room had changed, as well. All the old furniture she'd had as his live-in secretary was gone, of course.

The space had been turned into a bland guest room. Except…

She saw the brand-new elliptical wooden crib beside the bed, the changing table with diapers and baby clothes and everything else Robby might need. She exclaimed with delight as she touched the smooth wood. In the closet, she saw new clothes for her, as well. Gabriel had truly thought of everything. Going to the closet, she touched a black dress with a soft, satisfied sigh.

Then she saw the size on the tag.

Well, she thought with dismay, he hadn't thought of *everything*.

CHAPTER FIVE

TEN MINUTES LATER, Gabriel paced beneath the hot sun across his rooftop terrace. He stopped, staring down at Ipanema Beach across the Avenida Vieira Souto. He could hear the loud music from the crowds celebrating below. Lifting his eyes, he looked past the throngs of people, past the yellow umbrellas and food vendors to the shining waves of the surf, trying to calm his pounding heart.

Now Laura was here, everything would soon be sorted out. Oliveira and Adriana would both believe that they were in love. They had to believe. Otherwise….

No, he wouldn't let himself think about failure, not even for an instant. He couldn't lose his father's company, not now that it was finally within his grasp. He gripped the railing, glaring at the bright horizon of blue ocean. All along the coastline, tall buildings vied with the sharp green mountains for domination of the sky.

He'd changed into khaki shorts and an open, button-down shirt over a tank top, with flip-flops on his feet, Carioca-style. He paced his private rooftop. Bright sunlight reflected prisms from the water of his swimming pool. Turning back, he stared down blindly at the scantily clad women on Ipanema Beach, to Leblon to the west, ending in the stark, sharp green mountain of Dois Irmãos.

Gabriel had been only nineteen when he'd lost everything. His parents. His brother. His home. His hands tightened on the rail. When he'd had the chance to sell his family's business the day after the funeral, Gabriel had taken it. He'd fled to New York, leaving his grief behind.

Except grief had followed him. Consumed him. Even as he created an international company far larger than his father's had ever been, the guilt of what he'd done—causing the accident, but being the only survivor; inheriting his father's company, only to carelessly sell it—never left him. Never.

"Well, I did it," Laura gasped suddenly behind him. "Ten minutes."

"Very efficient," he said, turning to face her. "You should know that—"

His words froze in his throat.

Gabriel's eyes traced over her in shock as he watched her towel off her long wet hair. He took in the erotic vision of her obscenely full breasts overflowing the neckline of her black dress. He couldn't look away from the fabric outlining her full buttocks and hips.

"Where," he choked out, "did you get that dress?"

She stopped toweling her hair to look at him, tilting her head with a frown. "It was in the closet. Wasn't it for me?"

"Yes." He couldn't stop his gaze from devouring her curvaceous body. He became instantly hard, filled with the memory of how it felt to have her in his arms, for the most explosive sexual night of his life. *He wanted her.* Here in Rio, beneath the Brazilian sunshine, suddenly he could think of nothing but taking her, right here and now. He licked his lips and said hoarsely, "But I didn't expect it to look like *that*."

An embarrassed blush rose to her cheeks as she pushed up her black-framed glasses in a self-conscious gesture. "I gained a little weight with my pregnancy," she mumbled. "I'm not so thin as I used to be."

"No." Gabriel stared at her, feeling his body tighten with lust. "No, you're not."

Willing himself to stay in control, he pulled out a chair at the table next to the pool. "Maria made breakfast. Come and eat."

Laura scowled. "Is that an order?"

"Sim."

Carefully folding her towel and setting it on a nearby table—instead of just dropping it to the floor, as he would have done—she sat down.

"I probably shouldn't eat anything. Not if I'm supposed to wear a bikini," she said in a low voice. "I've tried to diet, but…"

"Never diet again," he said tersely. "You are perfect."

He pushed her chair back under the table. He paused, allowing his hands to remain on the back of the chair, next to her shoulders. He could almost feel the warmth of her soft skin.

She looked up at him over her shoulder with a scowl. "You're just being nice."

He stared down at her. "When have you ever known me to be nice?"

Her full pink lips suddenly curved into a smile as her blue eyes twinkled. "Good point." She tilted her head, considering. "So you really think I look…all right?"

"Hmm." His eyes lingered on her spectacular figure. She'd been beautiful before, but now, it was almost like torture to see her perfect female shape. Those hips. Her curvaceous bottom. Those breasts—!

She was almost *too* attractive, he thought. He wanted to convince Oliveira and Adriana he was in love with Laura, not have every other man on the Avenida Vieira Souta enjoy the luscious spectacle of her body. "You're fine," he said, irritated. "But that dress is unacceptable. We'll buy you something else when we go shopping today."

"Shopping. Right." Pouring milk and sugar into her cup, she stirred her coffee with a silver spoon. "I can hardly wait."

He sat down across the table. "You have nothing to worry about." He pushed the bread basket toward her. "It'll be fine."

She took a roll and sipped her coffee, and as they ate, Gabriel couldn't stop staring at her. Once, their relationship had been easy. A friendship. A trust. Now, he couldn't quite read her.

Strange.

For five years, Laura Parker had been the perfect employee. She'd had no life or interests of her own. She'd always been ready and waiting to offer her competent assistance for his latest emergency, whether it was a billion-dollar drop on a foreign stock exchange or a broken thread on his tuxedo.

Now…there was something different about her. Something had changed in her over the last year. He felt as if he didn't know her.

"How is your meal?" he said gruffly.

"Delicious."

"Try this." He handed her a bowl of pastries. Their fingers brushed and she jerked away as if he'd burned her.

He scowled at her. "We're attending Oliveira's party in three hours. No one will believe we are a couple if you jump every time I touch you."

Putting down her fork with a clang, she looked at him. "You're right."

He held out his hand across the table, palm up.

With an intake of breath, she placed her hand in his. He felt her tremble. Felt the warmth of her skin. A rush of desire went through him as his fingers tightened over hers. Coming to her side of the table, he pulled her to her feet.

For a moment, they stood facing each other beneath the warm, bright sun. A soft sea breeze ruffled her damp hair. She wouldn't meet his eyes. Her gaze seemed fixated on his mouth.

She licked her lips, and he nearly groaned.

"I passed your test," she whispered. "I'm touching you without flinching."

"Holding my hand is not enough."

She visibly swallowed, looking up. "What—what else?"

He put his arms around her, pulling her close. He felt the softness of her body, felt her curves pressed against him as he rested his hands on her hips. Her tight black dress squeezed her breasts still higher in the force of his embrace, plump and firm and begging for his touch. He stroked her cheek, tilting back her head. "Now I need you to look at me," he said in a low voice, "as if you love me."

Beneath her glasses, her wide-set blue eyes glimmered in the sunlight, shining like the sea.

"And I," he continued roughly, "am utterly, completely and insanely in love with you."

She trembled. Then she fiercely shook her head.

"This isn't going to work. No one will believe you'd choose me over her."

"You're wrong," he said. "Adriana is beautiful, yes. But that's all she is. While you…"

Laura stiffened in his arms, lifting her chin.

He cupped her head with his hands. "You are more than just a pretty face." He stroked her bare neck. "More than just a luscious body." He rubbed his thumb against her full, sensitive lower lip. "You are smart. And too kindhearted for your own good. You sacrifice yourself to take care of others, even when you shouldn't." He pressed a finger against her lips to stop her protest. "And you have something else Adriana does not."

"What?"

He looked down at her. "You have me," he whispered.

Gabriel felt her hands tighten around him.

"Can you do it?" he asked in a low voice. "Can you pretend you're in love with me? Can you make everyone believe that all you've ever wanted is for me to hold you like this?"

Her face was pale as she looked at him, trembling like a flower in his arms. When she spoke, her voice was almost too quiet for him to hear above the noise of the music and street party below. "Yes."

"Then prove it." He felt her soft curves pressing against his body, felt how delicate and petite she was in his arms. Laura was so beautiful in every way. He felt the press of her full breasts against his chest. Felt the tendrils of her long damp hair brush against his hands as he gripped her back. He breathed in the scent of her, lavender and soap, wholesome and clean.

He was hard for her. Rock hard. And yet she seemed to think she was inferior to Adriana da Costa, who aside from her beauty was nothing but a shallow, spoiled brat.

Suddenly Gabriel knew he had to tell Laura the truth.

"I want you, Laura," he said in a low voice. "More than any woman. I've always wanted you."

She gasped, her eyes wide. "You…"

Then her expression grew dull as the light in her eyes abruptly faded. "You're practicing again."

"No." He cupped her face roughly. "This has nothing to do with our business deal. I want you. I've spent the last year wanting you. And now you're in my arms, I intend to have you."

He saw her eyes widen beneath her glasses, heard her harsh intake of breath.

"But for now," he murmured, "I will start with a kiss."

Then he lowered his head to hers.

He felt her soft, warm lips tremble against his own. For a single instant, her body stiffened in his arms. He felt her hands against his chest as she tried to push him away. He just wrapped his arms around her waist more firmly and held her tight, refusing to let go.

Kissing her was even better than Gabriel had imagined.

It was heaven.

It was hell.

With a shudder and a sigh she suddenly melted against him. He ruthlessly pushed her lips apart, teasing her with his tongue, plundering the warm heat of her mouth.

His kiss became harder, more demanding, their embrace tighter beneath the white heat of the sun. Slowly, she responded. Her hands stopped pushing against his chest, and moved up to his neck, pulling him down to her. When she finally kissed him back, with a hunger that matched his own, a low growl rose in the back of his throat.

He forgot their affair wasn't real. He forgot the deal entirely. He felt only his masculine, animal need to have her, the need he'd denied himself for too long. Lust swarmed in his blood, pounding through his brain, demanding he take total possession of Laura in his bed.

CHAPTER SIX

THIS *couldn't be happening.*

Gabriel couldn't be kissing her.

But the part of Laura's brain that was telling her to push away, push away now, was lost in the scorching fire of his embrace. As his lips moved against hers, mastering and guiding her, heat seared down her body like a hot jungle wind.

Pleasure whipped through her, pleasure she'd felt only once in her life before. But this was even better than her memory. As they stood on the penthouse terrace, she grasped his open shirt, clinging for dear life. She felt the warmth of his body, the hardness of his muscled chest beneath his cotton tank top. His strong thighs in khaki shorts brushed like tree trunks against her legs. He towered over her, making her feel womanly and petite as he folded himself around her.

The hot, hard feel of his lips seared hers, causing sparks to shoot down the length of her body. Her breasts felt suddenly heavy, her nipples taut. A fire of ache raced to her deepest core as tension coiled inside her. She felt the rough sandpaper of his chin against hers and breathed in his intoxicating scent of musk and spice. Her knees shook beneath her. Her world was spinning.

Everything she'd wanted, everything she'd dreamed about for the past lonely year, and five years before that, was suddenly in her grasp.

His hands stroked her back through her black dress.

"Come to bed with me," he whispered against her skin.

Bed.

She sucked in her breath as reason returned. He was seducing her. And so easily. She'd made the mistake of giving in to her desire for him once, and it had changed the course of her life. She couldn't let it happen again. Never again…

With a ragged gasp, she pulled away from his grasp. Breathing hard, she glared up at him. "You don't seriously expect me to fall into bed with you after one practice kiss?"

His half-lidded eyes were sultry with confidence—*arrogance*—and his sensual lips curved into a smile. "Yes. I had rather hoped you would."

"Forget it."

"It would make our pretend affair more believable."

"By turning it into a real one?" she whispered.

He shrugged, even as the intensity of his gaze belied that casual gesture. "Why not?"

The early afternoon was growing hot, the sun and humidity alleviated only by the cooling trade winds off the Atlantic and the Janeiro River, for which the city had been named. Laura took a deep breath of the fragrant, fresh air redolent of spices and tropical fruits. How many times had she prayed that by some miracle, Gabriel would come for her?

I want you, Laura, more than any woman. I've always wanted you.

She pushed aside her own longing. She couldn't let herself want him. She couldn't. She lifted her chin. "Thanks, but I'm not interested in a one-night stand."

His black eyes glowed like embers. "I don't want a one-night stand."

She licked her suddenly dry lips. "You—you don't?"

He shook his head. "I want you to stay."

"You do?"

"I've missed having you as my secretary. And," he added, as she folded her arms furiously, "as my lover."

"Oh." Her arms fell back to her sides. She whispered, "And Robby?"

His jaw hardened as he looked away.

"The two of you can live in the apartment below mine," he said. "Your child need not inconvenience me at all."

Your child. Hot pride and anger rushed back to her, stiffening her spine. "You mean you will kindly overlook my baby in order to have me in Rio as your 24/7 employee and late-night booty call."

He stared at her, wide-eyed. Then he gave a sudden laugh. "I've missed you, Laura," he said softly. "No one stands up to me like you do. You're not afraid of me at all. You see right through me. I like that."

She jerked away from him, near tears and furious with herself. She couldn't believe she'd let herself get seduced by his sweet kisses, not even for an instant. Absolutely nothing had changed. Gabriel didn't want a wife or child. And for her, only a real family would do.

"Sorry," she said coldly. "But my days of being your

work slave and casual late-night lover are *over.* Don't you dare kiss me again."

But his hands only tightened on her. "I can and I will."

She exhaled in fury. "You have some arrogance to think—"

Seizing her in his arms, he kissed her at once, roughly, hard enough to bruise. Showing mastery. Showing possession. And to her eternal shame, when his hot lips were against hers, she could not resist. She sagged in his arms—and kissed him back.

"I want you, Laura," he murmured against her skin when he finally pulled away. "And I will have you. If not this instant, then soon. Tonight."

She shoved her hands against his hard chest, his deliciously muscular, taut body beneath the tight cotton tank top… Maybe it hadn't been so much a shove as a caress. Angry at herself, she stepped back from him, her cheeks hot. With more confidence than she felt, she said, "Not going to happen."

"We'll see." His voice held a smug masculine tone.

"Our deal had nothing to do with sex."

"Correct."

"I don't have to sleep with you."

He had the temerity to give her a sensual, heavy-lidded glance. "And yet you will."

"Ooh!" Clenching her hands into fists, she gave a little stomp of her heel and went back into the penthouse. She found her son still playing on the spotless floor in the kitchen as Maria washed the dishes.

Gathering her baby in her arms, Laura took Robby into the living room and sat down in a new rocking

chair by the wide windows overlooking the city. When
Gabriel followed her, she glared at him, daring him to
interrupt her time with her child. With a sardonic uplift
of his brow, he just turned away, disappearing down the
hall.

For long moments, Laura held her baby. She fed him,
rocking him to sleep, and suddenly felt like crying.

She couldn't let Gabriel seduce her. She could *not*. No
matter how much her body craved his touch. No matter
how her heart yearned.

Because her heart yearned for a lie. Gabriel would
never change. Getting close to him would only break
her heart—again. Break her heart, and possibly risk
custody of her son. If she fell into bed with Gabriel, if
she gave him her body, she feared she would also give
up the secret that had tormented her for over a year.

She looked down at the sweet six-month-old baby
slumbering in her arms. Gently, she rose to her feet
and carried him down the hall to her darkened bedroom and set him in his crib. She stared down at Robby
for a moment, listening to his steady, even breathing.
Then she stiffened when a shadow fell from the open
doorway.

"Time to go," Gabriel said behind her.

Straightening her tight dress over her hips, she walked
out of the bedroom and closed the door. She glared at
him, then glanced behind her. "I hate to leave him."

"Your son will be fine. Maria will be looking after
him. And anyway—" he lifted a dark eyebrow "—this
one night's work will allow you to give him a comfortable life."

She took a deep breath. "You're right. A million dollars is worth it." She lifted her chin. "It's even worth spending a night with you."

His lips curved into a sensual smile. "The whole night."

"Not going to happen."

"We'll see." He turned without touching her, and after bidding farewell to Maria, they took the elevator downstairs. Carlos had the Ferrari waiting in the alley behind the building, engine running.

"Obrigado," Gabriel said to him in passing, then held open the door for Laura. "If you please."

She tottered into the low-slung Ferrari, feeling squeezed like a sausage by the tight black dress and half expecting to bust a seam. Gabriel climbed in beside her and the red sports car roared away from the curb.

As he drove through the crowded streets, Laura stared out in amazement through the window. Rio de Janeiro always lost its mind and found its wildest heart during *Carnaval*, and this year that was more true than ever. Music wafted through the air, horns and drums to accompany people singing. Impromptu parades marched through the streets, and even those not on carnival floats from the prestigious samba schools often wore costumes that sparkled with sequins—and barely covered enough to be decent. Everyone became sexier, more daring versions of their regular selves. Laura took a deep breath. Even her.

"I'm taking you to Zeytuna," Gabriel said as he drove. "From there we'll go directly to Oliveira's pool party."

"Zeytuna?" She'd heard of the large, exclusive boutique, but had never shopped there. She licked her lips and tried to joke, "They sell magic bikinis, right?"

As he changed gears in the Ferrari, he glanced at her from the corner of his eye. "Yes."

Yes. Just yes. No encouragement. No reassurance. Laura tried not to think of her looming bikini face-off with Adriana da Costa and the sheer humiliation that was sure to follow. She bit her lip and changed the subject. "So what is our story?"

"Story?"

"When did we fall in love? So I'll know when people ask."

He considered. "We had an affair last year," he said finally. "You quit your job and left me when I wouldn't commit."

"Believable."

He glanced at her. "But I missed you. I've been secretly pursuing you for months—video chats, flowers, sending you jewelry and love letters and so forth."

"Sounds nice," she said, looking away.

"You invited me to your sister's wedding, and we fell into each other's arms. You surrendered to my charm and agreed to be mine at last."

"A true Valentine's Day fantasy." Her lips twisted as she looked back at him. "And Robby?"

Gabriel blinked, then his hands tightened on the steering wheel as he stared at the road. "Ah, yes. Robby."

"Everyone knows you would never date a woman with a child."

"Yes." He set his jaw. Then, relaxing, he shrugged. "It will only add to the credibility of the story. It makes you unique. I wanted you so desperately, I was even willing to overlook your baby."

"*Overlook* Robby? Thank you," she said, folding

her arms as she glared out the window. "Thank you so much."

"I do not appreciate your sarcasm."

She looked at him. "I don't appreciate you saying you'll *overlook* my baby—like you're doing me some big favor!"

He set his jaw. "And I do not appreciate the fact that there is a baby living in my house."

"Because you must never be inconvenienced," she said mockingly. "The great Gabriel Santos must never have even a hint of family domesticity in his selfish bachelor's penthouse!"

Silence fell over the Ferrari.

"You love your son," Gabriel said. It sounded like a question.

Pushing up her glasses, she glared at him. "Of course I love him. What kind of question it that?"

Gabriel's black eyes burned through her. "So how could you allow yourself to get pregnant without also giving him a father? You always told me you wanted marriage, Laura. A home near your family. A career that would allow you time to raise your children. How could you toss all that aside for the sake of a one-night stand?"

She swallowed, blinking back tears. Yes, how could she?

His eyes turned back to the road. "You quit without notice last year," he said coldly. "*That* was inconvenient."

She stiffened. "Inconvenient to replace me in your office—or your bed?"

His lips tightened. "Both."

"So difficult, and yet you didn't bother to even try to talk me out of it."

They stopped at a red light. He turned on her, his eyes glinting with fury. "I let you go, Laura. For your own good, so you could have the life you wanted. But instead of following your dreams, you threw it all away. You made my sacrifice worthless. How could you? How could you be so careless?"

"It was an accident!"

"I told you." His eyes were hard. "There are no accidents. Only mistakes."

"And I told you, my baby is not a mistake!"

"Are you saying you got pregnant on purpose?"

Her mouth went dry.

He waited, then the light turned green. His lip twisted as he turned back to the road. "Every child deserves to be born into a stable home with two parents. I'm disappointed in you, Laura. You should have been careful."

Laura stiffened. "Careful like who? Like you?"

"Yes."

She longed to have the satisfaction of wiping that scornful, judgmental look off his face. She wondered what he would say if she told him that he was the father.

But she knew the satisfaction would be short-lived. If he knew Robby was his child, he might feel duty-bound to take responsibility for a child he couldn't love, and be pinned down to a domestic life he'd never wanted. And he would hate not just Laura for that, he'd hate Robby, as well.

She had to keep the secret. *Had to*. Leaning back against the black leather seat, she pressed her lips shut. *Just a few more hours*, she told herself desperately.

Tomorrow she and Robby would be on the plane back home, a million dollars richer.

"I thought family meant everything to you."

She opened her eyes, blinking back tears. "It does."

"I thought you were better than that."

"Don't you think I want a father for Robby? Don't you think I want to give him the same loving family I had?"

"So why didn't you?" Gabriel took a deep breath and said in a low voice, "Badly done, Laura."

She started to deliver a sharp retort; then stopped when she saw the stark expression on his face.

"Why are you like this?" she said. "Why do you care so much?"

"I don't," he said coldly.

"You do. You've always acted like you despise the idea of matrimony and commitment and children—all of it. But you don't," she said softly. "You care."

Gabriel pulled the Ferrari to an abrupt halt. He didn't look at her. "We're here."

Blinking in surprise, she saw they'd arrived at the enormous, exclusive Zeytuna boutique in the Leblon district. Her door opened, and she saw a young, smiling valet in a red jacket. Gabriel handed him keys, then held out his hand to her.

"Come," he said coldly. "We haven't much time."

Reluctantly, Laura placed her hand in his, and felt the same shock of sensation, the brush of his warm skin and strong grip of his fingers around hers.

"Are you cold?"

"No," she said.

"You're shivering."

She ripped her hand away. "I'm just afraid we will fail. That *I* will fail."

"You won't."

She looked down at her tight black dress, seeing her big hips and oversize breasts and a belly that was far from flat. She thought again of competing against Adriana da Costa in a bikini, and shuddered. "I don't see how."

Gabriel's sensual lips curved up into a smile. "Trust me."

He folded her hand over his bare forearm as if she were a medieval French princess and he was her honored chevalier. He looked down at her with eyes of love, and even as she told herself that he was only practicing, this time the shiver was not in her body, but her heart.

Pretending to love him was too easy. She was playing with fire.

Just a few hours more, she told herself desperately. Then she'd never see him again. Her family would never need to worry about replacing parts on the tractor or losing their home after a bad harvest. They'd never need to panic when a glut on the market suddenly lowered prices of wheat to nothing. Her family would be safe. Her baby would be safe.

Her baby.

Laura swallowed. This was the first time she'd left Robby with a babysitter since he was born. It felt strange to be away from him. Strange, and dangerous to feel this young and free, with Gabriel beside her. He smiled down at her, and for an instant she was lost in his eyes, so dark and deep against his tanned skin.

It would be so easy to love him when he treated her like this. Even after she went home, she knew she would always remember his low, husky voice saying, *"I want you, Laura, more than any woman. I've always wanted you."* She would feel the heat of his body against hers when he'd seized her on the terrace and kissed her. She had new memories to add to the time they'd first made love, when he'd pushed her back against his desk, sweeping everything aside in his reckless, savage need. When their sweaty, naked bodies had clung together, their limbs intertwined in explosive passion.

Now, Laura's legs trembled as Gabriel drew her toward the two tall brass doors held wide by doormen.

"Boa tarde, Senhor Santos," the first doorman said, beaming.

"Good to see you again, Mr. Santos," the second doorman said in accented English.

Once they were inside the foyer, Laura looked up in amazement at a center courtyard two stories high, with a dome of colored Tiffany glass on the ceiling. But if the glamorous architecture was straight out of the nineteenth century, the boutique's clothes were as cutting-edge as anything she'd find on Fifth Avenue.

A bevy of pretty shopgirls rushed to wait upon Gabriel. "Allow me to help you, *senhor*!"

"No, me!" a second one cried.

"Senhor, I have something wonderful to show you!"

Laura scowled. She could just imagine what the eager girls wanted to show Gabriel. Turning, she glared at him. "How often do you come here?"

He snorted, hiding a grin. "Once or twice a month."

"Lingerie for all your one-night stands?"

"Suits for work. I'm known to tip well."

Laura looked at the fawning shopgirls, who were all staring at him with undisguised glee. "I bet."

"Sorry, girls," he said. "We already have an appointment."

"Mr. Santos," an older woman said in English behind them. "Welcome." She stepped forward with assurance, her red suit a perfect match to her short, sleekly coiffed gray hair. "I am ready to be of assistance."

"This is Mrs. Tavares," Gabriel told Laura. His hand tightened around hers as he turned back to the other woman. "And this is the girl I told you about. Laura Parker."

"Certainly, sir." Mrs. Tavares came closer. Gabriel stepped back, and Laura found herself standing alone, bereft of his strength, beneath the older woman's scrutiny. She examined a long tendril of Laura's mousy brown hair, then nodded. "Very fine material to work with, sir."

"Dress her for the beach."

"Which beach?"

"A pool party at a luxurious mansion on the Costa do Sul. It will be attended by famous beauties and rich men. Make her shine above the rest."

Still staring at Laura, the older woman stroked her chin thoughtfully. "How obvious do you wish her beauty to be?"

"Completely," he said.

"It will require help from a salon."

"As you wish."

The woman pulled the black-rimmed glasses off Laura's face.

"Hey!" Laura protested.

"And an optometrist."

Gabriel smiled. "I leave her in your hands."

Laura's cheeks were hot. The perfectly coiffed, elegant woman continued to walk around her, looking her up and down in the tight black dress, as if she were a handyman and Laura were a sad, decrepit old house in need of a complete remodel.

"This isn't going to work," Laura said, fidgeting uncomfortably. "I think you should go to the pool party without me. I'll just go to the Fantasy Ball later."

"You go to the Fantasia tonight?" Mrs. Tavares gasped. "The *Baile de Gala*?"

"Yes, and she needs a ball gown," Gabriel said. "Casual clothes as well. But she must be ready for the party in two hours."

Mrs. Tavares froze. "So little time?"

"Desculpa."

The woman tilted her head, considering Laura. "It will not be cheap. Or easy."

"Cost does not matter. Just results. Satisfy my requirements and you'll be generously rewarded."

The older woman's expression didn't change, but Laura saw her sudden stillness. Looking at Gabriel, she gave a slow, respectful nod. "It will be done, *senhor*, as you wish."

"My driver will pick her up in two hours."

With a clap of her hands, Mrs. Tavares turned and started barking out orders to the young shopgirls in Portuguese. With a second clap of her hands she scattered them.

"Tchau," Gabriel said to Laura, kissing her on both cheeks before he turned away.

He was abandoning her to face the sharks alone? Laura gasped, "You can't leave!"

"Missing me already?"

"Hardly!" she retorted witheringly, even as she looked around her nervously.

"You're in good hands," Gabriel said. "Carlos will bring you to Oliveira's mansion. I have business to attend to, unfortunately. But I'll be waiting for you at the party."

"But what if…what if you're disappointed? What if my makeover is a failure? What if—"

Gabriel leaned forward to whisper in her ear, "Have fun."

Fun? Laura glared at him, her heart in her throat. What kind of fun would it be to look like a fool, to be nearly naked in front of Rio's notoriously body-conscious crowd, to be compared to Adriana da Costa in a bikini? She shook her head desperately and said for about the millionth time, "This isn't going to work!"

He gave her an annoyingly confident smile. "You're going to love this."

"You will not be disappointed, Mr. Santos," the older woman said, gently pulling Laura back into her clutches. Laura was suddenly aware that there were twenty salesgirls hovering around her, while all the other customers were being chased out of this expensive, exclusive store.

The two-story luxury boutique had just closed—for her.

"No," she whispered, feeling scared that she would let Gabriel down. "You're wrong about me. I'll never be a beauty."

"You are the one who is wrong." Gabriel's eyebrows

lowered fiercely as he looked down at her, his dark black eyes glittering. "Today, the whole world will see how beautiful you really are."

CHAPTER SEVEN

OLIVEIRA'S party was in full swing when Gabriel arrived.

Security was tight for this event, one of the most coveted private parties of the *Carnaval* season. Not for tourists or international celebrities, this was for well-connected Cariocas, the richest local tycoons and their glamorous mistresses and wives.

Gabriel was grimly sure he'd gotten this invitation only so that Felipe Oliveira could taunt him in public that he'd decided to sell Açoazul SA to someone else.

And where was Laura? Gabriel cursed softly under his breath. He'd arrived ten minutes late, after an urgent phone call from London. He needed Laura here at once, so he could introduce her to Felipe Oliveira and try to undo the damage that Adriana had spitefully caused.

Oliveira's mansion was on the most beautiful stretch of the Costa do Sul to the north of Rio. The sprawling house was a white classical confection like a wedding cake, surrounded by multilevel terraces, with a large pool that overlooked a private beach. Oliveira had been a workaholic all his life, but now that he was in his mid-sixties, he'd apparently lost interest in business in favor of possessing—and pleasing—a woman half his age.

It was the only reason he'd finally offered to sell the company back to Gabriel after almost twenty years.

Gabriel stood on the upper terrace, looking down toward the pool where he instantly saw Oliveira, wearing baggy shorts and a button-down shirt. The man was deep in conversation with French tycoon Théo St. Raphaël, who was definitely not a local, and whose presence here could be for one reason only.

Gabriel ground his teeth. The Frenchman wore a sleek gray suit. He alone among all the guests was not even pretending to dress for a pool party. Gabriel's hands tightened on the railing. The aristocratic French bastard excelled at breaking companies up for parts. The two had tangled before, and Gabriel knew St. Raphaël would like nothing more than to steal Açoazul from under his nose. All the assets of his father's company would be scattered around the world, coldly dissected for St. Raphaël's profit.

Gabriel narrowed his eyes. He couldn't let that happen.

But where was Laura?

Scowling, he glanced at his watch. Carlos had texted that they were on the way. But Gabriel would have to start on his own. Grimly going down the stairs to the lower terrace, he started walking toward Oliveira and his French rival.

"Gabriel," he heard a woman's voice coo behind him. Setting his jaw, he turned with a scowl.

Adriana da Costa smiled up at him from a poolside cabana, where she was holding court in her tiny bikini. Five half-naked young men surrounded her, offering her food she would never eat in a million years. Gabriel saw one particularly hapless youngster trying to tempt her with a platter of bread and cheese. Bread and cheese?

Adriana's idea of a fattening meal was menthol cigarettes and a handful of raisins.

Lounging in her chair, she lazily stretched her skinny arm up over her wide-brimmed straw hat as she looked up at him. In her other hand, she was holding a glass of something that looked like water but was likely vodka on the rocks.

"What a lovely surprise," Adriana drawled. Her eyes raked over Gabriel's shorts and short-sleeved shirt, now open over his bare chest without the tank top. "I didn't know Felipe invited you." She smiled slyly. "I heard the two of you ran into some sort of...trouble."

Gabriel set his jaw. She knew perfectly well why he hadn't been able to close the deal. Since Gabriel had ended their short tumultuous affair, Adriana had been determined to get his attention, and now she had it. She clearly wanted to either have him back in her bed, or wreak her revenge.

How he despised her.

Curving his lips into a smile, he walked past the young men clustered around her and stood at the bottom of her lounge chair, near her perfectly pedicured feet. "Does Oliveira know you are keeping such company?"

"Oh, these?" She shrugged, indicating her admirers with a wave of her hand. "They are just my friends."

"You are an engaged woman. You should not have such friends."

"Go away, all of you," she told them in English. Pouting slightly, she sat back in her chair. "It is easy for you to say. You pushed me into an engagement that I never wanted."

"I would never push anyone into marriage."

"Dropping me like you did, what did you expect me

to do?" She sat up straight in her lounge chair, leaning forward to expose her cleavage to better advantage. "No man has ever left me before. You wouldn't return my calls. I fell into the arms of the first rich man who proposed to me!"

Gabriel set his jaw again. "And that is why you are trying to destroy my business deal with Oliveira?"

She shrugged gleefully. "I just told Felipe the truth—that we were once lovers."

"You implied more than that," he said. "You made him believe if I moved permanently to Rio, I would make it my mission to lure you into my bed."

Adriana looked up at him like a smug Persian cat, fluttering her long dark eyelashes. "Wouldn't you?"

He stared down at her, unable to believe her vanity. She'd been a pain in the ass as a mistress, possessive and jealous. But clearly, she still believed that he, like any man, must be lusting after her as a matter of course.

He was tempted to correct that impression, but if he did, she might do some real damage and lie to her fiancé, tell him that Gabriel had made a pass at her. Clenching his hands with the effort it took to hide his dislike, Gabriel forced himself to say pleasantly, "I will always treasure our time together, but that time is over. I am with another woman now. In a committed relationship."

"Committed? You?" Adriana stared at him, her eyes wide and shocked. It was very satisfying. For several seconds all he could hear was samba music from the live band. Seagulls flew overhead, their cries mingling with those of the guests and laughter of the Cariocas lying out in the sun. She licked her lips. "That's impossible," she said faintly. "You will never settle down."

"And yet I have."

"Who is the woman?" she demanded. "Do I know her?"

"My former secretary," he said. "Laura Parker."

Adriana sucked in her breath. "I knew it," she declared. Her eyes glittered. "I always knew there was something between you. Every time you ran to her in the middle of the night, every time you explained why she was the only woman who could possibly live in your flat, every time you swore your relationship was innocent, I knew you were *lying*!"

"I wasn't lying," he said. "At the time, she was just my employee."

"She was always more than that!"

"All right. We were friends," he said tersely. "But never more. Not until last year, when—"

"Spare me the details!" Adriana hissed.

A wide shadow suddenly fell between them from the front of the cabana, blocking the sun's reflection off the pool. "Is there a problem?"

Gabriel turned to see Felipe Oliveira standing behind him. His shapeless shirt covered his large belly, and his eyes were hard as bullets in his jowly face. He must have seen Gabriel come down the terrace steps and apparently make a beeline for Adriana. *Perfeito*, Gabriel thought, irritated.

"No problem." He glanced at Adriana, who'd folded her arms to look away in sulky silence. "I was just telling your future bride that her love for you has inspired me to make a similar commitment. My secretary and I have had an on-off affair for the last year, and I've asked her to move in with me."

Silence fell, until Adriana cried, "Move in with you?"

Oliveira stroked his double chin with shrewd watchfulness in his heavy-lidded gaze. "So you've decided to make a commitment to another woman. How romantic. How very…convenient."

The older man was no fool. Deliberately, Gabriel shrugged. "Laura is everything I've ever wanted."

Adriana muttered a blasphemous curse. "I always knew the little mouse was in love with you."

In love? Gabriel frowned. Adriana was mistaken. Laura couldn't love him. She was too smart for that. She knew his deep flaws far too well. Laura wouldn't give her heart to an undeserving man who would break it.

Or would she? He paused, remembering how she'd let herself conceive a child by a man who wouldn't marry her, a man she didn't even love.

Adriana said scornfully, "With her adoring, sickening gaze on you all the time, I knew it was just a matter of time." She gave him a hard look. "But your relationship won't last. Because we both know you care about only one thing."

Aware of Oliveira watching them, Gabriel stared down at her coolly. "And what is that?"

"Power. Glamour. Blatant sex appeal. And your secretary does not have it." Adriana tossed her head. "She's nothing but a drab little nobody who…"

She paused, tilting her head. Gabriel frowned, then he heard it, too—a low hum of male voices behind them, rolling across the pool and terraces like gathering thunder. Adriana leaned forward to look around the doorway of her cabana. Oliveira and Gabriel slowly turned.

A woman had just stepped out of the mansion, and

was coming down the stairs from the upper terrace toward the pool. She was wearing a tiny bikini, typical attire for Rio. Carioca women were among the sexiest in the world, and the women at this party were among the most beautiful in the city. One new beauty should have been nothing, and yet something about this particular woman caused every man who saw her to stop in his tracks.

Even the young men who'd hovered around Adriana suddenly were craning their necks to stare. A waiter who'd come to refill Adriana's drink accidentally poured vodka on her bare thigh, causing her to curse aloud as she rose to her feet. "Oh, you stupid—get away from me!"

But no one was looking at Adriana. Not anymore.

The beautiful new guest was petite and curvy, her hips swaying as she moved. Long honey-blonde hair hung in waves down her bare back. She had creamy skin, and beneath the triangles of her top, the largest, most perfect breasts any man could imagine.

Gabriel's jaw dropped as he recognized her, this woman coming around the pool toward the cabanas with such effortless grace. The woman who had brought Felipe Oliveira's exclusive, glamorous party to a standstill.

Laura.

Laura trembled as she walked in her high heels. She felt naked in her bikini, passing through the crowds of beautiful, glamorous people who one by one turned to gape at her. Her legs shook as she walked down the stairs toward the lower terrace, where cabanas overlooked the pool and private beach.

She walked past the musicians, past the buffet table, where a handsome, hawkish man in a gray suit stood staring at her. She stiffened as she walked passed him, her head held high though her cheeks burned. People's heads were turning sharply enough to cause whiplash. Men's eyes widened. Women's eyes narrowed. Laura's hand shook as she pushed her mirrored aviator sunglasses a little higher up her nose.

Wearing this tiny bikini was almost worse than wearing nothing at all. It had been crocheted of natural, wheat-colored yarn. She'd never gone out in public dressed in so little before. She had barely ever seen *herself* this naked, always averting her eyes from the mirror when she came out of the shower. Now, she could feel the hot sun of Rio burning against her skin.

Or maybe it was just the flush of heat caused by all the eyes roaming every inch of her, tracing the lines of her breasts, butt and legs.

Laura swallowed, wishing the earth would swallow her whole. She threw a glance of longing toward the Atlantic on the other side of the terrace gate. She had the sudden yen to throw herself in the water and start swimming for Africa.

But she forced herself to keep walking, looking for Gabriel to the right and left. She couldn't run away. He was paying her a million dollars, and she couldn't quit just because she was scared. She was on a job and she would earn her money. Every penny.

But she wished she knew what people were thinking. Were they staring because they thought she looked nice? Or because she looked so hideously bad? As soon as she was out of earshot, would they all dissolve into scornful laughter?

Mrs. Tavares had taken her into the center of a whirlwind at Zeytuna, barking orders in quick-fire Portuguese, and there had soon been five stylists surrounding her, doing her hair, hands, toenails. An on-call optometrist had come to fit her eyes for contact lens. Laura had tried on hundreds of potential outfits for the pool party, for the Fantasy Ball, casual clothes for later, even lingerie. Though she had protested at the lingerie, her every complaint had been ignored. Laura's mousy brown hair had been highlighted. The stylists had started to prepare a spray-on tan to darken her skin, until Mrs. Tavares had stopped them.

"No. Leave her pale. Her creamy beauty will stand out from the fake tans of all the rest."

Laura's makeup had been done to perfection, so lightly as to be barely visible, and yet somehow making her look…good.

Mrs. Tavares had ordered her to try on many bikinis before she'd finally been satisfied with this one. Laura couldn't tell the difference—they'd all just seemed to be tiny triangles of fabric, barely covering anything at all. But the Brazilian woman had chosen this one, crocheted of soft beige yarn. *"Perfeito,"* she'd said. "It shows you off to perfection, Miss Parker. You are soft, womanly, with those curves. You are *real*." Mrs. Tavares's thin lips had curved. "You will stand out."

It was true that Laura's breasts had always been somewhat on the generous side, and since she'd left New Hampshire to have a secretarial career in New York, she'd gone to a great deal of effort to hide them, to make sure it was her professional skills that attracted attention, not her body.

"You have the perfect figure," Mrs. Tavares had said

with satisfaction as they'd stared at the result of Laura's makeover in a full-length mirror. "A Marilyn Monroe for the modern age. The gold standard of femininity."

Laura didn't quite believe her. A lifetime of feeling plain and unfashionable, especially compared to the glamorous women of New York, had left it imprinted on her mind that she was the hardworking one. The smart one. Never in her whole life had she been the pretty one.

But of course Mrs. Tavares would give her compliments, Laura had told herself as Carlos drove her to the mansion. The woman had been hired to give Laura a makeover, so naturally she would try to make the best of things. Laura had taken her praise with a pound of salt.

But still, the older woman had almost managed to convince her. Laura had felt confident, even pretty, when she'd left the boutique. Now, beneath so many open stares, she felt shy.

And afraid. What if, after everything, she failed Gabriel? Would he refuse to pay her the million dollars he'd promised? Or worse, would he just shake his head and look at her with cool dark eyes and say in a low voice, "I'm disappointed in you, Laura. I thought you were better than this"?

It had taken more courage than she'd imagined even to get out of the Rolls-Royce. Carlos had held her door open for almost a full minute, conspicuously clearing his throat before Laura had gathered enough bravado to get out of the car and walk into the mansion with her shoulders thrown back. Now, beneath the eyes of so many glamorous people, she felt vulnerable. *Exposed.*

Where was Gabriel?

Laura's feet shook in her ridiculously high heels as she walked around the pool. She didn't dare meet anyone's eyes, for fear of the scorn or mockery she might see there. She kept walking, keeping her gaze over people's heads, looking for one man who would stand out above the rest. She ignored the low hum of voices around her. She held her hand above her forehead, shading her sunglasses, as she looked for him. Would he laugh when he saw her? Would he regret whatever madness had caused him to think, even for an instant, that she could convince the world she was the woman who'd finally vanquished his playboy heart?

The thought made her throat hurt. Her hand fell to her side. She swallowed, suddenly unable to take the strain of all those mocking eyes on her.

"Que beleza."

Hearing Gabriel's low, husky voice behind her, she whirled around. She saw him standing in the doorway of a large poolside cabana. He was wearing shorts and an open shirt that revealed his muscular chest, tanned and laced with dark hair. Beside him she recognized Felipe Oliveira, looking sweaty and suspicious. But she was so relieved to find Gabriel that she hurried forward, pushing her sunglasses up on her head with a relieved smile. "Oh, Gabriel. I'm so glad to find you. I—"

Then she saw the woman standing behind them in the cabana and drew back with an intake of breath. "Oh. Miss da Costa. Hello."

The supermodel folded her arms icily. "I think we're a little past the politeness of 'Miss da Costa,' don't you? You must call me Adriana now," she said, in the exact same tone one might say *Go to hell.*

Laura blinked beneath the woman's malevolent

gaze. Then she remembered Gabriel's words. *You have something Adriana does not. You have me.* Looking at Adriana's angry expression, Laura realized their plan was working. The supermodel clearly believed Laura was Gabriel's lover—and hated her for it!

Straightening her shoulders, she looked at Gabriel with a smile. "Sorry I'm late."

He kissed her cheek tenderly. "I waited thirty-eight years to find you, *querida*," he breathed. "What are a few minutes more?"

He put his arm around her. After smiling at each other, they both turned to see the effect.

Felipe Oliveira looked skeptical. Adriana was scowling, sticking out her lower lip.

"You can't really be moving in together!" she said.

Laura glanced at him. Moving in together?

"It's already done," Gabriel said. He looked down at Laura, and his dark eyes were hungry and tender as he stroked her cheek.

Adriana gave a forced laugh. "She's no one. Nothing."

Gabriel wrapped his arms around Laura's bare waist. She nearly gasped at the rough feel of his hands against her naked skin.

"I am the one who is nothing." His black eyes burned through Laura's soul. "Nothing without you."

It's an act, she told herself as her heart turned over in her chest.

"All this time, you were right in front of me," he murmured as his wide, rough hand traced softly down her cheek. "The woman of my dreams." He cupped her face, tilting up her chin as he suddenly smiled. "I would fight them all for you."

"Fight who?" she whispered.

Staring at her, Gabriel gave a sudden laugh. Turning, he silently pointed behind them.

Following his gaze, Laura saw all the gorgeous party guests whispering to each other around the pool, staring back at them.

Of course they would stare at Gabriel, Laura thought. He was the sexiest, most sought after bachelor on earth. But they weren't looking just at him. Even Laura, inexperienced as she was, could see that.

And she suddenly knew, down to her bones, that they weren't staring at her because she was *ugly*.

She suddenly blinked back tears. Her makeover had created the illusion that Laura was worthy to be Gabriel's mistress. For the first time in her life, she felt beautiful. It was dizzying. Electrifying.

But the feeling hadn't been caused by magic fairy dust. She looked up at him.

It was the magic of his dark, hungry gaze. The magic echo of his words.

All this time, you were right in front of me. The woman of my dreams.

She was dimly aware of Adriana's angry scowl. But Laura didn't care about her anymore. Everyone else around them faded into a blur.

She and Gabriel were the only two people on earth. His dark eyes met hers, and his gaze fell to her lips. With agonizing slowness, he started to move his head toward hers. She realized he was going to kiss her, and her heart pounded frantically in her throat.

"Am I to understand," Felipe Oliveira said in a gruff voice behind them, "that this girl, your supposed lover, used to be your employee?"

Straightening, Gabriel turned to him, and Laura was able to breathe again. She leaned her cheek against his chest, still dizzy from how close she'd come to being kissed.

"His employee?" Adriana sneered. "She was his *secretary*."

Gabriel gave her a cool smile before turning his focus back on his rival. "Laura was once my secretary, *sim*, for five years. But now she's so much more." Looking down as she nestled in his arms, he stroked her cheek and said softly, "Now…she's the woman who tamed me."

CHAPTER EIGHT

IT's only an act. Only an act!

But in spite of the constant repetition of those words, Laura's heart still didn't believe it as she looked up into Gabriel's dark eyes.

"Really," the other man drawled in accented English. His eyes traced over Laura. "She's certainly beautiful. But this is all too convenient." He folded his arms over his belly. "You've fabricated this affair, so I'll still sell you Açoazul."

Laura's pulse hammered in her chest. Convinced that their plan had failed before it had half started, she pulled away from Gabriel. But he held her tight in his powerful arms, even as he never looked away from the other man.

"Why would I do that?" Gabriel said coolly.

The man looked at Adriana's tall beauty, then back at Gabriel with a scowl. "You know why."

"You'd be a fool not to sell me Açoazul," Gabriel said sharply. "No other competitor has offered you a fraction of the price. Théo St. Raphaël certainly won't. Don't lose a fortune based on some unfounded fear!"

The older man stiffened. "I'm not *afraid*. And it's not unfounded."

Gabriel nuzzled her neck. "I'm not interested in any woman except Laura."

She leaned back against him, closing her eyes. The feel of his lips and the nibble of his sharp teeth against the sensitive flesh caused sparks to thrill down her body. She heard the other man hiss through his teeth, and opened her eyes. Felipe Oliveira and Adriana were staring at them with shock. Looking up at Gabriel, Laura shivered as a single bead of sweat trickled down her bare skin between her breasts. The air between them suddenly crackled with sexual energy.

"Come, *querida*," Gabriel said in a low voice. "It's getting hot. I need to cool off."

Wrapping her hand in his own, he pulled her away from the cabana and across the terrace through the open gate, past the security guards to the private beach. Turquoise waves pounded the white sand with a rhythmic roar. Laura glanced back at the party behind them. She and Gabriel were still in full view of the mansion and terraces as he led her across the sand.

"You did it," Gabriel said when they were out of earshot.

"Did I?" Looking up, she furrowed her brow. "He didn't seem to believe us."

"Of course he's suspicious. The man's not stupid. But we'll soon convince him we're in love."

"How?" she whispered.

He reached down and stroked a tendril of hair from her face.

"To think all this time I had such a beauty working for me," he breathed, then shook his head with a laugh. "I'm glad you didn't look like this when you were my secretary. I wouldn't have gotten any work done."

"You wouldn't?"

"It was hard enough as it was. You were always too pretty. I wanted you from the first day I met you, when you came up to my office wearing that old brown suit and big glasses."

He remembered the clothes she'd worn the day they met? "You don't have to talk like this." Her heart was hammering in her throat. "No one can hear us."

"That's why I'm saying it," he said. "Come on."

He yanked off his flip-flops and shirt, leaving them on the sand as he pulled her into the sea. Kicking off her high-heeled shoes, she followed him, almost willing to follow him into the very depths of the ocean as long as he kept hold of her hand.

He led her into the water, deeper and deeper still. She looked at him in front of her, and her eyes hungrily traced the hard curves of his muscular back, his strong legs. She felt the shock of cool water against her skin as they walked through the ocean waves, moving slower and slower until the water reached their thighs.

He glanced behind her. "They're still watching." He smiled. "You make this too easy. Any man would want you. Half the men here are in love with you already."

Laura swallowed, yearning to tell him she didn't care, that he was the only man she wanted, the only one she'd ever wanted. She'd once loved him with all her heart, this man with the warm dark eyes that made her melt, who whispered words of adoration, who made her body sizzle even when they weren't out in the hot sun.

Gabriel's sensual mouth curved. "And you've proved yourself every bit the skilled actress I hoped you'd be. The way you shivered and leaned back against me when

I kissed your neck, as if you were head over heels in love with me...they bought it all."

Except it hadn't been an act. Beneath the blazing sun, they stared at each other, thigh-deep in the cool turquoise water, swaying in the currents. She felt the splash of the cool waves against her hot, bare thighs.

He came closer to her. "The way you look at me sometimes..." His gaze searched hers. "It reminds me of something that Adriana said. As if you really..."

"Really what?" Laura whispered.

He pulled back, his self-mocking mask back in place on his darkly handsome face. "I think I really do need to cool off," he said with a laugh, and he fell back with a splash into the water.

When he resurfaced, Gabriel sprang from the waves like a god of the sea, scattering sparkling droplets as he tossed his black hair back. Rivulets streamed down his tanned, hard-muscled chest. She couldn't look away. She wanted him to kiss her. She wanted him to make love to her, hard and fast, slow and soft, and never stop. Most of all, she wanted him to love her.

He came toward her, his eyes dark. He took her in his arms, and she felt the hard muscles of his chest press against her bare skin. He looked down at her.

"I know what you're thinking," he said huskily. "I know what you need."

Her mouth went dry. "You—you do?"

Without warning, he lifted her up in his arms, against his wet, muscled chest. Her head fell back in surprise, and she had a brief image of the blue sea and distant green jungle before she realized what he meant to do. Holding her tightly in his arms, he fell back into the waves.

She had one instant to gasp in a breath before she felt the cool water splash against her skin and she was baptized by the waves.

When he lifted her back out of the sea, she sputtered in outrage, kicking her legs against his chest. "I can't believe you did that!"

"Why?" he said lazily. "Didn't it cool you off?"

"That's not the point!"

"It felt good. Admit it."

"It felt great," she muttered. "But you spent a fortune to get me to look pretty, and now you've ruined it. They spent ages getting my hair just right—"

"I haven't ruined anything." His arms tightened over her bikini-clad body. She saw they'd gone farther from the shore. The water now reached his waist, and she could feel the slide of the waves moving sinuously and languorously against her backside and thighs. Her cheeks grew hot as she realized the crocheted yarn bikini, with all its tiny holes, was transparent when wet. "I'm done with this party," Gabriel growled, looking down at her. His hands tightened. "I'm taking you home."

At the rough sound of his voice, a shiver went through her. Tension coiled low in her belly as his dark gaze devoured her with ruthless hunger.

As he started wading back through the waves, clutching her against his chest, she felt their overheated skin pressed together beneath the hot sun.

Against her will, Laura's gaze fell to his mouth, to the cruel, sensual lips that had kissed her with such passion. He looked down at her, then stopped. For several seconds, he just stood in the water, staring down at her.

Releasing her from his hold, he let her go, let her slide slowly down his body against him. She felt how much he desired her, felt his hard body beneath the water. His eyes were like fire.

Cupping her chin in his hands, he lowered his head to hers.

As he kissed her, she felt the hard press of his satin-smooth lips, the sweet, tantalizing taste of his tongue, the salty taste of his rough skin. She surrendered in his arms in the swaying ocean, floating on waves. Drowning in him.

As Gabriel kissed her, standing in the ocean, he felt the warmth of her naked skin in the swaying, cool water. He tasted the wet heat of her mouth. Suddenly, he knew he had to have her. Now.

He heard catcalls behind them in Portuguese and realized he'd forgotten about the party. He'd forgotten about Oliveira and Adriana. At this moment, he didn't give a damn about them.

He kept kissing Laura, even when she tried to pull away. She resisted. Relented. Surrendered. Then, with a gasp, she did pull away.

The waves rolled against their skin, pushing their bodies together as they stared at each other. Her eyes seemed to glimmer. With tears? Gabriel frowned. "Are you crying?"

"Of course not!" she said, rubbing her eyes.

He reached out to tilt her chin upward, forcing her to meet his gaze. "You're a terrible liar."

She looked away. "Don't women usually weep when you kiss them?"

Her tone was light, even sardonic. He felt as if he was in some strange dream as he looked down at her. This beautiful woman was Laura, and yet not Laura. "They usually weep when I leave."

She flashed him a glance. "If they're your employees, they're probably weeping with joy."

His lips tugged up into a grin against his will. *Meu Deus.* Even now, she could make him laugh, when all he could think of was dragging her back home, ripping off her tiny bikini and pulling her naked body into his bed. All he wanted was to be alone with her, to feel her soft limbs caress him, to pull her back into a red-hot kiss so explosive it burned him from within.

He would have her. Tonight.

I always knew the little mouse was in love with you.

He angrily shook away the memory of Adriana's words. Laura didn't love him. She couldn't. She was too smart for that. It wasn't love that existed between them. It was sex. Just sex. He shuddered. It would be, as soon as humanly possible.

"I'm taking you home," he said. "To bed."

The bravado fell from her beautiful face. She looked up, and her expression suddenly looked vulnerable. Young. The reflective waves of the water lit up her pale body, exposing her full curves, illuminating her beautiful face, which now seemed to hold new secrets.

"No," she whispered. "Please. I'm not like you. Making love…it means something to me."

Looking down at her beauty, Gabriel felt no mercy in his heart. She wanted him, as he wanted her. Why hold back? Why hesitate from taking their pleasure? Laura should belong to him, as she always had. She should be his. His unselfish act of letting her go last year had been a mistake.

And she'd had another man's baby. Sudden possessiveness raced through his body like a storm. Thinking of another man touching Laura left him in a rage. He wanted to get the memory of the other man off her skin. To make her forget anyone else had ever touched her.

With iron self-control, he took her hand. He heard her soft intake of breath as she stared up at him, her lips deliciously parted. His gaze fell to her mouth, but kissing her wouldn't be nearly enough. He led her out of the water and back to the sand. Stepping into his shoes, he grabbed his shirt, wadding it up in one hand.

"Where are we going?"

He glanced back at her. She looked as dazed as he felt. Her cheeks were flushed with passion, her lips bruised. "Home. Let Adriana believe we had to rush back to my penthouse."

"For an emergency?"

"I told you." He gave her a sensual, heavy-lidded look. "To bed."

He saw her shiver under the hot sun. Blinking, she knelt to pick up her high-heeled shoes. "But it's just a game," she whispered, sounding as if she were talking to herself as much as him. "It's not real."

Yet Gabriel was no longer sure. She'd come to Rio as his pretend mistress. Now he wanted to make it true. Where did the fantasy end and reality begin?

As he led her past security and across the lower terrace, he heard the whispers of the crowd racing ahead of them, a murmur rising like a wave of music. Gabriel didn't bother to glance at Felipe Oliveira or Adriana as he passed them. He was too infuriated by all the men staring at Laura. She did look beautiful with her long wet hair slicked back and beads of seawater sparkling on her skin like diamonds. And—Gabriel flinched—the yarn of her bikini was translucent when wet. Something he'd appreciated when they were alone, but now...

He bared his teeth at the other men as he led her across the terrace, a male predator protecting his chosen female. He climbed the stairs two at a time and entered the mansion, dripping water across the marble floors. As he led her toward the front door, he held her hand tightly. It felt so right in his. *Too* right.

He grabbed two towels from a uniformed attendant. "Tell my driver we are ready to depart."

The man hurried away. Gabriel took Laura outside to wait in the warm sun, away from prying eyes. Kneeling before her, he skimmed one plush towel over her bare skin, over her legs, her arms, the plump fullness of her breasts. Rising to his feet, he licked his lips and realized he was breathing hard.

He saw her swallow. Felt her tremble.

"Gabriel," she whispered, her voice hoarse, "Please..."

The Rolls-Royce pulled in front of the mansion, and Carlos leaped out to open the door, looking dismayed at his boss's early departure. He'd probably been playing dice with the other servants, Gabriel thought, but at this moment, he didn't give a damn about any man's pleasure but his own.

"Get in the car," Gabriel ordered Laura, his voice sounding admirably civilized compared to the roaring animal he felt like inside. When she didn't move, he grabbed her arm and pulled her roughly into the backseat.

As the driver closed the door behind them, Laura ripped her arm from Gabriel's grasp. "You don't need to be so rude!"

"Rude?" he growled.

"Yes, rude!"

Gabriel could tell she was hurt and angry. She thought he was being cruel. She didn't know it was all he could do not to push her back against the leather seat, to lay her flat on her back and rip off the little triangles of bikini. That all he wanted to do was taste those luscious breasts, throw himself over her, fill her completely. He clenched his hands into fists, shuddering at the sensual images that overwhelmed him. He wanted her—now. And he almost didn't care who saw them.

As Carlos started the engine, Gabriel forced himself to release her. He could wait until they got home. He could wait...

He repeated the mantra again and again as the car drove through the city. His body ached from the effort it took not to seize her in his arms. The slow drive though crowded streets, with police diverting traffic around sections closed for early evening parades, seemed to take forever.

Gabriel glanced at Laura sideways. The towel had slipped from her hands and the air-conditioning in the limo was no match for the way his temperature climbed every time he looked at her. Especially when he saw what the cold air was doing to her nipples beneath the bikini.

Water was still trickling from her wet hair, running slowly down her bare skin, down the valley between her large breasts. He wanted to run the edge of his fingertip down that trickle of water. He wanted to lap it up with his tongue. He wanted her spread naked across his bed, his body over hers, as he lowered his head to taste her, thrusting inside her, so deep, so deep...

As if she felt his gaze, she turned. Judging by the expression on her face, she hadn't been having such sensual images of him—oh no. She wanted to skewer him with a knife.

But as their eyes locked, her expression slowly changed. The glare slid away and her face turned bewildered, almost scared. With a visible tremble, she pulled the thick white towel tightly over her naked skin and looked out the window.

With a dark smile, Gabriel turned away.

She knew.

She knew what waited for them at home.

Memories of their one night together had caused months of hot, unsatisfied dreams for him. Now that he finally had her in Rio, he wasn't going to let her go. Not until he was completely satiated. He was done being unselfish when it came to Laura.

The car pulled up behind their building, but she didn't wait for Carlos to open her door. She flung it open herself and dashed out, heading for the private entrance.

It gave her a head start.

A low growl rose from the back of Gabriel's throat as he flung open his own door and raced out in grim pursuit. As he came around the car in the street, heading toward the curb, a red sedan nearly hit him. The driver honked angrily, but Gabriel didn't even pause, just leaped recklessly over the hood. He ran into his building's private lobby, across the marble floor. Ignoring the greetings of the guards, he ran for the private elevator just in time to see the silver doors slide together in front of Laura's face. Their eyes met for a single instant, and he saw the small smile that curved her lips. Then she was gone.

Gabriel cursed under his breath. He pressed the elevator button impatiently, multiple times, then rushed inside as soon as the door opened. When he arrived at the penthouse, he followed her voice.

"So Robby had a good day?" he heard her say from the terrace.

"Yes, Senhora Laura," Maria replied. "He had a good lunch, good play and is now having his second nap."

Breathing hard, Gabriel saw them through the windows, out on the terrace. The older woman was sitting in a lounge chair, with a glass of lemonade and the baby monitor on the table beside her, placidly knitting in the warm Brazilian sunshine.

"Did he miss me?" Laura's voice trembled. "Did he cry for me?"

"No, Mrs. Laura," she said kindly. "He had a happy day. But of course he will be glad to see his mama. He should wake soon. Perhaps you would like to take him on a walk?"

"Yes, I would like that. Thank you, Maria."

Laura turned and headed back inside. Gabriel ducked into the corner as she opened the sliding glass doors. Still holding her towel over her body, she started down the hall toward her bedroom.

He moved fast, springing like a jaguar. He heard her gasp as he shoved her through the open doorway of his room, pushing her against the wall. The towel dropped from her hands as he closed the door behind him with a bang. Grasping her wrists, he held her against the wall.

Without a word, without asking permission, he kissed her.

He felt the heat of her skin, covered only by the tiny bikini as he crushed her against the wall with his bare chest. Releasing her wrists, he grabbed the back of her head with his hand. Holding her tight against him, he kissed her savagely, hard enough to bruise, ruthlessly taking his pleasure.

CHAPTER NINE

WITH a gasp, Laura pulled back her hand and slapped his face.

"How dare you!" she cried.

The sound of the slap echoed in the bedroom. He stared at her incredulously, his hand on his cheek. Then his eyes narrowed. "Why are you pretending it's not exactly what you want?"

Laura sucked in her breath, feeling overwhelmed by need for what she could not—*could not*—allow herself to have. "Even if I want you, Gabriel, I know you're no good for me. It nearly killed me last year after our night together when you kicked me out of your life—"

"Kicked you out of my life?" he demanded. "You're the one who left!"

"You didn't try to talk me out of it. You didn't even ask me to stay!"

"I was trying to do what was best for you," he said. "I knew you wanted a husband, children. You needed a boss who didn't demand your life and soul. You needed a man who could love you as I cannot. So I gave you up, when it was the last thing I wanted! And what did you do?" He glowered. "You let yourself get pregnant by some cold bastard who cannot even be bothered to pay child support or visit his son!"

Tears streamed down her face as she shook her head. "Why do you keep torturing me about my pregnancy?"

"Because it means I sacrificed you for nothing!"

"Sacrificed?" she cried.

He grabbed her shoulders. "Don't you know how much I've wanted you, all this time?" His eyes searched hers fiercely. "Do you know how I've dreamed of you? In my office. In my bed!" His fingers tightened painfully on her shoulders. "If I'd known you would settle for so little, I would never have let you go!"

Panting with anger, they stared at each other in the shadowy bedroom, the only sound the violent rasping of their breath. His eyes were dark and furious with denied desire. His gaze fell to her lips.

"Laura..." he whispered.

She jumped when she heard Robby suddenly crying on the other side of the wall. All the shouting and the banging must have woken him.

"I'm not that virgin secretary anymore," she murmured, "free to make whatever stupid choices I want. I'm a mother now. My baby comes first." Setting her jaw, she pulled away from Gabriel. Stopping at the door, she looked back at him. "I gave in to passion once before," she said quietly. "And it nearly killed me."

Leaving him, she went to her own bedroom and locked the door behind her before she gathered her crying baby in her arms. Robby's plaintive wail instantly stopped as she cuddled him close. She breathed in the sweet smell of his hair.

She heard a low knock on the door.

"Laura." Gabriel's voice was muffled.

"Go away."

"I want to talk to you."

"No."

Silence fell on the other side of the door and she thought he'd left. She sat down in the rocking chair and held Robby in the darkness of the shuttered bedroom. Then Robby started to squirm and complain. Clearly, his nap was over and he was ready to play.

Setting her baby down on the carpet, with a pillow beside him in case he suddenly forgot how to sit and toppled over, she looked through the shopping bags that Mrs. Tavares had sent and selected some dark jeans and a white tank top. Pulling them on over a new bra and panties, Laura lifted her son onto her hip and quietly unlocked her door. Holding her breath, she peeked out into the hallway.

Gabriel stood leaning against the wall, waiting for her in jeans and a black T-shirt. His eyes were dark, almost ominous.

"Planning to sneak out?"

She took a deep breath, then tossed her head defiantly. "I'm taking my son for a walk."

"You need to get ready for the gala."

"It will just have to wait."

He stared at her, then set his jaw. "Fine. Then I'll come with you."

"Come with me?" she repeated incredulously.

He moved toward her quick as a flash, scooping Robby from her arms.

"Hey!" she cried.

Gabriel looked down at the baby, who was staring up at him with a transfixed expression. A shadow of a smile passed over Gabriel's handsome face. Turning, he opened the front closet and pulled out a folded stroller, an expensive brand that she would never have purchased on her own. Still holding the baby with one powerful arm, Gabriel opened the stroller with his other, in one easy gesture.

Her jaw fell. "How did you know how to do that?"

He shrugged.

She tried again. "Have you ever been around a baby before?"

He looked away. "It's madness outside. You are my guests. I will keep you safe."

"To protect us from a festival on Ipanema Beach? We're just going for a walk!"

"Funny. So am I."

"You're being ridiculous."

Putting Robby into the stroller, he clicked the baby's seat belt, then without a word, pressed the elevator button. The doors opened and he pushed the stroller onto it. Looking at her, Gabriel waited.

Exhaling, she followed him onto the elevator. The doors closed, leaving the two of them with only a baby stroller between them.

"Why are you doing this?" she said through her teeth.

"For my own selfish reasons, no doubt," he said dryly. "That is why I do everything, is it not?"

"Yes, it is." She bit out the words, then looked at him. "Why? Is there a chance Felipe or Adriana might see us?"

"There is always a chance," he said. "It's not impossible."

The elevator doors opened, and she grabbed the

handle of the stroller and pushed it through the lobby. Gabriel held the door open for her and they were out on the street.

Since she'd last been outside, the *avenida* had become even more crowded, filled with people celebrating *Carnaval*. Music was blaring, tubas and drums, as people sang and danced in the street with their friends, some of them wearing extremely provocative costumes as they gulped down *caipirinhas*, the famous Brazilian cocktail of lime and distilled sugarcane.

Laura and Gabriel walked down the beach to a slightly quieter area and found an empty spot past a big yellow umbrella. She saw families splashing in the surf with their children, as nearby, groups of young people drank together beneath the sun as they waited for the nighttime party to really begin, the women wearing tiny thong bikinis, the men in skintight shorts.

Laura took Robby out of the stroller, and when she looked around, Gabriel was gone. She placed her baby in her lap and Robby reached to take a handful of sand in his fist. She saw Gabriel across the beach, talking to a *barraqueiro*. A moment later, he was walking back across the beach toward her. He held up a plastic shovel and pail.

"I thought Robby would like to play," he said gruffly.

"Thank you," she said, shocked at his thoughtfulness.

He smiled, and the warmth of his suddenly boyish face as he held out the pail and shovel to Robby nearly made her gasp. As the baby happily took the shovel, Gabriel stretched out beside them and showed him how to dig in the sand.

Laura stared at him in amazement.

First he'd known how to handle the stroller. Then he'd thought of buying toys for their baby. He claimed he disliked children, so why was he acting like this?

Robby responded to his father's tutelage by first trying to chew on the shovel, then to eat the sand. Gabriel laughed, and with infinite patience, again showed him how to dig. Soon he had the baby in his lap. Robby was very curious about sand and kept dumping it on them both, then laughing uproariously. Soon deep male laughter joined with the baby squeals, and for Laura it was the sound of joy. She looked at Gabriel's handsome face, watching him as he smiled down at the child he did not know was his, and her heart filled her throat.

How could he not realize that Robby was his son?

"He likes you," she whispered. "And you seem to know how to take care of a baby."

Gabriel's dark eyes met hers. Then his expression abruptly became cold. He handed Robby back to her, causing the baby to give a little whine of protest. "No, I really don't."

All around them, she was dimly aware of the noise of the street party, of half-naked Cariocas tanning themselves beneath the sun, of people laughing and singing and making music all around them.

It wasn't too late for her to tell Gabriel the truth. She could tell him now. *By the way, Gabriel, I never took any other man as my lover. You were so careful to use protection, but guess what? You're Robby's father.*

How would he take that news?

He wouldn't be glad. Even in her most fantastic dreams she knew that. He'd told her a million times, in every possible way, that he didn't want a wife or children. Even today, when he'd asked her to be his mistress for real, he'd said he'd be willing to "overlook" her child. That he'd allow her baby to live in the downstairs apartment so he wouldn't be forced to endure his presence.

And worse. If there was one thing Gabriel resented almost as much as the thought of having a family, it was someone lying to his face. If he found out that Laura had lied to him for over a year, he would never forgive her. He would take responsibility for the child they'd created—yes—and he'd try to get some kind of custody. But he would not love their son. And he would *hate* her.

Tomorrow, she repeated to herself desperately. They would go home to their little farmhouse in the great north woods, safe and sound. She'd never have to see Gabriel again.

But that reassurance was wearing thin. Every moment she spent with Gabriel, seeing him with their son, she found herself wishing she could believe the dream. Wishing he could love them.

The truth about Robby hovered on her lips. But the rational part of her brain stayed in control, keeping her from blurting it out. If she told him the truth, only bad things could happen. And she'd no longer be in control of Robby's future.

Gabriel glanced at his watch. The sun had started to lower in the sky over the green Dois Irmãos mountain rising sharply to the west. "We should go. Your stylist is waiting at the penthouse."

"Stylist?"

He rose to his feet. "For the gala."

He held out his hand, and Laura hesitated. A wistful

sigh came from her lips. The brief happiness of feeling like a family was over. "All right."

She allowed him to pull her to her feet. Tucking a yawning, messy, sand-covered Robby back into the stroller, she followed Gabriel across the beach toward home. By now the avenue was so crowded that Gabriel had to physically clear a path for the stroller.

When they safely reached the opposite side of the street, he looked at her. "I'm looking forward to seeing your dress tonight." He gave her a sensual smile. "And seeing it off you."

He was so sure of himself it infuriated her. But as his dark eyes caught hers, her feet tripped on the sidewalk. He caught the stroller, grabbing her arm. Then, leaning forward, he kissed her.

"Nothing will stop me from having you," he whispered in her ear. "Tonight."

With an intake of breath, she felt butterflies of longing and sharp bee stings of need all over her body. Tightening her hands on the handle, she pushed the stroller as fast as she could toward the building. She told herself that the sexy, tender, strong man she'd just seen on the beach, playing with their baby son, was a mirage. She couldn't let herself be fooled by his act. Gabriel was always ruthlessly charming when he wanted something. And right now, he wanted her.

Gabriel Santos always won by any means necessary. Both in business and his romantic conquests. But once he'd had what he wanted, once he'd possessed her in his bed, he would be done with her. He would no longer be willing to tolerate the fact that she had a child. He would toss her out, or drive her out. He would replace her.

She licked her lips as he caught up with her. "What's going to happen tonight?"

His sensual mouth curved. "You already know."

She looked at his face. There was a five o'clock shadow on the hard edges of his jaw, giving his handsome face a barbaric appearance. "Felipe Oliveira is no fool. He's suspicious. What if after tonight, he still doesn't believe that you love me?"

"He will."

"And if he doesn't?"

Gabriel's dark eyes glinted with amusement. "Then I have a plan."

CHAPTER TEN

THE Fantasia gala ball was the single most sought-after invitation of Rio de Janeiro's *Carnaval*. Laura had read about it in celebrity gossip magazines in the United States. The glamorous event, held in a colonial palace on the Costa Verde south of Rio, attracted beautiful, rich and notorious guests from all around the world. And tonight, Laura would be one of them. Tonight, she would be Gabriel Santos's beloved mistress.

His *pretend* mistress, she corrected herself fiercely.

The door of the black Rolls-Royce sedan opened, and she and Gabriel stepped out onto the red carpet that led inside the palace, which had once been owned by the Brazilian royal family.

Gabriel looked brutally dashing in his black tuxedo. Laura felt his hungry gaze on her as he took her arm. She tried to ignore it, tried to smile for the benefit of the paparazzi flashing cameras around them, but her body shook beneath the palpable force of his desire.

I want you, Laura. And I will have you.

Liveried doormen in wigs opened tall, wide doors. Gabriel and Laura went down a gilded hallway, then entered a ballroom that sparkled like an enormous jewel box. Standing at the top of the stairs, Laura looked up in awe at the huge chandeliers glittering like diamonds overhead. From a nearby alcove, a full orchestra played, the musicians dressed in clothes of the eighteenth century, except with sequins and body glitter.

The guests milling around them drinking champagne, laughing, were in gowns and tuxedos that were even more beautiful. More outlandish.

As they paused at the top of the stairs, Gabriel turned to her. "Are you ready?"

Laura held her breath, feeling like a princess in a fairy tale, or maybe Julia Roberts in *Pretty Woman,* with her strapless red sheath gown and long white opera gloves that went up past her elbows. "Yes."

When Gabriel had first seen her in this dress, he'd choked out a gasp. "You are without question," he'd said hoarsely, presenting her with two black velvet boxes, "the most beautiful woman I've ever seen."

Now, Laura looked at him, tightening her hand over his arm as he escorted her down the sweeping stairs. A thick diamond bracelet now hung over her gloved wrist. Diamond bangles hung from her ears set off by her highlighted hair tumbling in soft waves down her shoulders.

She'd never felt so beautiful—or so adored. This ball was truly a fantasy, she thought in wonder.

Silence fell around them as Gabriel, the dashing, powerful Brazilian tycoon, led her onto the empty dance floor. Laura hesitated beneath the gaze of so many people. Then, seeing them, the orchestra changed the tempo of the music, and it was irresistible.

Within twenty seconds, other couples had joined them. By the second song, the floor was packed with people. But Laura hardly noticed. As Gabriel held her, she felt hot and cold, delirious in a tangle of joy and fear and breathless need.

He swirled her around on the dance floor, in perfect time with the music. She felt his heat through the sleek tuxedo that barely contained the brutal strength of his body, and all she could think about was the night he'd made love to her, when he'd pressed her against his desk and ripped off her clothes, taking her virgin body and making it his own. He'd filled her with pleasure that night. Filled her with his child.

Now, his dark eyes caressed her as he moved. Leaning her back, he dipped her, his handsome face inches from hers. Pulling her back to her feet, he kissed her.

His lips moved against hers, soft and warm, whispering of love that was pure and true. Promising her everything she needed, everything she'd ever wanted.

Promising a lie.

With an intake of breath, she jerked away from him, tears in her eyes. "Why are you doing this to me?"

"Don't you know?" he said in a low voice. "Haven't I made it clear?"

"We had a deal," she whispered. "One night in Rio. One million dollars."

"Yes." He looked down at her. "And now I'm not going to let you go."

She stared up at him, frozen, even as other couples continued to swirl around them in a dark, sexy tango.

"I'm not going to let you seduce me, Gabriel," she said, her voice shaking. "I'm not."

He looked down at her, his eyes dark with desire. He didn't argue with her. He didn't have to.

With a gasp, she turned and ran, leaving him on the dance floor. Looking wildly for escape, she saw open

French doors that led outside to some sort of shadowy garden. She ran for them, only to smack into a wall.

Except it wasn't a wall. A man grasped her shoulders, setting her aright as he stared down at her. "Good evening, Miss Parker."

"Mr. Oliveira." She licked her lips. Dressed in a tuxedo that only served to accentuate his bulk, he was drinking a martini beside the bar. Behind him, she saw the gorgeously pouting Adriana in a skimpy silver cutout dress that clung like spackle over her breasts and backside, leaving everything else bare down to her strappy silver high heels.

"Lovers' spat?" Felipe Oliveira said mildly.

Gabriel appeared behind her. He put his hands possessively on Laura's shoulders. "Of course not."

Swallowing, Laura leaned back against Gabriel, feeling the hardness of his body against hers, and tried her best to look as if her heart wasn't breaking. She forced her lips into a smile. "I, um, just wanted a little fresh air."

Gabriel wrapped his arms around her more tightly, nestling her backside firmly against his thighs as he nuzzled her temple. "And I wanted to dance."

Oliveira looked at them, his eyes narrowed. "You're both liars."

Gabriel shook his head. "No—"

"I'll tell you what is really going on," the older man interrupted. "You think I am stupid enough to fall for this. But if I sign those papers tomorrow selling you the company, you know what will happen?"

"You'll make a fortune?" Gabriel drawled.

His hooded eyes hardened. "You will end this charade and be once again free to pursue what does not belong to you."

Gabriel snorted. "Why would I possibly be interested in your fiancée, Oliveira, when I have a woman like this?"

The other man looked at Laura, then shook his head. "Santos, you change lovers with the rise of each dawn. Miss Parker is beautiful, but you will never commit to her for long. There is nothing you can say to convince me otherwise." He finished the last of his martini. "I will sell to the Frenchman."

"You will lose money!"

"Some things, they are more important than money."

Gabriel exhaled. Laura felt his body tense behind her, tight and ready to snap. "St. Raphaël is a vulture," he growled. "He will break my father's company up for parts, fire the employees, scatter the pieces around the world. He will crush Açoazul beneath his heel!"

"That is not my problem. I will not give you any reason to remain in Rio." Oliveira's jowly face was grim as he started to turn away, holding out his arm for Adriana, who could barely contain the smug look on her beautiful face.

They'd lost.

Laura's heart leaped up to her throat, choking her.

They'd failed. *She* had failed.

"You're wrong about me, Oliveira," Gabriel said desperately. "I can commit. I've always been ready to commit. I was just waiting for the woman I could love forever."

Frowning, the older man and Adriana glanced back at them. They stopped. Their eyes went wide.

As if in slow motion, Laura turned to face Gabriel, who was standing behind her.

Except he was no longer standing. He'd fallen to his knee.

He'd pulled a black velvet box out of his tuxedo pocket.

Opening it, he held up a ten-carat diamond ring.

"Laura," he said quietly, "will you marry me?"

Laura's jaw dropped.

She looked from the ring to Gabriel kneeling in front of her. She looked back at the ring.

I was just waiting for the woman I could love for- ever.

He'd changed his mind about love and commitment? Did he want her in his bed so badly he was willing to marry her?

He smiled, and everything else fell away. She was lost in his dark eyes.

"What is this?" Oliveira demanded. "Some trick? Now she's your pretend fiancée?"

Gabriel just looked at Laura. "Say yes. Make this an engagement party."

And Laura exhaled.

All her wedding dreams came crashing down around her. This proposal had nothing to do with love, or even sex. It was entirely about business.

This was his plan B.

Tears rose in her eyes, tears she hoped would appear to be tears of joy. Unable to speak over the lump in her throat, she simply nodded.

Rising to his feet, Gabriel kissed her. Tenderly, he placed the diamond ring on her finger. It fit perfectly.

Laura stared down at it, sparkling on her hand like an iceberg. It was beautiful. And so hollow.

"Hmm," Oliveira said, watching them thoughtfully. "Maybe I was wrong about you, Santos."

"You said you'd never marry anyone!" Adriana sounded outraged.

Never looking away from Laura's face, Gabriel smiled. "Plans change."

"But people don't," she spit out. "Not this much. You would never marry a woman with a baby!"

Stiffening, Gabriel turned to her.

"She has a baby," Adriana said spitefully to Oliveira. "They were seen together on Ipanema Beach. He just brought Laura here this morning, after they'd been apart for a year. Why would he suddenly decide he's in love with a woman after being apart for over a year? It's a trick, Felipe," she declared. "It's a lie. He's not committed to her. He won't commit to anyone."

"I can explain, Oliveira," Gabriel said through his clenched jaw.

Felipe Oliveira's jowly face hardened as he slowly turned to face his younger rival. "No," he said. "I'm afraid you can't. I don't appreciate this elaborate theater you've performed. The deal is officially off."

The man turned away. Laura saw Gabriel's frustration, saw his vulnerability and the desperate expression on his face as he lost his father's company forever.

"Wait," Laura gasped.

Snorting a laugh, Felipe Oliveira glanced back at her with amusement. "What could you possibly have to say, little one?"

"Everything that Adriana said is true," she whispered. "I have a baby. And I hadn't seen Gabriel since I left

Rio over a year ago. But there's a reason why he came for me. A very good reason he'd want to marry me."

Folding his arms over his belly, Oliveira looked at her with a shake of the head. "I am dying to hear it."

Laura didn't glance at Gabriel. She couldn't, and still say what she had to say. Closing her eyes, she took a deep breath. Then she spoke the secret she'd kept for over a year.

"Gabriel is the father of my baby."

CHAPTER ELEVEN

TREMBLING, Laura folded her arms.

"Ah," Felipe Oliveira said, stroking his chin with satisfaction as he looked from her to Gabriel with canny eyes. "Now I understand."

"No!" Adriana gasped. "It can't be true!"

Laura's gaze rested anxiously on Gabriel. His dark eyes were deep as the night sky. She saw him take a deep breath. Then slowly, very slowly, he came toward her. Never looking away from her face, he took her in his arms. Biting her lip in apprehension, Laura waited for his jaw to clench with fury and resentment. Waited for him to say something biting and cruel.

Instead, he gently kissed her cheek, then turned to face Oliveira and Adriana.

"We weren't going to tell anyone yet. But yes, Robby is my son. I wanted to wait until after our wedding to make it public. It seemed more proper."

"Proper?" Adriana sneered. "When have you ever cared about *proper*?"

Gabriel stiffened, glaring at her. "I have always cared about doing what is right," he said in a low voice. "I would never leave my child without a father, without a name."

"And yet," Oliveira said, shifting his savvy gaze between them, "you allowed your fiancée to raise your baby alone, for all these months."

Gabriel set his jaw. "I—"

"He didn't know about Robby," Laura interrupted in a whisper. "I didn't tell him. It wasn't until he came to my sister's wedding that he first saw his son. I knew Gabriel didn't want a family—"

"So he always insisted," Adriana said resentfully.

Gabriel's dark eyes glowed with warmth and love as he looked down at Laura, who was shivering in her red strapless gown and opera gloves. "But Robby changed my mind." He wrapped his warm, tuxedo-clad arms more firmly around her. "From the moment I saw Laura with our son, I knew I couldn't part with them. We were meant to be a family."

Laura blinked back her tears, hardly able to breathe as she heard the words she'd always dreamed of.

She'd told him the truth about Robby, and he knew it. She could see it in his eyes. Robby was his son. And this was Laura's reward for being brave enough to tell the truth. He wasn't rejecting her. He wasn't rejecting their baby.

All this time she'd thought it would be so hard to tell him the truth, but it wasn't. It was easy.

Staring at them, Felipe Oliveira stroked his chin. "You might be a bastard, Santos, but you wouldn't desert your son. Or your son's mother." He looked from Laura to Gabriel with a sly smile. "And I see the passion between you. I have been a doddering old fool to feel threatened. The two of you are in love." He gave a sudden decisive nod. "*Está bom.* We will sign the preliminary contracts tomorrow. Be at my lawyers' office at nine."

Gabriel put his arm around Laura's waist, smiling at the other man. "Sure."

Adriana glared at Laura. "You got pregnant on purpose! You tricked Gabriel into marriage!"

As Laura stiffened, Oliveira grabbed the supermodel's arm grimly.

"There's only one person you should worry about getting tricked into marriage," he said, "and that's me. I look at them—" he nodded toward Laura and Gabriel "—and I see love. I look at you, Adriana, and I see... nothing."

She stared at him, her eyes wide.

Oliveira lifted a white bushy eyebrow. "Our engagement," he said mildly, "is over."

He marched off across the ballroom. Adriana's cheeks went red as an amused titter flowed through the nearby crowd.

"Fine," she shrieked after him. "But I'm keeping the ring!"

Oliveira didn't even turn around. Frustrated greed filled Adriana's eyes, and with an intake of breath, she started to push forward. "Felipe," she whined, "wait!"

When they were alone in the crowd, Gabriel looked down at Laura. She took a deep breath, waiting for the onslaught of questions she knew were coming. "Oh, Gabriel. I know we have so much to talk about—"

"Wait." He glanced at the people around them, amused celebutantes and movie actors in designer clothes, rich and beautiful and dressed in sparkling, sexy gowns. "Come with me."

Grabbing two flutes of champagne from the tray of a passing waiter, Gabriel pulled her through the glorious, gilded ballroom, filled with music and magic, and out a side door.

The private garden was dark and quiet. Laura looked up and saw black silhouettes of palm trees swaying against the purple sky. The night was tropical and warm, and on the wild southern coast so far from the lights of the city, she could see stars twinkling down on them.

Biting her lip, she faced him. "So...so you don't mind?"

"Mind?" Smiling, he handed her a glass of champagne. His dark head was frosted with silvery moonlight as he leaned forward to clink his crystal flute against hers. "You are the most incredible woman I've ever met," he whispered. "Brilliant. Beautiful."

She stared up at him with trembling lips as joy flooded her heart. "You're not angry?"

"Angry?" His brow furrowed. "Why would I be angry? Because you lied?"

She licked her dry lips. "Yes."

He shook his head. "No, *querida*." His expression was tender. "I've just gotten everything I ever dreamed of. Because of you."

He drank deeply from his champagne flute, and she followed suit, her eyes wet with tears of joy. She'd never imagined he would react this way, not in a million years. What had she ever done to deserve this miracle—that Gabriel would so easily accept their child as his own? That he would be glad to be a father after all?

"I'm so happy," she whispered. Smiling, she wiped tears from her eyes. "I never dreamed you would react like this."

He looked down at her with a frown. "*Querida*, are you crying?"

"I'm happy," she whispered.

"So am I, my beautiful girl." He stroked her cheek, his fingertips lightly caressing her flushed skin. "You sexy, incredible woman," he breathed in her ear, causing prickles to spread down her body. Cupping her face, he lowered his mouth to hers. "I will never forget this night."

When he kissed her, his lips were hot and smooth on hers. He seared her with the sizzle of his tongue against her lips, teasing her. She gripped his shoulders, instinctively pulling him closer.

They heard a sudden burst of laughter as other guests came into the garden. Grabbing her hand with a low growl, Gabriel pulled her deeper into the trees, into a shadowy corner. Above them, palm trees swayed in the violet-smudged night. The other voices continued to come closer, and he pushed her all the way back against the palace wall. She felt the hardness of his body, the roughness of the stone behind her.

Without a word, he slowly kissed her throat. She closed her eyes, tossing her head back with a silent gasp. She felt his teeth nibble her neck, felt his hands skimming from her bare shoulders down the length of her arms, over her long white gloves. He kissed her bare collarbone, his hands cupping her breasts below the sweetheart neckline of her strapless gown. Pressing her breasts together, he licked the cleavage just above the red velvet, and she sucked in her breath.

Samba music poured out of the palace as the doors to the garden continued to bang open and more guests discovered the garden. Voices grew louder, laughing and sultry, murmuring in Portuguese and French, as other lovers approached their corner. Gabriel pulled away from her. "Let's get out of here," he growled.

She blinked at him, dazed with desire. "Leave the ball already? It's barely midnight."

Jerking her back against his hard body, he leaned his forehead against hers and whispered, "If we don't leave, I will take you right here."

Drawing in a breath, she saw his absolute intent to make love to her right here in the dark garden, against the wall, with people on the other side of the foliage and samba music wafting through the warm air. She gave a single nod.

Gabriel instantly grabbed her hand and dragged her through the garden, back into the ballroom. He pulled her through the huge, crowded space, wading against the flow of new arrivals. Laura heard people shouting greetings to him in a variety of languages, but he didn't stop. He didn't even look at them. He just pulled her relentlessly up the wide, sweeping stairs to the front door, where he tersely summoned his driver.

As they waited, they stood at the end of the red carpet, not looking at each other. His hand gripped hers, crushing her fingers through her gloves. She heard the hoarseness of his breath. Or maybe it was her own. Her heartbeat was rapid. She felt dizzy.

"What's taking so long?" Gabriel muttered beneath his breath. She felt his barely restrained power, felt the grip of his hand as if only sheer will kept him from turning to her and ripping off her slinky red gown, pushing her against the wall and tasting her skin, in front of all the servants, the valets and flash of the paparazzi's cameras.

It took three minutes before the Rolls-Royce sedan

pulled up and Carlos leaped out. Laura stared at the man's crooked tie. She saw a smudge of lipstick.

"Finally," Gabriel growled, grabbing his door.

"Sorry about the delay, *senhor*," Carlos said, casting a regretful glance back at the palace. Laura followed his gaze and saw a housemaid looking down from the second-floor window. Laura was so filled with joy, she couldn't bear the thought of everyone not being happy tonight. Standing on her tiptoes, she whispered in Gabriel's ear, "Give him the night off."

"Why?" he snapped. "I don't want to drive. I want to be alone with you in the back—"

"He was enjoying his time here." She tilted her head toward the window. "Look."

Gabriel glanced behind them, then instantly faced his driver, who'd just come around the car. "Carlos, you're dismissed."

"Senhor?" the man gasped in horror.

"Enjoy your night," he said. "I trust you can get a ride home tonight?"

Delight flooded the older man's face. "Yes, sir."

"I have an early appointment tomorrow. Do not be late." After opening the door for Laura, Gabriel walked around the car and climbed into the driver's seat.

Smiling at Carlos's dumbfounded expression, Laura fastened her seat belt, and Gabriel pressed on the gas. They drove down the tree-lined lane with a spray of gravel, and the flash of cameras from additional paparazzi parked outside the gate.

"I know a shortcut," Gabriel said a moment later. Turning off the busy main road, he drove down the rocky coast, the luxury sedan bouncing hard over the rough road. Laura looked out her window. The landscape was hauntingly beautiful, filled with trees and thickets of jungle that wound along the sharp cliffs overlooking the moonlit Atlantic.

She looked back at the dark silhouette of Gabriel's brutally handsome face, his Roman nose and angular jaw. She saw the tight clench of his hand on the gearshift, saw the visible tension of his body beneath his tuxedo.

As a warm breeze blew tendrils of hair across her face, she was so filled with joy she thought she might die. Life was wonderful, incredible, magical. How had she never fully realized it before?

It was Gabriel. He was the dark angel who'd changed her life forever. Her heart was his. Forever.

She loved him.

"Don't look at me like that," he said in a low voice, glancing at her. "It's a two-hour drive back to the city."

She sucked in her breath. "Can't you drive any faster?" she begged.

With a curse, he suddenly steered the car off the road with a wide spray of gravel, taking a sharp turn past a thicket of trees that ended on a dark bluff overlooking the wide ocean. He slammed on the brake and turned off the engine. The headlights went black, and with a low growl he was upon her.

But the front of the sedan hadn't been made for this. The two luxurious leather seats were separated by a hard center console, and the steering wheel pressed against Gabriel's hip. He'd barely kissed her before he was jumping out with a low curse. Opening her door, he yanked her out. She had one glimpse of the moon-drenched ocean beneath the cliff, and then he pushed her into the backseat.

He kissed her, his lips hot and hard against her, and covered her body with his own. She felt his weight against hers in the tight confines of the backseat. His scent of musk and soap mingled with expensive leather, the forest, wild orchids and the salty sea. The notched satin collar of his black tuxedo jacket moved against the bare skin of her shoulders. He gripped her gloved hands, pulling them back over her head, against the car window.

He kissed down her throat, his hands cupping her breasts through the corset bodice of her red dress. But their feet still hung off the end of the seat. His legs were dangling out of the car. And though the seat was comfortable and wide, he had scant space to brace his arms around her. With a low growl, he moved away, so fast he hit his head against the ceiling. He gave a loud, spectacular curse. She saw the flash of his eyes in the moonlit night.

"It's still not enough," he growled. "Not nearly enough."

He kicked the door wide open behind them. Taking her hand, he roughly pulled her out of the car. Kissing her, he pushed her back against the hood.

Laura gasped as she felt the warmth of the hard metal beneath her. Gabriel moved over her, kissing her lips, kissing her bare neck. Overhead, she saw the twinkling stars of the night sky as he peeled off her long white opera gloves one at a time, tossing them to the soft earth. She felt the shock the warm air against her bare skin. Standing up straight, he looked down at her as he yanked off his tuxedo jacket and tie, and she realized that he did not intend to wait until they got back to Rio.

Right here. Right now.

Below the cliff, she heard the roar and crash of the ocean waves pounding the shore. She heard the sounds of night birds and the chatter of monkeys from the stretch of dark forest behind them. She saw the flash of Gabriel's dark eyes in the moonlight as he bent over her, reaching around her to unzip her dress. He slowly pulled it down the length of her body. She watched in shock as he dropped the expensive dress to the ground. She was now lying on the hood of his Rolls-Royce, naked except for a white strapless bra, silk panties, white garter belt and white thigh-high stockings.

He gasped as he softly stroked her naked belly. "So beautiful," he breathed.

Swallowing, she looked up at him. The bright moon illuminated his black hair as his hands stroked her skin. Reverently, he undid the front clasp of her bra, pulling it off her body and dropping it, too, to the ground. She felt his shudder of barely controlled desire as he cupped her naked breasts in his hands. "I've wanted you so long," he said hoarsely. "I thought I would die of it."

Moving down her body, he licked the valley between her breasts, then took her nipple in his wet, warm mouth. As his tongue ran over her taut peak like a caress of silk, she felt his hands slide down to her hips.

Her own hands moved of their own volition, beneath his white tuxedo shirt to feel the smooth warmth of his skin, to feel the hard muscles of his chest beneath the scattering of dark hair. She unbuttoned his shirt with trembling hands as he breathed against her ear, tasting the sensitive flesh of her earlobe. He kissed a trail down her neck, to her breasts, as his hands moved between her legs, along the top edge of her garter belt and thigh-high stockings.

His fingers stroked over her silken panties, and her breath stopped in her throat. He reached beneath the edge of the silk, and she felt him stroke her lightly, so lightly, across her wet core. Her hips strained toward him but he took his time, holding back, stroking her. He slowly pushed two thick fingers an inch inside her.

She arched her spine against the hood.

Pulling back with a growl, he ripped off his white shirt, popping the cuff links. With a low curse in Portuguese, he bent over her once more. His bare chest was rough and laced with dark hair, his skin so warm as his muscles slid against the softness of her breasts. She felt him between her knees, his thickly muscled hips rough against her spread thighs. He leaned above her, standing beside the car. She gripped his shoulders as he kissed her neck, nipping the sensitive corner of her throat. With agonizing slowness, he kissed down between her breasts to her flat belly, past her white garter belt to the sharp edge of her hip bone. He kissed the edge of her white silk panties. Then he stopped.

She felt his warm breath against her skin above her thigh-high stockings. His lips slowly moved over the silk, kissing down her legs. Pushing them farther apart, he took an exploratory lick of her inner right thigh. As she sucked in her breath, he switched to her left thigh. She trembled beneath him, her breath coming in increasingly ragged gasps as his lips moved slowly higher on each side. He held her hips firmly, relentlessly, not allowing her to move away.

Pushing the silk of her panties aside, he paused, and

she felt his warm breath against her slick, sensitive core. He lowered his head between her legs, and still did not touch her, except with the soft stroke of his breath.

"Please," she gasped, hardly knowing what she was asking for. She grabbed his head, twining her fingers in his hair. "I—"

With ruthless control, he slowly pushed her wide with both hands. Lowering his head even more, he tasted her with the hot, wet tip of his tongue.

Pleasure ripped through her. With a cry, Laura flung her arms wide, desperate to hold on to something, anything, to keep herself from flying headlong into the sky. Her right hand found the car's metal hood ornament.

Gabriel's tongue moved against her, licking her in little darting swirls. Spreading her wide, he lapped at her with the full width of his rough tongue. As she cried out, he drew back, using just the tip of his tongue again to swirl against her in progressively tighter circles, until she twisted and writhed with the sweet agony of her desire. It was building—exploding....

"Stop," she gasped. "No." She gripped his shoulders, frantically pulling him up toward her, and he lifted his head. Undoing the fly of his tuxedo trousers, he yanked them down with his boxers. They fell to his black Italian leather shoes as he sheathed himself in a condom he'd pulled from his pocket. Leaving on her garter belt and stockings, he grabbed Laura by the hips and pulled her down to the very edge of the car hood, where he stood. Ripping the fabric of her panties in a single brutal movement, he pushed inside her in a single thrust.

She felt impaled by the way he filled her completely, so wide and big and deep. He gave a hoarse gasp and gripped her backside, lifting her legs to wrap around his hips.

Holding her against the hood, he thrust again, this time even deeper. He pushed inside her, faster and harder, squeezing her breasts as her hips rose to meet him. She felt tension coil low in her belly and held her breath as the sweet tension built, soared and started to explode.

Throwing her arms back on the hood, she closed her eyes and surrendered completely to his control. His hands moved to grip her hips again, speeding the rhythm as he rode her, so deep and raw that the pleasure was almost pain. So deep. So deep. Her body was so tense and tight and breathless that she didn't know how much she could take.

Her eyes flew open and she saw his face above her in the night, his features shrouded by shadow as he thrust so deep inside her that her heart twisted in her chest. He gasped her name and she exploded, clutching his shoulders as she heard a scream she didn't even recognize as her own voice. A man's voice joined hers as he plunged deeper into her one last time, thrust with a hard, ragged shout that echoed across the dark forest and crashing sea, causing startled birds to fly from the trees and disappear into the night.

Afterward, he collapsed over her, clutching her to him. Their sticky, sweaty skin pressed together as they lay on the hood.

When Laura came to herself, she realized she was wearing nothing but ripped silken panties and thigh-high stockings, beneath the dark Brazilian sky, on a remote stretch of coastline where any passerby could see them. She'd totally lost her mind. And it had been so, so good.

But Gabriel had won. He'd seduced her, just as he'd said. He'd possessed her.

And not just her body, but her heart.

She pulled away, intending to find her red gown in the darkness, to try to cover herself.

But he pulled her back into his arms on the long warm hood. "Where are you going?"

"You got what you wanted," she said bitterly. "You won." She shivered in the warmth of his arms. She'd surrendered and now she knew exactly the power he had over her—the power he would always have. She felt suddenly afraid of how vulnerable she was. He had her heart in his hands. "Now it's done."

"Done?" He gave a low, sensual laugh, then his hands tightened on her as he murmured, "*Querida*, it's only beginning."

CHAPTER TWELVE

By the time they arrived back in Rio two hours later, one thought kept repeating in Gabriel's mind. One thought over and over.

"Here," he said to her, covering her shoulders with his tuxedo jacket as they entered the lobby of his building. She threw him a grateful glance. Her red designer gown now hung askew on her body, the zipper broken from when he'd ripped the dress off her earlier.

As they passed the security guards, Gabriel glanced at them out of the corner of his eye. His white shirt was rumpled, the cuffs hanging open, his tie crumpled in the pocket of his trousers. Laura was looking at him breathlessly, her eyes luminescent, her makeup hopelessly smudged and her lips full and bruised.

He saw the security guards nudge each other with a smirk, and he knew he and Laura had fooled no one. There could be no doubt what they had been doing.

Normally he wouldn't care if people knew he'd taken a woman as his lover. But this was different. This was Laura. And one thought kept going through his mind, no matter how he tried to avoid it.

He never wanted to let her go.

Gabriel exhaled. When he'd taken her on the hood

of the car, beneath the night sky and in full view of the dark moonlit sea, he'd thought he would die of pleasure. Touching her naked skin, thrusting inside her until she screamed, holding her tight, the two of them joined together as one…

He shuddered. After that, he should feel satisfied, at least for the night. He should be satiated.

But he wasn't. Now that he'd had one taste of her, he only wanted more. And more. *He never wanted to let her go.*

Silently, they took the private elevator upstairs to the penthouse. The doors slid open, and he followed Laura inside. They found Maria quietly reading a book by the light of the lamp in the main room, beside the wall of windows two stories high.

The housekeeper rose to her feet, smiling. "The baby is sleeping, Mr. Gabriel, Mrs. Laura…" And then the older woman got a good look at both of them. She coughed, closing her book with a thump. "I will wish you both good-night."

"Thank you, Maria," Gabriel said gravely, and his former nanny scurried out, the elevator doors closing behind her.

After she was gone, Laura turned to him, a frown furrowing her brow. "You don't think she guessed about us, do you? You don't think she could tell?"

"Absolutely," he said, then at her horrified expression, he added, "not. Absolutely not."

She sighed in relief. "I'm going to go check on Robby."

Laura turned and went down the hall. He watched her go, watched the curves of her back and graceful sway of her body in his oversize tuxedo jacket as she moved like music. She stepped into the bedroom and disappeared. *Gone.*

His feet moved without thought, and he was down the hall and suddenly behind her in the darkened bedroom. He watched as she crept up to the crib and stood silently, listening to her baby's snuffling breaths as he slept. Gabriel came closer.

In the dim light of the tiny blue night-light plugged into the far wall, he could just barely see the sleeping baby. Robby's chubby little fist was tossed back over his head. His plump cheeks moved as his mouth pursed, sucking in his sleep. Gabriel heard the soft, even breathing of the child in the darkness, and something turned over in his chest. He felt the sudden need to protect this little boy, to make sure he never came to any harm.

Just as he'd once felt about his family.

The thought caused a raw, choking ache in his throat. Without a word, he turned and left.

He stood in the hallway for long moments, shaking. But by the time Laura came out into the hall a few moments later, he'd gathered his thoughts. Come to some decisions.

She closed her bedroom door softly behind her, then looked at Gabriel in the darkened hallway. "I'm so sorry about Robby," she said in a low voice. "I never should have lied, Gabriel. I was just so…scared."

Clawing back his hair, he gave a sudden laugh. "To tell you the truth, I was almost scared myself for a moment." He looked at her. "But it was brilliant of you to say I was Robby's father. It saved the deal. That was a stroke of genius, Laura."

Her beautiful face suddenly looked pale. "What?"

"It was the perfect lie. But don't worry. If Adriana

spreads the rumor I'm his father—and she likely will—I will not deny it." He set his jaw. "Since your baby's real father can't be bothered to give him a name, somebody has to do it."

She bit her trembling lower lip. "Gabriel—you never thought...for one moment...that it might be true? That Robby might actually be your son?"

He snorted. "No, of course not. If Robby were really my child and you'd lied to me all this time..."

"Yes?"

He shrugged. "I've destroyed men for less." Reaching forward, he smiled and stroked her cheek, then lowered his head to playfully kiss her bare shoulder. "But I knew Robby couldn't really be mine. We used protection. And you wouldn't lie, not to me. Other than Maria, you are the only person I trust in all this world. You are..."

But then he leaned forward, frowning at her. "You are crying again." He tilted his head, trying to see her face. "Is it from happiness?"

She looked away sharply, wiping her eyes. "Yes. Happiness."

"Good," he said. "Now." He stroked her cheek. "We must celebrate winning the Açoazul deal tonight." He gave her a wicked smile. "I can think of one way—"

"No," she blurted out. "I just need to—I need to...be alone."

Turning abruptly, she ran down the hall. He heard the soft whir of the sliding doors as she fled out onto the terrace. When he followed her moments later, she'd dropped his tuxedo jacket from her body. Her strapless gown was barely hanging on her full breasts, askew with the broken zipper.

"What are you doing?" he asked. "What's wrong?"

"Just leave me alone," she said. Her voice was low, almost grief-stricken. "Go to bed. I'll see you in the morning."

Her red dress suddenly fell to the ground, but she didn't seem to notice or care. He licked his lips, unable to look away from her half-naked body in the white bra and torn panties and thigh-high stockings. "What are you doing?"

She looked away. "I'm going to take a swim."

He smiled. "Wonderful idea. I'll join you."

"No!" she cried vehemently.

He blinked at her, frowning. "Why?"

For long moments, she didn't answer. He could hear the noise and music of the street party below them. She finally said in a low, muffled voice, "I need some time alone." When he didn't move, she choked out, "Just go away, Gabriel. Please."

Looking away from the illuminated turquoise water of the pool, she stared out at the vast dark ocean beyond Ipanema Beach. He'd seen a glimmer of tears in her eyes. And there was *no way* they were tears of happiness.

But she wanted him to leave. She'd made that clear. Setting his jaw, he turned and left her on the terrace, opening the sliding glass doors with a whir and closing them behind him.

Once inside, he stopped, clawing his hair back with one hand. He couldn't let it end like this. Did she have so much regret that she'd allowed him to make love to her? He turned around, intending to go back and argue, to plead.

Instead, he froze.

He saw her on the moonlit terrace, sitting on a lounge chair, her face covered by her hands. Then she dropped her hands. Squaring her shoulders, she started to roll down her stockings.

He stared at her, transfixed. She pulled off her garter belt and tossed that, too, to the limestone floor.

Rising, she stood in the moonlight. Now wearing nothing but her bra and panties, she walked to the edge of the illuminated pool. Ripples of water reflected tiny shimmers of light that moved across her naked skin. Gabriel stared at her as he touched the window, unable to move or even breathe as she stood on the edge of the pool, looking down into the water.

Then in a graceful movement, she dived in. She stayed underwater for so long that he was suddenly afraid. Sliding open the doors, he ran out onto the terrace.

He saw her sitting on the bottom of the pool, her eyes closed. It seemed to take forever before she finally rose to the surface with a gasp, her hair sleek and sopping wet.

Laura was facing away from him, the moonlight frosting her bare shoulders in silver. Her thighs spread wide as her legs chopped the water, which moved around her in illuminated ripples of blue.

He choked back a groan. He was hard and aching for her. There was no way he was leaving her now. Walking to the edge, he said, "Laura."

She turned to face him with a gasp. Her eyes were luminous, a dark shade of blue, as she tried to cover her breasts, treading water with her feet. "What do you want?"

Sitting on a chair by the pool, he looked down at her. "I want you to tell me what you're thinking."

"I'm thinking I want to be alone!"

"Tell me," he threatened. "Or I'll kiss it out of you."

Her eyes widened. Then she turned away. "Just go away."

But in spite of her defiant words, he heard a sob in her voice that caused his belly to clench. Had he done that? Had he caused it? His jaw set. Pushing the chair away, he rose to his feet. He calmly kicked off his black leather shoes.

"What are you doing?" she said, alarmed.

He didn't answer. Fully dressed in his tuxedo shirt and trousers, he jumped into the pool.

He'd been on the swim team in school, and was a fast swimmer underwater. He rose to the surface directly beside her, pushing her back against the hard edge of the pool. She gasped as she felt his hands on her.

"Tell me," he said grimly.

"No."

"Now."

Her eyes became wide and tearful. "I can't."

Gabriel looked at her, and again he had that same strange feeling in his chest, like a twist in his heart. Holding himself suspended in the water, he gripped the edge of the pool with both hands around her, trapping her. She had nowhere to escape.

"You're going to tell me." He felt the warmth of her curvy body against the sopping wet shirt now clinging to his chest. "Whatever it is."

He heard her intake of breath. Then she lifted her chin.

"It wouldn't do any good," she whispered. "Not to you. Not to anyone."

He growled in frustration. Holding on to the edge of

the pool with one hand, he cupped her cheek with his other palm. "Remember," he said roughly, tilting her chin. "You left me no choice."

And he ruthlessly kissed her.

Her lips trembled beneath his, soft and warm and wet. He moved his mouth against hers in a seductive embrace, luring her without force, tempting her with their mutual hunger, with the insatiable need between them. Deepening the kiss, he softly stroked down her cheek, down her neck. His hand went below the surface of the water and he stroked the side of her body, her plump breast beneath her nearly invisible silk bra, her taut, slender waist, the full curve of her hip.

With a shudder of desire, he pulled back to look at her.

In the moving prisms of light from the pool, he could hear the music and noise of the street party on the *avenida*. But here on the terrace of his penthouse, in the moonlit night, he saw only her. They were connected in a way he didn't understand.

He never wanted to let her go.

Reaching beneath her, he lifted her out of the pool. She was warm in his arms and her weight was light, barely anything at all, as he set her down gently on the limestone. He climbed out beside her, his wet tuxedo trousers and white shirt clinging to his skin. Impatiently, he pulled off the shirt, then yanked off his trousers with awkward force as the fabric clung stubbornly to his legs, nearly tripping him.

Laura, still sitting on the terrace floor in her transparent bra and panties, choked out a giggle.

"Laugh at me, will you, *gringa*?" Gabriel growled. He threw his sodden trousers on the floor, and his socks swiftly followed. He lifted her into his arms, holding her tightly against his naked body.

The laughter faded from her eyes, replaced by something hot and dark. Looking at him in wonder, she reached up and stroked the rough bristles of his jawline.

Just the gentle touch of her small hand sent his senses reeling, spiraling out of control. He wanted to push her into a lounge chair—that one, there at his feet—and throw himself on top of her, grinding into her, filling her until they exploded.

But he'd already done that once, on the hood of his car. No. Now, he would take his time.

Now, he would do it right.

Water trailed behind them as he padded naked across the terrace and back inside. The expensive rugs were left sopping wet with every step.

He looked down at her, this beautiful, soft, loving woman who had her arms wrapped around his neck and looked up at him with a mixture of apprehension, desire and wonder. He went down the hall to the master bedroom and set her reverently on his large bed.

He saw her lying across his white comforter, nearly naked, and he shuddered with need. Lines of silvery moonlight from his half-closed blinds slatted across Laura's bare skin, emphasizing the shadows of her full breasts and hips, and his whole body shook with hunger.

He needed her. *Now.*

"I'm going to get everything wet," she whispered with a nervous laugh.

"Good," he said roughly.

Her eyes were looking everywhere but at his naked

body, everywhere but the hard, huge evidence of his desire. There was no hiding how much he wanted her. Let her see. Let her know. He put his hand on the valley of bare skin between her breasts, and exhaled.

He could see her nipples through her wet silk bra. Beneath her transparent, half-ripped panties, he could see the dark curls of hair between her legs. He reached to rip off her bra, then stopped himself.

Take it slow. Do it right.

With iron control, he gently undid her bra and peeled it off her wet skin before dropping it to the carpet. Her panties were next—easy to remove those, as they'd already been ripped and only a few threads still held them together.

Looking at her now, naked and spread across his bed, he took a breath, struggling to stay in check. He wanted to throw himself on top of her and push deep, deep, deep inside until he felt her shake with joy around him. Instead, he forced himself to climb up beside her on the bed. Turning her against his naked body, he reached for her cheek and gently kissed her, long and slow.

His hand skimmed her side, caressing her. He took his time, kissing her, relishing the sweet taste of her lips, the warm wet pleasures of her mouth. He heard a sigh come from the back of her throat as she wrapped her arm around him, pulling him closer.

He throbbed against her soft belly, thick and rock-hard. But he made no move to throw her back against the bed. Instead, he just kissed her as if he had all the time in the world, exploring her mouth, biting her lip, nibbling her neck and chin, sucking the tender flesh of her ear. It nearly killed him to wait, but he owed it to her to take his time…take it—

He suddenly gasped as he felt her hand wrap around his hard, thick shaft. He jerked in her hand as she slowly ran her fingertips down his length. Her thumb gently touched the tip, and it became wet beneath her touch as a tiny bead like a pearl escaped. He gasped out a groan.

"Querida," he said hoarsely. "Don't... I can't..."

In a sudden movement, she flipped him on his back, pushing him against the pillows. He felt her lips move down his throat to his chest. He was suddenly in her power, and he felt it as she kissed his body. When her head slipped down past his taut belly, he gripped the goosedown comforter with white-knuckled control. Then he felt her tongue brush his hot, throbbing skin, licking the bead of moisture at the tip.

He gave a rough gasp and nearly lost it right then. Grabbing her shoulders, he pulled her up with force and lifted her hips over his body. He was blind with need, ready to thrust inside her, to impale her. He only knew he had to take her or die.

"Wait," she panted. Wrenching away from his grasp, she opened a drawer beside the bed. He saw a condom in her hand and realized he'd forgotten all about it.

He'd forgotten about it. If Laura hadn't stopped him, he would have made love to a woman without a condom for the first time in his life. He exhaled as he broke out into a sweat.

"There," Laura whispered. Finally, she lowered her body over his, allowing him to impale her, inch by inch.

His eyes rolled back and he closed his eyes. Yes. *Yes.* He was losing his mind. The more time he spent with her, the more he lost. And it was worth it. So worth it.

Slowly, she moved against him, pulling him deeper

inside her. Her thighs were clamped around his hips as she increased her rhythm and speed, riding him. Opening his eyes, he looked up at her, watching the sway of her enormous breasts as she moved over him. Her face was luminous. Her eyes were closed in ecstasy as she bit her full, bruised lower lip. He heard the intake of her breath, and he never wanted to let her go.

Ever.

His heart clenched in his chest. He couldn't let himself feel that way. He couldn't let himself feel anything but lust. Pure, raw sex.

He had to teach Laura her place. Show them both the true nature of the passion between them.

With a violent movement, he rolled her over on her back, so he was on top of her. Her eyes widened as he roughly gripped her shoulders. Then with a grunt he thrust inside her, hard and deep.

He gasped as he felt her body around him, hot and tight and silken and deep. She cried out from the force of his possession, but he didn't stop. He only rode faster, filling her with each thrust, deeper and faster, ramming himself inside her. He heard her shocked intake of breath and then she, too, began to grip his shoulders, her fingernails sharp in her answering frenzy of desire.

But it wasn't enough. He wanted to take off his condom, to feel her from the inside with his naked skin—

No.

The answer was like a blow. It was the one thing he could not allow himself to do. Ever. He could not be that close. He could not risk her conceiving a child.

Furiously, he rode her harder—faster—desperate to feel her tight sheath completely around him, to lose himself utterly inside her. As he slammed into her, he felt her fingernails cutting into the skin of his back. The pain only increased his pleasure as he rode her harder and harder until beads of sweat covered his forehead. He wanted to leave her raw, until he was utterly spent, until they both collapsed into oblivion.

He heard her cry out, her voice rising in a slow crescendo of joy. Tension sizzled down his body, leaving every muscle taut, crying for release. With a violent thrust, he filled her deeply, then held her tight as she screamed his name. He felt her convulse around him and could hold back no longer. With a savage, violent thrust, he filled her. He felt her hot and wet all around him and poured himself inside her with a shout, as his vision went black.

CHAPTER THIRTEEN

LAURA woke up with a start to see the soft curl of a pink sunrise through the windows. She sat up in bed abruptly, the blanket falling from her naked chest. Had she heard her baby next door?

She listened, and heard nothing except Gabriel's even, steady breathing beside her in the shadowy bedroom. Then she heard Robby's voice again.

"Ma...ma...ma!"

Quietly Laura rose from the bed and pulled a robe off the bathroom door hook. Leaving Gabriel's room, she went down the hall to her own, where she found her baby son sitting up in his crib. Whispering soft words of love, Laura took him in her arms. Holding him tenderly, she fed him, rocking him in the rocking chair. The baby, now yawning with a full belly, swiftly fell back to sleep.

But Laura knew she would not.

Putting him back in his crib, she went to the en-suite bathroom, closing the door silently behind her. She turned on the shower and dropped the robe to the floor. As the steam enveloped her body, she climbed into the marble shower. She washed her hair and stared bleakly at the wall.

She'd been so happy last night.

She'd been so *stupid*.

Of course Gabriel had thought she was lying when she'd claimed he was Robby's father. It had seemed a useful fabrication. Just like his marriage proposal.

She glanced down at the enormous diamond ring still on her finger. Her other hand closed around it with a sob. It had all felt so real. She closed her eyes, leaning her head back in the hot water. When she'd realized he still didn't believe he was Robby's father, her heart had split in two. She'd fallen into the pool, sinking into the water, hoping to forget her pain the way she did at the pond back at her farm.

But it had been Gabriel's touch that had made her forget, the searing heat of his dark eyes as he'd carried her to bed. For a few hours, she'd managed to forget her heartbreak, forget that she was in love with a man who didn't want her or their child. She'd managed to forget she'd be leaving him in the morning, with a lie forever between them.

He'd taken her in his arms and kissed her, his lips so gentle and tender and true, and she'd forgotten everything but that she loved him.

His hands had stroked her naked skin as he'd kissed her, his body hard and hot against hers on the bed. She'd lost her mind. Then she'd taken things into her own hands. Literally. A half-hysterical laugh escaped her. She remembered the hard, silky smooth feel of him in her grasp. The taste of the single gleaming bead on the tip of his throbbing shaft. She remembered the rough way he'd reacted, pushing her down against the bed and savagely thrusting deep inside her until she exploded with pleasure, blinding sweetness tinged with bitter salt like tears.

She blinked back tears as she stared across the steamed-up shower. It was morning now. Her left hand closed over the ten-carat diamond sparkling beneath the running water. Their night in Rio was over. Time to give back the ring. Time to take back her heart.

As if she could.

She'd go back home to her family's farm. Back to her lonely bed. Only now it would be worse than before. Because now she knew she'd always love him. Now, she'd never be free.

Who is the father of your baby, Laura? Will you ever tell?

She turned off the water and dried her hair with a thick white towel. She put on the plush white robe and left her bedroom, closing the door softly behind her.

Going to the kitchen, she turned on a light and made coffee. As it brewed, she poured milk and sugar into a big mug, then filled it to the rim with the hot, bitter brew. Blowing on the steaming liquid, she stood for a moment, alone in the house of sleeping males.

This could have been her home. They could have been her family. If only she'd fallen in love with a man who actually loved them back, a man who wanted a wife and child.

Carrying her mug, she went outside to watch the sun rise over the Atlantic. It was the last morning she would ever spend with both Robby and his father under the same roof. The last day she'd ever see the man she would always love.

She felt the soft wind, the breeze off the sea, and looked down at the beach below. She looked down. The party had ended, leaving only litter rattling along the empty street.

"There you are."

She turned to find Gabriel behind her in drawstring pajama bottoms. Her eyes unwillingly lingered on his bare chest before she met his gaze. His dark eyes twinkled at her as he held up a steaming cup of coffee. "You made coffee. Thank you."

She took a sip from her mug, relishing the burn against her tongue. "Sure." She drew a deep breath and turned back to the view of the ocean. "It was the least I could do before I go."

"Go?" There was something odd in his voice.

She turned back to face him, startled. "In a few hours, you'll sign the papers to buy your father's company. And Robby and I will go home."

Gabriel's handsome face looked suddenly grim. Setting down his coffee, he put his hands on her shoulders and gazed down at her. "I don't want you to leave."

"We had our night. It's over." She swallowed back her own pain, tried to smile. "We both knew it wouldn't last."

"No."

Laura gave him a trembling smile. "It was always meant to be this way."

"No," he repeated roughly. "Stay."

"As what?"

"As…as my mistress."

She licked her lips, yearning to agree, yearning to say anything that would give her relief from this heartbreak. But she knew that staying here as Gabriel's mistress wouldn't end her pain. It would only prolong it.

"I can't," she whispered. "I would always be waiting for the day you'd tire of me, and move on to another."

He searched her gaze. "Can't you live in the moment? Just live for today?"

Blinking back tears, she shook her head.

"Why?" he demanded.

For an instant, she almost laughed. He looked like a spoiled child deprived of his favorite toy. Then she sobered. "I don't want to raise Robby that way. And because…"

"Because?"

She took a deep breath. Taking her heart in her hands, she looked up at him.

"Because I love you," she whispered.

His dark eyes widened. "You—love me," he repeated.

She nodded, a lump in her throat. "I left you last year because I knew you could never love me back. You've told me so many times you will never love anyone. Not a wife." She trembled, lifting her eyes to his. "Not a child."

He stared at her, and Laura waited, breathless with the hope that he might deny it, that he'd say his time with Robby had changed his mind.

"There's more to life than love, Laura," he said, pulling her into his arms. "There's friendship, and partnership, and passion. And I can't do without you, not anymore. I need you. Your truth. Your goodness. Your warmth." He gave her a humorless smile. "It warms even my cold heart."

She caught her breath, then rubbed her stinging eyes. "I'm sorry, but I can't do it, Gabriel. I can't," she choked out. "I can't just stay here, loving you, while you give me nothing in return but the knowledge that you'll someday leave—"

He gripped her shoulders. "Marry me."

Her eyes and mouth went wide. "What?"

"Marry me." He picked up her left hand, looking down at the diamond on her finger. His lips curved upward. "You already have the ring."

"But I thought your proposal was a lie!"

"It was."

She shook her head tearfully. "So why are you saying this? We're alone. You've already convinced Oliveira. You don't need to pretend, not anymore!"

"I'm not pretending." Bending his head, he kissed her hand, making her tremble with the sensation of his warm lips against her skin. He looked up. "I need you, Laura," he said huskily. "I don't want to lose you. Marry me. Now. Today."

She licked her lips, feeling like she were in a dream. "What about Robby?"

Setting his jaw, Gabriel straightened.

"Perhaps I can't love him. But I can give him my name. I can give you both the life you deserve. And I can be faithful to you, Laura. I swear it."

It was so close to everything she'd ever wanted. Gabriel would be her husband. He would be a father, at least in name, to their child. And if some part of her warned that this was a fool's bargain, to marry a man who could not love her, she still couldn't resist. Her heart overrode her reason and she succumbed to the temptation of her heart's deepest desire.

With a tearful sob, she flung her arms around him in her bulky white cotton robe, kissing him as the sun finally broke, vivid and golden, over the fresh blue Atlantic.

"Yes!" she cried with a sob. "Oh, yes!"

CHAPTER FOURTEEN

Two weeks later, Laura stared at herself blankly in the mirror.

An elegantly dressed bride in a long, white lace veil and satin sheath gown stared back at her. It still didn't feel right. She picked up her neatly bundled bouquet of white roses and looked back in the mirror.

It was the morning of her wedding. In less than an hour she would have everything she'd barely dared to dream of—she'd be Mrs. Gabriel Santos. Robby would have his father.

So where was the joy? She should have been ecstatic with bliss and hope. So why, looking at herself in this beautiful dress, standing in a suite of this beautiful rented mansion outside her village, did she feel so... empty?

Gabriel had wanted to marry her immediately, in Rio, but he'd quickly given in to Laura's begging when she'd asked to have their wedding in New Hampshire, so her family could attend.

"We can get married in New Hampshire, of course we can, if that's your wish," he'd told her. "But after the ceremony, we must live in Rio. Do you agree?"

She'd agreed. She'd been lost in romantic bliss, and

all she'd thought about was getting married to the man she loved, in a beautiful wedding surrounded by friends and family.

She hadn't bothered to think about what would happen afterward. Gabriel had already signed the preliminary contracts to acquire Açoazul SA, and he now planned to merge the company with Santos Enterprises and permanently move the headquarters from New York City to Rio de Janeiro.

Starting tomorrow, she and Robby would live far away from her family, far from the people who actually loved them. Laura would be the wife of a man who didn't love her, a man who would offer only financial support to the child he didn't know was his son. A child he could never love.

Now, Laura was dressed in an exquisite 1920s-style designer gown and her great-grandmother's old lace veil. In ten minutes, she would go downstairs to get married in this beautiful place. The Olmstead mansion was a lavish house of forty rooms built by a now-bankrupt hedge fund manager, currently rented out for weddings. It sat among acres of rolling hills with its own private lake, a winter wonderland. And after the elegant ceremony in the gray stone library filled with flowers, a reception would follow in the ballroom, a lavish sit-down dinner of steak, lobster and champagne.

Laura had fretted about having such a luxurious wedding, worrying she'd steal her little sister's thunder from two weeks ago. Gabriel had smiled and picked up the phone. Within minutes, he'd arranged to send Becky and her new husband to Tahiti on honeymoon, via his private jet. He'd created college funds for young Margaret and Hattie, to allow them to go to university.

For their mother, he'd completely paid off the mortgage on the farm, and even helped out Ruth's dearest friend, a neighboring woman with a sick child, by paying for medical care.

All of this, and he'd still deposited the agreed-upon million dollars into Laura's bank account.

"A deal's a deal," he'd told Laura when she'd thrown her arms around him with a sob of delight. "I will always take care of you. That means taking care of your family."

Laura bit her lip, furrowing her brow as she stared at herself in the mirror. She had everything she'd ever wanted. And yet...

"Your family," Gabriel had said. Not *our* family.

He didn't love her. He didn't love Robby. And he still didn't know the truth.

What difference does it make? she argued with herself. Her love for Gabriel could be enough for both of them. He would still provide for Robby financially, living in the same house, acting exactly like a father in so many ways. What difference did the truth make?

Except it made a huge difference. In fact, truth was everything. Because without truth, how could there be love?

Her troubled eyes looked back at her in the mirror.

But if she told Gabriel now that he really was Robby's father, if he knew she'd lied to him all this time, she might lose everything she had. He would never forgive her for the lie. He might—almost certainly *would*—call off the wedding. Why would he take her as his wife if he couldn't trust her? Then he might sue for custody of Robby, and take her baby away from her out of duty—or even a desire to punish her.

But her conscience stung her. Didn't Gabriel deserve to know the truth before he pledged himself to her for the rest of his life?

She heard a knock, and her mother's smiling face peeked around the door. "All ready, sweetling? Your sisters are waiting and eager to be bridesmaids."

Laura took a deep breath, clutching her bouquet in her cold, shaking hands. "Is it already time?"

"Just a few more minutes. The last guests are arriving now…" Then, as Laura turned to face her in her 1920s-style gown and her great-grandmother's long veil, Ruth gasped, and her eyes filled with tears. "Oh, Laura," she whispered. "You're beautiful."

Laura's lips trembled as she smiled. "You look amazing, too, Mom."

Her mother shook her head dismissively at the compliment, then came forward to embrace her, looking chic in pearls and a mother-of-the-bride suit of light cream silk. "I'm going to miss you and Robby so much when you're in Rio," she choked out. "You'll be living so far away."

Laura fought back tears. Though she adored the energy of Rio, the warmth of the people and the beauty of Brazil, the thought of moving permanently to the other side of the Equator, far from her family and home, caused wrenching pain in her heart. If her husband loved her, it might be endurable. But as it was… Choking back a sob, she squeezed her mother tight and tried to reassure her. "We'll be just a quick plane ride away."

"I know." Her mother pulled away with a smile, even as her eyes glistened with tears. "My consolation is that I know you're going to be happy. Really, truly happy." She paused. "Gabriel is Robby's father, isn't he?"

Laura sucked in her breath. "How did you know?"

Her mother's smile widened. "I've got eyes, haven't I? I see how you are together. How you've always been. He's crazy about you."

Apparently her mother didn't see as much as she thought. Blinking back tears, Laura swallowed and said over the lump in her throat, "We have some...problems."

Her mother laughed. "Of course you do. There were times I was ready to kill your father. But now—" her voice broke "—the problems we had seem small. I would give anything to have him here again, arguing with me." She paused. "I know love isn't simple or easy. But you'll do the right thing. You always do."

Laura swallowed yet again. "Not always."

Ruth smiled. "Your father used to call you Little Miss Trustworthy. Of all my children, you were the easiest to raise. And now, the hardest to let go." Her mother shook her head, wiping away her tears. "Look at me. Here I am, making a mess of myself after Gabriel bought me this expensive dress."

"You're calling him Gabriel," Laura said.

"Well, what else would I call my son-in-law?" She kissed her daughter on the cheek. "He's not your boss now. A husband is quite a different matter." With a little laugh, she turned to leave in a soft cloud of lavender perfume. "Husbands need to be reminded not to take themselves too seriously."

"Wait," Laura whispered.

Her mother stopped at the door. "Yes, sweetie?"

Laura clenched her hands. The bodice of her wedding gown suddenly felt inexplicably tight.

She was standing on a precipice and knew it. The

choice she made today would change the entire course of her life. And her son's life, as well.

You'll do the right thing. You always do.

"I need to see Gabriel," she choked out. "Will you send him up to me?"

Her mother frowned. "Right now? It's bad luck to see the bride. Can't it wait an hour?"

In an hour, they'd be married. Not trusting her voice, Laura shook her head. With a sigh, her mother closed the door. Five minutes later, Gabriel appeared.

"You wanted to see me, *querida*?" he said huskily.

A lump rose in Laura's throat as she looked at her handsome husband-to-be, at the brutal power of his body barely contained in the sophisticated tuxedo. She was suddenly reminded of the last time he'd been in a tuxedo, when he'd kissed her in the shadowy gardens at the Fantasia Ball, then made love to her on the hood of his car overlooking the dark, moonlit ocean...

She set her bouquet on the vanity. "I need to ask you something."

His lips curved as he came up to her, stroking her face. "What is it, *minha esposa*?"

His wife. She swallowed, looking up at him.

"Do you love me?" she whispered.

He stiffened. Staring down at her, his handsome eyes became expressionless and dark. She waited, her heart pounding.

"I thought we agreed," he finally said. "I care for you, Laura. I admire you and I always will. I lust for you and want you in my life."

Her heart fell to her white satin shoes.

"But you don't love me," she said softly.

He set his jaw. "I told you from the start. I can't love anyone. Not a wife. Not children."

"But we will have them…"

"No," he said. He came closer, putting his hands on her shoulders as he searched her gaze. "Is that why you sent for me before the ceremony, to ask if I might want children someday?"

She nodded tearfully.

He took a deep breath. "I'm sorry, Laura. I thought you understood. Though I can offer you marriage, nothing else has changed. I still cannot offer you love. Or more children."

She blinked, staring up at him in shock. "No more… no more children?"

He shook his head.

"But why?" she cried.

He dropped his hands from her shoulders.

"You should know, before you marry me, why I will not change my mind." His jaw clenched as he turned away from her. Outside the windows, rolling white fields were dotted with black, bare trees. "My parents and brother died when I was nineteen. Because of me."

"I know you've spent your whole life trying to regain what you lost," she said. "But it wasn't your fault they died!"

"I was driving the car that killed them." His black eyes were bleak. "My brother had just eloped with a waitress who'd had his baby while we were away at university. He'd been living with her for months, keeping it secret from our parents that he'd dropped out of school. I visited their flat in São Paulo, where they were living with their baby daughter, barely surviving on the wages he could make as a laborer. This from my brother—who should have been a doctor!"

Laura took a deep breath. "So that's how you know how to play with a baby," she whispered. "You'd spent time with your niece."

He gave her a smile that broke her heart. "Yes," he said in a low voice. "But when my brother decided to marry the woman, I was sure she was a gold digger. I dragged my parents to São Paulo to break up the wedding, and we convinced Guilherme to come back with us to Rio. I hated the thought of my brother giving up all his dreams, just because he'd accidentally gotten some woman pregnant."

"Right," Laura said over the lump in her throat. "A child doesn't matter to you. Not like a career."

His jaw clenched as he turned away. "It was raining that night," he said in a low voice. "I was driving the car so my parents could convince my brother to see reason." Gabriel gave a hard laugh. "But instead, Guilherme convinced *them* he needed to go back and marry Izadora. 'Turn the car around,' they told me. I looked into the rearview mirror to argue. I looked away from the road only for a second," he whispered. "Just a single second."

He stopped, his face grief-stricken.

Laura stared at him, feeling sick.

"I slammed on the brakes. I turned the wheel as hard as I could. But the tires kept sliding, right off the cliff. I heard my mother scream as the car rolled, then we hit the bottom. They all died instantly. But not me." He looked at her bleakly. "I was lucky."

"Oh, Gabriel," she whispered, coming close to him.

She tried to put her arms around him, to offer comfort. But his body was stiff. He pulled away.

"I was wrong about Izadora. At my brother's funeral she wouldn't even look at me. I offered to buy her a house, set up a trust fund for my niece, but she refused with angry words. I'd taken her husband from her, taken the father of her child, and she told me she hoped I would rot in hell."

Laura shuddered.

"She eventually married an American and moved to Miami. My niece is grown now." He took a deep breath, and she saw that his eyes were wet. "She's almost twenty, and I haven't seen her since she was a baby."

"You haven't?" Laura said in shock. "But she's your only family, your brother's child!"

His jaw clenched. "How could I see her?" he demanded, turning on her. "Why should I be allowed to spend time with my niece, when it was my thoughtless action that caused her to lose her father? Her grandparents? They never got to see her grow up. Why should I?"

"But, Gabriel...it was an accident. You were trying to help your brother. We all make mistakes with the people we love. Your brother would forgive you. Your family loved you. They would know your heart. They'd know you never meant to—"

"I'm done talking about this," he growled, raking his hair back with his hand. He set his jaw, and his dark eyes glittered. "You wanted to understand why I never want children. I've told you why."

She closed her eyes, drew a deep breath. Tears streamed down her face as she opened her eyes.

"It's too late," she whispered.

"What do you mean?" he demanded. "Too late? What are you saying?"

She lifted her chin. "I've never had another lover, Gabriel. How could I, when I never stopped loving you? It's always been you. Just you."

He stared at her. His dark eyebrows came together like a storm cloud. "That's impossible," he said angrily. "Robby—"

"Don't you understand?" She shook her head tearfully. "Robby is your son."

The echo of her words hung in the air between them like a noxious cloud.

Gabriel stared at her, then staggered back.

"What?" he choked out.

"Robby is your—"

"I heard you," he cried, putting his hands over his ears. But he couldn't stop his mind from repeating those words. *Robby is your son.* "You're wrong. It's impossible."

"No," Laura said quietly. "Didn't you notice how he looks so much like you? That he was born exactly nine months after our night together? How could you not know? How could you not see?"

He shook his head. "But—but it can't be," he gasped. "I was careful. I used protection."

She shook her head. "Condoms have been known to fail—"

"Only to people who use them incorrectly," he muttered. "I do not."

"But even then, three percent of the time they—"

"No." He held out his hand, blocking her words. He

felt as if he couldn't breathe, and loosened the tie on his tuxedo. "I can't be his father. I can't."

Laura took a deep breath. She looked so beautiful in her white gown and veil. He'd never seen her look so innocent, so beautiful. So deceitful.

"I know this must come as a shock to you," she said softly. She gave him a tremulous smile. "It was a shock for me, too. But Robby's not an accident. He's not a mistake."

"Then what is he?" Gabriel demanded.

She looked up at him, her blue eyes luminous.

"A miracle," she whispered.

Images of Robby's chubby, smiling face went through his mind. His dark hair, his inquisitive dark eyes. *Of course* Robby was his son. Pacing, Gabriel raked his hair back with his hand. How could he have not seen it before?

Because he hadn't wanted to see it, he thought grimly. Because having a child, when he'd killed his parents and prevented his brother from raising his, was the one thing he could not allow himself to do.

"I destroyed my own family," he said in a low voice, staring blindly through the windows toward the wintry hills. "I don't deserve another."

Laura came slowly toward him, her beautiful face filled with tenderness and love, her eyes glowing with light.

"What happened that night was an accident. It wasn't your fault. But you've buried yourself in the cemetery with them, not allowing yourself to be happy or loved, always punishing yourself—"

"Not punishment. *Justice*," he said in a low voice, feeling as if his heart were being ripped out of his chest. "If I hadn't tried to talk Guilherme out of having a family, if I hadn't tried to talk him out of committing to his wife and baby, they would all be alive. Why should I enjoy the life I denied my own brother?"

"Your brother is gone. He forgave you long ago. But we're still here, and we need you," she said. She took a deep breath and lifted her tearstained eyes to his. "Please, Gabriel. I love you. Love me back."

His jaw hardened as he stared down at her.

"Don't use the word *love*," he said harshly. "You lied to me. And you turned me into a liar, as well. I said I would never have a wife. Now look at me." Rage burned inside him as he gazed down at his tuxedo. He ripped the tiny rose boutonniere out of his lapel. "Just look at me!"

She went pale beneath her wedding veil, and the beautiful light in her eyes dimmed. "I'm sorry. It's why I didn't tell you I was pregnant. I knew it wasn't what you wanted, that you'd feel trapped by duty to a child. But—" she took a deep breath "—I couldn't marry you. Not without telling you the truth."

"Thank you," he said coldly, pacing the carpet. He stopped. His body felt chilled, as frozen as a New Hampshire winter. Maybe because of the icy dagger she'd just plunged through his back. "Thank you, Laura, for being so trustworthy and decent."

She flinched. Her eyes were red, her beautiful face swollen with tears. "I understand if you want to back out."

"Back out?"

"Of the wedding," she whispered.

He saw the way her petite, curvaceous body was shivering in her wedding dress. He forced himself not to care. What difference did her feelings make to him anymore? His lips curved as he looked at her scornfully. "I'm more determined to marry you now than ever."

She licked her lips and he saw a tremulous hope in her blue eyes. "Because you love Robby?"

He stared at her. "Because he's my duty."

Tears fell unchecked down her face as she clutched her arms together over her exquisite beaded gown. "Can't you even try to love him?"

"The deal stands," he said coldly. "I will still marry you. I will still take care of your son."

"*Our* son!"

For a long time, she stood, staring at him. Her lips parted to speak, and his cell phone rang in his pocket. Emotionlessly, he turned away from her. "Santos."

"I'm afraid I have to back out of our deal, Santos."

Gabriel recognized the voice at once. Felipe Oliveira. His eyes widened in shock as he stepped away from Laura. "Is that some kind of joke, Oliveira?" he growled into the phone. "Some attempt to drive up the price? Because you've already signed the papers."

"Just the preliminary papers. And Théo St. Raphaël has just offered me three million euros more for Açoazul than you. Best of all, he's throwing in his prize vineyard to sweeten the offer." The man gave a laugh. "I've always wanted to make my own champagne, and his vineyard is legendary."

"You can't do that!" Gabriel exploded. "We signed a contract!"

"A preliminary contract," the man pointed out gleefully. "All I need pay for reneging on the terms is a small penalty—a million American dollars. Which St. Raphaël has also offered to cover."

Gabriel cursed aloud. "But why? Why betray me like this, Oliveira, after we helped you see Adriana's true nature?"

The older man cackled. "Now that I'm rid of her, I suddenly find I'm interested in business again. Sorry, Santos." He paused, then said with greater seriousness, "Sorry, young man. But you'll live to fight another day."

"I'll leave within the hour," Gabriel said desperately. "I can be in Rio by tonight, and we can talk further—"

But Oliveira had hung up. Gabriel stared for a long moment at the phone in his hand. He felt dizzy with the vertigo of how much he'd lost in the last two minutes.

He'd lost...*everything*.

He whirled on Laura, who was staring up at him with big eyes. "Let's get the wedding over with," he growled, stomping toward the door. "As soon as it's over, we're leaving for Rio."

Her trembling voice stopped him. "No."

He frowned, looking back at her from the doorway. "No? What do you mean, no?"

She licked her lips, coming closer. Her eyes were luminous in the morning light.

"I could accept you not loving me," she said. "I told myself that my love could be enough for both of us." Her eyes narrowed, glittering like a frozen blue sea. "But I can't accept you not loving Robby. He can't just be your *duty*."

"I just found out he's my son," he retorted, "after a year of your lies. What do you expect from me? That I declare my love and fall at your feet?"

She looked at him, and her lips trembled in a smile. "That would be nice."

He shook his head angrily. "Accept what I can give you. And be grateful!"

"Grateful?" she cried. With an intake of breath, she held up the hem of her wedding dress and marched right up to him. Her beautiful face was outraged. "I waited five years for you to love me," she said. "I dreamed of you for the whole last year! All I wanted was for you to marry me…"

"And I will," he said impatiently. "Come on."

"But I was wrong." She lifted her chin. "Love is what matters. Without love, this marriage is nothing but a lie." She shook her head fiercely. "And I won't let Robby settle for that. I won't let him grow up wondering why his father doesn't love him, why his parents' marriage is so strained, what he's done wrong!"

Gabriel stared at her. It suddenly seemed as if an ocean divided them. He reached out his hand. "Laura…"

She slapped it away. "No!"

He glared at her. "I don't have time for this."

"So go."

He briefly considered the idea of dragging her forcibly down the aisle. But she was surrounded by farmers and ranchers and strong neighbors with guns, while to their eyes he was just some stranger who was taking her and Robby away.

But he wasn't just a stranger. He was Robby's father.

Gabriel sucked in a deep breath, overwhelmed by the flood of emotion in his heart. He couldn't give in to the feeling. *Couldn't…*

Grabbing her wrist, he started to pull her towards the door. "We will marry, then leave for Rio—"

She ripped her arm out of his grasp. "I'm not going."

"You're being ridiculous. Don't you understand? Oliveira is backing out of the contract! If I don't change his mind, I'll lose everything!"

"I understand," she said softly. "You should go."

"I'm not leaving the country without you and our son."

"I'm not marrying you. Not like this."

"You're being selfish!"

Laura swallowed, her cheeks pink. He could see he'd hurt her with the accusation. But she wasn't going to let him manipulate her so easily. "I'll never try to stop you from seeing Robby whenever you want. Our lawyers can work out some arrangement. But I won't marry you, and I won't leave the people who love us for someone who doesn't."

"So that's it?" he said incredulously. "You're giving me an ultimatum?"

"Yes." Her eyes filled with tears as she gave him a trembling smile. "I guess I am."

Gabriel swallowed against the sudden lump in his throat. He couldn't force her to marry him. He couldn't seduce or charm or bully her into it. When did she get so steady? When did she get so strong?

Raking his hair back, he looked at her. "Laura," he said slowly. He exhaled a deep breath. "I can't do it. What you're asking. I wish I could, but I can't. I can't... love you."

Pain flashed across her face, raw and sharp. Then she straightened her shoulders in her wedding gown.

Reaching up, she pulled the vintage lace veil off her elegant blonde chignon. Her blue eyes were stricken but steady.

"Then I'm sorry," she said quietly. "But if you can't love us…you can't have us."

CHAPTER FIFTEEN

GABRIEL had to hurry. Every second he wasted with Laura was like a grain of sand falling through a fatal hourglass. He had to leave at once.

And yet he couldn't.

Leaving her felt like a death. He took a deep, shuddering breath. "This isn't over," he said hoarsely. "I'll be back after I close the deal in Rio."

"Of course." Laura's shoulders straightened, even as her lower lip trembled. "I will never stop you from seeing Robby. I hope…I hope you'll see him often. He needs his father."

Gabriel heard the music start to play downstairs and thought of the guests surrounded by white roses and candlelight, waiting for the wedding ceremony to begin. He clenched his hands, feeling that same strange spinning, sinking feeling in the region of his chest.

"Remember," he said tersely, looking at her. "This was your choice. I wanted to marry you."

She swallowed as tears streamed unchecked down her pale cheeks. "I'll never forget that."

No, he thought suddenly. It couldn't end like this. Not like this!

With a sudden, ragged breath, he seized her in his

arms. Pressing his lips against hers, he kissed her with every ounce of passion and persuasion he possessed. He never wanted to let her go.

She was the one to pull away. He saw tears falling down her cheeks as she stepped back, out of his reach. "Goodbye."

He sucked in his breath. But there was nothing he could do. Nothing to be done. "I'll be back," he said heavily. "In a few days."

She gave him a wan smile. "Robby will be glad whenever you choose to visit."

He left the room. Went out the door. Walked past her mother, who was waiting at the bottom of the stairs. He went outside into the cold winter air to the limo waiting outside. Gabriel felt a sudden pain in his chest when he saw that someone—one of Laura's friends, perhaps—had written Just Married across the back window in white shaving cream, and attached aluminum cans to the back bumper to drag noisily down the road.

His hands clenched as he flung himself heavily into the backseat of the limo. Carlos, who'd apparently been texting someone as he waited in the driver's seat, jumped.

"Mr. Gabriel! What are you doing, so soon…? And where is Mrs. Laura?"

"She's not coming," he replied tightly. His throat hurt. "And she's not *Mrs.*"

"But *senhor*… What happened?"

Gabriel looked bleakly out the window, at the beautiful fields of endless white. "Just go."

Laura stood by the closed door until the sound of Gabriel's footsteps faded away.

Sagging into a chair, she covered her face with her hands. She'd been happy to be a bride, a single mother no longer—so pleased to finally leave the scandal behind her. She thought of her baby, downstairs now with one of her cousins, and a sob came from her lips.

But she'd had no other honorable choice. If she'd been willing to accept a life without love forever, what would that have done to her soul? What would that have taught her son?

She'd done the right thing. So why did she feel so awful?

She heard the door squeak open and looked up with an intake of breath.

Her three sisters, all dressed in elegant bridesmaid gowns, stood in the open door with their mother. "Why did Gabriel storm off like that?" Ruth asked tremulously. Then she saw Laura's tearful face. "Oh, sweetheart!"

A moment later, Laura was crying in their arms as they hugged her, and her scowling little sister Hattie was cursing and offering to go punch Gabriel in the face. That made Laura laugh, but the laughter turned to a sob. Wiping her eyes, she looked up at them.

"What do I do now?" she whispered.

Her mother searched her gaze. "The wedding is off? Is it for sure?"

Laura nodded with a lump in her throat. "He said he didn't love me, that he would never love me. Or Robby, either."

Her mother and sisters stared at her with a unified intake of breath. Then Ruth shook herself briskly.

"Well then. I'll go downstairs, tell everyone to head home."

Laura folded her arms, her belly sick with dread and

grief. "It'll cause such a scandal," she whispered. She stared at the patterns on the carpet as the full horror built inside her. "Just when all the rumors were coming to an end."

"Weddings get canceled all the time," Becky said staunchly. "There's nothing scandalous about it."

"Zero scandal," Hattie agreed quickly, pushing up her glasses. "It's totally uninteresting."

"Not even as interesting as when Mrs. Higgins's cow knocked over the Tast-E Burger truck," Margaret added.

"It'll be all right, sweetheart," her mother said, softly stroking Laura's hair as she sat beside her. "Just stay here. I'll handle everything."

It was very tempting. But with a deep breath, Laura shook her head.

"I'll ask your uncle, then," Ruth said quickly. "He's waiting to walk you down the aisle. He can simply make a little announcement and—"

"No," Laura choked out. "I did this," she whispered, rising to her feet. "I'll end it."

Climbing onto his private jet at the airport five miles away, Gabriel nearly bit the stewardess's head off when she offered him champagne. As she scurried off to the back cabin, he grabbed the entire bottle of Scotch from the galley and gulped straight from the bottle, desperate to feel the burn. But when he pulled the bottle from his lips, he realized the pain in his chest had only gotten worse.

It was his heart. His heart hurt.

"Ready, sir?" the pilot said over the intercom.

"Ready," Gabriel growled. Falling into the white

leather seat, he took another gulp of the bottle and stared out his window.

He felt as if he were leaving part of himself behind. His wife. His child.

Robby. His *son*. Gabriel still couldn't believe it.

He didn't want to go.

I have to, he told himself angrily. *I have no choice.* He remembered how his parents had taken Gabriel and Guilherme to visit the factories of Açoazul Steel. It had been truly a family company. His father had been president, his mother vice president of marketing. "Someday, boys," his father had said, "this company will be yours. Your legacy."

The jet's engine started. Closing his eyes, Gabriel leaned his head into his hands. He still remembered the sound of his father's laugh, the tender smile in his mother's eyes. They'd been so proud of their strong, handsome, smart sons. He could still hear his brother saying, at twenty years old, "I never intended to have a family so soon, but now I can't imagine it any other way. I'm happy, Gabriel. I am."

Grief gripped Gabriel's chest. Why hadn't he believed him? Why had he been so sure that *he* was right, and his brother wrong?

"Robby's not an accident. He's not a mistake."

He suddenly saw Laura's beautiful face as she'd stood in the morning light, wearing a wedding gown as luminescent as New England snow.

"Then what is he?"

She'd looked up at him. *"A miracle."*

He blinked, staring at the porthole window as the jet's roar increased. Last year, he'd let Laura go because he'd wanted her to find a man who could love her. He'd wanted her to be happy. He'd been so angry when he'd thought she'd thrown her dreams aside and fallen into bed with a man who didn't deserve her.

But she'd loved Gabriel himself all this time. She'd loved him without hope. She'd taken care of their baby all on her own, while carrying such a heavy weight on her shoulders at home. She'd assumed from the start that she and Robby were on their own.

Gabriel was the man who didn't deserve her.

He'd tried to offer her money. His name. But that wasn't what Laura wanted. She wanted his love. She wanted...a family.

Gabriel set down the bottle. His body felt hot and cold at once.

The jet lurched forward, taxiing toward the runway.

He gripped the armrests. He had to go back to Rio, or he'd lose his family's company forever. Açoazul SA would be dismantled. He would lose his last link to his family.

The jet started to go faster down the runway, and he sucked in his breath.

His family.

He'd told himself for twenty years that he didn't deserve another family. And yet, like a miracle, he had one.

He had a family. Right here and now. And he was choosing to leave them.

He sat up straight in his chair. His breathing came hard and fast. What about his family's legacy?

Legacy.

He had a sudden flashback of a million small memories of warmth and joy and home. Visiting the steel factory. Sitting on his father's shoulders at *Carnaval*, watching the parades go by. Vacations in Bahia. Dinner together each night. A life of love and tenderness. Until he'd made one dreadful mistake.

"Your brother would forgive you. Your family loved you," he heard Laura's warm, loving voice say. *"They would know your heart."*

The jet hit full throttle, racing down the runway faster and faster, preparing for takeoff.

And Gabriel suddenly realized he was about to make the worst mistake of his life. And this time it wouldn't be an accident, a car spun out of control on a rainy road by a nineteen-year-old boy. This time it would be a stupid, cowardly decision made by a full-grown man.

He hadn't wanted another family.

But he had one.

Gabriel saw the white fields fly past the window. The jet started to rise, lifting off from the ground, and he leapt to his feet with a scream.

"Stop!"

CHAPTER SIXTEEN

LAURA hesitated outside the closed doors of the huge, flower-strewn library, frightened out of her mind.

She could hear the rumble on the other side of door, the mutters and whispers. The wedding had been scheduled to start thirty minutes ago, and everyone was obviously starting to assume the worst.

But there was no way around it. She had to get through it. With a deep breath, she pushed the doors open.

The enormous two-story library had been modeled after an old English abbey with walls of gray stone. It was now festooned with white roses and candles, with hundreds of chairs set up to create an aisle down the middle.

At the sight of the bride standing at the end of the aisle, musicians hastily began to play "Jesu, Joy of Man's Desiring" on guitars and violins. Laura stopped the music with a chopping gesture across her neck.

Silence fell. She could have heard a pin drop as three hundred pairs of eyes turned to her.

She trembled, passing a hand over her eyes. Then she heard her baby cry out halfway down the aisle. Going swiftly to her cousin Sandy, who held him in her lap,

Laura took her son in her arms. Robby looked dapper in a little baby tuxedo just like his father's, complete with rose boutonniere. She smiled through her tears. For an instant, she just held her baby in her arms, feeling his soft skin and breathing his sweet smell.

Then, squaring her shoulders, she slowly turned to face her family and friends.

"Thank you all for coming," she said loudly, then faltered. "But I'm afraid… Afraid that…"

"What?" her great-aunt Gertrude demanded loudly from the back. "Talk louder!"

Laura's knees grew weak. Did she really have to announce to all her friends and relatives that the only man she'd ever loved had just left her at the altar? How had she ever thought this was a good idea?

"Did he leave?" one of her hotheaded cousins demanded, rising to his feet in the front row. "Did that man desert you?"

"No," she cried, holding up her hand. Even now, she couldn't bear for them to think badly of Gabriel. He'd always been honest with her from the beginning. She was the one who'd arrogantly tried to change him, who'd thought that if she loved him enough, he might love her back. She was the one who'd thought if he knew Robby was his son, he might change, and love the child he'd never wanted. "You don't understand," she whispered. "I told him to go. I made him leave—"

"You couldn't," a husky voice said behind her. "Though you tried."

With a gasp, she whirled around.

Gabriel stood in the double doorway, dark and dashing in his tuxedo. And most incredible of all, he was smiling at her, smiling with his whole face. Even his black eyes held endless colors of warmth and love.

"What are you doing here?" she murmured. "I thought you were gone."

He started walking toward her.

"I couldn't go," he said. "Not without telling you something."

"What?"

He stopped, halfway down the aisle.

"I love you," he said simply.

She swayed on her feet. She was dreaming. She had to be dreaming.

He caught her before she could fall. "I love you," he murmured with a smile, and he looked down at the baby between them. "And I love my son."

There was an audible gasp. Gabriel looked around him fiercely.

"Yes," he said sharply. "Robby is my child. Laura was afraid to tell me about Robby, afraid I wouldn't be able to measure up to be the man—the father—he needed." Gabriel looked back at her. "But I will. I will spend the rest of my life proving I can be the man you deserve."

A sob escaped Laura's lips. Reaching up, she put her hand to his cheek, looking up at him. "You love me?"

He pressed his hand over hers. She saw tears in his eyes. "Yes."

She blinked, sucking in her breath. "But what about the deal in Rio?"

He looked down at her. "I don't care about it. Let the Frenchman have it."

She gasped, shaking her head desperately. "But you've tried to get the company back all these years.

It's all you wanted. All you've dreamed about day and night!"

"Because I thought it was my family's legacy." He reached down to cup her cheek. A smile curved his sensual lips. "But it wasn't."

"It wasn't?" she whispered.

"My family loved me, and I loved them," he said. "No accident can ever change that. I will honor their memory for the rest of my life. I will honor them by living as best as I can until the day I die." He took her hand tightly in his own, looking down at her. "And today, I will start the rest of my life loving you."

"I love you...." she choked out. "So much." She swallowed, then shook her head. "But we can get married later. We should leave for Rio at once. I don't want you to lose your company, your family's legacy—"

"I haven't lost it. I've found it at last. My family's legacy is love," he said. "My family's legacy—" he lifted his shining eyes to her face "—is you."

The autumn leaves of New Hampshire were falling in a million shades of red, gold and green against the cold blue sky when Gabriel and Laura returned home from New York.

Laura sighed with pleasure as their SUV rounded the bend in the road and she caught her first glimpse of the old Olmstead mansion on the hill. It was the Santos house now. The day after their wedding, Gabriel had bought it for her as a present.

"It's too big," she'd protested. "We can't possibly fill all those rooms!"

He'd given her a sly, wicked smile. "We can try."

And they had certainly done their best. In fact, they'd

done excellent work on that front. Laura blushed. Since they'd moved into the house in March, they'd made love in all forty rooms, and also in the secret nooks of the large sprawling garden. They'd shared many warm evenings on the banks of their private lake, swimming and talking and watching the stars twinkle in the lazy summer night. One big pond, she thought, for what was sure to be one big family. She smiled. She would some-day teach her own children to swim there, as her father had taught her.

She'd been in New York City with Gabriel for only a single night, but she was already glad to be back home. She hadn't known it was possible for a man to fuss so much over his wife.

As the SUV stopped, she started to open the door, but Gabriel instantly gave her a hard glare. "Wait."

Laura sat back against her seat with a sigh.

He raced around the SUV and opened her door. Gabriel held out his hand, and his dark eyes softened as he looked down at her. She placed her hand in his, and felt the same shiver of love and longing that she had the very first time she'd touched his hand, in the days when she was only his secretary.

After helping her from the SUV—it wasn't as easy as it used to be—he closed the door behind her. He fol-lowed her constantly, anxiously, always concerned about her safety and comfort. It might have been irritating, if it wasn't so adorable.

"I can close my own door, you know," she observed.

He stroked her cheek, looking down at her fiercely. "I have a lot to make up for. I want to take care of you."

Glancing at the sweeping steps that led to the front

door, she lifted her eyebrow wickedly. "Want to carry me up the stairs?"

Grabbing her lapel, he pulled her against his dark wool coat. "Absolutely," he whispered, nuzzling her hair. He gave her a sensual smile. "Especially since the next flight of stairs leads straight to our bedroom."

Lowering his head to hers, he kissed her.

His lips were hot and soft against her own, and a contented sigh came from the back of Laura's throat. As he held her, a cold wind blew in from the north around them, scattering the fallen leaves and whispering of the deep frost that would soon come to the great north woods. But Laura felt warm down to her toes.

"You're a furnace," Gabriel said with a laugh as he pulled away. Then he smiled. "I think the baby is glad to be home."

"So am I," she said, then laughed. "For one thing, you won't be trying to throw yourself in front of trucks, trying to protect me on the crosswalk."

"Fifth Avenue is insane," he muttered.

"Yeah, all those crazed tourists and limo drivers," she teased. Turning, she started to walk toward the front steps. She was excited to see Robby, after his first overnight apart from them. He'd had two loving babysitters fighting over him, Grandma Ruth and nanny Maria. "Thanks for a lovely night. It was nice."

"Yeah." Lifting a dark eyebrow, he grinned wickedly, clearly remembering their time alone together in front of the fire last night.

She elbowed him in the ribs. "I meant with the girls."

"Right." He cleared his throat. "Your sisters seem to

be settling well. It's the first time I've seen them since they started college."

"You're not in New York very much these days," she teased.

"I have better things to do than work," he growled. "Like make love to my beautiful wife." Grabbing her again by the lapels of her warm camel-colored coat, he kissed her again, long and hard, before she pulled away.

"You are insatiable!"

He gave a dark, wicked grin. "I know."

A flash of heat went through her. After they'd married that blustery day in early March, he'd made love to her without protection for the first time. The sensation was so new to him that they hadn't left the bed for a full week after their wedding. In some ways, Laura thought, she'd been his first, just as he'd been hers. And they'd gotten pregnant on their honeymoon.

Laura put a hand on her jutting belly. Their baby, a little girl, was due in just a few weeks.

"Thanks for moving up here," she whispered. "I am so happy to be close to my family."

His eyes met hers. "So am I. And I have you to thank for that."

Maybe it was pregnancy hormones, but Laura still felt choked up every time she thought of the three girls now living in the same city, all going to college. Two of them were her sisters. Brainy Hattie had transferred to Columbia University, and eighteen-year-old Margaret had opted for NYU.

But the greatest miracle of all—Gabriel's young niece, Lola, was now at Barnard.

Last spring, shortly after Laura had found out she was

pregnant, she had tracked down Izadora, Lola's mother, and invited their family to come up for a weekend visit to New Hampshire in the private jet. To Gabriel's shock, they'd accepted.

After twenty years, Gabriel had finally made peace with Izadora and met her American husband, a restaurant owner in Miami. Gabriel had hugged his young niece for the first time since she was a baby. And he'd convinced Izadora to allow him to create a trust fund for Lola. "It's what Guilherme would have wanted," he'd said gravely, and put like that, how could Izadora refuse? Lola was now at Barnard College studying art.

"All this family around us." Wiping away her tears with a laugh, Laura shook her head and teased, "And you paying for three students at college already. Robby will probably want med school. And now this little one. Are you sure you're ready for more?"

Gabriel put his hands on her swelling belly beneath her long T-shirt. At nearly nine months along, she could no longer button her wool coat. Half the time she was too hot to wear it, anyway. "Just a few weeks now," he whispered. Dropping to one knee, he impulsively kissed her belly.

"Gabriel!" she gasped with a laugh, glancing up at the big windows of the house.

Her husband looked up at her. His eyes glowed with tenderness and love. "I'll be here this time, *querida*," he said in a low voice. "Every step of the way."

"I know," she said, her throat choking with tears of joy. Tugging him to his feet, she wrapped her arms around his neck and kissed him. And as the cold wind blew, carrying dry leaves down their long driveway, she felt only warmth and love in the fire of their embrace.

And Laura knew two things.

The fire between them would always last.

And second, that they had an excellent chance of filling all forty rooms.

To Love, Honour
and Betray

JENNIE LUCAS

To my husband.
Thanks for Europe.
Thanks even more for home.
Thanks for making all my dreams come true

CHAPTER ONE

CALLIE WOODVILLE had dreamed of her wedding day since she was a little girl.

When she was seven, she placed a long white towel on her head and walked down an imaginary aisle in her father's barn, surrounded by teddy bears as guests and with her baby sister toddling behind her, chewing on flower petals from a basket.

At seventeen, as a plump, bookish wallflower with big glasses and clothes hand-sewn by her loving but sadly out-of-date mother, Callie was mocked and ignored by the boys at her rural high school. She told herself she didn't care. She went to prom with her best friend instead, an equally nerdy boy from a neighboring farm. But Callie dreamed of the day she would finally meet the darkly handsome man she could love. She knew that somewhere out there in the wide world, he waited for her, this man who would wake her with the sensual power of his kiss.

Then, when she was twenty-four, that man had come for her.

Her ruthless billionaire boss had kissed her. Seduced her. He'd taken her virginity, as he'd already taken her heart, and for one perfect night she was lost in passion and magic. Waking up in his arms on Christmas morning, in the luxurious bedroom of his New York brownstone,

Callie thought she might die of pure happiness. For that one perfect night, the world was a magical place where dreams came true, as long as your heart was pure and you truly believed.

One magical, heartbreaking night.

Now, eight and a half months later, Callie sat on the stoop outside her former apartment on a leafy, quiet street in the West Village. The sky was dark, threatening rain, and though it was early September it was hot and muggy. But her cleaned-out apartment felt almost ghostly in its emptiness, so she'd come outside to wait with the suitcases.

Today was her wedding day. The day she'd always dreamed of. But she'd never dreamed of this.

Callie looked down at her secondhand wedding dress and the wilting bouquet of wildflowers she'd picked from the nearby community garden. Instead of a veil, pearl-laced barrettes strained to hold back her long, light brown hair.

In a few minutes, she'd marry her best friend. A man she'd never kissed—or even *wanted* to kiss. A man who wasn't the father of her baby.

As soon as Brandon came back with the rental car, they'd be wed at City Hall, and start the long drive from New York to his parents' farm in North Dakota.

Callie closed her eyes. *It's best for the baby,* she told herself desperately. Her baby needed a father, and her ex-boss was a selfish, coldhearted playboy, whose deepest relationship was with his bank account. After three years of devoted service as his secretary, Callie had known that. But she'd still been stupid enough to find out the hard way.

A car turned off Seventh Avenue onto her residential street in the West Village. She saw an expensive dark luxury sedan and watched it go by, then exhaled. It wasn't Eduardo's style of car, and yet, as clouds covered the noonday sun, Callie looked up at the sky and shivered. If her ex-boss ever found out their single night of passion had created a child…

"He won't," she whispered aloud. Last she'd heard, he was in Colombia, developing offshore oil fields for Cruz Oil. After Eduardo possessed a woman in bed, she was pretty much dead to him, never to be remembered again. And though Callie had witnessed this scores of times during her time as his secretary, she'd still thought that she might be different. That she would be the exception.

Get out of my bed, Callie. She'd still been naked and blissful and sleepy in the pink light of Christmas morning when he'd shaken her awake, his voice hard. *Get out of my house. I'm through with you.*

Eight and a half months later, his words were still an ice pick in her heart. Exhaling, Callie wrapped her arms around her baby bump. He would never know about the life he'd created inside her. He'd made his choice. So she'd made hers. There would be no custody battle, no chance for Eduardo to be as domineering and tyrannical a father as he'd been a boss. Her child would be born into a stable home, with a loving family. Brandon, her best friend since the first grade, would be her baby's father in all the ways that counted, and Callie would be a devoted wife to him in return. In every way but one.

She'd been doubtful at first that a marriage based on friendship could work. But Brandon had assured her that they didn't need romance or passion to have a solid partnership. "We'll be happy, Callie," he'd promised. "Really happy." Over the months of her pregnancy, he'd worn her down with kindness.

Now, as Callie leaned back against their suitcases on the stoop, her eyes fell on her Louis Vuitton handbag. Brandon kept telling her to sell it. It would look ridiculous on the farm, she knew. It had been a gift from Eduardo last Christmas. *Totally unnecessary*, she'd wept, amazed that he'd noticed her gaze lingering upon the shop window months before. *I reward those who are loyal to me, Callie*, Eduardo had replied. *A woman like you comes along only once in a lifetime.*

Squeezing her eyes shut, Callie turned her face upward, feeling the first cool raindrops against her skin. Such a ridiculous trophy, a three-thousand-dollar handbag, but it had been a hard-won symbol of her hours of devotion, of their partnership. But Brandon was right. She should just sell it. She was done with Eduardo. With New York. Done with everything she'd once loved.

Except this baby.

A low roll of thunder mingled with the honk of taxis and distant police sirens on Seventh Avenue and the hiss from the subway vent at the end of the street. She heard another car pull down the street. It stopped, and she heard a door slam. Brandon had returned with the rental car. It was time to marry him and start the two-day journey to North Dakota. Forcing her lips into a smile, she opened her eyes.

Eduardo Cruz stood beside his dark Mercedes sedan, powerful and broad-shouldered in an impeccable black suit.

The blood drained from Callie's cheeks.

"Eduardo," she breathed, starting to rise. She stopped herself. Maybe he couldn't see her pregnant belly. She prayed he couldn't. Wrapping her arms loosely over her knees, she stammered, "What are you doing here?"

Silently Eduardo stepped onto the sidewalk. His long-limbed, powerful body moved toward her with a warrior's effortless grace, but she felt every step like a seismic rumble beneath her.

"The question is—" his dark eyes glittered "—what are *you* doing, Callie?"

His voice was deep, with only a hint of an accent from his childhood in Spain. It was a shock to hear that voice again. She'd never thought she would see him again, outside of her haunted, sensual dreams.

She lifted her chin. "What does it look like I'm doing?" She jabbed her thumb toward the suitcases. "Leaving." Her voice trembled in spite of her best efforts, and she hated Eduardo for that, as she hated him for so much else. "You've won."

"Won?" he ground out. He slowly circled her at the end of the stoop. "A strange accusation."

Beneath his gaze, her body shuddered with ice, then fire. She stiffened, glaring at him. "What else would you call it? You fired me then made sure no one else in New York would hire me."

"So?" he said coldly. "Let McLinn provide for you. You are his bride. His problem."

A chill went down her spine.

"You know about Brandon?" she whispered. If he knew about her coming marriage, did he also know about her pregnancy? "Who told you?"

"He did." He gave a harsh laugh. "I met him."

"You met? When? Where?"

Eduardo gave her a hard smile. "Does it matter?"

She bit her lip. "Was it a chance meeting...or..."

"You might call it chance." His casual drawl belied the cold accusation in his eyes. He looked up at the expensive town house behind her. "I stopped by your apartment and was surprised to find you had a live-in lover."

"He's not my—"

"Not your what?"

"Never mind," she mumbled.

Eduardo moved closer. "Tell me," he said acidly, "did McLinn enjoy living here? Did he relish living in the apartment I leased as a gift of gratitude for the secretary I respected?"

She swallowed. A year ago, she'd been living in a cheap studio in Staten Island, so she could send most of her salary to her family back home. Then Eduardo had surprised her with a paid yearlong lease for a gorgeous one-bedroom apartment close to his own expensive brownstone on Bank Street. Callie had nearly wept with joy, believing it was proof that he actually cared. She'd later realized he'd only wanted to eliminate her commute so he could get more hours out of her.

"What could you possibly have to say to me now?" She frowned. She'd been home all week—packing boxes, directing the movers, being informed by the airlines that she was too pregnant to fly, calling car rental agencies. "When were you even here?"

"While you were in bed," Eduardo ground out.

Her heart lifted to her throat.

"Oh," she whispered. It suddenly made sense. She slept in the bedroom, while Brandon had the couch. "He never mentioned meeting you. But why? What do you want?"

His black eyes glittered at her. He was staring at her as if she were a stranger. No—as if she were a bug beneath his Italian leather shoe. "Why didn't you ever tell me about your lover? Why did you lie?"

"I didn't!"

"You hid his existence from me. The very day after you moved into this apartment, you had him move in with you. But you never mentioned him, because you knew it would make me question your commitment and loyalty."

She stared at him then her shoulders sagged. "I was

afraid to tell you." She swallowed. "You're so unreasonable in your demand for absolute loyalty."

His mouth was a grim line. "So you lied."

"I never invited him to move in! He...he surprised me."
After Callie had called Brandon in North Dakota to tell
him about the apartment her generous boss had just leased
for her, he'd shown up on her doorstep the next day, telling
her he was worried about her in the big city. "He missed
me. He was going to get his own place, but then he couldn't
find a job...."

"Right," Eduardo said sardonically. "A real man finds
a job to support his woman. He doesn't live off her severance package."

She gasped at the insult. "He's not like that!" Throughout
her pregnancy, Brandon had cooked, cleaned, rubbed her
swollen feet, held her hand at the doctor's office. All the
things that she'd have wanted her baby's real father to do,
if he'd been anyone besides Eduardo. She scowled. "In
case you haven't noticed, there aren't many jobs in New
York for *farmers!*"

"So why stay in New York?"

Soft, lazy raindrops fell around them, pattering against
the hot sidewalk. "I wanted to stay. I hoped I would find
a job."

"And so you have. As a farmer's wife."

"What do you want from me? Why did you come—
just to insult me?"

"Oh, didn't I mention why?" His eyes were cold and
black. "Your sister called me this morning."

A chill went through her.

"Sami—called you?" Callie's conversation with her sister last night had ended badly. But Sami wouldn't betray
her. She wouldn't...would she? She licked her suddenly
dry lips. "Um. What did she say?"

"Two very interesting things that I could hardly believe." Eduardo took a step closer to her on the stoop and said softly, "But clearly one of them is true. You're getting married today."

Her body started to shake. "So?"

"You admit it?"

"I'm wearing a wedding gown. I can't exactly deny it. But how does that affect you?" Her lips trembled as she tried to shape them into a mocking smile. "Mad because you weren't invited?"

"You sound nervous." He slowly walked a semicircle around the end of the stoop. "Is there something you are keeping from me, Callie? Some secret?" He moved closer. "Some lie?"

She felt a contraction across her body, her belly tightening. Braxton-Hicks contractions, caused by stress, she told herself. Fake labor, the same that had sent her racing to the hospital last week, only to have the nurses sigh and send her home. But it hurt. One hand went over her belly; the other went to her lower back as she panted, "What could I possibly have to hide?"

"I already know you're a liar." A beam of golden light escaped the gray clouds and caressed his handsome face, leaving dark shadows beneath his cheekbones and jawline as he said softly, "But how deep do your lies go?"

The wilted bouquet of wildflowers nearly fell from her numb fingers. She gripped them more tightly in her shaking hands. "Please," she whispered. "Don't ruin it."

"Ruin—what—exactly?"

Her teeth chattered. "My…my…" *My life. And my baby's life.* "My wedding day."

"Ah, yes. Your wedding day. I know how you used to dream about it." He looked down at her. "So tell me. Is it everything you hoped it would be?"

She felt painfully conscious of the used wedding dress, several sizes too large, with a lace and polyester bodice that kept sliding off one shoulder. She looked down at the wilting flowers, at the two shabby suitcases behind her.

"Yes," she said in a small voice.

"Where is your family? Where are your friends?"

"We're getting married at City Hall." She lifted her chin defiantly, pushing aside the sudden desire to cry. "We're eloping. It's romantic."

"Ah. Of course." He showed his teeth in a smile. "The wedding would not matter to you and McLinn, would it, as long as you have your honeymoon."

Honeymoon? She and Brandon planned to break up their drive on a pull-out sofa at his cousin's house in Wisconsin. Passion was nonexistent between them—she thought of Brandon like a brother. But she could hardly admit to Eduardo that there was only one man on earth she'd ever wanted to kiss, only one man she'd ever dreamed about: the man glaring cold daggers at her right now. "My honeymoon is none of your business."

Eduardo snorted. "Anything for you would be romantic where Brandon McLinn is concerned. Even an ugly dress and a bouquet of weeds. He's always been the one you wanted. Even though he is a man without a job, unable to stand on his own two feet. You *love* him—" his voice was scornful "—though he is barely a man."

Callie's jaw clenched. She started to rise to her feet then she remembered she couldn't let him see her belly. Trembling with fury, she glared up at him. "Rich or poor, Brandon is twice the man you'll ever be!"

Eduardo's eyes burned through her. Then he spoke coldly.

"Stand up."

She blinked. "What?"

"Your sister told me two things. The first is true." Raindrops splattered noisily into the trees above. "Stand up."

Callie sucked in her breath. "Forget it! I'm not your secretary, I'm not your lover…I'm your *nothing*! You have no power over me, not anymore. Stop harassing me before I call the police!"

Eduardo's dark eyes glittered as he moved closer, standing over her, so close his pant legs brushed her knees. He leaned forward. "Are you pregnant with my baby?"

Staring up at him, Callie sucked in her breath. He *knew*.

Her sister had betrayed her. She'd told Eduardo everything.

She'd known Sami was angry, but she'd never thought she'd do it. Yesterday, her sister had called to wish her good luck on her trip. Callie had been jittery and afraid she was about to make the worst mistake of her life. When she'd heard her sister's loving voice, she'd blurted out her plan to elope with Brandon because she was pregnant by her boss. Sami's reaction had been furious.

I won't let you trap Brandon this way, with a baby that's not even his!

Sami, you don't understand –

Shut up! Even if your old boss is a jerk, it's his baby and he deserves to know! I won't let you ruin so many lives with your selfishness!

Callie had been shocked, but she'd never once thought Sami would go through with her threat. Her baby sister adored her. She'd trailed after Callie and Brandon every day for years with hero worship in her eyes. She might be angry, but she'd certainly never betray her. Or so she'd thought.

She'd been wrong.

"Are you?" Eduardo demanded harshly.

Callie felt another hard contraction. She tried to breathe through it, but the childbirth classes she'd attended with Brandon seemed useless. The fake contractions, which were supposed to get her body ready for eventual labor weeks in the future, were getting stronger.

"Very well. Do not answer," Eduardo said coldly. "I would not believe a word from your lying mouth, in any case. But your body…" He stroked her cheek, and an electric current coursed through her. Callie looked up with a gasp, her lips parted. "Your body won't lie to me."

He removed the bouquet of wildflowers from her unresisting hand and dropped it to the ground. Taking both her hands in his own, palm to palm, he gently lifted her to her feet.

Callie stood before him on the sidewalk, shaking and vulnerable and clearly pregnant in an ugly white wedding dress. Closing her eyes, she waited for the explosion.

But when he spoke, his voice was cool. "So it is true. You are pregnant." He paused. "Who is the father?"

Her eyes flew open. "What?" she stammered.

"Is it me? Or McLinn?"

"How can you ask…?" She faltered, blushing. "You know I was a virgin when we…when we…"

"I thought you were, though I wondered later if I'd been deceived." He set his jaw. "Perhaps you were saving yourself for your wedding night, and the day after we made love, you went home to your fiancé, and lured him into bed. Perhaps in a fit of remorse, or perhaps to hide what you'd done in case there was a child."

"How can you even say that?" she gasped. "How can you think I'd do something so disgusting—so low?"

"Is the child is mine? Or is it McLinn's?" His gaze was like ice. His sensual lips twisted. "Or do you not know?"

Her heart wrenched.

"Why are you trying to hurt me?" She shook her head. "Brandon is my friend. Just my friend."

"You've been living with him for a year. Do you expect me to believe he slept on the couch for all that time?"

"We took turns!"

"You are lying! He is *marrying* you!"

"Out of kindness, nothing more!"

He gave a harsh laugh. "*Por supuesto*," he mocked, folding his arms. "That is why men marry. To be *kind*."

She stepped back from him. Her throat throbbed with anguish. "My parents don't know I'm pregnant. They think I've just given up the job hunt and decided to move home." Her eyes burned as she shook her head fiercely. "I can't go back there as an unwed mother. My parents would never live it down. And Brandon is the best man on earth. He—"

"I don't give a damn about him. Or you. I care about one question. Is. This. Baby. Mine?"

Callie took a deep breath. "Please don't," she whispered. She despised the pleading note in her voice but couldn't stop herself. "Don't make me give you an answer you don't want. Let me give her a home. A family."

"Her?"

She could have kicked herself. Reluctantly she looked at him. "I'm having a baby girl."

He exhaled, setting his jaw. "A girl."

"It doesn't matter! You don't want to be tied to me. You've made that clear! She's nothing to you, any more than I am. You must forget you ever saw me—"

"Are you out of your mind?" he growled, grabbing her shoulders. "I won't let another man raise a child that could be mine!" He searched her gaze fiercely. "When is the baby due? What is the exact date?"

Thunder rolled across the dark clouds hanging low over

the city. Callie felt herself on a precipice of a choice that would change everything.

If she told Eduardo the truth, her baby would never enjoy the idyllic childhood that Callie had had, surrounded by endless prairie, playing in her father's barn, knowing everyone in their small town. Instead of parents who were best friends, her precious child would have parents who hated each other, and a tyrannical, selfish father.

If only she were the liar Eduardo thought she was, Callie thought miserably. If only she could give him a false date, and say Brandon was the father!

But she couldn't lie. Not to his face. Especially not about something like this. Grief twisted her heart as she whispered, "September 17."

Eduardo stared down at her. Then his eyes narrowed and the grip on her shoulders tightened.

"If there's even the slightest chance McLinn is the father, tell me now," he ground out. "Before the paternity test. If you're lying—or if you are simply wrong—and this baby is not mine, I will destroy you for your lie. Do you understand? Not just you, but everyone who loves you. Especially McLinn."

Her throat ached. She knew her ex-boss's ruthlessness. She'd seen him use it against others for three years, and finally—inevitably—against her. "I would expect nothing less."

"I will take your parents' farm. McLinn's. Everything. Do you understand?" His dark eyes glittered. "So choose your words carefully. Tell me the truth. Am I the—"

"Of course!" she exploded. "Of course you're the father! You're the only man I've ever slept with! Ever!"

Staggering back a step, Eduardo stared down at her. His jaw hardened. "*Still*? Do you honestly expect me to believe that?"

"Why would I lie? Do you think I actually *want* you to be her father?" she cried. "I wish with all my heart it was Brandon, not you! He's the one I want—the one I trust— the best man in the world! Instead of a selfish workaholic playboy who turns on everyone in his life, who doesn't trust anyone, who has no real friends—"

Her voice cut off as his fingers tightened into her flesh. "You were never going to tell me about the baby, were you?" His voice was dangerously soft. "You were just going to steal my child from me and put another man in my place. You were going to erase me completely from her life."

A shiver of fear went through her, but she glared at him. "Yes! She'd be better off without you!"

He sucked in his breath then bared his teeth into a smile.

"And that," he said, his black eyes gleaming, "is your greatest lie of all."

They stood glaring at each other on the sidewalk, like mortal enemies. She heard the soft patter of heavy raindrops sliding from the green leafy trees above the brick town houses, and she knew he was right.

For eight months, Callie had told herself that Eduardo wouldn't want a baby. That his workaholic bachelor lifestyle would be hampered by a child. That he would be a horrible father and she was doing the right thing for everyone. But part of her had always known that wasn't true. After being orphaned himself, and brought to New York at the age of ten, Eduardo Cruz would want to be a father. He'd never surrender a son or daughter.

It was just *Callie* he would sweep aside and discard.

And that was what frightened her. With Eduardo Cruz's wealth and power, if he took her to court to battle for full custody, there was no question who would win.

His dark eyes cut her to the bone. "You should have told me the day you realized you were pregnant."

She looked up at him, her heart twisting beneath the weight of guilt and regret and the grief of broken love. "How could I," she whispered, "after you abandoned me?"

His eyes widened. Then he glowered at her, his expression merciless. "You are clever and resourceful. You could have found a way to contact me. But you did not. You tried to hide her, as you hide everything."

She felt another sharp pain as her belly tightened. "And now I've told you the truth, will you try to take her from me?"

His jaw tightened. Then a smile curled his lips. Reaching out his hand, he stroked her cheek. A sizzle of electricity spun across her skin, vibrating down her spine, and she was filled with longing and desire, irrepressible need like fire. All her traitorous body wanted to do, even now, was turn toward him like a flower toward the sun.

"You will be punished, *querida*," he said softly. "Oh, yes."

Callie stared up at him, breathless beneath his touch, trapped beneath the dark force of his gaze. Then she exhaled when she saw a cheap two-door hatchback driving up her street. The cavalry had come to save her. She nearly sobbed with relief. "Brandon!"

Eduardo whipped around. A low, guttural word came from his lips, a word in Spanish she'd only heard him use when he'd just lost a huge deal, or the time a brokenhearted starlet had tried to break into his bedroom. Turning back, he grabbed Callie's handbag, then her arm. "Come with me."

Before she even knew what was happening, he'd pulled her across the sidewalk and opened the back door to his black sedan. "Start the engine," he ordered his driver.

Realizing his intent, she desperately tried to rip her arm away. "Let me go!"

But Eduardo's grip was like steel. He shoved her into the backseat and climbed in beside her, crowding her with his massive body that seemed far too big for the space.

Eduardo leaned over her, his eyes black with fury as he gripped her wrists. "I'm not giving you another chance to hide my baby."

Callie breathed in the woodsy, exotic scent of his cologne, overwhelmed by his closeness, by the sensation of his thigh pressed against hers. It was just as she'd dreamed about in the years she'd worked for him, and unwillingly dreamed every night in all the months since he'd fired her. Their faces were inches apart. Callie's heart thumped in her chest. She felt lost in a dream.

Then Eduardo closed the door with a bang behind him.

"Drive," he told his chauffeur tersely.

"No!" With an intake of breath, she whirled around in the backseat. Her last vision through the back window was of Brandon standing by the rental car with his door ajar, staring after her with his black-framed glasses askew, his expression anguished. Beside him, their two old suitcases still sat forlornly on the curb.

Their car turned the corner, and Brandon was gone. Callie's body felt tight with pain that seemed to emanate white-hot from her heart as she turned back to Eduardo with a choked sob. "Take me back. Please."

His eyes were merciless. "No."

"You've kidnapped me!"

"Call it what you want."

"You can't keep me against my will!"

"Can't I?" he said softly.

She shivered at the look in his eyes. He turned away

as if bored, but she saw the hard set of his jaw, heard the clipped tension of his voice as he said coldly, "You will remain with me until the matter of the baby is resolved."

"So I'm your prisoner?"

"Until my paternal rights are formalized—yes."

"So you don't believe I'm a liar after all," Callie said bitterly.

"Not about the baby. But there are all kinds of lying. You lie with silence. I wonder," he said blandly, "if there's anything else you've been hiding from me? My perfect, loyal secretary."

She wrapped her arms over her belly, which felt hard and tight beneath the polyester blend of her wedding dress. "What do you know about loyalty? You've never been loyal to anyone but yourself!"

"I was loyal to you, Callie," he said in a low voice. "Once."

Staring into his fathomless dark eyes, she was suddenly lost in memories of their days together, in the office, sharing sushi at midnight, traveling the world on his private jet.

"That was when I mistakenly believed you were worth it." His tone hardened. "I learned my lesson."

"What lesson?" she cried out, bewildered. "The instant I slept with you, I went from being your trusted secretary to a disposable one-night stand. After everything we'd been through together, how could you treat me exactly like all the rest?" She lifted her tearful gaze to his and spoke from the heart. "Why did you sleep with me?" she whispered. "Did you ever care for me at all?"

He stared at her.

"You were a convenience," he said roughly, turning away. "Nothing more."

The words felt like a knife blade in her heart, serrated, rusty, tearing through her flesh. She'd loved him with such devotion, and the night she'd given him her virginity, she'd thought a miracle had happened: that he'd fallen for her, too.

"Every woman in this city thinks she can tame you. The rich, handsome playboy," she choked out. She shook her head. "The truth is you'll never trust anyone long enough to care. You desert a woman the instant you've had your minute of cheap pleasure!"

Eduardo's eyes narrowed. Then his gaze traced slowly over her lips, her neck, her breasts.

"Longer than a minute, I assure you," he drawled. "Or don't you remember?"

Their eyes met, and her cheeks flooded with warmth. Heaven help her, but she remembered every hot, sensual detail of the night he'd made love to her. She still dreamed of it every night against her will. How he'd stroked her virginal body, how he'd peeled off her clothes and kissed every inch of her skin, how he'd made her scream with pleasure, crying out his name as he suckled her, as he licked her, as he filled her until she wept with mindless joy.

Heaven help her, but she couldn't forget.

His gaze dropped. Callie sucked in her breath when she realized the neckline of her tatty, oversize wedding dress had slid down her shoulder to reveal far too much of one plump breast and a full inch of her white cotton bra. She yanked the neckline up, scowling. "I can't believe I ever let you seduce me."

"Seduce?" His lips twisted with amusement. "What a charming description. I didn't seduce you. You jumped into my arms the instant I touched you. But call it *seduction*, if it makes your conscience easy."

She gasped in outrage. "You are such a—"

"Oh, I'm sure you regretted it afterward. McLinn must have taken it hard." He shook his head. "Amazing," he mused, "to think he was willing to marry you while you were pregnant by another man. He must be insanely in love with you."

A twinge of unease went through her. "He's not in love with me. He's my best friend."

"And you must have felt so guilty." Reaching over, he twirled a tendril of her brown hair. "So full of remorse that you ruined your chaste, loyal, boring love affair of years for a single night of hot, raw lust with me."

She jerked away. "You are so full of yourself to think—"

"Why did I treat you exactly like the rest? I'll tell you." Eduardo's eyes met hers evenly. "Because you are no different."

"I hate you!"

He snorted a laugh, but his eyes were icy. "Then we agree on something at last."

Tears fell down her lashes as she looked down, suddenly deflated. "All I wanted was to give my baby a good home," she whispered. "But now, instead of two loving parents, she'll be pulled like a tug-of-war rope between a mother and father who hate each other. Two parents who aren't even married. The world can be cruel. She'll be called *illegitimate*. She'll be called a bastard..."

Eduardo's eyes widened. "What?" he exploded.

"She'll always feel she's not good enough, as if she were some kind of accident, some kind of mistake. When the truth is you and I are the ones to blame." She looked up at him with a sob. "I don't want her to suffer. Please, Eduardo. Can't you just let me marry Brandon? For her sake?"

He looked at her for a long moment, his expression half-wild.

Then his jaw set. He abruptly leaned forward in his seat to say something in rapid-fire Spanish to his chauffeur then turned away, dialing into his phone and speaking again in the same language, too fast for her to understand. Praying she'd made him see reason, that he'd changed his mind and would let her go, she watched him, tracing the harsh lines of his silhouetted face, the handsome, sensual, cruel face she'd once loved with all her heart.

When Eduardo turned back to her, his dark eyes were strangely bright. "I have happy news for you, *querida*. You are going to be married today after all."

She let out a sob of joy. "You're taking me back to Brandon?"

He gave a hard laugh. "You think I would allow that?"

Callie frowned, confused. "But you just said—"

"You are going to be married today." Eduardo gave her a smile so icy cold it reminded her of the winter wind whipping across the empty, frozen prairie. "To me."

CHAPTER TWO

CALLIE gasped. Marry Eduardo? The father of her baby? Her ex-boss? The man she despised more than anyone on earth?

Shocked, she stared at him as she waited for the punch line. Licking her lips nervously, she finally said, "I don't get the joke."

Eduardo's lips curved humorlessly. "It's not a joke."

She spread her arms wide in the backseat of the car. "Of course it is!"

Eduardo grabbed her left hand, looking down at her cheap engagement ring with its microscopic diamond. "No, Callie, *that* is a joke."

Trying to rip her hand from his grasp, she glared at him. "A ring is a symbol of fidelity, no wonder you hate it!"

"You'll have a real one."

"I'm not going to marry you!"

"Oh, right. I forgot you're a *romantic*. I should ask you properly," he said sardonically. His dark eyes gleamed as he wrapped her hand in his own and pressed it against his chest. Before her horrified eyes, he went down on one knee in the back of the car. "*Querida*, my darling, my dear, will you do me the deep, deep honor of becoming my wife?"

She felt the heat of his hard chest through his suit, and her heart fluttered—even as her cheeks burned at the mockery in his voice. Anger gave her strength, and she jerked her hand from his grasp. "Go to hell!"

He moved back to his seat. "I'll take that as a yes."

Rain pattered against the roof of the car, horns honking around them as the car moved through traffic. The rain-splattered streets passed in a gray blur.

Callie realized Eduardo meant it.

He actually wanted her to be his wife.

"But you—you don't want to get married!" she stammered. "You've said as much to every woman you've dated. You practically had it tattooed on your chest!"

"I always planned to marry the mother of my children."

"Yes—but you wanted to marry some ritzy Spanish duchess!"

The edges of his lips lifted. "The best laid plans," he said. "You are having my child. We must wed."

He made it sound like a punishment—for him. She lifted her chin. "Gee, thanks," she said sarcastically. "I'm touched. Five minutes ago, you didn't even believe you were the father. You said you wouldn't believe a word I said. Now you want to marry me?"

"I've decided that not even you, Callie, would lie to me about our baby's paternity. Not when the truth is so clearly unpleasant to you."

She folded her arms, glaring at him. "I'm having your baby, all right, but nothing on earth could make me be your wife."

"Strange. You were keen to get married a few minutes ago."

"To Brandon!" she cried. "I adore him. I'd trust him with my life!"

"Spare me his list of virtues," Eduardo said, sounding bored. "Your love makes you blind."

"He might not be rich and heartless like you, but that's

exactly why he'll make a wonderful father. Far better than—"

She cut herself off as a painful contraction arced through her body.

"Far better than me?" Eduardo said with dangerous softness. "Because I am not good enough to be her father. And that was your excuse for lying to me and marrying your lover."

"He's not my lover—"

"Perhaps not physically. But you *love* him. So you were going to steal my child. And you accuse me of being heartless," he said contemptuously. "You are breathtaking."

The words were not a compliment.

Callie held her breath as new pain assailed her. Her baby wasn't due for two and a half weeks, but this was starting to feel very different from the Braxton-Hicks contractions she'd had last week. *Very* different.

Was it possible…?

Could it be…?

No! She forced herself to take a deep, calming breath. It couldn't be real labor. It was sixteen days too soon. Stress was causing her body to react, that was all. She had to calm down, for the baby's sake!

She shifted in the backseat of the car, trying to alleviate the stabbing pain in her lower back. "You don't want to raise a baby and you certainly don't want me as your wife. It's only your masculine pride that makes you—"

"My masculine pride." Eduardo bared his teeth into a smile. "Is that what you call it?"

"You don't want to marry me, I know you don't. You're just in shock. You haven't had time to think what it would mean for you to raise a child. To have a family."

"You think I've had no time to consider what it means

for a child to feel abandoned by his parents? To feel alone? To have no real home?"

Callie closed her mouth with a snap. Of course he knew. Licking her lips, she tried helplessly. "I could give our baby a wonderful home—"

"I know you will." His eyes were fathomless and stark. "Because I will provide that home. As her father."

There was no winning this war. Now that Eduardo knew about her pregnancy, he would never give up his rights as a father.

"So what do we do?" Callie said miserably.

"I told you. Marry."

"But I can't be your wife."

"Why?"

"I—I don't love you."

"Good," he bit out. "Your sainted McLinn can keep your love. Just your body and your vow of fidelity are enough."

Her heart was pounding in her throat. "You really want to marry me?" she whispered. The thought made her tremble. In spite of everything, she couldn't forget the romantic dreams she'd once had of Eduardo taking her in his arms and saying, *I made the worst mistake of my life when I let you go, Callie. I love you. Come back to me. Be mine— forever.* "As in forever?"

Eduardo gave an ugly laugh. "Be married to you forever? No. I have no desire to live the rest of my life in hell, chained to a woman I'll never be able to trust. Our marriage will last just long enough to give our child a name."

"Oh." She shifted in her seat then frowned. That changed things a bit. "Like—like a marriage of convenience?"

"Call it what you like."

"For a week or two?"

"Let us say three months. Long enough for it to actually

look like a real marriage. And for our baby's first months to be the best possible, with us both in the same home."

"But—where would we live? My lease is gone. You sold your brownstone in the Village."

"I just bought a place on the Upper West Side."

She blinked. "You were moving back to New York, because you thought I'd be gone."

His lips twisted. "I bought it as an investment. But you are correct."

Callie stared up at him, her heart pounding. "This is never going to work."

"It will."

She took a deep breath. *Marriage.* Would it be good for their baby, as Eduardo believed? Or would it only make their frayed relationship even worse, creating yet more accusations and distrust between them?

"But how would our marriage end?" she said. "With an ugly divorce—throwing plates and screaming at each other? That wouldn't help anyone, least of all my baby."

"*Our* baby," he corrected, then bared his teeth in a smile. "Our prenuptial agreement will outline our divorce. We will agree from the beginning how it will end."

"Plan our divorce before we're even wed? That seems so sad…."

"Not sad. Civilized." He lifted a dark eyebrow, rubbing the rough, dark edge of his jawline. He gave her a tight smile. "Since we are not in love, there will be no hard feelings when we part."

Three months. Callie swallowed. She tried to imagine what it would be like to live in Eduardo's house. Even as his secretary, she'd never lived with him on such intimate terms. And though she was no longer the naive, trusting girl who'd fallen in love with him so stupidly, he still had such frightening power over her. Callie's foolish, traitorous body yearned for him like a sugary, buttery cake that was impossibly bad for her but she couldn't stop craving just the same.

"And if I refuse?" she whispered. "If I get out of this car and flag a taxi back to Brandon?"

His expression cooled.

"If you are truly so selfish that you'd put your desire for love ahead of the best interests of our child, I will have no choice but to question your fitness as a mother, and challenge you for full custody." She started to protest, but he cut her off calmly. "I have limitless funds and the best law firm in the city at my disposal. You will lose."

She felt another contraction and this time, the pain was so deep and sustained that she closed her eyes, bracing her body against it as she panted, "You're threatening me?"

"I'm telling you how it will be."

"We're here, sir," Sanchez, the driver, said from the front seat, as he pulled the sedan to the curb.

Looking out her window, Callie saw the same courthouse where she'd gotten a marriage license yesterday with Brandon. The thought of deserting her best friend to marry Eduardo was insane. But she could either become Mrs. Eduardo Cruz for three months, living in the same household and sharing custody of their newborn, or she could possibly lose her child forever.

"And…afterward…" she said haltingly, "how would we arrange custody?"

Eduardo gave her a smile that didn't meet his eyes. "Once you show that our child means more to you than some lover, and that you are a reasonable and concerned parent, I am sure we can work something out." As Sanchez got out of the front seat and walked around to open the door, Eduardo's voice turned hard. "You have thirty seconds to decide."

Shivering, she stared at him with her hands wrapped over her belly. She felt her baby moving inside her, and she was desperate to protect her. She glared at him, feeling trapped and frightened and furious all at once. "You've left me no choice."

The door opened behind Eduardo.

"I knew you'd see reason," he said sardonically. Climbing out, he turned back, holding out his hand. "Come, my bride."

For an instant, Callie was afraid to touch him—afraid of what it did to her. But as he waited, she reluctantly put her hand in his own. His hard, hot palm pressed against her skin, his larger fingers intertwined around hers. As he pulled her from the car to the sidewalk, she looked up at his face, remembering the first time she'd touched his hand.

Callie Woodville? The powerful CEO of Cruz Oil had been visiting his outpost in the Bakken fields of North Dakota. Callie was the local office liaison, sent from the nearby town of Fern. He'd held out his hand, looking sleek and urbane in a black suit, with his helicopter still noisily winding down behind him. *I've heard you run the entire office here, and do the work of four people.* His sudden, gorgeous smile lit up his darkly handsome face. *I could use an assistant like you in New York.*

She'd looked into the warmth of his dark eyes. Dazzled, she'd taken his outstretched hand. And that had been it. The thunderbolt she'd always prayed for. She'd loved him from that first moment. How she'd loved him...

Now, with Eduardo's hand still wrapped around hers, Callie was barely aware of people rushing by them on the busy New York sidewalk. The two of them were connected like the moon and the sun, as stars and comets streaked around them in the vastness of space. The two of them. Just like always.

But his handsome face had changed over the last year. It was subtle. Perhaps no one else would have even noticed. But she saw the tighter set of his jaw. The deeper crinkle around his hard eyes. His high, angled cheekbones seemed chiseled out of stone, and so did his jawline, already dark with five o'clock shadow. At thirty-six, he was even more ruthless and powerful than she remembered. His masculine beauty was breathtaking. Looking up into his deep black eyes, Callie trembled. It would be too easy to fall under his spell again, and forget the way he demanded total devotion from others, while offering none in return.

Eduardo's expression darkened. Reaching down, he tucked a tendril of her wavy brown hair behind her ear. "You will be mine, Callie. Only mine."

A shudder went through her. She was helpless, lost in his gaze. Lost in his touch. Lost in her traitorous heart's memory of how, for years, she'd lived for him, only for him.

A cough behind her broke the spell, causing her to jump away. An unsmiling bald man in a plain blue suit stood behind her. She recognized John Bleekman, Eduardo's chief attorney.

"Hello, Miss Woodville," he said expressionlessly.

"Um. Hello," she said, wondering why he was there.

He turned to Eduardo, holding out a file. "I have it, sir."

Taking the file, Eduardo opened it and glanced over the papers for several minutes. "Good." He handed it to Callie. "Sign."

"What is it?"

"Our prenuptial agreement."

"What? So fast?"

"I had Bleekman start drawing up the draft after I spoke with your sister this morning."

"But you didn't even know if it was true about the baby–much less that you wanted to marry me!"

"I always like to be prepared for every possibility."

"Yes." She scowled. "To make sure you get your way."

"To mitigate risk." He pushed a fountain pen into her hand. "Sign it. And we'll go get our marriage license."

Callie looked through the thick stack of papers of the prenuptial agreement. She started to read the first paragraph. It would probably take an hour to read it all. Frowning, she thumbed through the pages uncertainly. She saw the amount of money he intended to give her as alimony and child support and looked up with a gasp. "Are you crazy? I don't want your money!"

"My child will grow up in a safe, secure, comfortable home. That means she must never worry about money. And neither can you." He set his jaw, watching her with visible annoyance as she turned back to page two and continued reading through the document. "Do you intend to read every single word?"

"Of course I do." Lifting her head, she glared at him, even as pedestrians jostled them on the sidewalk. "I know you, Eduardo. I know how you operate—"

Her voice choked off as another sharp pain hit her body, so intense her spine straightened as she nearly gasped aloud. The contractions were getting worse. Surely this wasn't Braxton-Hicks. She was in labor. Real labor. The baby was on her way. Callie put one hand over her belly and exhaled through her teeth.

"What's wrong?"

Eduardo's voice had changed. Trying to hide the pain rolling through her in waves, she looked up.

His handsome face was looking down at her with concern. He was worried about her. His dark eyes were warm, warm as they'd been during the time when she'd been his infallible secretary, when she'd been the one woman he needed, the only woman he trusted. Before they'd slept together in the happiest night of her life, and then she'd lost everything.

The intensity of his gaze caused her heart to twist in her chest. She could cope with his cold anger or cruel words, but not his concern. Not his kindness. A lump rose in her throat, and she suddenly had to fight tears.

"Nothing's wrong," she said. "I just want to get this over with." Gripping the pen, she turned to the pages marked with yellow tags and rapidly scrawled her signature. It was all she could do to keep the pen steady, with her knees shaking. She shoved both the signed prenuptial agreement and pen against Eduardo's chest, then turned away to focus on her breathing.

Breathe in, breathe out. She tried to let the pain go through her without fighting it or tensing her muscles, but it was impossible. *Stupid useless breathing classes!*

"You didn't read it," Eduardo said behind her, sounding almost bewildered. "That's not like you."

A policeman mounted on horseback came clopping in their direction, even as yellow taxis and large buses whizzed down the street, honking noisily. But all the moving colors of the busy world seemed to slide like water around her. She didn't answer.

Eduardo touched her shoulder, turning her around. "Callie," he said huskily. "What is it?"

She couldn't speak over the ache in her throat. She'd loved him, in spite of his faults. She'd thought she was his one indispensible woman. Until he'd discarded her. She couldn't let herself care for him. And she couldn't let herself believe, even for an instant, that he cared for her.

"I just hate you, that's all," she bit out, pulling away. Pain ebbed from her body, and she exhaled, forcing her shoulders to relax. "Let's just get this sham of a wedding over with."

Without waiting for him, she started walking up the steps toward the courthouse.

"Fine." When he caught up with her, the brief concern in his voice was gone. He strode ahead to open the door, and when she saw his face, it was hard and cold again. She was glad. She couldn't bear his tenderness, not in his eyes and not in his voice. Even after all this time, it twisted her heart into a million pieces.

Three months, she told herself, her teeth chattering. *Then I'll be free.*

She followed him into the courthouse, with his lawyer trailing behind. Twenty-two minutes later, they walked back out with the license. Callie knew it was exactly twenty-two minutes, because she'd started timing her contractions with her watch.

Eduardo didn't touch her as they walked down the steps. He didn't smile. He barely looked at her. After bidding the lawyer farewell, he led her toward the black car at the curb. "I have made arrangements for us to be married privately at my home," he said coolly, as if discussing a business arrangement. Which, Callie reminded herself savagely, was exactly what it was.

She tried to follow, desperate to get their nightmare wedding over and done with, but another contraction hit her. Panting, she grabbed his arm. "I don't think I can."

He looked at her, his eyes flinty. "It's too late for second thoughts."

Sun burst through the clouds as light rain fell, sprinkling against her hot skin. She felt the contraction build inside her, and she could no longer deny what was happening. She gripped his jacket sleeve tightly. "I think...I think I'm in labor."

He sucked in his breath, searching her gaze. "Labor?"

Wheezing, she nodded. As the pain built, her knees went weak beneath her and she felt herself start to collapse toward the sidewalk.

Then she felt Eduardo's strong arms around her as he lifted her against his chest. It felt good, so good, to be cradled in his arms that she nearly wept. He looked down at her, his jaw tight.

"How long?" he demanded.

Her body was starting to shake with the pain and she saw from his expression that he could feel it, too. "All… day…I—I think…"

"Damn you, Callie!" he said hoarsely. "Why do you hide everything?"

She was in too much agony to answer. His jaw clenched and he turned away, racing to the curb. "Sanchez! Door!" he shouted, and his driver sprang into action. Seconds later, she was in the backseat of the black sedan. Eduardo took her hands in his own as he asked urgently, "Which hospital, Callie? The name of your doctor?"

She told him, as Eduardo turned to shout the information at his driver, growling at him to drive faster, *faster*.

"Just hold on, *querida*," Eduardo said softly to her, stroking her hair. "We're almost there."

But Callie was lost in pain as the car flew down the streets of New York, taking sharp turns and honking wildly until the car sharply stopped. The car door flung open, and she was dimly aware of Eduardo shouting that his wife needed help, help *now* dammit!

"But I'm not your wife," Callie breathed as she was wheeled into the hospital. She looked up at him, blinking back tears even as the pain started to recede. "We only have a license. We're not married."

Callie heard him gasp before she was whisked away by

a nurse to a private examination room. As the contraction eased, she changed into a hospital gown. When the nurse came back through the door, Callie got a single glimpse of Eduardo pacing in the hallway, barking madly into a phone at his ear. Then the door closed, and the round-faced, smiling nurse came to check her. She straightened. "Six centimeters dilated. Oh, my goodness. This baby is on the way. We'll notify the doctor and get you to your room. I'm afraid it might be too late for anesthesia…"

"Don't—care—just want my baby to—be all right…" But before Callie had even been wheeled to her private labor and delivery room, the new contraction had already begun. Each one was worse than the last, and this one hit her so badly it made her whole body shake. Rising to her feet, reaching toward her bed, Callie covered her mouth as nausea suddenly roiled through her.

Quickly Eduardo came behind her. He snatched up the trash can and gave it to her just in time for her to be sick in it. Afterward, as the pain receded, Callie sat down on her hospital bed and cried. She cried from pain, from fear, and most of all from knowing that she'd just been vulnerable in front of Eduardo Cruz…and was about to be even more vulnerable.

But there was no way out now.

Only one way through.

"Help her!" Eduardo bit out at the nurse, who gave him an understanding smile.

"I'm sorry. I don't think there's time for meds. But don't worry. The doctor is on his way.…"

Eduardo snarled a curse that involved the doctor's lacking moral qualities, intelligence and bloodline. Growling, he went to the door and peered out into the hallway for the third time before Callie heard him mutter, "Thank God. What took so long?"

"All good things take time." A smiling, white-haired man in a suit followed him back into the private delivery suite. Eduardo went to Callie, who was stretched out across the hospital bed with her feet in stirrups, taking deep breaths and trying to relax before the next contraction.

"That's not my doctor!" she cried.

Eduardo knelt beside the bed. "He's going to marry us, Callie."

She looked between them in shock. "Right now?"

He gave her a crooked half smile, pushing sweaty tendrils of hair off her face. "Why? Are you busy?"

Callie looked at the trim man with the white beard and bow tie. "Is he authorized to just randomly marry people?"

The corners of his lips quirked. "He's a justice of the New York Supreme Court. So yes."

"There's a twenty-four-hour waiting period after the license—"

"He's waived it."

"And my previous license—"

"Handled."

"Everything always goes your way, doesn't it?" she grumbled.

Leaning over the hospital bed, he kissed her sweaty forehead. "No," he said in a low voice. "But this time it will." He turned back to the judge. "We are ready."

"The doctor will be here any second," the nurse warned.

"I'll do the express version, then." The judge stood in front of the beeping, flashing displays that monitored both Callie's heart rate and the baby's, and gave the plump nurse a wink. "Will you be my witness?"

"All right," the nurse said with a girlish blush. "But make it quick."

"Quicker 'n quick. So. We're gathered here in this hospital room to marry this man and this woman." The judge peered down at Callie's huge belly. "And none too soon, I'd say…"

"Just get on with it, Leland," Eduardo snapped.

"Do you, Eduardo Jorge Cruz, take this woman—what's your name, my dear?"

"It's Calliope," Eduardo answered for her through clenched teeth. "Calliope Marlena Woodville."

"Is it really?" The judge looked at her sympathetically through wire-rimmed glasses. "How very unfortunate for you."

"From my mother's—favorite soap opera," she panted.

"Right. So do you, Eduardo, take this woman, Calliope Marlena Woodville, to be your lawfully wedded wife?"

"I do."

Callie felt the pain starting to build again, and grabbed Eduardo's shirt. Looking at her, he put his hand over hers, then said angrily to the judge, "Hurry, damn you!"

"And do you, Calliope Woodville, promise to love Eduardo Jorge Cruz, forsaking all others, till death do you part?"

Eduardo looked down at her with his dark eyes. Once, this had been all Callie ever wanted, to promise her love and fidelity to him forever. And now it was happening. She was promising to love him forever, though she knew it was a lie.

It *was* a lie, wasn't it?

"Callie?" Eduardo said in a low voice.

"I do," she choked out.

Eduardo exhaled. Had he wondered, for a brief instant, if she might refuse? No, impossible. He was too arrogant, too sure of his control over women, to ever doubt….

"I see you already have the ring," the judge said, then blinked in surprise at the tiny diamond on Callie's hand.

"I must say, Eduardo," he murmured, "that's unusually restrained for you."

She was still wearing Brandon's engagement ring! Horrified, Callie tried to pull it off her swollen finger, but it was stuck. "I'm sorry—I...forgot..."

Without a word, Eduardo eased the ring from her finger and tossed it in the trash. "I will buy you a ring," he said flatly. "One worthy of my wife."

"Don't worry." She gave him a weak smile as she felt the pain start to build again. She panted, "Our marriage will be so short it really doesn't matter..."

"That's the spirit," the judge said jovially. "Ring can come later. Or not. Well, kids, we'll just skip through and assume the part about forsaking all others and staying together for better or worse. And since with Eduardo I already know it'll be for richer, not poorer, I reckon that's about it."

Callie stared at the judge, then Eduardo. The wedding ceremony had passed by in a flash. Just a few words spoken, and two lives—soon, three—forever changed. How could something so life-changing be so fast?

The judge gave them a big grin. "You may now kiss the bride."

She nearly gasped. *Kiss?* She'd forgotten that part! He was going to kiss her?

Eduardo turned to her. Their eyes met. He slowly leaned over the bed, and for an instant, all the pain fled Callie's body in a breathless flash.

When his mouth was an inch from hers, he hesitated. She could feel the warmth of his breath against her skin, causing prickles up and down the length of her body.

Then he lowered his lips to hers.

Eduardo kissed her, and prickles turned to spiraling electricity, sizzling her nerves like a current sparking up and down her body. His lips were hot and soft, in pledge of their promise, inflaming her senses from within. It lasted only a brief moment, but when he pulled away, Callie's hands were shaking, and not from pain.

"Congratulations, you crazy kids," the justice said, beaming at them. "You're married."

Married. Callie's body flashed cold over the magnitude of what she'd just done. She'd married Eduardo. She was his wife.

Just for three months, she reminded herself desperately. The prenuptial agreement had been clear about the timetable. At least in the paragraphs she'd skimmed before the contraction had hit her... She tensed as another contraction hit, burning through her like wildfire. She gasped, biting back a cry as her doctor came in, a brown-haired man in his late fifties. Glancing at the monitors, he checked her. Then he smiled. "Seems you're good at this, especially for a first-time mother. All right, Callie. Time to push."

Her eyes went wide as fear ripped through her. Instinctively she reached for Eduardo's hand, looking up at him with pleading eyes.

Eduardo took both her hands in his. "Callie, I'm here." His voice was deep and calm as his dark eyes looked straight into hers. "I'm right here."

Panting, she focused only on his black eyes, letting herself be drawn into them. As she started to push, bringing her baby into the world, she'd never felt any pain so deep. She gripped her new husband's hands so tightly she thought she'd break his bones, but Eduardo never flinched, not once. He never left her. As she held on to him for dear life, nurses moving around them at lightning speed, monitors beeping, she focused through her tears on his single, blurry image. Eduardo was her one solid, immovable focal point.

He never looked away.

He never backed down.

He never left her.

And in the end, the pain was worth it.

A healthy seven-pound-eight-ounce baby girl was finally placed in Callie's arms. She looked down at her daughter in amazement, at the sweetest weight she'd ever known. Cuddled against her chest, the baby blinked up at her sleepily.

Leaning over them, Eduardo kissed Callie's sweaty forehead, then their baby's. For a long, perfect moment, as medical personnel bustled around them, the newly married couple sat together on the bed with their brand-new baby.

"Thank you, Callie, for the greatest gift of my life," Eduardo said softly, stroking the baby's cheek. He looked up, and his dark, luminous eyes pierced her soul. "A family."

CHAPTER THREE

EDUARDO CRUZ had always known he'd have a family different from the one he'd grown up in. Different.

Better.

His home would have the joyous chaos of many children, instead of a lonely, solitary existence. His children would have comfort and security, with plenty of food and money. And most of all: his children would have two parents, neither of whom would be selfish enough to abandon their children.

The first time Eduardo had seen a truly happy family, he'd been ten, hungrily trolling the aisles of a tiny grocer's shop in his poor village in southern Spain. A gleaming black sedan had pulled up on the dusty road, and a wealthy, distinguished-looking man had entered the shop, followed by his wife and children. As the man asked the shopkeeper for directions to Madrid, Eduardo watched the beautifully dressed woman walk around with her two young children. When they clamored for ice cream, she didn't yell or slap them. Instead she'd hugged them, ruffled their hair then laughed with her husband as he'd pulled out his wallet with a sigh. Handing out the ice creams, the man had whispered something in his wife's ear as he wrapped his arm around her waist. Eduardo had watched as they left, getting back in their luxury car and disappearing down the road to their fairy-tale lives.

"Who was that?" Eduardo had breathed.

"The Duke and Duchess of Quixota. I recognize them from the papers," the elderly shopkeeper had replied, looking equally awed. Then he turned to Eduardo with a frown. "But what are you doing here? I told your parents they'd get no more credit. What's this?" Grabbing the neck of Eduardo's threadbare, too-short jacket, he pulled out the three ice cream bars melting in his pocket. "You're stealing?" he cried, his face harsh. "But I should have expected it, from a family like yours!"

Humiliated and ashamed, Eduardo's heart felt like it would burst, but his face was blank. At ten years old, he'd learned not to show his feelings from a mother who raged at him if he laughed, and a father who beat him if he cried.

Scowling, the shopkeeper held up the ice cream bars. "Why?"

Eduardo's stomach growled. There was no food at home, but that wasn't the reason. He'd been sent home from school early today for getting into a fight, but his father hadn't cared about what had caused the fight. He'd just hit Eduardo across the face and kicked him from the house. He was too disabled—and too drunk—to do anything but lie on the couch and rage against his faithless wife. Eduardo's mother, who worked as a barmaid in the next village, had been coming home less and less, and three days ago, she'd disappeared completely. The boys at school had taunted Eduardo. *Not even your mother thinks you're worth staying for.*

When he'd seen the *Madrileños* eating ice creams, Eduardo had had the confused thought that if he took some home, his family might love each other, too. *¡Idiota!*

Crushing, miserable fury filled him. He suddenly hated them—all of them.

"Well?" the grocer demanded.

"Keep it, then!" Reaching out a grubby hand, Eduardo knocked the ice cream bars to the floor. He'd turned and run out of the shop, running as fast as his legs could carry him, gasping as he ran for home.

And it was then he'd found his father...

Eduardo blinked. He looked around the comfort and luxury of his chauffeured, three-hundred-thousand-dollar car. His eyes were strangely wet as he looked down at his two-day-old baby, sleeping peacefully in her car seat as Sanchez drove them home from the hospital.

Her childhood would be different.

Different.

Better.

He'd never let the selfishness of adults destroy her innocent happiness. He would protect her at all costs. He would kill for her. Die for her. Do anything.

Even be married to her mother.

As the car drove north on Madison Avenue, Eduardo's eyes looked past the baby to Callie on the other side. He'd once thought she was the only person he could really trust, but the joke was on him.

She'd lied to his face for years.

And not just to him. A few hours after the birth, Callie had called her family to tell them about her new marriage and new baby. White-faced and trembling, she'd refused to speak to her sister then started crying as she spoke to her mother. When Eduardo had heard her father yelling on the other line, leaving Callie in tearful, pitiful sobs, he'd finally snatched the phone away. He'd intended to calm the man down. But it hadn't exactly turned out that way.

He scowled, remembering Walter Woodville's angry

words. Setting his jaw, Eduardo pushed the memory aside. The man was clearly a tyrant. No wonder Callie had learned to keep things to herself. His eyes narrowed.

Then he looked back at his sleeping daughter, and his heartbeat calmed. For the past two days he hadn't been able to stop staring at her tiny fingers. Her plump cheeks. Her long eyelashes. The way she unconsciously pursed her tiny mouth to suckle, even while she slept.

Eduardo took a deep breath.

He had a child. A family of his own.

He had a wife.

He'd married Callie to give their baby a name, he reminded himself, then he scowled. And yet she was still nameless.

He glared at his wife and bit out, "María."

Callie looked back sharply, her vivid green eyes glinting like emeralds sparkling in the sun. "I told you no. My baby will not be named after your Spanish dream wife. No way."

He exhaled, regretting he'd ever told his trusted secretary that he wished to marry María de Leondros, the young, beautiful Duchess of Alda. They'd only met socially once or twice, but marrying her would have been a satisfying way to prove how far he'd come since the days he'd stolen ice creams. "María is a common name," he said evenly. "It was my great-aunt's name."

"Bite me."

"You're being jealous for no reason. I never even slept with María de Leondros!"

"Lucky her." She folded her arms, glaring at him. "My daughter's name is Soleil."

Irritated, Eduardo set his jaw. Was it so strange that he wished to name his child after his Tía María, who'd brought him to New York, who'd worked three jobs to support him? María Cruz had encouraged him to see his high-school job pumping gas in Brooklyn not as a dead-end, but a place to begin. After she'd died, he'd gone from driving a gas truck, to owning a small gasoline distribution business, which he'd sold at twenty-four to become a wildcatter. His first big find had been in Alaska, followed by Oklahoma. Now Cruz Oil had drilling operations all over the world.

Yet Callie stubbornly refused to be reasonable. Instead she pushed for the name *Soleil,* which meant nothing personal to anyone—she'd just found it in a baby name book and liked the sound! He set his jaw. "You are being irrational."

"No, you are," she retorted. "You're already giving her a surname, and I chose her name months ago. I'm not changing it because of your whim."

He lifted his eyebrows incredulously. "My *whim*?"

"Soleil is pretty!"

"Did it, too, come from your mother's favorite *tele-novela*?"

"Go to hell," she said, turning to stare out the window as they drove through the city. Silence fell in the backseat. Eduardo took a deep breath, clenching his hands into fists. His wife's stubbornness exceeded common sense! Because of her, they'd had to leave the hospital without yet filing a birth certificate.

His jaw set grimly, he turned back to her. "Callie—"

But her eyes were closed, her cheek pressed against the car window. He heard the rhythm of her breathing, and realized to his shock that she'd fallen asleep in the middle of their argument.

He looked at her beautiful face, against the backdrop of Central Park, the vivid green trees and lawn reminding him of her eyes. Her light brown hair fell in soft waves against her roses-and-cream complexion. As usual, she wore no makeup, but no ingénue on Broadway could hold a candle to her natural beauty. She wore the baggy knit pants and long-sleeved T-shirt his staff had brought to the hospital, but he knew the hidden curves of her generous figure would put any scrawny swimsuit model to shame.

For months he'd tried not to remember her beauty, but being this close to her, the reality overwhelmed him. His wife was the most desirable woman on earth. Even with those dark hollows beneath her eyes.

A sharp edge rose in his throat. Turning, he looked out at the brilliant dappled early evening light glowing gold through the trees. Callie had given birth to their child without anesthesia. He still couldn't comprehend that kind of bravery, that kind of strength. For the last two nights, as he'd slept in a chair beside her bed, Callie had barely slept at all. The baby had had some difficulty learning how to nurse, and Callie had been up almost every hour. He'd offered to help, and so had the nurses, but she'd insisted on doing everything herself. "She's my baby," Callie had whispered, her face pale with exhaustion. "She needs me."

Looking at Callie now, asleep with her face pressed against the window, Eduardo was forced to acknowledge feelings he'd never thought he'd feel for her again.

Admiration. Appreciation. *Respect.*

Things she'd clearly never felt for him.

"I've heard all about you, Eduardo Cruz." Walter Woodville had hissed over the phone two days ago. "Do you expect me to be grateful to you for doing the honorable thing and marrying my daughter?"

Eduardo knew Callie's family meant everything to her, so he'd contained his temper. "Mr. Woodville, I understand your feelings, but surely you can see…"

"Understand? Understand? You seduced my daughter. You used her and tossed her aside." Walter Woodville's voice was sodden with anger and grief. "And when you found out she was pregnant, you weren't even man enough to come and ask me for her hand. You just selfishly took her. *You stole my daughter.*"

Those particular words ripped through Eduardo like a blade. Then rage built through him in turn. "We never expected it to happen, but I have taken responsibility. I will provide for both Callie and the child—"

"*Responsibility,*" Walter spat out. "All you can offer is money. You might own half our town, but I know the kind of man you really are." The old man's voice caught, then hardened. "You'll never be a decent husband or father, and you know it. If you're even half a man, you'll send her and the baby home to people who are capable of loving them."

Then to Eduardo's shock, the man had hung up, leaving him standing in the hospital room, staring at his phone, wide-eyed with rage. No one spoke to him like that—well, no one except Callie.

But the old man wasn't afraid of him. He knew Eduardo's faults and flaws. And there could be only one person who'd told him.

Funny to think how he'd once trusted her. He'd wanted her in his bed almost from the start, but he'd needed Callie Woodville so much in his office, in his life, that he'd forbidden himself to ever act on his desire.

Until last Christmas Eve.

In a lavish, gilded ballroom of a Midtown hotel, Eduardo had found himself stone-cold sober at his own Christmas party, surrounded by Cruz Oil's vice presidents and board members and their trophy wives. The men in tuxedos, the women dripping diamonds and furs, had danced and drunk the spiked eggnog, alternatively boasting about the latest promising data in Colombia or gleefully discussing the expensive toys they planned to buy with their next stock bonuses.

Eduardo had watched them. He should have been in his element. Instead he'd felt lost. Disconnected.

He had everything he'd ever wanted. He controlled everything; he was vulnerable to no one. He'd thought being strong and powerful and rich would make him content, or at least, impervious to pain. Instead he just felt…alone.

Then he saw her on the other side of the ballroom.

Callie wore a simple, modest sheath dress. She stopped, her emerald eyes wide, and a flash went through him like fire.

In this cavernous ballroom, filled with tinsel and champagne and silvery lights, nothing was warm. Nothing was real. Nothing mattered.

Except her.

"Excuse me." Shoving his untasted glass of mulled wine into his CFO's hands, he'd walked straight through the crowd. Without a word, he'd taken Callie's hand. He'd pulled her out of the ballroom, and she didn't resist as he led her out into the white, icy winter night. Not waiting for his limo, he'd hailed a taxi to Bank Street, where he'd carried her to his bed. There, amid the breathless hush of midnight, he'd made love to her. He'd taken her virginity. He'd held her tight, so tight, as if she were a life raft that might save him from a devouring black sea.

He'd never felt anything like that night, before or since. Their passion had resulted in a baby.

It had resulted in a wife.

Eduardo's eyes narrowed as he looked at Callie, still sleeping as the car exited Central Park into the city streets of the exclusive Upper West Side.

You seduced my daughter, Walter Woodville had accused. The truth was that she had seduced Eduardo. With her innocence. With her warmth. With her fire.

But she was a liar. She'd hidden so much from him. He could never trust her again.

Only his baby mattered now. With her dark hair, she was his spitting image. Eduardo had known she was his child long before that morning's paternity test confirmed it. But if Sami Woodville hadn't called him two days ago out of the blue, his baby would be living in North Dakota right now. She'd be Brandon McLinn's daughter.

Eduardo's jaw clenched. Even if Callie was in love with another man, he could hardly believe she'd betrayed him so deeply. But he didn't have to trust her. He had a private investigator on staff who could tell him everything he needed to know about Callie. He'd never be fooled by her again.

He would keep his friends close, his enemies closer and his wife the closest of all.

The sedan arrived at his twenty-floor building on West End Avenue. As Sanchez opened the door, Eduardo carefully, breathlessly, lifted his sleeping baby out of the car seat. He walked slowly so he didn't wake her, cradling her head against his chest as the doorman held open the door. The baby was so tiny, he thought. So helpless and fragile. And he loved her. Love swelled his heart until it ached inside his ribs. He let himself love her as he'd never loved anyone.

His plump, gray-haired housekeeper, Mrs. McAuliffe, was waiting in the luxurious lobby. "The nursery is ready. Och, what a sweet babe!"

"Do you know how to hold a baby?" he demanded.

"Why, I'm insulted, Mr. Cruz! You know I raised four children of my own."

"Here." Gently he thrust the sleeping baby into her arms, watching anxiously. As the older woman cooed softly in admiration, Eduardo turned and raced back outside.

The September sun was still hot, pouring golden light through the white clouds. His driver was reaching for his wife's door when Eduardo stopped him. "I'll do it, Sanchez."

"Of course, sir."

Eduardo looked down at Callie through the car window. Her head had fallen back, her beautiful face now leaning against the leather seat. Dark, long eyelashes fluttered against her pale skin. She looked so young. So tired.

As he lifted her into his arms, she stirred but did not wake. Her eyelashes fluttered and she murmured something in her sleep, nestling her cheek against his chest as her wavy light brown hair fell back on his shoulder.

She weighed next to nothing, he thought. Looking down at his wife, his heart gave a strange thump. While Sanchez drove the car to the underground garage, Eduardo carried Callie inside. He took his private elevator to the top floor.

He'd closed on this two-story penthouse a week ago as an investment. The penthouse had been languishing on the market for two years with a thirty-six-million-dollar price tag before he'd bought it for a steal, at the fire sale price of twenty-seven million. He hadn't intended to live here for long. But now…his plans were rapidly changing.

"I'll take the baby to the nursery, sir," his housekeeper said softly when he came out of the elevator. He nodded then carried his wife across the large, two-story foyer with its Brazilian hardwood floor in a patterned mosaic. Going up the sweeping stairs, he started down the hall toward the guest room.

Then he stopped.

The master bedroom would be better for Callie in every way. It was larger, with a huge en suite bathroom and a wall of windows overlooking the city and the Hudson River. Most importantly, it was adjacent to the study, which had been turned into the nursery. Shifting Callie's weight in his arms, Eduardo turned back. Carrying her into his bedroom, he put her down on his king-size bed. *Sí.* It was better.

Callie shifted, murmuring in her sleep as she turned on his soft feather pillow with its thousand-thread-count Egyptian cotton pillowcase. Eduardo closed the heavy curtains around the windows, darkening the room. He covered her sleeping form with a blanket, then for a long moment, he looked down at her, listening to her steady, even breath.

He'd only meant their marriage to last three months. He hadn't thought he could endure it for longer.

But in the forty-eight hours since the birth, his perspective had changed.

His daughter was small and innocent and oh, so fragile. Eduardo knew what it meant to feel like unwanted baggage, like a stray without a home. He wanted his daughter to feel safe and protected, not split between divorced parents, between two lives. He wanted her to have not just a name, but a real home. A real family.

And no matter what Eduardo thought of Callie, he knew she loved their baby. He'd seen it in the way she'd fought through the pain of childbirth with such bravery. In the way she'd sacrificed her own body, her own sleep and peace, in order to nurture and cherish their child. Even in the way she'd fought with him over her name.

Eduardo's jaw set. If Callie could endure pain, so could he. He turned away. There would be no divorce. They both would sacrifice. He would give up his desire for a wife he could trust. She would give up her dreams of love. Love was an illusion, anyway.

Responsibility was not.

She might not like his plan. Eduardo exhaled, remembering her horrified reaction when he'd first proposed marriage. She wouldn't accept a permanent union without a fight. So he would give her time to accept their loveless marriage. To appreciate what he could offer. To forget the people she'd left behind.

His hand tightened on the doorknob. He'd give her the agreed-upon three months to see the benefits of their marriage. And if, at the end, Callie still wanted her freedom?

He glanced back through the shadowy bedroom with narrowed eyes. Then he'd ruthlessly keep her prisoner, like a songbird in a gilded cage. Walking into the hallway, Eduardo shut the double doors behind him with quiet, ominous finality.

Now that Callie was his wife, he never intended to let her go.

CHAPTER FOUR

CALLIE sat up straight in bed.

Disoriented, she put her hands to her head, feeling dizzy and half-asleep as she looked around the strange, dark room. Where was she? How did she get in this bed? Her breasts were full and aching, and she was still dressed in the same long-sleeved T-shirt and knit pants she'd worn from the hospital. She had no memory of how she'd gotten here, but she'd thought she heard her baby crying....

Her baby! She sucked in her breath. Where was her baby?

"Soleil?" she whimpered. She jumped up from bed and screamed, "Soleil!"

Light flooded the room from the hallway as double doors opened. Suddenly Eduardo's arms were around her.

"Where is she?" she cried in panic, struggling in his arms. She looked up at the hard lines of his face, half-hidden in shadows. "Where have you taken her?"

"She's here." Eduardo abruptly released her, crossing the bedroom to fling open a door. "Here!"

Her baby's cries became louder. With a gasp, Callie ran through the door. As he turned on a lamp, she saw the bassinet. Sobbing with relief, she scooped her baby up into her arms.

The baby's cries subsided the instant she was cradled

against her mother's breast, but she was clearly hungry. Callie sat down in a soft glider near the lamp and started to pull up her T-shirt. She stopped, looking up awkwardly at Eduardo. "I need to feed her."

His dark eyes shimmered in the dim lamplight. "Go ahead."

"You're watching."

"I've seen your breasts before."

She glared at him. "Turn around!"

He lifted an eyebrow then with a sigh he turned away.

Once he was safely facing the other direction, Callie lifted up her shirt, pulled down her nursing bra and got her baby latched on to her breast. She flinched at first then relaxed as her tiny daughter started gulping blissfully.

"Sounds like she was hungry."

"Don't listen!" Callie cried, annoyed.

He gave a low laugh. "Sorry."

Moments passed in silence, and Callie took a deep breath, suddenly ashamed. "I'm sorry about earlier. I just panicked. I woke up in a strange place and didn't know where I was."

His spine stiffened, but he didn't turn. "You fell asleep in the car, on the way home. I carried you upstairs. Don't you remember?"

The last thing she recalled was arguing with him as they drove through Central Park. He'd been pressuring her about their baby's name—as if Callie would ever name her sweet newborn after a spoiled Spanish heiress! But the soft hum of the engine had been hypnotic.

"I guess I was tired." She rubbed her hand over her eyes. "I slept so hard that I almost thought you'd drugged me so you could steal the baby. Funny, right?"

His voice was cold. "Hilarious."

"I'm sorry," she whispered. "I didn't mean to accuse you of..." Her throat constricted.

He turned to face her, but he definitely wasn't looking at her breasts. "Of stealing the baby?"

She swallowed. "Yes."

His eyes glimmered in the dim light. "Don't worry about it."

He was being nice, which made her feel even worse. For months, she'd hated Eduardo, calling him a coldhearted jerk to her parents and friends, telling them stories about his worst flaws, telling herself he didn't deserve to be a father.

But *she* was the coldhearted jerk. Her lips parted. If not for Sami's meddling, she would have done the dreadful thing she'd just accused him of: she'd have stolen their baby. He never would have even known he had a daughter.

How could Eduardo stand to look at her?

"I was wrong not to tell you." It took all her courage to meet his eyes. "I'm so sorry. Can you ever forgive me?"

"Forget it," he said harshly. He folded his arms. "We both made mistakes. It's in the past. Our marriage is a fresh start."

"Thank you," she whispered, feeling like she didn't deserve his generosity. Awkwardly she looked around them. The nursery was straight out of a celebrity magazine, with soft yellow walls, stuffed animals, and the sleek comfort of an expensive designer crib and bassinet. "This is nice."

"I had my staff redecorate the study while we were at the hospital."

"Your staff?"

"Mrs. McAuliffe."

"I've always known I liked her," Callie said with a

smile, trying to lighten the mood. "So next door is the guest room?"

He shook his head. "It's the master bedroom."

Her heart plummeted. "I…I was sleeping in your bed?"

"*Sí.*"

"Oh." She swallowed and tried to pretend it was no big deal that she'd slept sprawled across the same bed where Eduardo Cruz slept naked every night, when he wasn't entertaining lingerie models. Feeling self-conscious, she moved her baby to the other breast, quickly covering up any flash of skin with her cotton shirt. Cheeks flaming, she glanced up at Eduardo, but thank heaven, he was carefully looking away. "Well, thanks," she said with forced cheerfulness. "I'll move to the guest room later."

"You will stay in the master bedroom," he said evenly, "close to our baby."

"Then where would you sleep?" A sudden dreadful thought struck her. "You surely can't think you and I will—"

He cut her off. "I will take the guest room."

"I don't want to inconvenience you."

"You won't." Coming forward, he touched the infant's soft, downy head. "I want you to be here. Both of you."

Looking up at him, she breathed, "You—you do?"

"Of course I do." Eduardo looked at her, and his dark eyes cut straight through her heart. "I've dreamed of having a family like this. Of keeping them safe and warm. Protecting them." He squared his shoulders. "And I will."

The cold, ruthless edges of his expression had melted away, changing to something warm, something fiercely tender. He looked like another man, she thought in wonder. The man he might have been if his childhood had been less of a tragedy.

Compassion mixed with longing and the echoes of her love, rising in her heart. But she couldn't let it win. She wouldn't. She took a deep breath. "Thanks for taking such good care of me." With a trembling smile, she looked down at the baby falling asleep in her arms. "And Soleil."

"Marisol," he said abruptly.

She blinked. "What?"

"Marisol. It's a classic Spanish name. A blend of your favorite name—Soleil—and my aunt's name. María."

Callie licked her lips. "Marisol," she tried. She didn't hate it. She tried again, "Marisol...Cruz."

"Marisol Samantha Cruz," he said softly.

She looked up, her eyes wide with shock. "After my sister?"

"She brought our family together."

"Sami betrayed me!"

"She's family. You will forgive her." He looked down at her. "We both know you will."

Callie stared at him in consternation. No. No way! She'd never forgive her sister for going behind her back and telling Eduardo about the baby—never!

And yet...

How could she be angry at Sami for betraying her, when telling Eduardo the truth had been the right thing to do? Even if Sami's motives hadn't been totally pure. A tremble went through Callie. Even if her sister's motivation had only been because she was in love with Brandon.

Sami was in love with Brandon. Callie had to face it. For years, she'd seen the way Sami hung on Brandon's every word, but she'd told herself it couldn't possibly be serious. Her sister had a crush. Puppy love. Callie hadn't seen the truth. She doubted Brandon did, either. They'd never noticed Sami's devoted, anguished love, right in front of their very eyes.

But Brandon deserved to be loved like that, as every husband wanted to be loved by his wife. Callie had been selfish to accept his proposal, to think, even for an instant, that friendship would be enough for a marriage. How could she have even thought of allowing him to make that sacrifice? A sob escaped her throat. She'd very nearly ruined so many lives.

Looking down, Eduardo put his hand gently on her shoulder.

"I've heard you talk about your little sister for years," he said quietly. "You send her gifts, write her letters. You're putting her through college. We both know you're going to forgive her."

Callie looked up at him, blinking back tears. "You're right," she whispered. "I was so angry at her. But she didn't do anything wrong." She closed her eyes. "It was all me."

Silence fell. When she opened her eyes, Eduardo's forehead was furrowed, as if he couldn't understand her. Their eyes met, and she felt that strange tugging at her heart. With an intake of breath, she turned away. "Fine."

"Fine?"

"Her middle name can be Samantha." Callie touched her baby's plump, soft cheek. "Marisol Samantha Cruz."

"I don't believe it." A ghost of a smile lifted the corners of Eduardo's lips. "Are we in agreement? I can fill out the birth certificate?"

Looking up at him, she smiled back. "Yup."

"Wonders never cease." For a long moment, their eyes met in the soft light of the nursery, with their baby slumbering between them. Then clearing his throat, he glanced at his platinum watch. "It's nearly ten. You must be starving."

"Not really…" As if on cue, her stomach growled. "I guess I am."

"I'll make you something."

"You? You'll cook?" she said faintly.

She must have sounded dubious, because Eduardo smiled. "I am not completely helpless."

"You must have changed a lot in the last nine months. The man I knew could barely find his own kitchen." She shook her head with a snort. "I'm amazed you even survived without me."

He looked at her.

"It wasn't easy," he said gruffly. Turning, he paused at the door. "Come down when you are ready."

Callie stared at the empty doorway, bewildered at this friendlier mood between them. Looking down at her sleeping newborn, she rocked back and forth in the soft cushioned glider, cuddling her close. She gazed in wonder at her downy dark hair. Her daughter had Callie's snub little nose and round face, with her father's dark coloring and olive-colored skin. She would be a beauty. How could she not be, with such a father?

In all the years Callie worked for Eduardo, she'd never once seen him put someone else's comfort above his own. But in the last two days, he'd asked her to marry him. He'd slept in a chair for two nights at the hospital. He'd brought her to his home. Turned his study into a nursery. He'd given Callie his bed while he himself was relegated to the guest room down the hall. He'd asked her to teach him how to swaddle their baby and change her tiny, doll-size diapers. Coldhearted billionaire tycoon Eduardo Cruz, changing a baby's diaper? That was something she'd never imagined in a million years!

It won't last, Callie told herself fiercely. When the novelty wore off, Eduardo would chafe at the responsibility and intimacy of family. He would crave the freedom of sixteen-hour workdays and endless one-night stands. He would return to the selfish, cold playboy he was at heart. Very soon—likely before the three months was even up—

he would divorce Callie, and be relieved to make his parental support of Marisol the distant, financial kind.

Once that happened, Callie and her baby would go back to North Dakota. To her family. To the people who loved her.

Or did they?

She swallowed. Her phone call to her family, just hours after the birth when she was still exhausted and in pain, had officially been a disaster. Callie tried to explain that she'd just had a baby and gotten married to a man they didn't know except by reputation, and planned to live in New York for the foreseeable future. Her mother had just sobbed as if her heart was breaking. As for her father...

Her shoulders tightened. Her father never reacted well when his wife was crying. But he'd never spoken to Callie like that before—as if she were such a disappointment he didn't even want to call her his daughter. As if he yearned to disown her.

An ache filled her throat. She'd never planned to get pregnant, but keeping her baby a secret had just made it a million times worse. And that phone call had changed something between them. She felt estranged from her family, and it was like half her heart was missing.

But she also felt angry. How could her family have turned on her like this? They were supposed to love her. Why couldn't they see her side?

And her father had been so harsh to Eduardo. Callie still didn't know exactly what he'd said. She just remembered how Eduardo's expression had changed when they were talking on the phone, from conciliation to cold fury.

Walter Woodville had never liked the way Cruz Oil had swept into their town, bulldozing through the county with money and influence, luring young people from family farms with the promise of high-paying jobs. But Callie had made that initial dislike worse. Her cheeks burned as she recalled her bitter words about Eduardo after he'd fired her. Was it any wonder that stalwart, old-fashioned Walter, who'd married his high school sweetheart and still farmed land once owned by his grandfather, had been horrified by the idea of such a man knocking up his daughter, and worse—marrying her?

And as for Brandon...

Her cheeks reddened further with shame and regret. Brandon was certainly back in North Dakota by now, after driving across the country alone. She wondered what he'd told her parents. What he felt inside. Was he worried about her? Was he angry? Or worse—brokenhearted?

Amazing to think he was willing to marry you while you were pregnant by another man. He must be insanely in love with you.

Callie shook Eduardo's words away. Brandon wasn't in love with her. Friends just tried to help each other. But no—that was a cop-out. She swallowed. He'd been kind, and she'd taken advantage. She needed to call him and beg for forgiveness.

Another person she'd hurt. She slowly rose to her feet, her body sore, her legs shaking with exhaustion. As she tucked her sleeping daughter into the bassinet, she suddenly remembered the tender light in Eduardo's dark eyes when he'd held Marisol for the first time. Remembered how he'd dozed on a chair in their hospital room, cuddling their daughter against his naked chest so the baby could feel the warmth and comfort of skin on skin. Strange. In this moment, she felt closer to Eduardo than anyone else. Eduardo.

Creeping softly out of the nursery, she went to the bedroom, where she found the suitcase of new clothes his staff had brought to the hospital. Opening it on the enormous bed, she selected a pink cashmere lounge set and sighed. It probably cost the equivalent of a week's salary. But the cashmere felt soft.

Taking a hot shower in the marble en suite bathroom was pure heaven. After combing her wet hair, Callie put on the soft cashmere set over a white cotton t-shirt and went downstairs.

It wasn't just a penthouse, she thought in amazement. It was a mansion in the sky. She went down the sweeping stairs to the great room, with a fireplace and floor-to-ceiling windows that showed the sparkling lights of New York City by night.

"What do you think?"

She jumped and turned. Eduardo walked toward her with two martini glasses. He was wearing dark jeans and a black T-shirt that showed off his exquisitely muscled body. "It's incredible," she breathed. "Like nothing else I've seen."

"Good." He gave her a slow-rising smile. "I'm glad you like it, since it's yours." She blushed, but still couldn't look away from his powerful body, or the masculine beauty of his face. *Hers*. If only that were true!

He held out an orange-filled martini glass. "Here."

"I can't drink while I'm nursing."

He held up his own drink, a clear martini with an olive. "This is mine." He pushed the orange-colored drink into her hand. "This is juice."

"Oh. Thanks," she said, suddenly realizing she was dying of thirst. She drank it all in one swallow, then wiped her mouth and realized she was hungry, too. "Something smells delicious from the kitchen," she said hopefully, setting down her glass.

Eduardo was staring at her. "I made quesadillas and rice."

"Great!"

"You might not like them." He smiled again, but for the first time she noticed that his smile didn't reach his eyes. His hand was gripping the stem of his martini glass, his shoulders tense. "Like you said, I'm helpless in the kitchen. Not like some men, who are undoubtedly born chefs."

Callie frowned, puzzled at his sudden change in mood. "Is something wrong?"

He showed his teeth in something like a smile. "Not a thing."

"You just seem—strange."

"I'm fine. Shall we have dinner?"

"Sure," she said reluctantly. Maybe she was so tired she was starting to imagine things. Or maybe it was her guilt talking. With a sigh, she looked around. "Have you seen my purse? I just need to make a quick call."

"Your family?"

"No," she said, irritated at the suggestion. "I called them from the hospital and look where it got me. No. Brandon."

Eduardo's dark eyes flashed in the shadowy room. "No."

"He must be back in Fern by now. I'm sure he's worried about me, and I'm worried about him—"

"He's fine," Eduardo said coolly. He finished off his martini and placed the empty glass on the marble mantel. "I just spoke with him."

She stared at him. "You did?"

"He'd been calling for hours. I got sick of the phone ringing. Ten minutes ago, I answered the phone and told him to stop."

"What did he say?"

"An earful," he said grimly. He set his jaw. "What exactly did you tell him about me?"

Her cheeks grew hot. "I was angry after you fired me. I might have called you a world-class jerk."

"A jerk?"

"And a workaholic with no heart, who lures a new woman into bed each night, only to put her out with the trash each morning," she whispered. She shook her head. "I'm sorry. I shouldn't have said it."

Eduardo gave her a hard smile. "You just told him the truth." Reaching for his empty martini glass, he pulled the olive off the toothpick with his white teeth and slowly chewed. "I am all of those things. Just as you are secretive, naive and ridiculously sentimental."

Protestations rose to Callie's lips then faded. After the way she'd acted, how could she argue with that—any of it?

He came closer, his face silhouetted by the huge windows that sparkled with the lights of the city. "But we must endure it."

"Endure it?" she whispered.

"Each other," he said coldly. "For Marisol's sake."

Pain cracked through her heart. Just a moment before, she'd been filled with hope. But now she saw she really was alone. No one was on her side. No one.

Stiffening, she held out her hand. "Give me my phone."

"No."

"Fine," she bit out. "I'll find it myself."

Moving through the swinging door, she went into a large, luxurious kitchen, with top-of-the-line appliances, a wine fridge, and a pizza oven, overlooking the sparkle of the city and black void of the Hudson River. Her eyes widened as she saw her bag on a granite countertop. She snatched it up, digging all the way to the bottom.

"It's not in there," Eduardo said, watching her.

Still digging, she didn't bother to look up. "Where is it?"

"I threw it away."

Her hand stilled. "Are you kidding me?"

His voice was like ice. "I won't let you call him."

"You can't stop me!" Her eyes were wide as she gasped with outraged fury. "You had no right!"

"I'm your husband. I had every right."

"I'll get a new phone!"

His black eyes glittered. "Try it."

"This is ridiculous. I'm not your prisoner!"

"For as long as we are married, I expect your loyalty."

"He's my best friend!"

"And you are my wife."

"You can't possibly feel threatened by—"

"No, why would I?" His voice was low and full of dislike. "Just because he is the man you *adore*, the man you *trust*, the man you wanted to be Marisol's father. The man you tried to marry two days ago."

"Only because I was pregnant—"

"You were engaged *years* ago, Callie," he snapped. "Before I even met you!"

Her mouth fell open. "What?"

Eduardo leaned his hand on the kitchen countertop. "Last Christmas Eve, when we made love," he ground out, "I couldn't sleep with you in my bed—"

"So why didn't you kick me out?"

He ground his teeth. "I went for a walk. I decided to stop at your apartment to collect a few of your things. I was going to ask you to stay. I never expected to find a man living there with you."

"You—what?"

His jaw was hard as he shook his head. "After our years together, I'd actually thought I could trust you. But just hours after you gave me your virginity, I met your live-in love. Your longtime fiancé."

She gaped at him.

"What, no witty comeback?" he jibed.

"Brandon wasn't my fiancé. Not back then!"

His eyes grew wild. "Stop it, damn you! Will you never stop lying? *I met him!*"

"But we only got engaged a few weeks ago!"

Eduardo folded his arms, his expression as hard as the wooden floors. "Then how do you explain it? Either you are lying, or he was. Which is it?"

She licked her lips. "Brandon wouldn't lie," she said weakly. "Unless—" She covered her mouth with her hand.

If we're not married by thirty—Brandon had taken her hands in his own—*let's marry each other.*

Sure, she'd laughed. On the night of their senior prom, thirty had seemed a million miles away. *Why not?*

She'd thought it was a joke. But could Brandon have taken it seriously? Could that be why, the day after Eduardo had gotten her an apartment, Brandon had suddenly shown up in New York with no job and a suitcase full of jeans? Because he'd heard in Callie's voice that she was falling completely in love with her boss, and wanted to protect his territory?

No. It couldn't be. Brandon loved her as a friend. Just a friend!

She glared at Eduardo. "Either you misunderstood him, or Brandon was trying to warn you off. To protect me from a sleazy boss."

"Sleazy?" he gasped.

She folded her arms. "But there's never been anything romantic between Brandon and me. Let me call him and prove it!"

"He's in love with you." His eyes were like ice. "You're either lying, or blind. But I won't be played for a fool ever again. You will not communicate with McLinn in any way.

Not by phone, by computer or via carrier pigeon. And not through your parents. Do you understand?"

Callie couldn't believe he was being so unreasonable. Tears rose to her eyes. "But I just left him there," she whispered. "Standing in the street on our wedding day. He deserves an explanation!"

"He saw you leave with me. That is all the explanation he needs. And if not…" He allowed himself a cold smile. "I just told him everything he needs to know."

A chill went down her spine. "What did you say to him?"

Turning away, he scooped up quesadillas and rice on a plate and shoved it toward her on the countertop. "It's simple. Contact him during our marriage, just once, and you are in breach of our agreement."

"Fine, I'll be in breach! Keep your stupid alimony. I don't care about your money!"

"Do you care about custody?"

She sucked in her breath. "What?"

He lifted an eyebrow. "It seems you did not read our prenuptial agreement very carefully before you signed it."

She struggled to remember the words of the prenup, but the truth was she'd barely skimmed the first pages. "I was in labor! In pain, under duress! Whatever I may have signed, it will never stand up in court!"

He gave her grim smile. "Shall we find out?"

Callie couldn't believe he could be so heartless. No, on second thought, she could. What she couldn't believe was her own stupidity—in believing it was possible for Eduardo Cruz to be anything *but* heartless! Blinking back tears, she tried to keep her voice from trembling. "Just let me talk to him once. You can listen on the other line. I just need to tell him I'm sorry." She closed her eyes. "When I think of what I did to him…"

"Yes, I can only imagine how badly you feel," Eduardo said sardonically. "Knowing you caused him pain by flinging yourself enthusiastically into bed with me and conceiving my child instead of his. A pity raising Marisol is now a responsibility more important than the romantic longings of your heart!"

His sardonic tone tore at her soul like nails on a chalkboard. "Why do you even care?" she spat out. "Our marriage will be over in months. For that matter, why did you even marry me? Why make such a song and dance about giving our child a name and a father and a home, when we both know you'll never last for long?"

His hand tightened into a fist on the counter. "What are you talking about?"

"I know you too well," she said. "I know the life you love. Traveling around the world, beating your competitors, buying expensive toys you barely take time to enjoy, any more than the women whose names you can't remember. Keeping score with your billions in the bank." She lifted her chin. "Am I leaving anything out?"

His dark eyes were cold. "My priorities have changed."

"For how long? A few days? A week? How long will you last before you abandon us?"

"*Abandon*?" he ground out. "You mean, how long until I let you rush into another man's arms?"

She shook her head. "I'm sick of your stupid jealousy!"

"And I'm sick of constantly being told it's impossible for me to be a decent husband, oh, no, not like some unemployed farmer who hangs on your every word. Too bad for you he's not Marisol's father!"

It was the last straw.

"Yes, it is!" Callie cried, blinking back tears. Grabbing her plate of quesadillas and rice—which indeed looked very poorly cooked—she yanked violently through the cupboards until she found a fork, then stomped across the kitchen. Stopping at the swinging door, she turned and yelled, "Three months can't come soon enough!"

Then with a sob, she ran upstairs, where she could eat and cry in peace with the one person in this world who still loved her—her baby.

CHAPTER FIVE

Three months later

IT HAD been a horrible three months of watching Eduardo be a perfect, loving, devoted father to their baby, who'd gone from tiny newborn to chubby baby who slept better through the night. Three months of being treated with distant courtesy as his wife. Three months of being tortured with memories, of silent hurt and anger and repressed longing by day—and haunted dreams at night. Three months.

Over.

Looking at herself in the bedroom mirror, Callie zipped up her silver dress, a slinky, strapless gown with a sweetheart neckline that emphasized her bustline. She put on the three-carat diamond stud earrings that matched the ten-carat diamond ring on her hand. Leaning forward, she applied mascara and red lipstick. Stepping back into crystal-studded high heels, she straightened. She stared at her own unsmiling image.

It was like looking at a stranger.

Callie thought of herself as plain and plump but the mirror now plainly told her otherwise. Her light brown hair was long and lustrous, blown-dry straight twice a week at the best salon on the Upper West Side. Her arms and legs had become toned and sleek from carrying Marisol and taking her on long autumn walks. She went to the park almost every day, rain or shine, eager to escape the penthouse, where she felt useless, trapped in the same house as a husband who did not care for her.

But her transformation into his trophy wife was complete. She no longer looked the part of the farm girl, or even the secretary. She was Mrs. Eduardo Cruz. The oil tycoon's unloved wife.

But tomorrow morning, her three-month marriage sentence would be over. She and her baby would be free.

Callie's green eyes were pools of misery.

Every night, she'd slept alone in his big bed as he slept in the guest room down the hall. Every day when Eduardo came home from work—earlier than he ever had, before dinner—his face lit up with joy as he scooped Marisol up in his arms. At night, when the baby couldn't sleep, she heard him walking the halls, cuddling her against his chest, singing her to sleep in his low baritone. Callie had a million new memories that would always twist her heart, because after they divorced, she'd never see them again.

Eduardo had been unfailingly courteous. He'd never brought up Brandon, her family, or any other subject that might cause an argument. Instead, every night as she sat beside him at the dinner table, he read the paper over dinner and kept the discussion to small talk. And her gaze unwillingly traced the sensual curve of his lips and shape of his hands, her body electrified with awareness as she breathed in his masculine scent and felt his warmth.

He never touched her. All he expected of Callie was for her to take care of their child and occasionally accompany him to charitable events. As they were doing tonight.

In the intimate world of New York society, the official Christmas season was kicked off in early December by the annual Winter Ball, which raised money for children's

charities across the five boroughs. Tonight was the last
night Callie would wear an elegant gown and accompany
Eduardo in his dashing tuxedo. The last night she'd have
to look up at her husband and pretend her heart wasn't
breaking.

Tonight was the end.

Fitting that their marriage would end at a Christmas
party, she thought dully. Just as it had begun with one.
Tomorrow, as outlined by the prenuptial agreement, she
would move out and Eduardo would begin divorce proceedings.

Standing in front of her bedroom mirror, Callie exhaled.
She didn't believe for a single second that he'd been faithful to her. She knew him too well. He wasn't the type of
man who could go without physical release for a month,
much less three. He must have had lovers since their marriage—but where? How? It tortured her.

She put a trembling hand to her forehead. What did she
care? Tomorrow, she'd be packing for North Dakota. For
home. She missed her family. Sami. Her mother. Brandon.
Even her father. She'd missed so much. Harvest. Autumn.
Apple dunking and hot mulled cider. Thanksgiving with
her father carving the turkey and her mother's prize-win-
ning pumpkin pie. But she'd been resentful and angry.
She'd wanted them to call and apologize. They had the
number. But they hadn't called, and neither had she.

But tomorrow, she'd go home. She'd noted the date in
her planner and circled it with a black pen. This sham marriage would be over.

No doubt Eduardo, too, had been watching the calen-
dar. He'd done a wonderful job as a father but he must
be exhausted, hiding his love affairs, working only nine
hours a day instead of his usual sixteen, eating dinner at

home every night. Honestly, she'd never expected him to last this long.

Callie shivered as if she felt the cold December wind blowing through the canyons of the city.

He'd never tried to touch her during their marriage, not once. They'd only had that single night together, the night they'd conceived Marisol. One perfect night, the fulfillment of all her innocent dreams. One night. And so much she would never forget. The sudden hot hunger of his gaze across the hotel ballroom. The warmth of his sensual lips as they kissed in the back of a taxi heading south on Fifth at a breakneck pace. The woodsy, clean scent of his black hair as he carried her up the stairs to his bedroom and how silky it had felt clutched in her fingers as he covered her naked body with his own. The low rasp of his breath as he cupped her breasts. His hard gasp as he pushed inside her. The sound of her own scream ringing in her ears as her world exploded like fireworks, like a million dreams coming true at once.

Tomorrow, she'd go home and try to find a regular job. She'd face her family. She'd forget Eduardo. She had to; otherwise the rest of her life would be bleak...

"*Querida*."

She whirled around. Eduardo was standing in the open doorway of the master bedroom, wearing a well-cut black tuxedo. He looked so devastatingly handsome that her heart lifted to her throat.

His eyes were as black as his jacket. His dark, short, wavy hair set off his handsome, chiseled face to perfection. As he came into the bedroom, the muscles of his powerful body seemed barely constrained by the civilized, sophisticated tuxedo.

He slowly looked her up and down, and his eyes seemed to devour her in the floor-length silver dress. "You look ridiculously beautiful," he said huskily. "Every man will envy me tonight."

"Oh," she said in shock, and blushed. She had no idea how to react. He'd never said such a thing to her before. On this, the last night of their marriage, she suddenly felt as awkward and self-conscious as if they were on a first date. "Thank you. Um. You, too."

He smiled. "I brought you a gift."

Pulling a black velvet box from his tuxedo pocket, he opened it in front of her. Her jaw dropped when she saw the priceless emerald and diamond necklace sparkling inside.

She looked up with a gasp. "That's—that's for me? Why?"

He gave a low laugh. "Do you really need to ask?"

She bit her lip. "Is it like—a going-away present?"

"No." He shook his head then gave her a charming, crooked grin. "Think of it as an early Christmas present." Setting down the box on the bed, he pulled the necklace from the black velvet setting. "May I?"

Nervously she held up her long brown hair and allowed him to place the necklace's heavy weight around her neck and latch it in the back, shivering as she felt his strong, warm hands brush against her nape. It was the first time he'd touched her in months, and it caused a tremble to rise from deep inside her. Moving away, she glanced at herself in the mirror. She put her hand over the green jewels sparkling in the light from the black wrought-iron chandelier.

"It's beautiful," she said over the lump in her throat.

Their eyes met in the mirror. The smile left his face.

"Not half as beautiful as you," he said in a low voice. "No other woman can compare."

He was standing behind her, so close their bodies could almost touch. Sensual need suddenly poured through her, so intense and deep that it made her knees weak. She closed her eyes.

"Why are you being nice to me?" she choked out. "Why now? When it's the end?"

Coming behind her, he put his hands on her bare shoulders. "Who says it's the end?"

She felt the weight of his hands on her skin and breathed, "The prenuptial agreement."

Eduardo turned her around, and she opened her eyes. She could feel the heat radiating from his body. Feel its answering, unwilling fire in her own.

Nervously she licked her lips. His gaze fell hungrily to her mouth. "You have to know what I want," he said softly.

His freedom, she thought unhappily. While as for her... The time of their marriage had only taught her to crave him again. To yearn. To want.

"Of course I know," she said, and tried to laugh. "It must have felt like the longest three months of your life."

He stroked her cheek. "It has."

She swallowed. "Three months of waiting, and waiting..."

"Three months of hell," he agreed.

She exhaled, blinking back tears as all her worst fears were proven true. "Well, tonight it will end."

His dark eyes tracing her face, her cheeks, her lips. "Yes," he said softly. "It will."

Shaking, she turned away, picking up her satin clutch off the bed. "I'm ready."

"Good." His sensual mouth curved as he held out his arm. "Mrs. Cruz."

Breathlessly she took his arm. He led her downstairs to the penthouse foyer, where they bid farewell to Mrs. McAuliffe, who would watch their sleeping baby. Eduardo pulled Callie's white fur wrap from the closet and placed it gently around her. She felt the weight of his hands against her shoulders and shivered, remembering last night's dream that had felt so real, when she'd imagined his naked body over hers. With a tremble, she glanced down at his thick fingers spread across the white faux fur. Heat flashed across her body as she remembered the sensation of his fingertips against her skin. Shuddering, she pulled away as they took the elevator downstairs and went outside.

"Good evening, Mr. Cruz, Mrs. Cruz," the smiling doorman said, tipping his cap. "Have a wonderful night."

"Thank you, Bernard." Eduardo put his hand on the small of Callie's back, guiding her to the black limo waiting at the curb. Sanchez held open the door as she climbed into the backseat, exhaling as she pulled away. And yet, as they drove through the sparkling, snowy city, every inch of her body was aware of her husband beside her. She didn't relax until the car stopped, and she could escape the tight space beside him.

The Winter Ball was being held at a glamorous old hotel on the edge of Central Park. As Callie walked through the lobby on her husband's arm, her fingers barely touching his sleeve, she looked up at the soaring, frescoed ceilings in awe. Cruz Oil's Christmas party last year had been huge, but it was nothing compared to this, the most lavish social event of the season. As they entered the enormous ballroom, she saw a winter wonderland. White twinkling lights sparkled from black bare trees, in front of a white background illuminated with pale lavender light. Winter was Callie's favorite season, December her favorite month, and she gasped with wonder at the fairy forest of white.

Then the fantasy came crashing down as she saw the guests milling around them: gorgeous, skinny socialites and powerful men, the type who'd all gone to prep schools and Ivy League colleges, who'd come from the best families and summered together in Kennebunkport and Martha's Vineyard. And who was she? Nobody.

Back at the penthouse, Callie had felt pretty; but here, she felt chubby and awkward. Scrawny, tall models seemed to circle them like sharks, looking hungrily at Eduardo.

"Do you know them?" she whispered, clutching his arm as he led her past them through the crowd.

"Who?"

"Those women who are staring at you."

He glanced over at the gorgeous supermodels. "No."

"Oh." She swallowed. Was he telling the truth? Or just trying to spare her feelings? She felt an ache in her throat, wondering if he'd had affairs with any of them. If he hadn't, he was probably counting down the moments until their divorce, marking out his future sexual conquests. And who could blame him? Three months without sex would be was a long time for a man like Eduardo.

But not for her. Callie had only had one sexual experience in her whole life. And with the only man she'd ever wanted. She'd tried not to care, told herself their marriage was just a sham. But just the thought of him jumping into bed with any one of those gorgeous, hard-eyed women made her want to throw up.

But Eduardo wasn't looking at the models. He was looking at Callie. "Can I get you a drink?"

Nervously she nodded, and when Eduardo brought her a cup of punch in a crystal glass, she gulped it down.

"Be careful with that," he said, sounding amused as he sipped his own Hendrick's martini, garnished with a slice of cucumber. "It's stronger than you think."

But Callie was tired of being careful. The punch tasted fruity and tart and sweet, with a little bit of bite. It tasted like temptation. Finishing it off, she held out her glass. "Please get me another."

He shook his head, looking down at her with dark eyes. "Take care, *querida*."

"I'm tired of taking care," she whispered. "Just for this one night, I want to be reckless."

Eduardo gave her a slow grin. "As you wish."

Turning, he went toward the bar. When he returned, the intensity of his gaze flooded her with heat.

"Here," he said in a low voice, holding out her drink. Their fingers brushed as she took the glass, and she shivered.

For weeks, he'd treated her with distant civility. She might as well have been one of his staff, the nanny who cared for his child. But tonight... Tonight he was looking at her. Really *looking* at her. As if he wanted to rip off her dress, kiss every inch of her skin, and make her lose her mind with pleasure.

He left me, she reminded herself fiercely. *I mean nothing to him. He only slept with me in the first place because I was* convenient.

"Thanks," she muttered, taking the glass. "What's this drink called, anyway?"

His lips quirked. "It's called a Rudolph."

"A Rudolph? Why?"

"It'll make your nose red and you fly all night."

"Oh," she muttered. Ask a silly question. Knocking back her head, she drank deeply, aware of his gaze upon her face, her neck, her breasts. She kept drinking until the cup was empty, and she had no choice but to meet his eyes. His dark eyes caressed her face.

"Have you ever had a hangover before?"

"No."

"Want one?"

She'd never experienced a hangover, but the idea of waking up with one tomorrow sounded appealing. It would be a welcome distraction from their impending divorce. "Maybe."

Music from the orchestra swelled across the ballroom and he held out his hand. "Dance with me."

Shaking her head, she looked toward the gorgeous cluster of supermodel-types on the edge of the dance floor, who were still watching Eduardo with voracious eyes. "Why don't you ask one of them?"

He frowned at her then glanced over before setting his jaw. "Why would I?"

"They seem to know you."

"Lots of people know me."

A lump rose in her throat. "Why don't we just end the charade? You don't need to be so discreet. I know perfectly well that you've had lovers during our marriage."

His eyes turned sharp. "Who told you that?"

"No one had to tell me. We haven't been having sex, so I assumed..."

"You assumed wrong."

For a long moment, they stared at each other.

"Are you really telling me the truth?" she whispered, her heart in her throat. "But it's impossible. There must have been someone else!"

His dark eyes burned like fire. "So that is what you think of me." His voice was low and terse beneath the rising music. "That while insisting on your absolute fidelity, I would cheat on you and betray our marriage vows?"

"What else do you expect me to believe? I know you, Eduardo. There's no way you've been celibate for the last three months, especially when women throw themselves at you! No man could resist that. Especially not—"

"Especially not me?" he said with dangerous quietness.

She shook her head tearfully. "You got what you wanted. Our baby has your name. Now all your friends have seen

me, they'll know you did the right thing by our baby, and
they'll know why our marriage didn't last."

"Which is?"

"Just look at me!" Starting to feel dizzy from the alcohol and the heat of the ballroom, she looked down at her
overflowing curves in the tight dress then gestured toward
him. "And look at you!"

Eduardo's brow creased as he looked down at his tuxedo, then back at Callie in her silver gown—the gown
that had made her feel so pretty at the house but that now
only seemed to emphasize her overblown figure compared
to the stick figures of the models. He shook his head. "I
don't understand."

"Oh, forget it!" she choked out. "It doesn't matter. Not
anymore!"

But as she started to leave, she felt his larger hand en-
fold her own. Taking the empty glass from her, he set it
on the silver tray of a passing waiter and pulled her into
his arms. His dark eyes searched hers. "I never betrayed
you, Callie."

She licked her suddenly dry lips. "Why would you be
faithful to me?"

"If you have to ask, you don't know me at all." His hand
tightened on hers. "Dance with me."

Callie stared up at him, her heart in her throat. She
knew she should refuse. Her mind was reeling at the
thought that he'd been faithful to her. Without her anger,
she was vulnerable. She had nothing to defend her. The
marriage would end tomorrow. She was so close to being
free. She couldn't let him any closer now. She should run,
as fast and hard as she could.

But as he led her to the dance floor, she couldn't resist,
any more than she could resist breathing.

"All right," she whispered. "Just once." *To say good-bye*, she told herself.

Turning to her, Eduardo pulled her against his body. All around them, pale purple shadows moved against soft lavender lights, and the white bare trees looked like lacy latticework beneath twinkling white stars. Surrounded by couples swaying to music, they began to dance. Eduardo held her tightly, nestling her against the white shirt of his tuxedo. She felt his warmth. His heat. She felt the strength of his arms around her.

Callie closed her eyes, pressing her face against his chest. She felt strangely safe. Protected. She felt as if she'd gone back in time, to that one perfect night when she'd felt he cared.

For the next two hours, they never left the dance floor, and Callie was lost in the haze of a perfect, romantic dream. As Eduardo held her, as she swayed in her silver gown, she looked up into his handsome, sensual face and everything else fell away. She barely heard the music. She and Eduardo were alone, in an enchanted winter forest.

And she realized she loved him.

She'd never stopped loving him.

Callie froze, staring up at him as unseen couples whirled around them in the violet shadows.

"What is it, *querida*?" Eduardo said softly, looking down at her.

Callie licked her lips, feeling dizzy and hot all over. She couldn't let herself love him again. She couldn't be that stupid. She couldn't.

"What are you trying to do to me?" she said hoarsely. "What are you doing?"

Eduardo stood still on the dance floor, looking down at her. A tremble went through her as a current of awareness sizzled down her veins. Her mouth felt suddenly dry as he stroked her cheek.

"What am I doing?" His dark eyes searched hers, and he whispered, "I'm kissing you."

Callie couldn't move, couldn't breathe, as he lowered his mouth to hers.

She felt the heat of his sensual lips like satin and the warmth of his breath in an embrace that swirled around her body with breathless magic. She felt his hard, hungry lips against her own. Felt the scratchy roughness of his chin, as his hands ran softly through her hair, then down the bare skin of her back.

His kiss was exactly how she remembered. Exactly how a kiss should be. His deeply passionate embrace didn't just promise pleasure—it whispered of eternity. And against her will, words filled her soul that were an incantation in her heart.

I love you, Eduardo.

I never stopped loving you.

Oh, God. Could he feel it on her lips as he kissed her? Had her own body betrayed her?

"I want you, Callie," he murmured against her skin.

She saw the blatant desire in his dark eyes and suddenly felt like crying.

"How can you torture me like this," she whispered, "when we both know in the morning you'll only toss me aside? I gave you my devotion. And you treated me like trash!"

"Callie!"

"No!" She ripped away, not wanting him to see the anguish in her eyes. She couldn't bear that final humiliation. Turning, she ran off the dance floor. Pushing through the crowd, she rushed through the ballroom, running past the coat check without stopping for her wrap. She ran blindly through the lobby and out of the hotel, into the street, where she was nearly run over. A taxi driver honked and yelled at her angrily, but she barely heard him. She crossed the street to Central Park.

The park looked almost eerie in its snowy whiteness beneath the black, bare trees, just like the illusion inside the ballroom, but dangerous and cold, the real thing.

Moonlight filled the dark sky, illuminating the small clouds around it, making them glow like pearls in black velvet. As Callie ran, she wept, and it wasn't soft, feminine weeping, but big gulping sobs. Wiping her eyes, she glanced behind her.

And saw Eduardo following, an ominous figure in black.

She gasped and started to run, tripping on her shoes as she ran deeper into the park. She raced headlong down the windswept path, knowing that if he caught up with her, he would see her shameful love for him and he'd see her pathetically broken heart.

One of the high-heeled shoes fell off her feet. Turning around, she started to go back for it, but when she saw him right behind her, she kicked off her other shoe instead and turned back to run. The frozen, snow-kissed path felt like cold knives against her bare feet, the silver dress dragged against her legs and the winter air bit against her naked shoulders.

Then Eduardo caught up with her. His powerful arms lifted her off the frozen ground.

"Go away." Crying, totally humiliated, she struggled against his hard chest. "Just leave me alone!"

"You think you're disposable to me?" he said grimly, looking down at her. The moonlight gave his black hair a silver halo, like a sensual, dark angel come to lure her to hell. "Is that what you think?"

"I know it!"

"You just had my baby," he ground out, his dark eyes glinting. "I'm not a brute. I wasn't going to force myself on you!"

She tried to kick her way free. "Of course not, when you have half the supermodels of this city queued up outside our door. How can I ever compete with that? You said it yourself—you can't wait to divorce me!"

"Oh, my God." His jaw clenched. "Do you know how much I've wanted you? How long? Do you?" he thundered.

She stared at him, shocked at his fury.

His voice dropped. "I've wanted you for a year, Callie. And I've waited for you. For a year."

"No," she whispered. "It's not true."

What she saw in his dark eyes made her shiver all over. "My God. How can you not know? How have you not seen it?"

Her heart nearly stopped in her chest. She licked her dry lips. "You haven't tried to touch me, not once. You've barely even looked at me."

"You were a new mother. You were drowning." Reaching out, he brushed long brown tendrils off her shoulders. "You didn't need me trying to seduce you, placing more demands on you when you were only getting four hours of sleep. You didn't need a lover. You needed a partner. You needed me to be a good father."

She stared at him.

"And you were," she choked out tearfully. "The best father Marisol could ever have had."

Callie heard his intake of breath, felt the way his hands tightened on her as he held her against his chest. Looking down at her, his angled face was in dark silhouette.

"Thank you," he said softly. All around them, the winter landscape glowed in the moonlight.

"You really—wanted me?" she whispered.

He gave a harsh laugh. "I tried not to. Told myself that our night together was meaningless. Reminded myself that you were a liar engaged to another man, and you'd betrayed us both when you gave me your virginity."

Ice flashed through her. "I—"

"But I couldn't forget you. No matter how I tried." He shifted her weight against his chest. "There has been no other woman since the night you were in my bed," he said roughly, looking down at her. "Do you understand what I am telling you? No other woman."

She stared at him. "But…but it's been a year."

His dark eyes looked through hers. "Yes."

Callie couldn't believe what she was hearing. She licked her lips. "But those pictures of you with that duchess in Spain…"

"She is beautiful," he whispered. He shook his head. "But she left me cold."

Tears spilled unheeded down Callie's cheeks, freezing against her skin as she looked up at her husband. "No. No, it can't be true. You can't have been celibate for a year, wanting me—"

"You don't believe me?" he said grimly. He released her, slowly letting her slide down his body to her feet. "Then believe this."

And lowering his head, he pulled her body roughly against his, and kissed her once more, hot and hard.

CHAPTER SIX

CALLIE's mouth parted in a gasp as she felt the smooth satin of his lips, the sweet rough fire of his tongue. She felt the warm strength of his arms around her, and in the dark, cold solitude of Central Park, surrounded by snow and the bare black trees of winter, she felt an explosion of heat.

Murmuring words in Spanish, Eduardo tightened his embrace as he held her against his chest. She dimly felt the icy wind against her cheek as tendrils of her light brown hair blew all around them, but the sensation of his lips against hers felt like a thousand flickers of fire.

As he kissed her, a sigh escaped her lips and she tilted her head back to deepen the embrace. Feeling his body so strong and hard against hers, her endless longing could no longer be repressed. With a soft moan, she wrapped her arms around his neck. She no longer felt the cold air against her skin, the frigid ground beneath her feet. She barely heard the distant traffic of the city and the wind through the bare trees. The night was frozen and dark, but Callie felt hot as a summer's day, lit up from within.

Eduardo's hands stroked her back, down her bare arms. Prickles of need spiraled through her everywhere he touched. Everywhere he *didn't* touch.

His lips gentled against hers, seducing and enticing where they'd once demanded and taken. Memories of another winter night went through Callie, leaving her lost in time, as if all the grief and pain of the last year hadn't happened, and she'd teleported back into the most perfect night of her life.

She wrapped her fingers in his hair. He felt so good, so powerful and masculine. His warrior's body made her feel feminine and small, and as he kissed her, as his sensual mouth moved against hers, she was completely beneath his control....

Then, with a harsh intake of breath, Eduardo pulled away. Taking his phone from his pants pocket, he dialed. "Sanchez," he panted, never looking away from Callie. "Outside. At the corner."

Hanging up, he put the phone in his pocket and reached for her, lifting her back into his arms.

"You don't need to carry me," she whispered. "I'm not cold."

He looked down at her almost pleadingly. "Let me."

Exhaling, she relaxed into the warmth of his arms, and Eduardo carried her back down the path, stopping to pick up each of her shoes, holding Callie with one arm as if she weighed nothing at all. When they reached Central Park South, he put the high-heeled shoes on her feet and gently set her down on the sidewalk.

"Thank you," she said, shivering, but not from cold.

Without a word, he pulled off his black tuxedo jacket and wrapped it around her bare shoulders and sparkling silver dress. His eyes were dark, his voice deep. "Never thank me. It is what I want to do. Take care of you."

Callie swallowed, her mouth dry, her heart pounding as she leaned against him. Thick snowflakes, illuminated by streetlights, started to fall from the dark sky. Was it really possible that Eduardo had been celibate for a year, longing for her? That he'd known the same feelings she had… The lonely bed, the regret, and most of all: the end-less craving…?

Her mind told her it was impossible, but his kiss had told her differently.

"Callie," he whispered. "You know what I'm going to do to you when we get home."

Her heartbeat went crazy, her breathing became quick and shallow and she felt a little dizzy. He wanted her. She wanted him. But the last time he'd made love to her, the joy and heartbreak had nearly killed her. Their marriage was ending in just a few hours. She was so close to being free…

But suddenly, freedom from Eduardo sounded like death. Wrapping her arms around him, she placed her cheek against his white tuxedo shirt and closed her eyes, listening to the beat of his heart. They remained there, holding each other silently, as the soft snowflakes fell in their hair and tangled in their eyelashes.

"The car's here." His voice was hoarse. She opened her eyes and he led her into the backseat of the limo. As Sanchez drove them from the curb, Eduardo didn't seem to care who might see as he turned to her. Reaching out his hands, he cupped her face. He lowered his head toward hers.

At the last instant before their lips touched, she turned her head away. "I can't."

"Can't?" he said hoarsely. "Why? Because—because you love someone else?"

She looked at him in the backseat of the car. His face was so impossibly handsome that her heart twisted in her chest. Every inch of her body was crying out to be in his arms, but lifting her chin, she forced herself to say, "I'm afraid."

He blinked. "Afraid?"

Afraid it will rip my heart apart so thoroughly that the

pieces will never be glued back together. "I'm afraid…it wasn't part of our deal." She swallowed. "Our marriage is in name only."

Eduardo's sensual lips curved. "What gave you that idea?"

"At the courthouse, when we got the marriage license, you said—"

"*You* called it a marriage of convenience. Which it is. But I never said it would be a marriage in name only. I promised to remain faithful, and I have. But I cannot suffer, wanting you, for the rest of my life."

"You don't have to. Tomorrow is our three-month anniversary. Our marriage is over." She paused, suddenly confused by the look in his eyes. "Isn't it?"

"No." His eyes glittered in the Christmas lights as they drove through the city. "There will be no divorce."

Time seemed to stop for Callie.

Behind his head, she dimly saw the bright lights illuminating the colorful displays in shop windows. "But you said three months!"

"I changed my mind." He scowled at her. "From the day I held our baby, I knew that whatever I'd once planned, our marriage would be—must be—permanent. That is the best way to raise our child. The only way. I'd hoped you would come to realize that."

"But you said you'd divorce me," she whispered. The will-o'-the-wisp Christmas lights seemed to be dancing away, disappearing along with her dreams of returning home to her family. "You promised. You said our marriage was just to make our child legitimate, to give her your name!"

His eyes had turned utterly cold, his body taut beneath his tuxedo. "You should be pleased," he said stiffly. "As my wife, you have everything you could possibly want. A fortune at your disposal, beautiful homes, servants, clothes and jewels."

"But what about…" Her throat closed and she looked away. "What about the people I love?"

"You'll love your children," he ground out.

Wide-eyed, she turned back to face him. "Children?" she stammered. "As in…more than one?"

He narrowed his eyes. "It is lonely to be an only child. Marisol needs siblings. Sisters to play with. Brothers to protect her."

Callie stared at him, remembering what she'd heard about Eduardo's poverty-stricken childhood in Spain, about his mother who'd run off with her lover, and his proud, humiliated father, who'd shot himself in the aftermath with an old World War II rifle. At ten years old, Eduardo had been shipped off to a great-aunt he'd never met in New York, and even she had died when he was eighteen. He had no one. He was alone.

She couldn't even imagine it. As much as the restrictive rules of her old-fashioned parents had chafed her, and as much as her little sister had irritated her on a regular basis, Callie couldn't imagine being an only child—and an orphan to boot, whose parents had both chosen to abandon her. Sympathy choked her, but then she hardened her heart. "So just like that, you expect me to agree? You expect us to remain married, to have more children? To plan it all in such a cold-blooded fashion?"

Glaring at her, he sat back in the car seat, folding his arms. "Marisol will be wanted. She will be safe and loved. She will have two parents and a home. There will be no divorce."

Horrified, Callie stared at him.

Stay Eduardo's wife?

Forever?

Her heart twisted in her chest. It was all like some strange dream. For a moment she was mesmerized by his certainty. Perhaps Eduardo was right. Perhaps it would be better for Marisol…better for everyone.

But how could she stay married to him, loving him as she did? He still wanted to be married to her for one reason only: to give their child a good home. How could Callie spend the rest of her life giving him her love, when all he wanted was—at most—her body?

Could she sacrifice her heart, and all hope of ever being loved? Could she spend the rest of her life feeling unloved and alone, in order to give her child the home she deserved?

Swallowing, Callie lifted her chin. "My family would have to be part of Marisol's life. And mine. I miss them. My parents and my sister and—" She cut herself off, but too late.

A sneer rose to his lips. "And Brandon McLinn, of course. His light still glows so brightly in your heart." He set his jaw, turning away. "You disappoint me."

Controlling herself with a deep breath, she didn't rise to his bait. "It was unreasonable of you to block me from seeing him. The only reason I went along with your demand was because I knew that as soon as the three months was over I could—"

"Yes." His eyes were hard as he glared at her. "I know exactly what you were planning to do."

The limousine stopped and Sanchez opened the door. Miserably she followed Eduardo out of the car. Why did he always take things so wrong? Why did he persist in being jealous of Brandon?

Eduardo didn't even look at her as they walked through the lobby of their building. The hot passion of Central Park seemed to have evaporated like smoke. He pressed the button, and they stood without touching, waiting silently in front of the private elevator.

Then he abruptly turned to face her, his hands clenched.

"I've left you alone too long," he ground out, his eyes dark. "I was trying to give you space to grieve the past and accept your new life. To embrace your future as my wife." Furiously he seized her in his arms. "But I see I took the wrong path with you. I should have staked my claim long ago."

Callie stared up at him, her eyes wide with shock. "You can't—"

Tightening his grip on her, he brought his mouth down on hers in a hard, punishing kiss. Trembling, she tried to push him away, but he was too strong for her. Especially when his lips tasted like sweet fire...

The door to the elevator opened with a *ding*, and Eduardo lifted her up into his arms. He looked down at her fiercely.

"Tonight, wife," he growled, "I'm taking back my bed."

The elevator door hadn't even closed before he was pressing her against the mirrored wall, his mouth hard and hungry against hers. Callie had given up any thought of resisting. In fact, she'd given up any thought altogether. Wrapping her arms around his neck, she returned his kiss with equal hunger. He released her, letting her body slide down his, and she felt his hard desire for her. She felt hot, wearing his tuxedo jacket, and through the thin cotton of his shirt, she felt the strength and heat of his body as he held her tight and kissed her, so long and hard and deep that she prayed he'd never let her go.

At the *ding* of the elevator, he picked her up and carried her wordlessly through their massive foyer, beneath the crystals of the shadowy chandelier above. His black eyes never left hers as he carried her up the curved, sweeping staircase. His gaze reached into her heart, taking brutal possession of her soul.

"Och, you're home early!" Downstairs, Mrs. McAuliffe came out into the foyer, her voice cheerful. "The baby's sleeping and happy and—oh."

As if from a distance, Callie heard the woman's shocked intake of breath, saw her turn and flee back down the shadowy hall toward her own rooms on the first floor. But for once in her life, Callie wasn't embarrassed. She couldn't care. All that mattered was this.

Without a word, Eduardo carried her up the last stairs and down the hall to the master bedroom. He set her down on her feet beside the king-size bed. She glanced down at the mattress, remembering how she'd slept alone for all the nights of their marriage. But she would not be alone tonight.

Her husband caressed her hair, tucking tendrils behind her ear. She shivered as his rough fingertips brushed her sensitive earlobe, and his hand slowly moved down her cheek to her throat, beneath the expensive diamond-and-emerald necklace to the sensitive corner between her neck and shoulder. His body towered over hers as he pulled his oversize tuxedo jacket off her shoulders, dropping it to the floor.

Walking around her slowly, he stroked the bare skin of her shoulders. Fire raced up and down her body as he finally faced her, cupping her face. He lowered his mouth to hers.

His lips were soft and warm, rough and hard all at once, searing through her body like lava, melting her core from within. Her full breasts ached, crushed against his muscled chest. He reached around her, and she heard, and felt, the pull of the zipper. Suddenly the weight of the silver strapless gown fell to the hardwood floor.

Stepping back, Eduardo looked at her in the moonlight. "You're beautiful," he said hoarsely. "I've waited for you so long. Too long…"

Yanking off his black tie, he tossed it to the floor. But as he started to unbutton his tuxedo shirt, his hands seemed clumsy. She looked at his fingers and realized they were shaking, just as hers were. With a low curse, he finally just ripped off his shirt, popping the buttons with brute force and kicking the expensive garment away. She nearly gasped at the beauty of his incredible upper body in the moonlight. The muscles of his chest were hard and defined, from his broad shoulders to his nipples and the dark arrow of hair that traveled down his flat, hard belly.

Wearing only trousers, he came closer, running his fingers along the curve from her waist to her hip. His gaze devoured her in the plunging strapless bra and matching panties. Beneath his gaze, she should have been acutely aware of her body's every flaw, and yet she saw the hunger in his eyes and she'd never felt more womanly or desirable.

A low growl escaped Eduardo's lips. Grabbing her hips with both his hands, he pulled her to the bed. Sitting down on the edge, he lifted her into his lap, so she straddled him.

Wrapping his hands in her hair, he pulled her head down and kissed her fiercely. She kissed him back with equal force, gasping at the sensation when her naked belly brushed against his bare chest. He cupped her breasts over her silky strapless bra. Her nipples tightened to agonizing points, her breasts heavy and tight. Reaching around her with one hand, he unhooked her bra. His first sight of her full breasts, swollen to twice their normal size from nursing, made him gasp. He slowly reached to cup her bare skin. His large, rough hands caressed her naked breasts and Callie's body went tight, as a hot current of electricity traveled from her nipples to her toes, sending spirals of hot, aching need to her deepest core.

"So beautiful," he breathed again. The bed was covered in a pool of silvery light, leaving the two of them in their own magic world as he pushed her back against the pillows.

Never taking his gaze from hers, he stood beside the wall of windows overlooking the entire Upper West Side, and removed first his trousers, giving her a glance of his powerful legs and trunklike thighs, then his silk boxers.

Callie's heart lifted to her throat as her husband stood before her, utterly naked and unashamed.

The moonlight frosted his naked chest, giving him an otherworldly appearance, like a powerful warlord from the mists of legend, a fierce barbarian king. He looked dark, handsome and powerful, illuminated by a gleam of silver. He looked like a dark knight from a fantasy. He moved toward her, and her whole body—down to her soul—trembled from within. And in the magical silvery light, his erection jutted from his body, proud and hard and every bit as huge as she'd remembered.

A spasm of fear went through her. After childbirth, what if it hurt to have him inside her? What if he was rough? What if he even tried to be gentle but was still just so big that he split her apart?

Eduardo moved over her on the bed. She sucked in her breath as he stroked her cheek, slowly kissing down her neck. She tilted back her head as she felt his lips caress her skin, gasping as she felt his hands' featherlike touch, cupping her breasts. Lowering his head, he kissed one breast, then the other, and slowly stroked down her body, down her collarbone, down the soft curve of her belly. Tension coiled low and deep inside her, and hardly knowing what she was saying, she breathed, "Yes…"

"You're mine, Callie. Only mine." He put his hand on her cheek, his eyes dark. "Tell me…"

"I'm yours," she whispered, her voice choking on a sob. *Of course* she was his. She'd been his from the moment he'd first taken her hand, when he was the CEO of a global multibillion-dollar company and she was just his secretary.

Lowering his mouth to hers, he kissed her, long and deep. His tongue teased hers, lightly at first, then plunging deeper into her mouth as their tongues intertwined, slick and hot and wet. She felt his hand stroke her, moving softly down her belly. His fingers moved along her hip, over the top edge of her panties, and she shivered, aching for him. His hand moved so slowly, so lightly. He stroked down the side of her hip, over her thigh, between her legs. As he continued kissing her, she felt his hand move with agonizing slowness up the inside of her thigh, and held her breath…

But he moved his hand away, cupping her breast. She exhaled, pulling him closer, wanting to feel his weight on her. But he wouldn't be distracted. His hand moved back to her inner thigh, traveling upward frustratingly slowly as she held her breath. Finally he stroked over her panties. He teased her. She gasped as he gently cupped the mound between her thighs.

Kneeling between her legs on the king-size bed, he pulled her silk panties down, down, down. She felt the soft fabric slide like a whisper down her skin. Suddenly naked beneath him, she felt him climb naked on top of her, lowering his head to kiss her. His tongue moved between her lips, his mouth stretched her wide. And she felt him hard and thick at the entrance to the hot center that ached between her thighs. Every inch of their bodies, her soft curves and his hard, muscled form, seemed fused together with need, sweat and fire. Only one part of them had yet to be joined. One part on fire with need. She felt him, huge and hard, nudging against her wet, hot core.

But she was afraid. She braced for him to thrust himself inside her, cleaving her tender flesh, but instead, exhaling, showing visible control, he slowly thrust a single inch inside her. She gasped. She felt so wet, enfolding his enormous shaft. He pushed further, to two inches. He was so thick it ached a little, stretching her, but as he slid inside, it felt good. So good. Just like the first time...

Then she remembered. With a sudden cry, she lifted up on her elbows and breathed, "Condom?"

His dark eyes narrowed, and then he scowled. "I forgot..." He started to reach toward his nightstand. Then he looked down at her with a sensual, slow-rising smile. "I do not need a condom, *querida*. Ever again."

"You—don't?"

"You are my wife." He pulled back his hand, and his expression turned wicked as he looked at her with heavily lidded eyes. "I want to get you pregnant. Now."

"Now?" she said, her eyes wide. It was too soon. She hadn't even had a period yet, since the birth of her baby three months ago. She shook her head. "I'm not ready..."

"We have eight bedrooms," he insisted. "I want to fill them. I want the noise and joy of many children. And I want you as their mother." As he held her wrists, holding her down to the bed, his dark eyes seared hers. "Let me fill you with my baby, *querida*."

Callie stared up at him, feeling pinned to the bed. Was she ready to make that lifelong commitment to Eduardo that he wanted? Ready to be bound to him even further? Even deeper?

He pushed himself back into her, and she closed her eyes, gasping with pleasure. He felt so good inside her. Farther and deeper sounded like all she'd ever wanted. She tried to think about the decision that had to be made but her rational mind fell away as he gripped her hips tight. His huge shaft slowly filled her, inch by inch, sliding through her tight, wet passage.

She gripped his shoulders, her fingernails digging into his skin as she arched her back, her head tilted back. Her whole body was taut and aching with need for more, just a little more. She wanted him to fill her all the way, to ram himself deeply inside her. Her breasts swayed as he penetrated her. Her nipples were taut as he lowered his head to lick one rosy peak. With his rough mouth on her, his hips took decisive action. He thrust deeply inside her, all the way to the hilt, and she nearly screamed with pleasure.

But even then, reality intruded. She'd made this mistake once. Not again. Never again. Her fingers gripped into his shoulders, and she opened her eyes, pushing him back.

"Condom," she panted.

For a long moment, he stared at her. Then his eyes narrowed. Rolling off her, he grabbed a condom from the nightstand and sheathed himself in a quick movement, rolling it down over his thick shaft in the manner of a man who'd done it many, many times. Then he climbed back on top of her. Anger seemed to seep from his body, and Callie licked her lips, wanting to repair the mood between them.

"Thank—"

He put his finger roughly on her lips. "Don't," he ground out.

Gripping her hips with his hands, he thrust himself inside her, all the way to the hilt. She gasped, forgetting their argument, forgetting everything as he rode her, hard and deep. A shudder built inside her, a tremble like an earthquake as he filled her, like an underground river bursting from the cracks of a dam. She felt tension ratchet higher and higher inside her, shaking her. Her head fell back as she held her breath, climbing higher and higher still. She closed her eyes as her lips parted in a soundless cry.

Then it was no longer silent, and she screamed, clutching his shoulders as she exploded.

A low, answering cry came from his lips. His hard, handsome face was pale, as if he'd held himself back by only the slenderest thread. But as she shook and tightened around him in ecstasy, he surrendered. He thrust inside her one last time, impaling her so hard and deep she felt split in two, and he filled her with a hoarse shout, his eyes closed, his face euphoric. Almost reverent.

Collapsing over her sweaty, exhausted body, he held her against his chest. "You will belong to me," he whispered. "You'll soon surrender."

Turning toward him, Callie pressed her cheek against his bare chest. Her own heartbeat roared in her ears. As she drowsed in his powerful arms, exhausted and protected by the warmth and strength of his naked body, she knew it was already true. It had always been true.

Her heart had surrendered long ago.

CHAPTER SEVEN

CALLIE woke up with a start. What time was it? Was that her baby crying?

She rose blearily from bed before she was even quite awake. The moonlight had moved across her bedroom, so she must have slept. With a gasp, she remembered how her husband had just made love to her. She glanced back at the bed with her heart in her throat and a smile on her lips.

The bed was empty. Eduardo was gone.

She glanced at the clock over the mantel on the bedroom's fireplace. Three in the morning. Where could he be? Why would he leave her in the middle of the night, after he'd so thoroughly reclaimed his bed?

Her cheeks grew hot at the memory of last night. He'd claimed her in a way she'd never forget.

Then her baby wailed again from the nursery, louder this time. She hurried through the adjacent door, turning on a little lamp shaped like a giraffe that gave a soft, golden light. She picked up her baby. "It's all right," she soothed. "Mommy's here. I'm here." Cradling her chubby three-month-old baby in her arms, Callie carried her to the gliding chair near the window. As she nursed her child, the baby's complaints faded. Looking down at her, Callie was lost in wonder at her baby's beauty, at the long black eyelashes she'd gotten from Eduardo brushing against her plump cheeks. One of her baby's tiny hands gripped her finger.

We have eight bedrooms. I want to fill them.

What would it be like, Callie thought, to have a whole houseful of babies like this? To have a large family? An adoring husband?

Slowly her eyes looked around the cheerful nursery. It was warm and luxurious, but she would have liked to create her baby's nursery herself, even with just a bucket of paint, a sewing machine and her own two hands—not paying someone else to do it, but doing it herself as a labor of love. Next time, she promised herself. Then stopped.

Next time.

Could she really stay married to Eduardo, knowing he would never love her? He knew how to make love...oh, yes. She shivered, closing her eyes as she remembered how he'd caressed her last night. Remembered the feel of his body against hers. The husky sound of his voice as he'd said, *You belong to me.*

He knew how to make love.

But she'd never seen him truly care for anyone. Except their baby.

Was their lust, and mutual care for their child, enough to sustain a marriage when their values were so different?

After her baby nursed back to sleep, Callie left her on her back in the oval-shaped crib, careful not to wake her. She'd likely sleep another four hours now, or maybe more. Every night, she slept a little longer. Her baby had become an excellent sleeper.

And maybe she would be now, too. Closing the nursery door softly behind her, Callie smiled. The last few hours, after falling asleep in Eduardo's arms, had been the best sleep she'd had all year.

He wanted her to be his wife forever. He wanted them

to be a family. And she'd loved him for years. Even when she'd hated him, it had been the hurt of a woman who'd been rejected from the person she loved most.

Maybe it could work. Maybe it could be enough.

Or maybe, somehow, he would grow to love her, as she loved him. She closed her eyes, hugging herself at the thought. If there was even the slightest chance of him loving her someday, she would have married him at once. Remembering, she bleakly opened her eyes. No wonder Eduardo had called her *naive* and *ridiculously sentimental*.

Where was he, anyway? She looked around her dark, empty bedroom. Where could he be at this time of the night?

Maybe he'd gone to the kitchen for a snack.

Pulling on a soft blue chenille robe, she went downstairs, but the kitchen was dark and empty. Walking past the wall of windows with its magnificent view of the city, she went down the hall to his home office, then to the theater room, then even past Mrs. McAuliffe's suite. She could hear the older woman's soft snoring muffled through the door. Puzzled, Callie finally went back upstairs.

Glancing in the empty guest rooms, she had just decided to phone their bodyguard in his separate apartment downstairs when she heard Eduardo's voice in the guest room.

"Nothing has changed." His voice was the smooth, arrogant tone she remembered. "Nothing."

With an intake of breath, she pulled back from the doorway, leaning against the wall of the dark hallway with one hand over her mouth and the other over her heart.

"Don't call here again," he growled, and hung up.

A little squeak escaped her lips. Who was Eduardo talking to? An old lover? Was that why he'd snuck out of bed to talk to someone in private, so his wife couldn't hear? Even as Callie tried to tell herself that she was overreacting, that he could be talking to anyone, her heart was gripped with fear.

There has been no other woman since the night you were in my bed. Do you understand what I am telling you? No other woman.

She exhaled as the vise grip on her heart loosened. Eduardo was not a liar. If anything, he was cruelly honest. As his secretary, she'd seen him callously dispose of one lover after another, plainly telling them to their faces that he was bored with them, or that he had absolutely no intention of being faithful. He was not a liar.

But then, he'd never had to lie. He'd never been married before.

"What are you doing awake?"

With an intake of breath, she saw him in the doorway, looking down at her with dark eyes. "Um…" Her fingers fidgeted with the belt of her blue chenille robe. "I got up to feed Marisol and you were gone."

"I didn't want to wake you." His handsome face was impassive. "I couldn't sleep."

"Oh. I'm sorry." She bit her lip, feeling guilty that she'd slept so well. "Is something wrong? Was I snoring, or…"

He gave a low laugh then shook his head soberly. "I just don't sleep well with other people in my bed. I have never managed it."

She frowned. "Never?"

"Have you ever heard of me letting a woman sleep over?"

Callie stared at him, remembering when he'd been her boss, the most heartless playboy in the city. "N-no," she said hesitantly. She gave him an awkward smile. "You were kind of famous for your one-*hour* stands, actually."

He leaned against the door frame, looking down at the floor. "It's hard to let down my guard."

"Even with me?"

He looked up. "Especially with you," he whispered.

The low lights of the hallway caused hard shadows across the angles and planes of Eduardo's face. His jawline was dark with stubble, giving him a piratical air. He looked like a pirate all over, in fact. A sexy, dangerous, hard-bodied pirate. Without thinking, she put a hand on his warm, hard, bare chest above drawstring cotton pajama pants slung low on his slender hips.

"Is there anything I could do to help you sleep?" Realizing how blatant that sounded, she blushed. "I mean, could I get you some warm milk or something?"

"No," he said abruptly then amended, "but thanks."

She looked at him. "Why didn't you kick me out?" she whispered. "Last Christmas, the night I stayed at your house?"

His eyes met hers. "You weren't just some starlet I picked up at a gala. You were important to me. I wanted you to stay."

"You did?" she breathed. "Why?"

"Don't you know?" Pulling her into his arms, he lifted her chin to meet his gaze. Then he smiled…the charming, megawatt smile that always twisted her heart in a million pieces. "I need you, Callie."

Eduardo looked at his wife in the shadows of the hallway. Her pale cheeks were rosy, her emerald eyes bright, and her light brown hair, long and wavy, fell over the shoulders of her blue robe. She was so sexy, so soft and desirable. He'd just had her, and already he wanted her again. He wanted her even more.

Callie's eyes filled up with tears.

"You need me? I thought…I thought you only wanted me here because of the baby."

He moved toward her, gently brushing her hair off her shoulders. "That's not the only reason."

Trembling, she looked up at him. Words seemed to tremble on her lips, but at the last moment, she turned away. Staring down the dark, quiet hall, she wrapped her arms around her body. The sleeves of the blue chenille robe hung long over her wrists, making her look like a kid playing dress-up.

"I want to stay with you," she said softly. "And be your wife."

Eduardo's heart rose with fierce triumph. "*Querida*— "

She held up her hand. Her green eyes were luminous. "But I will no longer neglect and ignore my friends and family just to coddle your insecurity."

Her harsh words were like a slap across the jaw. His eyes widened then narrowed. "*Coddle* my *insecurity*." His voice was low and dangerous. "You mean how I've forbidden you to talk to Brandon McLinn."

"Yes."

Jaw tight, he took a step toward her. "You should just let him go."

"No." Her eyes glittered defiantly. "He's my friend."

"Friend!" he snarled. He shook his head. "He told you'd been engaged since high school. He said even if you'd fallen into bed with me, I meant nothing to you and that you'd soon be done with me—"

Eduardo stopped, his jaw tight, his heart pounding. He hadn't meant to say so much. Brow furrowed, Callie came closer, and the soft light from the guest room illuminated her pale, beautiful face. She gave an awkward laugh.

"Want to hear a funny story? At senior prom, we made this silly pact that if we weren't married by the time we were thirty, we would marry each other."

"You're only twenty-five."

"Yes, I know. I'm starting to wonder if perhaps Brandon was—" she licked her lips uncomfortably "—well, maybe threatened by you."

Suddenly it all made sense.

Eduardo sucked in his breath. "You weren't in love with him, were you? He was trying to get rid of me, and it worked." He clawed back his hair with his hand. "Once I was out of the way, he used your pregnancy as an excuse to move in for the kill."

Drawing back in confusion, Callie shook her head. "He loves me, yes, but like a brother!"

"I was such a fool." Pacing two steps down the hall, he could hardly believe his own stupidity. That night, that beautiful Christmas Eve night when they'd first made love, when he'd taken Callie's virginity, he'd thought their relationship might be different from all the rest. But he'd thrown away that precious connection—based on the insinuations of his rival!

"Brandon McLinn is in love with you," he ground out. "I saw it in his face."

"He must have been trying to protect me."

"You may be blind to his true feelings. I am not." His eyes narrowed. "You will never contact him again. Or your family."

"What?" Callie's mouth fell open. "What does my family have to do with anything?"

Eduardo couldn't explain, or she would find out everything he'd been keeping from her—for her own good. "I am your husband. You will trust me and obey."

"Obey?" Callie glared at him, folding her arms. "What century are you in? You might be my husband, but you are no longer my boss!"

"Am I not?" he said softly. He reached his hand to her cheek, stroking softly down her neck. She closed her eyes, and he felt her shudder beneath his touch. "I am trying to protect our family. I have my reasons. Believe me."

But Callie stiffened, stepping back, out of his reach. "No."

His eyes widened then his brows lowered. "No?"

"I want to be your wife, Eduardo. I do," she whispered. "But I have to see my family. And Brandon."

"I could take you to court. The prenuptial agreement—"

"So do it." She looked at him evenly. "Take me to court."

She was calling his bluff. He had no desire to sue his own wife, the mother of his baby. And now they both knew it. He exhaled, clenching his hands. "I will not allow you to—"

"It's not a question of you *allowing* me. I'm telling you. I need a relationship with my family—including Brandon—and so does Marisol. I'm going home to visit my family. You can divorce me. But you can't stop me."

Checkmate, he thought, almost with despair.

He still couldn't forget—or forgive—the way her parents had treated Callie when she'd called them just two hours after the birth, anxious to tell them about the baby. She'd had every reason to relax and get some rest, but instead she'd tried to share the joyous news with her mother and father. She'd been left sobbing with grief. The memory still made his jaw clench.

Eduardo had always dreamed of having a family of his own. A family that was kind and loving, not cruel or harsh as his own had been.

He wouldn't let anyone make Callie cry like that. Ever.

Staring at her, a thought took hold of his brain. Morally reprehensible—but then, he thought grimly, he was already in so deep he might as well go a little further.

It was for her own good, he repeated to himself. For her own good, and the safety of their little family.

"Have you considered, *querida*," he said in a low voice, "that perhaps they might not want to see you?"

Callie looked at him with stricken eyes. "What?"

It was cold, it was cruel, it was wrong. But he pushed aside his twinges of conscience. He had to be ruthless. "Has McLinn contacted you once in the last three months?" He tilted his head. "Has anyone in your family tried to call you back, even once?"

Her folded arms fell, and she looked uncertain. "No." Swallowing, she blinked fast. "But I can't blame them. I let them down."

"No," he said sharply. "You had a baby. You got married. And when you tried to share that news with them, they ripped you apart."

She took a deep breath. "I know it might seem that way…"

"They were cruel to you." He could still remember the rasp of her father's voice. *You'll never be a decent husband or father, and you know it. If you're even half a man, you'll send her and the baby home to people who are capable of loving them.*

"I'll make them forgive me." Callie's emerald eyes glittered suspiciously. "I have to try."

As she turned away, he grabbed her arm. "Write to them first."

She turned back to face him. "What?"

"If you show up in person, who knows how they'll react? What if they shut the door in your face? Do you really want to risk it?"

Callie looked pale, staring at him.

"Write first," he said smoothly. "It's the best way to gather your thoughts. And give them time to consider theirs."

"Well." She took a deep breath, her expression crestfallen. "Maybe you're right." She looked down at her feet. "I would die if they shut the door in my face. Or if they refused to see Marisol. I can't even imagine it. But then," she said unhappily, "I thought they would call me before now...."

He put his hands around her shoulders. "Write to them."

"You think so?"

"Absolutely."

She bit her lip. "Even Brandon?"

Exhaling, jaw tight, he gave a single nod.

She sighed. "All right."

"All right?"

She looked up. Her green eyes were bright, her cheeks flushed. "Thank you," she said haltingly, "for helping me. I don't know what I'd do without you."

Eduardo had never seen her look so beautiful. Mesmerized, he reached down to stroke her cheek then pulled her into his arms. He felt her soft breasts press against his chest, and breathed in the floral and vanilla scent of her hair. He felt the warm whisper of her breath against his bare chest, and his drawstring pajamas suddenly felt three sizes too tight. "I told you," he said hoarsely. "I don't want your thanks."

"But—"

"Don't." Especially since he had no intention of allowing her letters to reach her family—or McLinn. He put his palm against her cheek, his fingers threading through her hair. "You are my woman, Callie. I would do anything to keep you safe and happy."

Looking up at him, she suddenly blurted out, "Who were you talking to on the phone?"

He stared at her. "What?"

Looking grumpy, she folded her arms. "I wasn't going

to ask," she sighed. "I was going to be totally stoic and silent about it."

"Oh, *querida*." Smiling, Eduardo stroked her cheek. She was so transparent. He loved that about her. "You wondered if I was talking to some woman?"

"The thought crossed my mind. Every woman wants you...."

"And I want only one woman in the world." Lifting her chin, he looked straight into her eyes. "I am yours and only yours, my beautiful wife. I will never betray you, Callie."

"You won't?"

"I was just talking to a rival...who lives far away."

"Oh," she said. With a sigh of relief, she hugged him, pressing her face against his bare chest.

Stroking her back through the soft chenille robe, Eduardo exhaled at how close it had been. She must have heard the end of his phone call. If she'd heard the whole conversation, she wouldn't have been worried about some imaginary woman. No, it would have been far more dire.

"Try to contact my wife again," Eduardo had growled, "and you'll regret it."

"You can't keep me from her. We both know you're not good enough. You'll never make her happy." McLinn's voice had been angry, and with an edge of desperation that had grown over the months Eduardo had blocked the man's letters and phone calls. Yesterday, there had even been an attempted delivery of a cell phone in a padded envelope. His bodyguard had opened the package while Callie was upstairs getting ready for the Winter Ball.

An hour ago, Eduardo's anger had finally boiled over. Rising from their bed as Callie slept, he'd used the number from his investigator, and called McLinn's cell phone in the middle of the night.

The young farmer had actually threatened him, saying he was going to call the police and claim Callie was being held against her will. Against her will!

Eduardo narrowed his eyes. The police he could deal with. But McLinn had threatened to return to New York. He could not guard Callie at every moment in the city, keeping her from any unexpected meeting. Nor could he risk letting her talk to McLinn. He could only imagine what the man would tell her.

He needed a third option.

From the day they'd wed, he'd assigned the same investigator who got dirt on business competitors to keep track of his wife and all her family. Eduardo had burned the angry letters sent by her father, the pleading tearstained cards from her mother. He'd tossed her sister's bouquet of sappy flowers shaped like a pink baby carriage in the trash.

At first he'd done it because he didn't trust Callie. Then he told himself he was just trying to protect her. Sure, her father was trying to be nicer now, but even Eduardo's own parents had had their good days. He wouldn't allow them access to Callie until he knew for sure they wouldn't hurt her again.

But deep in his heart, he knew that wasn't the only reason.

You weren't even man enough to come and ask me for her hand. The memory of her father's cold words still rankled in his mind. *You might own half our town, but I know the kind of man you really are. You'll never be a decent husband or father, and you know it.*

To Walter, as to many others, Eduardo was just a selfish, demanding tyrant, the foreign CEO that his employees obeyed—but despised.

So be it. Eduardo didn't need the man's respect. But he

wouldn't let anyone insult his wife. Or cause them problems that could tear his family apart.

Stroking her back, Eduardo took a deep breath. He was starting to trust Callie again. But he didn't trust the world. Whenever he let himself care for someone, they disappeared from his life. He wouldn't let that happen. Not this time.

"Eduardo?"

Callie was looking up at him in the shadowy hallway, her brow furrowed. Her robe had fallen open slightly to reveal her plump breasts, and suddenly he knew exactly what he needed. He pulled her closer, stroking the edge of her neckline as he murmured, "You said something about helping me sleep?"

"Er." She suddenly blushed. "I just thought…"

"Yes." Grabbing her hand, he led her back to the master bedroom. Pulling the robe off her unresisting body, he pushed her back against the bed. His wife looked like an angel in the moonlight, he thought, her light brown hair silver twined with gold, her pale skin luminous. Her breasts were huge, their full rosy tips bright and vivid against her white skin.

Eduardo kissed her hard and deep. He felt her respond, kissing him back with equal fire, and wanted her as if he hadn't already been satiated that night. He wanted her even more than he did yesterday, and all the year before that. Her small hands roamed his body, stroking his naked chest, caressing his shoulders, his back. He exhaled when she ran her fingers lightly over his backside then groaned aloud as she ran her hand questingly over the hard shaft beneath his drawstring pajama pants. Her face was rapt as she stroked his hard length through the fabric. He grabbed her wrist.

"I do not know—how long I can last," he groaned.

She gave him a smile full of infinite feminine mystery. "So don't."

"*Querida*—"

She unlaced his pants and pulled them down his hips, to his thighs. His hard shaft sprung free from the fabric, and she looked down at him with awe. Reaching out, she took him fully in her hands.

"Callie," he breathed. Her touch felt too good, causing him to jerk involuntarily beneath her stroke. His heart was pounding. He wanted to bury himself deep inside her, impale her, fill her to the hilt now—now—*now*! "What are you—?"

Her eyes were dark and full of need as she pulled him over her onto the bed. "Take me," she whispered.

A low growl rose in his throat as he looked down at her, spread across the bed for his pleasure. He didn't even take the time to pull off his pajama pants. He couldn't. Leaving them across his thighs, he positioned himself and thrust inside her, filling her.

She gasped, gripping his shoulders. Her face filled with anguished ecstasy, and for a moment he thought he'd gone too far, too deep. He started to withdraw.

"No." Gripping her fingers into his flesh, she started to move beneath him. "More."

He pushed inside her again, and she moaned. He rode her, harder and faster, until the bed frame rocked loudly against the wall.

"Stop!" she whispered, looking up at him. "Don't wake the baby!"

He exhaled in a surprised laugh then, leaning forward, kissed her forehead tenderly. Gripping her hips, he slowly thrust inside her in a controlled movement. Somehow the silence just deepened the pleasure. Made it forbidden. He rode her wet and hard until she gripped his upper arms and he heard her soundless scream of pleasure. With a rush of ecstasy, he slammed into her one last time with a shuddering, silent gasp as his whole world shimmered and exploded.

He fell on top of her. It might have been minutes, or an hour, later before he was aware he might be crushing her beneath the weight of his body. He didn't know how much time had passed, which was strange. For one precious moment, it had almost felt like sleep....

He started to move away from her, but she grabbed his arm. "Stay with me."

He hesitated. He knew he wouldn't be able to sleep beside her. But in this moment, he could deny her nothing. Without a word, he rolled back and pulled her to his naked chest, spooning her smaller body with his larger one.

She turned around in his arms. "I love you."

Shocked, he stared down at her in the dark bedroom. Her beautiful, round, upturned face was glowing, tears sparkling down her cheeks in the moonlight.

"I love you, Eduardo." Closing her eyes, she pressed her cheek against his bare chest. "I never stopped loving you, and I never will."

A tremble went through his body as he stroked her hair. Hearing those words on his wife's lips—the words he'd detested and avoided hearing from any other woman—was a sudden, precious gift. Sweet beyond measure.

Poison in his heart.

Now he had even more to lose. Even more to protect. His arms tightened around her. Would she still love him if she found out what he'd done? After Brandon McLinn explained it to her in the most destructive way possible?

He said with forced cheerfulness, "What do you think about spending Christmas in the south of Spain?"

Pressing her face against his chest, she gave a contented sigh. "Spain?"

He stroked her back, keeping his voice casual. "I have a villa on the coast, not too far from my old village." *And five thousand miles from Brandon McLinn.* "What do you say?"

She smiled up at him sleepily. "I'll go anywhere with you."

Eduardo gloried in his wife's generous spirit and trusting heart. Callie knew his flaws better than anyone. And yet somehow she'd chosen to love him.

It was the most precious gift he'd ever received. And the one he least deserved.

Within minutes, she fell asleep in his arms. Eduardo stared out the windows at the dark city and the vast blackness of the Hudson River. It was cold December, when night lasted forever and spring was a distant promise. She loved him. And it was like hot summer to a half-frozen man.

He would never let her go. Ever. Even if it cost his very soul.

In the darkness, his eyes hardened.

He wouldn't lose her. Not now. Not ever.

CHAPTER EIGHT

SITTING by their pool overlooking the Mediterranean, Callie was trying—again—to convince her body to tan in the warm Spanish sun. She glanced back toward their luxurious, enormous villa, where her baby was taking her afternoon nap. Callie loved it here. All right, she was still shockingly pale, but she'd never been so happy.

Or so sad.

In the four months since they'd left New York, her handsome husband had taken their family all over the world via private jet, to all the glamorous places she'd once dreamed of as a girl. They'd spent Christmas here at the villa, decorating their enormous Christmas tree with oranges. On Christmas Eve, they'd gone to a candlelight service, then after putting the baby to bed she and Eduardo had a midnight supper by candlelight. It had been a special, sacred night between them, the one-year anniversary of the first time they'd made love.

When she woke the next morning, Eduardo was gone, as always. Getting Marisol from her crib, she'd gone downstairs to discover an obscene number of gifts beneath their Christmas tree, and beside it, a debonair Santa with twinkling black eyes, in a red suit far too large for his sleek physique and a fake white beard over his chiseled jawline. Marisol had laughed in wonder and delight, and so had

Callie. Santa had presented their baby with so many expensive toys and clothes that it could have satisfied a child army. Marisol had responded by playing with the tissue paper and then trying to chew on her own shoe.

Callie had giggled. "See what happens when you spend too much money on a baby, Santa?"

Santa turned to her. "And I have something for you, Mrs. Claus, er, Cruz."

Reaching into his big black bag, he'd pulled out a key chain that had her initials, "CC", created in what looked to be diamonds and gold. She'd taken the key chain with an incredulous laugh.

"It's beautiful...but are you crazy? People lose key chains. I'll be scared to use this."

Santa smirked. "The key chain isn't the gift. Look again."

Frowning, she looked down at the ridiculously expensive gold-and-diamond key chain and saw the key. Her mouth went dry as she looked up. "What's this?"

He gave her a sudden wicked grin. "Go outside."

Still in her red-and-green flannel pajamas, she'd lifted their baby on her hip, and gone out into the courtyard of the villa, with Santa close behind. Even on Christmas Day, the Spanish sun was warm, and the air smelled of orange groves and the ocean. She'd stopped abruptly in the dusty courtyard.

There, with a big red bow on the hood, she saw a brand-new Rolls-Royce.

"The silver reminded me of you," he murmured softly behind her. "It's the color of the dress you wore to the Winter Ball a few weeks ago. You sparkled like a diamond. You shone like a star."

Turning to face him without a word, Callie pulled down

his white beard. Eduardo's handsome face was revealed, his dark eyes glowing with admiration.

"And every day, Mrs. Cruz," he said, stroking her cheek, "you're more beautiful still."

With an intake of breath, she threw one arm around his neck and, standing on tiptoe, gave Santa the kiss of his life. It wasn't until Marisol began to squirm and complain that Callie recalled that she was squashing their baby, and that she probably shouldn't let her baby see her kissing Santa Claus anyway.

Callie drew back with tears in her eyes.

"Thank you," she whispered, then shook her head with a laugh. "But I'm afraid you're going to be very disappointed with my gift to you."

"What is it?"

"Soap-on-a-rope and a really ugly tie," she teased.

"Oh, yeah? I've been needing those."

She smiled at him. In reality it was a homemade coffee mug she and Marisol had made together, etched with her baby's tiny handprints, which she knew he'd love.

He sobered. "You give me a gift every day, Callie," he said softly. "By being my wife."

She'd looked at him, her heart in her throat. Then her smile faltered. "I just wish I'd heard from my family today."

Eduardo's eyes darkened, and he gave her a tight smile that didn't meet his eyes. "Do not worry, *querida*. I am sure you will hear from them soon."

But she hadn't, not in all the months since then. She'd sent her parents and her sister a letter every week, filled with photographs of Marisol and of their life in Europe. She'd told them how the baby was growing. She'd told them about Marisol's first tooth, the first time she'd turned over in her crib, the first time she'd sat up by herself. She'd described everything that had happened over the seven months of her baby's life. Callie had even poured out her feelings about Eduardo, her former boss, whom she'd once tried to hate but now loved. She wanted to undo the damage she'd once done, and let them see Eduardo as he really was: a good man.

In response to all her carefully written letters, she'd gotten only cold silence.

She tried not to let it bother her. When Eduardo was home, he gave her and the baby his full attention. He'd needed to take business trips again, to the Arctic and Colombia and elsewhere. But whenever he traveled to a destination he thought his family might enjoy, he brought Callie and Marisol along, traveling on the private jet with a full staff and Mrs. McAuliffe in tow. It was amazing.

They'd spent Valentine's Day in Paris, in a royal suite at a five-star hotel with a view of the *Tour Eiffel*. After the baby was asleep, Eduardo had surprised Callie with a romantic, private dinner for two in their suite. She shivered, remembering champagne, chocolate-dipped strawberries and hot kisses that had lasted for hours.

Most recently, they'd gone to Italy. In Venice, he'd rented a palace overlooking the Grand Canal and they'd shared a romantic gondola ride; in Rome, Marisol had had her first taste of lemon gelato, which she'd savored by letting it dribble down her chin.

Such adventures they'd shared as a family. Growing up on her parents' rural farm, the farthest Callie had ever traveled as a child was to the county fair. She'd never have imagined she'd someday have a life like this. International. Glamorous.

Now, the afternoon sun lowered behind the swaying palm trees as Callie sat beside the gorgeous infinity pool back at their villa. She turned her face toward the blue sky.

Taking a drink of cold, lemon-flavored water, she closed her eyes, stretching out on the lounge chair, relishing the warm Spanish sun on her cheeks.

Seven months of marriage and she still wasn't pregnant. But Eduardo never seemed to tire of trying. He wanted her pregnant. Each night, after they made love, he held her till she slept before he slipped away to the nearest guest room to sleep alone. She hated waking up alone. But that was a tiny thing, nothing really, compared to the multitude of joys in her life, with her baby and husband she loved.

But she still missed the family she'd left behind in North Dakota. It was a heartache that never quite went away.

Her letters hadn't worked, in spite of her best efforts. Her eyes flew open and she stared up at the blue sky. Maybe it was time to do something drastic.

"Callie."

She heard her husband's voice across the pool. Lifting her head, she smiled as she watched him walk toward her, wearing only swimming trunks that showed off his tanned, magnificent body. She could not look away from his hard-muscled torso, powerful arms and strong thighs. The sensual way he moved seduced her—without him even trying!

"I like seeing you by the pool," he said appreciatively. Lifting a dark eyebrow, he looked over her pale body in her tiny bikini. "You look hot, in all those clothes."

She giggled. "You always say that. You told me I looked hot when it was pouring rain in London in January. I was shivering like a drowned rat and you started taking off my clothes!"

"I'm always available to help take off your clothes." Taking her hand in his own, he said innocently, "Care for a nice refreshing swim?"

Eduardo had a look in his dark eyes that made her suspect their "nice refreshing swim" would soon lead to rampant nakedness for them both. The heat in his gaze left her breathless. Her husband didn't seem to see any flaws in her post-pregnancy figure. He called her *beautiful, gorgeous*, and *irresistible*, and once she was naked in his arms, he told her so with his body.

"All right." Smiling, Callie let him pull her to her feet and lead her into the pool. The bobbing water felt cool against her bikini and sun-warmed skin. Once in the deep end of the pool, he pulled her into his arms and kissed her.

His lips felt hot and hard against hers. She clung to him as he kissed her, relishing the feel of his hard, muscled body towering over her petite frame. She loved him so much. And though he hadn't spoken those three words back to her, she was convinced it was just a matter of time...

He pulled back with a shiver. "Oh, *querida*," he said hoarsely. "I'm going to miss you."

"Miss me?" She blinked. "Where are you going?"

As they held each other in the pool, the water bobbing against her breasts, he stroked her cheek with a scowl. "Marrakech. To complete a business deal."

"Morocco? For how long?"

"Hard to say. The man is unpredictable. The negotiations might last a day—or a week."

"A week? A full week at the villa without you? I can't face it."

"I'll miss you, too."

She took a deep breath. "But it might be the perfect time for me to visit my parents. I'll just take the other jet while you're gone..."

He frowned. "What?"

She met his eyes. "I've been writing my family every week for four months. It's not working. I need to go see them."

Eduardo stared at her. Was it just her imagination, or did some of the color disappear behind his tan? "Absolutely not."

"Why?" She tilted her head, folding her arms. She'd expected a fight and was ready for it. "You won't exactly miss us. You'll be in Morocco."

"Maybe I'd like you and Marisol to come with me. Marrakech is beautiful in April."

"That wasn't your plan a minute ago."

"Plans change."

As the cool water of the pool bobbed around them, they glared at each other. Above them, the wind blew through the palm trees, and she could hear the roar of the distant ocean as seabirds cried out mournfully across the cloudless blue sky.

And Callie broke. "I miss them, Eduardo." She unfolded her arms, blinking back tears. "I don't know what else to do. I miss them."

He set his jaw. "I thought you were happy here—"

"I am. But I *miss* them. Every hour. Every day. It's like a hole in my heart." She put her hand over his chest. "Right here." Tears streamed down her cheeks as she looked up at him. "I can't stand the silence. I feel lost without them."

Eduardo stared at her for a long moment. Then, closing his eyes, he exhaled.

"All right," he said in a low voice.

"All right?"

He looked down at her. "Not McLinn. But your parents and your sister—yes."

"I can go see them in North Dakota?" she breathed, hardly able to believe it.

"But I don't want you and Marisol so far away from me. And I need to be in Marrakech tomorrow…"

Her heart, which had been rising, suddenly pinched. She said dully, "So I should put off my visit."

"No." Taking her in his arms, he gently lifted her chin. "I will charter a jet to collect your family. If they agree, they will meet us in Marrakech tomorrow. How about that?"

She stared at him, shocked.

"You will see them. And they will get a chance to meet me." His jaw clenched as he looked away. "Not just as the CEO who owns the oilfields outside your town, but as your husband. As Marisol's father." He looked back at her, his darkly handsome face suddenly uncertain. "Is... is that satisfactory?"

"Satisfactory!" she cried. She threw her arms around him in the pool and kissed him, over and over, kissed his cheeks, his forehead, his chin. "Oh, Eduardo, I love you so much. Thank you, my darling, thank you!"

He straightened in the pool. His hard-muscled body dazzled her. Droplets of water cascaded down his tanned skin, sparkling in the sun as he lifted her up, wrapping her legs around his waist.

"This time," he whispered, "I'll let you thank me."

And he kissed her, long and hard, beneath the waving palm trees and the hot Spanish sun.

Many hours later, Eduardo looked down at his naked wife, sleeping in his arms in the darkness of the bedroom. It was past midnight. And he wanted to sleep with her.

Not just make love to her. Making love was easy. Callie was damn beautiful. A man would have to be dead not to want her constantly. Especially when she was happy, as she'd been today.

She'd been so thrilled to speak with her parents on the phone that afternoon. She hadn't noticed how shocked her parents were to hear from her, and learn she was in Spain. But after tears on both sides, the Woodvilles had agreed to take his chartered jet and join them in Morocco, after a quick stop at the American consulate to get their very first passports.

Later that evening, as Eduardo discussed necessary travel arrangements with his assistant, Callie had bounced off the walls with excitement and joy. After dinner, they'd played with the baby, given Marisol a bath and put her to bed, and then Callie had grabbed his hand and pulled him to bed, too. Even after making love for hours, for the second time that day, it had still taken unusually long for Callie to fall asleep in his arms: a full ten minutes.

That was hours ago. Eduardo looked bleakly across the luxurious master bedroom of the villa. God knew he'd tried to make himself sleep. But it was always the same. After they made love, he would hold her, his body relaxed, his soul in perfect, blissful peace. He would cherish her in his arms, so soft and willing and warm. But the instant he closed his eyes, sleep disappeared. He tried to relax, but his muscles became tight until beads of sweat broke out on his forehead.

He'd never slept with any of the women he bedded. But he'd never wanted to. He'd thought it would be different with Callie. But even with her, he still couldn't let down his guard completely. Eduardo exhaled, knowing he wasn't going to be able to sleep tonight, either. He should get up and go to the guest room to sleep, like usual.

Yet he wanted to sleep with his wife.

He wanted to deserve her.

Since the day they'd wed, Eduardo had done everything he could to keep his family safe and happy. He'd supported Callie in every way.

Except one. None of her letters to her family had ever

left the house. And she'd never gotten any of their mail, forwarded from New York. When Sami Woodville had tried to phone his office, he'd instructed his secretary to block her calls. When she'd called his cell phone, he'd changed his number.

A cold chill went through his body. Would Callie ever forgive him when she discovered what he'd done? Would she understand that he'd done it for one reason: to protect their family?

He'd been ruthless for a reason. But when Callie had wept with grief in the pool today, something had snapped inside him, and he couldn't do it anymore—even though he knew all hell would break loose when she spoke with her parents and put two and two together. It was remotely possible for the mail service to misplace a letter, but not scores of them. Callie would soon figure out who'd had means and motive to suppress them.

Eduardo stared bleakly at the bedroom ceiling.

He should tell her himself what he'd done, rather than letting her figure it out. Rather than—say—letting Brandon McLinn be the one to tell her. His jaw tightened. He was sick of feeling the ghost of McLinn always at his back. Tired of waiting for the moment when Callie would finally be disgusted by Eduardo's flawed soul and leave. Tired of feeling Brandon McLinn always waiting in the shadows, ready to take Callie away the instant he made a mistake.

Was this that final mistake?

His arms tightened around Callie.

Her parents and sister were already somewhere over the Atlantic, but his investigator was having trouble tracking down Brandon McLinn. He believed the young farmer might be on his way, even now, to southern Spain, since he'd discovered their villa's location from Callie's family.

Eduardo allowed himself a grim smile. By the time he arrived here, Callie would be in Morocco.

The smile faded as he looked at Callie's slumbering, trusting face. He should pull his private investigator off Brandon McLinn, along with Walter, Jane and Sami Woodville. He should stop going through his wife's mail or screening her calls at the villa. He should just take a deep breath, and trust her. Trust everyone.

But he couldn't. It would mean flying blind. If Eduardo didn't know the future, how could he prevent catastrophe? How could he keep his family safe? How could he make sure she would never leave, never break his heart; never break Marisol's?

Listening to her quiet, even breathing, he squeezed his eyes shut. His whole body was tense, and sleep danced away from him, mocking him.

Wearily sitting up, Eduardo watched the gray light of dawn through the windows, and heard the faint call of morning birds above the roar of the ocean. He put his head in his hands. He wanted to deserve her. He wanted to trust her.

He wanted to love her.

"Eduardo?"

He felt a gentle hand on his back. He turned, and saw Callie looking up at him with luminous eyes. "What is it?"

He looked down at her. She was naked, and beautiful, and unafraid. He said in a low voice, "I had a dream that you left me."

Her eyes went wide. She sat up, shaking her head. "No." Reaching for him, she pulled him back into the soft comfort of her arms. "That will never happen. Never."

Reaching out, he twined his fingers in her hair. "My parents loved each other once," he said. "They wanted a child. They built a home. Then they grew apart, twisted by secrets and lies. My mother met a new man, and my father was destroyed by it. Everything ended."

Callie took both his hands in her own. "That won't happen to us."

Blinking fast, he looked out at the gray dawn. "I had a dream."

Callie stared at him, suddenly frowning.

"But you don't sleep," she said slowly. "You don't dream."

Eduardo turned to her. She was so beautiful, his wife. So gentle and kind. She believed the best of everyone, even when they didn't deserve it. He took a deep, shuddering breath.

"I do now," he whispered.

CHAPTER NINE

CALLIE's hands and feet bounced rhythmically against the interior of their four-wheel drive as they drove from the Marrakech airport. Eduardo, who was driving beside her, reached out and stilled her knee with his hand.

"Sorry." She looked up at him with an apologetic smile. "I'm excited."

"Yes." He smiled back at her, his dark eyes warm. "I know." Then a troubled shadow crossed his expression, and he turned away to focus on the road, gripping the wheel.

Business negotiations usually didn't faze Eduardo. Callie wondered why he seemed so tense. He generally relished a good fight. Shrugging it off, she cooed at their baby in her car seat behind them. Through the back window she saw the other vehicle following with their staff and bodyguards as they drove past the twelfth-century ramparts of the medina to the vast sprawling palm desert beyond. The sky was blue above the distant, snowcapped Atlas Mountains.

She turned back to her dark, impossibly handsome husband beside her. He was wearing a business suit, but his dark coloring and black hair made him look like a sheikh. In her own long purple caftan, with the window rolled down and the warm Moroccan wind blowing through her hair, she felt like a cosseted Arabian princess at his side.

It was officially the happiest day of her life. After today, she'd have no reason to ever be sad again.

"Thank you," she said for the millionth time.

Eduardo gave her a sideways glance. "Stop."

"You don't know what this means to me—"

"I mean it." His jaw was tight as he turned off the main road to a guardhouse. Pulling up to a heavily scrolled metal gate, Eduardo spoke in French to a security guard, who with a very deep bow, swung open the gate. Eduardo drove up a long sweeping driveway with the other car behind them.

Callie looked up through the front windshield, her eyes wide when she saw the enormous Moroccan *riad*, two stories tall and surrounded by gardens. Willowy palm trees graced the edges of large swimming pool that sparkled a brilliant blue in the sun. The grand house itself was the combination of traditional Moroccan architecture and old French glamour. Craning her head, Callie looked up with awe at the home's soaring curves and the exquisitely detailed scrollwork. "What is this place?"

"In the 1920s it was a hotel. Now it belongs to Kasimir Xendzov, who loaned it for our visit."

"He's not staying here?"

"No."

She turned to Eduardo in shock. "Why would he leave a place like this?"

He shook his head. "He is in the city as little as possible. He prefers to live like a nomad in the desert." His lips curved. "Like those sheikhs, in the romance novels you love."

"But he's Russian?"

"The local people call him the Tsar of the Desert."

"Oh." The romantic phrase made her shiver. "What's he like?"

"Kasimir? As cold and heartless as his brother. You remember Vladimir Xendzov?"

She tilted her head. "Prince Vladimir? The man who stole the Yukon deal from us?"

"He's not really a prince, no matter what he says. But yes. They're brothers. They've spent the last ten years trying to destroy each other."

Callie stared at him, aghast. "That's awful!"

Eduardo smiled with satisfaction. "A fact that will help me get what I want."

"Prince Vladimir was vicious," she said, troubled. "Corrupt. Definitely unsafe."

"And not a prince."

She pressed her lips together. "Is it smart to make a deal with his brother?"

"Don't worry. We are safe here. Kasimir is our host. His honor is at stake." Pulling the car up to the front of the house, he turned off the engine. Getting out, he handed the keys to a waiting servant. Callie stepped out behind him with her seven-month-old baby in her arms, and heard the soft water of a fountain. She looked at the huge house beneath the hard blue sky of the desert, and saw a shadow move in the window.

"Are they here?" she whispered.

Eduardo gave her a single, silent nod, and an involuntary shiver went through her. She walked towards the *riad*, her baby against her hip, her husband and bodyguards following behind them.

The house seemed Moorish in design, with a flat roof and intricate tile work. They walked through the soaring arches to the door. Inside, the walls were decorated with floral and geometric motifs, intertwined flowers and vines in green, red and gold-leaf paint all the way to the ceiling. Past the foyer was a cloister, an outdoor walkway built around a lush courtyard garden. Callie took a deep breath of the fresh air, listening to the sound of a burbling fountain mingling with birdsong.

Then she heard a woman's scream.

Whirling around, Carrie instinctively held up her arm, protecting her baby from the unseen danger.

But there was no danger, just her sister, racing at her full blast!

"Sami," Callie cried then she looked behind her and saw the smiling eyes of her parents. "Mom! Dad!"

"Callie." Her mother was openly weeping as she pulled her into her arms. "And is this your baby? My grandchild?"

"Yes, it's Marisol," Callie choked out. Her mother sobbed, wrapping Marisol and Callie into a hug with Sami. Her father wrapped his large form around the whole family and she saw to her shock that he, too, was weeping— something she'd never seen in her whole life.

"I missed you all so much," Callie whispered. She glanced at Eduardo out of the corner of her eye. He was standing back, watching them from the shadows.

"It's my fault." Pulling off his John Deere cap, her father rubbed his gray head with the heel of his hand. "I never should have written that nasty letter, chewing you out. It was just your Mom kept weeping, and you know I can't think straight when she's crying. I don't blame you for the silent treatment." His voice caught. "I wouldn't have written me back, either…"

Callie had no idea what he was talking about, but it felt so good to be with her family and have them clearly happy to see her and the baby. Marisol, looking at all the crying adults around her, gave a little worried whimper, looking up at Callie for reassurance. "It's all right," she told her, smiling. "It's finally all right."

As Jane Woodville held out her arms, tears were streaming down her plump cheeks and she looked like a slightly more wrinkled version of her granddaughter. "Can I hold her?"

The baby looked uncertain at first, but within sixty seconds, Jane had won her trust. Ten minutes later, Sami and then Grandpa Walter held her, and they heard Marisol's sweet baby giggle. Callie looked at her family, and could hardly believe that she'd been apart from them for seven months. They were the best, kindest people in the world.

Except for her husband. She looked at Eduardo adoringly, but he remained back in the shadows across the room.

"Mari—Marisol?" her father asked uncertainly.

Callie turned back, smiling through her tears. "Marisol Samantha Cruz."

"You named her after me?" Sami blurted out, her face screwed up with tears. "How could you forgive me? I was so selfish. I told myself calling your old boss was the right thing to do, but the truth is I didn't want you to marry Brandon." She sniffled. "How can you stand to look at me?"

"It *was* the right thing," Callie said through her tears. "Eduardo and I were meant to be together, and thanks to you we are. We're happy. Really happy…"

Callie looked back at Eduardo. He was still standing by the door, his arms folded as he watched the family reunion. Why didn't he come over to join them? It was strange. Any normal person would have come over to be part of the group. But Eduardo chose to be standoffish, to watch from a distance.

Her mother, standing beside her, followed her gaze.

"He loves you," Jane said softly.

Callie looked at her wistfully. "How can you tell?"

Jane smiled. "I see it in the way he looks at you. Like his

heart's nigh about to break." Reaching out, she squeezed her daughter's hand. "I still can't believe we're in Morocco. I always told your father that someday we'd travel and see the world. He said he'd do it as soon as it was free." She chuckled mischievously. "Eduardo's jet was the answer to my prayer."

The two women laughed, hugging each other, and for the rest of the afternoon, the family talked and giggled as Kasimir Xendzov's well-trained servants served refreshments and drinks. Eduardo continued to remain out of the circle, out of the group, until he finally disappeared all afternoon with his assistants to work on the deal. His behavior bewildered Callie. Was he just trying to give her some space with her family? But didn't he realize that he, too, was part of the family now?

After a delicious dinner of couscous and lamb, Callie said good-night to her jet-lagged parents and sister as they turned in to their luxurious bedrooms. After giving Marisol a bottle, she tucked her into a crib next door to their own large bedroom on the other side of the *riad* from the rest of her family. For the first time all day, Callie was alone. She looked at the large bed, covered with dark blue pillows. Fading sunlight fell upon the blanket in a pattern from the carved lattice window. She touched the bed. The mattress felt soft.

She heard a noise behind her. Jumping, she turned around.

Eduardo stood in the doorway. His eyes were dark, his expression set, as if braced for bad news.

"There you are," she said, furrowing her brow. "Where have you been? Why didn't you come talk to my family?"

"I didn't want to intrude."

Callie frowned, feeling puzzled by the strangeness of

his tone. She shook her head. "But you're part of our family now."

The door closed behind him as he came toward her in the bedroom. His voice was stilted. "Your family isn't rich."

She drew back, confused at the turn in conversation. "No. Especially not these days. My parents' farm has had a rough couple years...."

He came closer, something strangely intense in his dark eyes. "But you all still love each other."

"Of course we do," she said, bewildered. "Like you said—we're family."

His jaw twitched as he rubbed his wrist. In the shadowy bedroom, she saw the flash of his platinum watch. "Growing up, I thought money made a family. That it made people actually love each other enough to stay."

Callie's breath suddenly caught in her throat. "Money has nothing to do with it. Don't you know that?"

Eduardo gave her a tight smile.

"I'm glad you spent time with your family today. I have work to do before I meet with Xendzov tomorrow. Get some rest."

As he turned away, Callie stared after him, shocked. It was the first night she could remember when he hadn't wanted to accompany her to bed at night, to make love to her, to hold her until she slept.

He stopped at the door. "We need to talk," he said heavily. "Tomorrow. Then we'll see." He took a deep breath. "Afterward, I hope you will still..."

His voice trailed off. For a long moment, he stared at her, his eyes glittering in the shadows. Then he turned away, closing the bedroom door between them.

Callie was hardly able to sleep that night without him beside her. In the morning, she hurried down for breakfast, but he never appeared. She found out he'd left at dawn with his team of administrators and lawyers to work on the business deal with their invisible host, the mysterious Kasimir Xendzov. She thought it was strange, because Eduardo had seemed so determined to talk to her. About what?

And then she knew.

Was Eduardo finally going to tell her he loved her?

Joy filled her, followed by certainty. What else could it be? She was filled with happiness, counting down the moments until she'd see him again. She spent an enjoyable morning with her baby and family, sharing breakfast in the courtyard garden, walking around the estate, swimming in the pool. After lunch, as her parents took an afternoon nap with their grandbaby, Callie and Sami decided to explore the *souks* of Marrakech.

As the two sisters wandered the narrow, mazelike streets of the medina, Callie's heart was light. They walked through the outdoor markets, investigating booth after booth of copper lanterns, terra-cotta pots, embroidered *jellabas* and coral beads. She constantly checked her new cell phone in her handbag, just to make sure Eduardo hadn't called for her, but in the meantime, she was happy. Wearing a floppy pink hat, a billowy blouse and long skirt, with her wide-eyed sister at her side, Callie felt almost like a child again, when she and Sami went on "expeditions" across the wide fields and brooks of their family farm.

She suddenly froze in the middle of the outdoor market. Feeling prickles on her neck, as if someone was watching her, she whirled around.

But she only saw her bodyguard, Sergio Garcia, following at a discreet distance through the crowded medina. Eduardo never let her go anywhere without a bodyguard, and often more than one. Still, even as the afternoon passed and the hot Moroccan sun lowered to the west, the cold prickles on her neck didn't go away.

"So you really forgive me?" Sami asked softly.

Kneeling as she looked through a selection of copper lanterns, Callie smiled up at her sister. "I forgave you long ago—the day I named my daughter."

Sami's young face was dubious. "But if you forgave me, why didn't you write back?"

Callie straightened, frowning. "You wrote? When?"

"Lots of times! I even sent flowers! But other than the day Marisol was born, when you called us, we never heard a word. Not me, not Brandon, not even Mom and Dad!"

Callie gaped at her. "I wrote you letters every week! I sent hundreds of pictures!"

"We never got anything."

A shiver of ice went down Callie's spine. "Strange," she said faintly then tried to push it away with a smile. "But it doesn't matter anymore, does it?"

"We were worried about you," Sami said softly, clawing back her hair. "I'm glad you at least called us from the hospital when Marisol was born. Brandon arrived two days later and was so upset. He made it sound as if you'd been, well—" she bit her lip "—kidnapped."

Callie looked at her. "Have you been spending a lot of time with Brandon?"

Sami's cheeks turned pink. "Yeah."

"You're in love with him." It was a statement, not a question.

Sami stared at her then burst into tears. "I'm sorry," she whispered, wiping her eyes. "I've loved him for years." She tried to smile. "All the time that he loved you."

Callie shook her head. "I keep telling people—Brandon and I are just friends!"

Sami gave a hoarse laugh. "Man, you're dumb. Just as dumb as he was."

"*Was*? Have you told Brandon how you feel?"

"Not yet." Sami looked away. "I'm scared. We've spent a lot of time together lately, ice skating, looking at the stars, running errands. Whatever." She shivered beneath the fading afternoon sun of the Marrakech market. "Once, I almost thought he was going to kiss me. Then he turned away and started talking about you."

"He did?" Guilt went through Callie. "He must hate me."

"He hates Eduardo. Not you."

"Then why didn't he ever write me?" Callie whispered.

Sami looked at her as if she were crazy. "He did. I know he did. He showed me the letters."

The strange feeling went through Callie again, a dark cloud like a shadow over the sun. How was it possible that her family hadn't gotten any of her letters? Or that Callie hadn't gotten any of theirs?

Pushing the thought away, she turned back to Sami, putting her hand on her shoulder. She said firmly, "You should tell him how you feel."

Sami's eyes lit up then faded. "But what if he's not interested? What if he just laughs at me?"

"He won't."

"Yeah, but what if he does?"

"Life is short. Don't waste another day. Call him. Call him now."

"You're right." Sami stared at her then suddenly hugged her tight. "Thank you, Callie." Pulling away, she wiped her eyes. "I'll go back to the house. And call him in private. Oh," she breathed, wiping her shaking hands on her jeans, "am I really going to do this?"

"Sergio!" Callie called, wiping tears from her own eyes as she waved the bodyguard over. "Please take my sister back to the house."

"And you, Mrs. Cruz," Sergio Garcia said, his expression a smooth mask.

"I haven't finished my shopping."

"I can't leave you alone here, *señora*."

"I'll be fine," Callie said impatiently. She motioned to the busy *souk*. "There's no danger here!"

The bodyguard lifted an eyebrow. Turning away, he used his cell phone and spoke in low, rapid Spanish. Hanging up, he turned to Sami with a broad smile. "*Sí*. I can take you home, *señorita*."

"Thank you," Callie said, surprised. He'd never been so reasonable before. "Would you mind taking these bags back with you?"

"*Por supuesto, señora.*" Garcia took her purchases, gifts for her parents, clothes and toys for Marisol, even a silver *koumaya* dagger for Eduardo. "Stay right here, Mrs. Cruz, in the open market."

"I will." Callie hugged her sister and whispered, "I think you and Brandon are perfect for each other."

"Thank you," Sami breathed fervently. "I love you, Callie." Then she was gone.

Callie was alone. She took deep breaths of the exotic, spicy scent of the air, of the distant leather tannery, of flowers and musky oriental perfumes. No bodyguard. No baby. Not even her husband. Callie was alone in this exotic foreign market. After so many months, the sudden freedom felt both disorienting and intoxicating.

Smiling to herself, she ignored the shouts of sellers trying to get her attention and walked through the market, feeling light as a feather on air as she continued to shop for gifts. Who knew if she'd ever return to Morocco again?

Her eye fell upon a tiny star carved in wood. It reminded her of Brandon's hobby that Callie found intolerably boring—astronomy. Thinking of him, a pang went through her.

Why didn't he ever write me?

He did. I know he did. He showed me the letters.

With a ragged breath, Callie lifted her gaze to the sky, turning toward the fading warmth of the sun. Above the busy, crowded, chaotic *souk*, a bird flew toward the distant Atlas Mountains. The setting sun had turned the snow-capped peaks a deep violet-pink.

"Callie."

She sucked in her breath. Slowly she turned.

Brandon McLinn stood in front of her.

Time slowed as he came toward her, tall and thin, standing out from the rest of the crowd in his cowboy hat, plaid flannel shirt and work-worn jeans. He stopped in front of her.

"At last," Brandon breathed, his eyes wet with tears. "I've found you."

"Brandon?" she whispered, her throat choking. "Is this a dream?"

"No." Smiling through his tears, he put a skinny hand on her shoulder. "I'm here."

"But what are you doing in Morocco?"

His hand tightened. "It took a miracle, all right," he said grimly. His eyes narrowed beneath his black-framed glasses. "No thanks to that Spanish bastard."

Callie gasped. "Don't call him that!"

He blinked, frowning. "But you hate him. Don't you? You said he was a playboy, that he had coal instead of a heart...that he couldn't be loyal to anything but his own fat bank account!"

Hearing her own words thrown back at her hurt. She

closed her eyes against her own cruelty. "He's not like that," she said over the lump in her throat. "Not really. He's—changed."

"Must be Stockholm Syndrome," Brandon snorted then his voice grew serious. "I've been so worried about you, Callie. I just let him take you away. I didn't save you."

Callie opened her eyes in shock. "*You* felt guilty?"

"I swore I'd leave no stone unturned, until you and your baby were back home. Safe, and free."

Smiling through sudden tears, she put her hand over his. "But we are safe. And free. I know our marriage had a rocky start, but he's been nothing but good to us."

"Good?" Brandon's jaw hardened. "He's had me followed for months."

"Followed?" she echoed.

"When Sami told me she was leaving for Marrakech, I skipped out in the middle of the night, slipping past the man watching my house. I drove to Denver and booked a flight. I've been staying at a hotel off this square, following your movements through Sami's messages."

"You knew I'd be at the market." Callie stared at him. "It was you I felt, watching me. Following us."

"Hoping to get you alone." He looked down at her, his eyes owl-like beneath his glasses. "I tried to contact you. Letters, phone calls. I tried everything short of a singing telegram. Last December, he called me in the middle of the night, warning me off. I threatened to call the police in New York. So he spirited you overseas. For the last four months, I had no idea where you even were!"

Callie remembered the night she'd caught Eduardo talking on the phone to a rival, he'd said, who lived far away. That very same night, he'd suddenly suggested they go to Spain. Once there, he'd never let her out of his sight, or even let her drive her own car, without a bodyguard. He'd said it was to keep her safe.

But safe from whom?

"I promised myself I wouldn't abandon you," Brandon said. "I've been waiting...praying...desperate. All the time he kept you prisoner."

Prisoner. Callie stared at him with a sick feeling in her belly. She was starting to think that Eduardo's planned talk later didn't involve him taking her in his arms and declaring his eternal love.

"I always knew the man was bad news." Brandon narrowed his eyes. "From the moment I first heard you talk about him. When he leased you that apartment in the Village, I knew he wanted you." His voice became bitter. "And from the sound of your voice, I knew you would let him."

"So you told Eduardo we were engaged," she said slowly. "The night he stopped by the apartment, you said..."

"I just told him the truth," he said stubbornly. "We *were* engaged. We said, if neither of us were married by the time we were thirty..."

"That was a joke!"

"It was never a joke to me." He looked down. "But I guess it was to you."

She stared at him, her cheeks aflame, unable to speak.

"I loved you, Callie," he said gruffly. "Since we were kids, I loved you."

She felt a lump in her throat, remembering their childhood. Chasing fireflies on warm summer nights. Watching fireworks on the Fourth. Christmas dinner with her cousins, aunts and uncles, turkey and stuffing and homemade pumpkin pie, sledding with her sister down McGillicuddy's hill. Even going out with Brandon's telescope at night and looking at stars until she wanted to claw her eyes out. It had been wonderful.

Her throat hurt. "I should have known. I'm sorry. But…I don't feel that way about you."

"Yeah. I figured that out." He took a deep breath then gave her a sudden crooked smile. "I've started to think that maybe I should look for someone who can love me. Who can see me. As more than a goofy, dependable friend."

Her heart broke a little in her chest. She tilted back her floppy pink hat. "Brandon—"

"But first I'm taking you and the baby home. We'll get you a good divorce lawyer. I don't care how much money Cruz has, the courts will see that you are in the right."

"You don't understand—"

"You don't have to be scared. We'll be with you every step of the way. Me. Your family—"

"I'm in love with him, Brandon," she blurted out. At his intake of breath, she lifted her eyes miserably. "I love him so much I think I might die of it. Every day all I can think is that I would do anything, absolutely anything, to make him love me back."

Brandon stared at her, his face pale. His Adam's apple bobbed then he looked at his feet as he said in a low voice, "I remember that feeling."

"I'm so sorry." Reaching out, she pulled him into her arms as she wept. "Forgive me."

For a moment, he accepted the comfort of her arms. They held each other, like kids dodging a storm.

"How can you love a man like that?" Brandon said in a low voice. "I accept that you can't love me. All right, fine. But a man who keeps you prisoner? Of all men on earth, you choose Cruz? A cruel, selfish beast of a man?"

Her heart lifted to her throat. "You don't know him,

Brandon. He's been hurt in the past. But he's not selfish and he's not cruel. If you only knew. He has such a good heart—"

Her voice ended in a gasp as Brandon was violently wrenched from her arms.

"Don't *touch* my wife!"

Turning in shock, Callie saw Eduardo's handsome face distorted with rage. A beam of blood-red light covered his black, civilized business suit, from the sun setting fire to the west.

"No, Eduardo, no!"

But he didn't hear her. Drawing back his fist, he punched Brandon so hard across the jaw that the other man, totally unprepared, dropped like a stone into the dust.

"No!" Callie shrieked. Around the *souk*, people stared at them across the busy, crowded market, speaking in a cacophony of languages. Fist raised, Eduardo started for Brandon again.

Callie ran between them, so fast her hat fell off her head. Holding up both her arms, she cried, "Don't!"

Eduardo whirled on her, his black eyes so hot that she should have burned to ash. "You told him to meet you here!"

"No, of course I didn't!" Looking at him, all Callie could suddenly think of was how he'd been lying to her face for months. How he'd caused her family pain. Forcing herself to take a deep, calming breath, she knelt down in the dust and checked on Brandon, who was knocked out cold but seemed otherwise fine. Rising to her feet, she glared at Eduardo. "Brandon couldn't contact me. A fact you know well."

Eduardo stared at her, breathing heavily. "What did he want from you?"

She lifted her chin. "To help me go back to North Dakota and file for divorce."

"And what did you say?"

"What do you think I said?" she cried. "I said no! Because I'm married to you. I have a child with you. I love you! Of course I told him no. Are you out of your mind?"

Baring his teeth, Eduardo grabbed her arm and pulled her away from the staring eyes of the *souk* and down the warren of streets to the parked car. Pushing her inside, he started the engine. It was only after they were back on the road that he spoke to her through gritted teeth.

"I found you in his arms."

Callie whirled on him. "I was comforting him!"

"I *trusted* you," he ground out.

"Trusted me?" She looked at him, tears in her eyes. "That's a joke! You never trusted me. You kept me a virtual prisoner, locked away from my family. Did you think I wouldn't find out?"

Eduardo looked at her, his handsome face pale beneath his tan. Setting his jaw, he didn't answer.

"When I think of all the time I spent," Callie whispered. "Sending them picture after picture, letter after letter." She looked up at him fiercely. "And the whole time, you were keeping them away, and me, locked away in your own little cage!"

He turned his eyes grimly back to the road. As he drove from the fortified gates of the medina toward the sprawling palm desert, he was silent, his jaw tight.

"You're not even trying to deny it," she said, tears streaming down her face.

He changed gears with more force than necessary. "I was going to tell you about it," he retorted. "It's why I told Sanchez he could leave you there. I wanted to surprise you at the market, and take you out to dinner just the two of us, so we could talk in private. So I could try to make you understand."

"I understand, all right!"

His hands clenched on the wheel. "I was trying to protect you. To protect all of us."

"Brandon said he was followed. Did you have me watched, too? What about my family?"

Eduardo looked at her then looked away.

"Keith Johnson had the detail," he said flatly.

The hot Moroccan air blew through the car window, whirling over her skin. "Keith Johnson?" she faltered. "But you use him to gain information on your rivals. On your enemies." She looked at him. "Which one am I?"

"You're my wife," he said tightly. "I was trying to keep you safe."

Her emotions were so jumbled she felt numb. "Safe!"

He glanced at her out of the corner of his eye. "What was I supposed to do?" he said roughly. "Let another man destroy our marriage?"

Callie's throat hurt. She closed her eyes, hearing the purr of the engine and soft whirr of the tires against the road.

"No," she whispered. "You destroyed it yourself."

She looked at him, and his dark eyes burned through her. Then wordlessly, he looked back at the road as the car turned into the gatehouse and drove up the sweeping entrance to the *riad*.

"We left Brandon," she cried. "Injured in the medina…"

"I'll send someone to check on him," Eduardo said coldly, not looking at her. "I wouldn't want your *best friend in all the world* to be left abandoned and alone."

Parking the car, he turned off the ignition and got out. Callie didn't move. She stared at the beautiful tile work of the grand home, at the green gardens and swaying palm trees above the blue-water pool. This place truly was paradise.

Her hands were shaking. She felt chilled to the bone.

The car door opened.

"Come, *querida*," Eduardo said quietly, reaching for her hand. She did not resist as he pulled her from the SUV and into the house. Inside the *riad*, all was quiet. Perhaps her parents and baby were sleeping. Callie heard only the soft burble of the fountain from the courtyard garden.

She felt her husband's hand in her own, as strong and protective around hers as it had ever been. But everything had changed. Was it only that morning that she'd been so happy, feeling like all her dreams were coming true? As Eduardo led her through the cloistered walk around the interior courtyard, she felt cold in the fading light of the sun.

"Why did you do it?" she rasped. "Why?"

Eduardo stopped.

"I'm tired, Callie," he said wearily. "Tired of trying to keep you. Tired of feeling like I'm failing. Tired of knowing, whatever I do, it won't be good enough."

"I did nothing but love you."

"Love is nice." His eyes glittered like hot coals as the edges of his lips curved. "Love changes nothing."

She stared at him, her heart chilled. "Is that what you think?"

"It's what I know," he said grimly, and that was the end. Her heart frosted over.

"You were right about one thing," she said. "Brandon was in love with me. But you've been so wrong about the rest. You are a wonderful father, Eduardo. But—" she gave him a trembling smile "—a terrible husband."

Hearing the noise of servants down the hall, he pulled her into their bedroom, closing the door behind them.

Looking down at her in the shadows, he spoke in a low voice.

"I always knew that someday you would see through me."

She felt trails of ice on her cheeks and lifted her hand to discover she was weeping. She loved him. But she wouldn't be his prisoner. Not anymore.

"I loved you, Eduardo." Her voice choked. "I loved you so."

His handsome face was hard with anguish. "*Loved*?"

"I would have done anything to make you love me," she whispered. "Anything." With a deep breath, Callie looked up at him through her tears. She squared her shoulders. "But I won't be your prisoner." Pulling off her diamond ring, she held it out to him with a trembling hand. "So I can't be your wife."

CHAPTER TEN

IT WAS like a punch through Eduardo's gut, a blow so deep it reverberated against his spine.

When he'd found Callie embracing McLinn, it had been like walking into a nightmare and seeing his worst fear come to life. He'd felt fury that he'd never known. He'd wanted to kill the man with his bare hands. And he might have done it, if not for Callie.

Now, sinking down on the bed, Eduardo stared at the ten-carat diamond ring twinkling in his palm. And realized that seeing Callie with another man had only been his *second*-worst fear.

Somehow, he'd always known this day would come. It was almost a relief to get it over with, rather than always wondering when it would happen. When she would leave him. His hands tightened over the ring, feeling the hard diamond bite into his palm. He spoke over the razor blade in his throat.

"I will start divorce proceedings tomorrow."

Her lips parted. "What?"

"I'll do what I should have done a long time ago." He looked at her. "Set you free."

Tears streaked her pale, beautiful face like stardust in the fading red twilight outside the latticed window. "I just can't live with a man who doesn't trust me. Who tries to control every aspect of my life."

"I understand." He gave her a grim smile. "I told you on our wedding day that when our marriage ended, the prenuptial agreement would see us through."

His wife looked white and wan, standing beside the bed. She looked like a ghost. "I didn't think you would let me go so easily."

He tried to ignore the fierce, white-hot blade of pain that entered his body.

"I am tired," he said harshly, "of always wondering what you're thinking. What you're doing. Tired of waiting for the day you'll wise up and leave." Rising to his feet, he cupped her cheek. She shuddered a little, turning toward his touch like a flower. He said hoarsely, "It's almost easier this way."

"And Marisol..." she whispered.

The knife twisted in his chest. Dropping his hand, he stepped back. "We will always be her parents. We'll be respectful of each other, for her sake. I will pay child support. We will share custody."

"Right," she said, looking dazed. "Right."

"And if there is another child..." His lips curved humorlessly. "This time, you will tell me, *si*?"

"Yes. Yes, I will." Callie's lovely, round face looked bewildered as she swayed where she stood, like a drunk who'd lost her balance.

"You and your family can return to North America tomorrow."

She turned, walked two steps then looked back at him. He could see her shaking. "And Brandon?"

"Ah, yes." He smiled grimly. "Brandon. As you said, he is a member of your family, is he not? As I," he added lightly, "never was."

She swallowed then looked up at him pleadingly. "You won't...won't do anything to hurt him?"

Reaching out, Eduardo brushed some long wavy tendrils of light brown hair off her shoulder. Even now, saying goodbye, he was mesmerized by Callie's beauty. Now more than ever. When he was losing her forever.

"Of course I will not hurt him. I'm not the monster you seem to think." He remembered how he'd been tempted to kill the man just hours before, and shook his head with a hard laugh. "Well. I have no reason to hurt him now. Our marriage is over. We are free."

"Free..." she whispered.

McLinn's harsh words from long ago went through Eduardo's mind. *You can't keep me from her. We both know you're not good enough for her. You'll never make her happy.* And he realized that he'd always agreed. But he'd tried to keep Callie just the same. Selfish and wrong, when he knew he'd never be able to love her the way she deserved. Christ—he couldn't even sleep in the same bed.

"Yes. You're free." Eduardo turned away, making his voice deliberately casual as he said, "Marisol fell asleep in her playpen, in your parents' room. Do you want to see her?"

Callie did not answer. She just looked at him, her green eyes dark as a midnight sea. Her beautiful, grief-stricken face was more than Eduardo could bear. It had to end, he thought heavily. So let it end. Merciful and quick.

Taking his wife's limp hand, he pulled her out of their bedroom and through the deepening shadows of the courtyard. Midway through the garden, she stopped. He looked back at her in the twilight, surrounded by the shadows of palm trees and the soft cool burble of the fountain. Crystalline tears sparkled down her pale cheeks, glimmering in the fading moonlight.

"I'm sorry," she whispered, her eyes luminous. "So sorry."

Exhaling, Eduardo slowly pulled her into his arms. She pressed her face against his heart, which felt like it was breaking beneath his ribs.

Her voice was sodden, muffled against his shirt. "I didn't want it to end this way…"

His arms trembled around her. He thought of all his mistakes, everything he'd done wrong from the beginning, all the things he would have changed if he could. But the truth was he didn't know how. He couldn't trust anyone—especially not someone he loved. Because deep in his heart, he didn't believe in happy endings, only bad ones. Ones that felt like this.

"It was never your fault," he said, stroking her hair. "Just mine. All mine."

Hearing Callie sob, his throat constricted, and he wanted to cut out his ears, his eyes, rather than be faced with the pain he'd caused her. Desperately he pushed his feelings away, just as he'd done his whole life. Lifting her chin, he gave her a crooked smile. "Our marriage wasn't all bad, was it?"

"No," she whispered, searching his gaze in the shadows. "Most of it was wonderful."

"We gave our daughter a name. We will still give her a good home."

"Yes," she agreed. "But two homes. Apart."

He gave her a single unsteady nod then looked away, afraid of what she would see in his eyes. Afraid to speak and have her hear weakness in his voice. For long moments, he held her in the deepening shadows of the courtyard, listening to the water of the cool fountain as they stood in silence. Above them, palm trees waved against the deepening violet night.

Eduardo closed his eyes, breathing in the scent of her hair. Feeling the sweet softness of her body against his, knowing he was holding her for the last time.

It was best for her to leave. It was the only way to spare them both unnecessary pain. But the thought of it felt like death.

"It's all right," he said, gently brushing the tears from her cheeks, though he knew it would never be all right again. "You'll go home. You'll be happy there, just like you were."

"Yes, I will." She wept.

He heard the hoarseness of her voice, and knew what the words cost her. Emotion rushed through him, and before he could stop himself, he cupped her face in both his hands. "But before you leave, there's one thing you have to know. One important thing I've never said." He looked down at her. "I love you."

Callie sucked in her breath, her eyes wide.

"I love you as I've never loved anyone." He looked down at the flowers at his feet. "But I can't love you without hurting you. Without hurting both of us. Without being a man I don't want to be." Looking at her stricken face, he whispered over the razor blade in his throat, "That's why I'm letting you go."

In the shadows of the garden, Callie's eyes were deep emerald, like an ancient forest older than time itself. Her beauty was like an ache in his heart. Unwillingly he lifted his hand to her cheek, touching the softness of her skin as he looked into her eyes, connecting them soul to soul. Beneath the violet-tinged sky swept with stars, he heard the howl of the wind, shaking the palm trees above.

"I'm sorry I couldn't love you as you deserve," he said hoarsely. "I always knew I didn't deserve you. And I knew, from the beginning, that it was a matter of time—"

Standing on her toes, Callie cut off his words by covering his mouth with her own.

Her lips were soft and sweet, trembling against him. He felt the warmth of her body against his, and a surge of anguished need rushed through him like an overflowing river. A gasp came from the back of his throat, and he wrapped his arms around her, pulling her against him tightly as he returned her kiss hungrily. On her lips, he tasted salt with the sweet and no longer knew if they were her tears, or his own. All he knew was that he was kissing her for the last time and he had to make it last forever. He had to kiss her so deep and hard that he'd possess this memory for all time, not just on his lips, but in his heart.

Eduardo's fingers twined through her long hair as they embraced, their bodies pressing together as they clutched each other mindlessly in front of the courtyard fountain. He felt the tangled smoothness of her hair, breathed in her scent of flowers and vanilla that mingled with the exotic spices of the desert wind. He stroked down her back, marveling at her shape as he wrapped his far larger body around the small woman who'd conquered him so completely. Looking at her, touching her soft skin, feeling her breasts against his chest, he kissed her with anguished passion. Need burned away every other thought or desire of his soul, except to possess her.

With a gasp, he pulled away. Looking down at her beautiful face, he saw the shadows of the rising moon move against her skin; saw the breathless, aching need in her eyes. Without a word, he lifted her up into his arms. He carried her silently to their bedroom.

For the last time, he took Callie to bed.

Setting her down on the mattress, beneath the pattern of moonlight through the latticed window, Eduardo pulled off her blouse, kissing her neck, her shoulders, her arms.

He pulled off her skirt, stroking the length of her legs, kissing the sensitive spot behind her knees with a flick of his tongue. He pulled off her lacy white bra, cupping her breasts, suckling her until she gasped.

"Callie," he said hoarsely. "Look at me."

She obeyed, and her beautiful eyes shimmered with tears as she watched him move down her body, pulling her panties down her legs. Still fully dressed in his black suit, he kissed her naked body. Up her calves. Her inner thighs. He paused at the crux of her thighs, letting the warmth of his breath curl between her legs, inhaling the tantalizing scent of her.

Pushing her thighs apart with his hands, he bent his head and tasted her, stretching her wide. She was sweet and smooth as satin. He nestled himself between her thighs and flicked the tip of his tongue against her hard, aching core. He felt her writhe beneath him, bucking her hips to escape the intensity, so he held her hips against the bed, forcing her to accept the full rough pleasure of his tongue. He stroked her, lapped her. When she was dripping wet and trembling, he pushed three fingers a single inch inside her.

Panting for breath, she threw out her hands, gripping the soft cotton blankets as he suckled her hard pink nub, swirling his tongue in featherlight circles and pressing his fingers deeper and deeper inside her. Callie's hands tightened on the blankets, her back arching, as if only her grip kept her from flying off the bed. He heard the long gasp of her breath, felt her body lifting from the mattress, higher, higher, felt her body grow tense and tenser still. Until she exploded.

Her soft, wet walls contracted tightly around his fingers as she cried out, twisting her body from side to side, in a symphony of mindless, helpless pleasure. He watched her face. He'd given her that pleasure. He'd made her weep with grief. But at least he'd also made her scream with joy. As she opened her eyes, still panting for breath, her expression was almost bewildered as she looked up at him. "I love you," she whispered.

Cupping her face, he looked down at her. "I know."

She stroked his face, his hair, his neck, his jacket. He lowered her mouth to hers, and she kissed him back almost savagely. He felt her tongue, her teeth. He felt her need for him. He felt her heart. Fully dressed, he moved against her, his erection hard and throbbing against her thighs.

A sob come low from her throat. She flung her arms around his neck, pulling him down against her with sudden desperation. Her fingers frantically attempted to pull off his tie, to unbutton his shirt. Pulling away from her, he yanked off his coat and tie. He ripped his civilized white shirt and tailored trousers and silk boxers to the cool tile floor.

Naked, he faced her, his soul as bare as his body. Without a word, he lowered his mouth to hers, stroking her, telling her with his touch everything he could not trust himself to put into words.

Covering her body with his own, he felt her full breasts against his chest, felt her soft, feminine curves sway against his hardness. The satin-smooth skin of her inner thighs stroked the hard length of his shaft, and her wet core tantalized his aching tip alluringly. He heard her gasp with need as she twisted her body beneath him, gripping his hips with her hands, trying to pull him closer, spreading her thighs in unconscious seduction.

But he did not want to take her. No. Not yet. Beads of sweat covered his forehead as he held himself apart from everything he wanted most. This was the last time he would possess her, and he wanted to make it last forever. As long as she was in his arms, he would not have to face the heartbreak and grief that waited for him on the other side. He would not have to face the dark solitude without her...

She stroked his back, her breasts plumping against his chest. He felt the sweaty heat of her skin, heard the breathless hush of her sigh. Gripping her shoulders, he closed his eyes, trying to resist. But she knew him too well. She moved beneath him, suckling his earlobe, breathing on his neck as she ran her hands on the back of his upper thigh, below his buttocks, between his legs. She stroked him—and he felt the hot, wet core of her slide against him—pulling him inside—

With a choked gasp, he surrendered. His body took over. With a low growl, he grabbed her shoulders and plunged himself inside her in a single deep thrust. Her body tensed, then melted, parting for him, accepting him, embracing every inch of his thick length. Pulling back, he thrust again with a gasp, and again, riding her. His every muscle was taut in the exquisite precipice between agony and pleasure. Six thrusts and only the grimmest vestige of self-control kept him from exploding inside her. But he had to make it last. He had to. He could not live without her....

Rolling onto his back, he lifted her over him, impaling her. Her thighs gripped his hips as he let her control the rhythm and speed. After months of bed play, his once-virgin secretary had become a fiery seductress. He thought having her on top would slow him down, make him last. But instead, as she pushed herself against him, he filled her harder and deeper than he ever had. Her heavy breasts swayed back and forth against his face as she rode him, going deeper with each thrust, until he closed his eyes, panting beneath the brutal onslaught of pleasure. Reaching his hands behind him, he gripped the headboard of the bed.

Harder, deeper. And wet, so wet. As she slammed

against him, her walls wrapped around him, tight, so tight, pulling him into an abyss of mindless pleasure. His eyes rolled back as he gripped her hips with his hands, his whole body shaking with the agony of need. He felt her quicken and pulse around him as she flung back her head and screamed with joy. Looking up at her, seeing her beautiful face filled with ecstasy, her eyes closed as if in prayer, he could no longer resist. With one last savage thrust he exploded inside her, riding the wave with her. His hoarse cry mingled with hers as he came and came and came, never looking away from her beautiful face.

And Callie collapsed on top of him, clutching him to her hot, sweaty body, happiness pouring out of them both like radioactive light.

Afterward, Eduardo held her. For the first time, he was grateful knowing that he wouldn't be able to sleep beside her. He could hold her all night. He'd watch her gentle face slumber beneath the latticed moonlight. She felt so soft in his arms. So warm. So sweet. His eyelids became heavy as he held her. Closing his eyes, he kissed her temple, breathing in the vanilla and floral scent of her hair. He loved her so much he thought he could die of it. He would hold her all night long. He'd relish every hour. Every minute…

Eduardo woke with a gasp.

The pink light of morning poured in through the window as he realized that he'd slept beside his wife for the first time.

In panic, he looked at her side of the bed.

It was empty. For the first time, Callie had been the one to rise in the middle of the night. She'd been the one to leave. And as the first wave of anguish hit his body, he knew this was how he'd always known he would be.

Alone.

CHAPTER ELEVEN

CALLIE sat at the kitchen table of her parents' farmhouse and looked at the papers in her shaking hands. The words seem to swim in front of her eyes.

Divorce papers.

"It'll be quick and painless," her lawyer had assured her when he'd given her the file. "I marked each place for you to sign with a yellow tab. All the tough questions were already dealt with in the prenup. You'll share custody, switching visitation each week, and with Mr. Cruz's extremely generous level of alimony and child support you'll be the richest woman in Fern County." The lawyer gave her a sudden sharp grin. "Good thing every divorce case isn't so quick and painless, or else I'd be bankrupt."

Quick. Painless. Callie heard a wheel squeak as her nine-month-old daughter crossed the floor in the antique walker used by three generations of Woodville babies. Marisol giggled at the sound, and her laughter was like music. Callie smiled at her daughter through her tears.

"Pa-pa-pa?" Marisol said hopefully.

Callie's smile faded as she looked down at the papers. "Soon, sweetheart," she said over the lump in her throat. "You'll see him tomorrow." Marisol would be flown back to New York for a week with Eduardo, and Callie would have to endure seven long, aching days without her child.

Then the next week, they would switch, and it was Eduardo who would be alone.

He'd been fair. More than fair, allowing Callie to live at such a distance, using his private jet to shuttle Marisol between North Dakota and New York. Callie had no idea what they'd do when it was time for Marisol to start school, but something would surely be worked out. Money, it seemed, could solve any problem.

Except this.

Callie didn't want his money. She wanted him. She was still in love with him.

But he'd let her go.

She hadn't seen Eduardo for two months, since she'd left Marrakech with her baby, Brandon and her family. Since then, their only point of contact had been through their lawyers. Even Marisol's pickups and drop-offs each week were handled by Mrs. McAuliffe.

Callie hadn't seen him. But each night, she dreamed of him, of their last night together, when they'd kissed in the shadows by the fountain. When they'd made love so passionately and desperately the bed seemed to explode into fire. When he'd huskily spoken the words she still, against her will, held to her heart.

I love you. I love you as I've never loved anyone. But I can't love you without hurting you.

Once, she would have given ten years of her life to hear Eduardo say he loved her. Now, the words were poison. She'd cried for weeks, till there were no tears left. But there was no other answer. She couldn't live as his prisoner. And he couldn't risk giving her his heart if she wasn't.

Two teardrops fell on the divorce papers spread out across her parents' blue Formica table. When she'd come back home, part of her had hoped she might be pregnant, which would at least give her a reason to talk to her husband again. But even that hope had failed her.

"Ma-ma?" Marisol's dark eyes, exactly like her father's, looked up at her mother with concern.

"It's all right," Callie whispered, wiping her eyes and giving her daughter a tremulous smile. "Everything is fine." All she had to do was sign the papers and her lawyer would file them. She'd be Callie Woodville again. Callie Cruz would disappear.

Across the small kitchen, where it sat in a small woven basket, the gold and diamond double "CC" key chain flashed at her in the morning light. It seemed forlorn and out-of-place in the key basket, amid the clutter of pens, sticky notes and unpaid utility bills around the twenty-year-old phone. But even her keychain wasn't as out-of-place as the shipment that had arrived at their rural North Dakota farm yesterday. Picking up her steaming mug of coffee, Callie went to the kitchen window and pushed aside the red gingham curtain.

Outside, beside her father's red, slightly rusted 1966 pickup truck, her sleek silver car was now parked in front of the barley field.

Callie closed her eyes. She'd never thought she would have the strength to leave Eduardo.

But then, she never thought he'd let her go.

And he'd already moved on. She'd already seen pictures of Eduardo in a celebrity magazine, attending a charity gala in New York with the young Spanish duchess. Callie wondered if they'd marry, once his divorce to her was final. Her heart twisted with jagged pain at the thought, and for the first time, she truly understood what Eduardo must have felt when he'd thought she was in love with Brandon.

How hard it was, to set the person free that you loved most on earth. But Eduardo had done it.

Now so must she.

Callie heard an engine coming up the long driveway. Looking back out the window, she smiled. About time. Taking another sip of her coffee, Callie watched Brandon and Sami leap out of the Jeep.

Brandon's heart hadn't remained broken for long. Since their return from Morocco, now freed of his guilt and concern over Callie, he'd finally allowed himself to give his heart to the young woman who'd been his constant companion for nine months. Yesterday, he'd asked Sami to marry him.

Their parents had been cautious at first, then ecstatic. News of the engagement had rapidly spread across Fern, and thanks to Jane's eager posting, to all her internet friends, across the world. Callie swallowed, feeling a little misty-eyed. *Engaged.* Her best friend and little sister were planning to be married in September.

As the two vagabonds traipsed through the door, Callie shook her head with a wry laugh. "Engaged or not, sis, Mom and Dad are not happy you stayed out all night."

"It was totally innocent!" Brandon protested. Then his full cheeks blushed beneath his black-framed glasses as he gave Sami a sudden wicked grin. "Well, *mostly* innocent…"

"We were up at McGillicuddy's Hill," Sami said quickly, "to see the comet away from the lights. There were so many stars." She looked dreamily at her fiancé. "Brandon knows all the constellations. We just lost track of time…"

"Good luck explaining that to Dad."

"Dad knows he can trust Brandon," she protested. She turned to him. "Like I do. With my life."

Brandon looked back at Sami with love in his eyes. Taking her hand in his own, he kissed it fervently. And Callie suddenly felt like an intruder, standing in the cozy, warm kitchen in her old purple sweatpants and ratty T-shirt. "All right," she said awkwardly. "You should talk to him, though."

"Where is he? Out in the fields?"

Callie nodded. "Alfalfa by the main road."

"Don't worry." Brandon clutched Sami's hand. "You won't have to face him alone."

"I know."

As he pulled his car keys out of his pocket, they turned toward the door. On impulse, Callie blurted out, "Wait."

They paused, staring at her questioningly. Crossing to the key basket, Callie took the "CC" keychain and held it out to them. "I want you to have this."

"What?" Sami exclaimed. "Your car?"

Brandon glowered. "Why?"

"It's—" Callie grasped at straws "—an engagement gift."

"Are you kidding?" Sami blurted out.

"We don't need anything from *him*." Brandon looked mutinous. It was possible he still nursed a grudge. "My Jeep works just fine."

Sami turned to him. "Think of it as compensation for him punching you," she said hopefully.

It didn't help her case. Brandon scowled.

"Please take it." Callie shook her head. "I hate looking at it. It makes me remember..." Her voice trailed off, as she felt overwhelmed by sweet memories of the Christmas day Eduardo had dressed in a Santa suit and given it to her. How happy they'd been... She gave them a tremulous smile. "Sell it. Use the money however you like."

The young couple looked at the dangling gold-and-diamond keychain.

"We could buy land," Sami said.

"A farm of our own," Brandon breathed. He blinked then snatched the keychain from her hand. "Very well. We accept." He paused, tilting his head with a grin. Then he sobered. "Thanks, Callie. Thanks for being the best friend I've ever had." He turned to Sami. "Till now."

And then they were gone, racing out of the farmhouse to the car parked near the barn. Their conversation floated back to Callie on the June breeze.

"One ride before we sell it?"

"Let's go the long way, past the Coffee Stop!" Sami giggled. "I want to see Lorene Doncaster's face when she sees me in this thing...."

"Your father will forgive us for being out all night. I'll explain. It was the fault of the stars..."

The fault of the stars. Alone in the kitchen, Callie stood in the warm sunlight of her mother's cheerful kitchen. She looked back at the divorce papers. She saw the black, angular scrawl of Eduardo's signature. He'd asked for a divorce. It was the only thing to do.

Wasn't it?

She picked up the pen in her trembling hand. She looked down at the empty line beneath his black signature.

Was their marriage really nothing more than a nine-month mistake?

She exhaled, closing her eyes.

Then, an hour later, she got a call that changed everything.

"Good progress today. So, same time next week?"

Eduardo nodded, pulling on his jacket. He left the therapist's office and took a deep breath of the morning air. The June sky was bright blue over Manhattan.

"Sir?" Sanchez stood ready at the curb, waiting beside the black Mercedes sedan.

Eduardo shook his head. "Think I'll walk."

"Very well, sir."

Eduardo walked slowly down the street, feeling the sun on his face, hearing the birds sing overhead. A bunch of laughing schoolkids in identical uniforms ran by him on the sidewalk, reminding Eduardo of the *Madeline* book he'd read to his two-week-old daughter, to the great amusement of his wife.

He stopped, feeling a sudden pain in his chest.

He would see Marisol soon, he reminded himself. His jet was already gassed up and ready at a private airport outside the city. He glanced at his platinum watch. Mrs. McAuliffe was likely headed for the airport now, if she wasn't there already, preparing to make the long flight across the country and back. She would collect the baby from his soon-to-be ex-wife. From the woman who still haunted his dreams.

Blankly Eduardo stared up at the green trees above the sidewalk. The trees looked exactly like they had in early September, when he'd first shown up in the West Village demanding marriage. On the day when, in the space of a few hours, he'd gained both a wife, and a child.

His stomach clenched. He suddenly couldn't bear the thought of going back to work. All those hours of work, all those days and years, and for what? He was a billionaire, and yet he envied his chauffeur, who went home every night to a snug little home in Brooklyn with a wife who loved him and their three growing children. Eduardo had a huge penthouse on the Upper West Side filled with art and expensive furniture, but when he was alone, the hallways and rooms echoed with the laughter of his baby. Of his lost wife.

Soon to be *ex*-wife.

He clenched his hands into fists. Had Callie signed the papers yet? Why hadn't she signed them?

It had been two weeks since he'd signed the divorce

papers, and the waiting was slowly driving him mad. He wanted it done, finished. Every day he was still married to Callie was acid on his heart, making him question if he'd made a mistake, if there was still a chance she might have forgiven him—if he could have earned back her trust.

He clawed his hair back with his hand. No. No way. She was probably engaged to Brandon McLinn by now and planning their wedding. McLinn's steadfast loyalty had triumphed at last. And unlike Eduardo, McLinn fit into Callie's world as Eduardo never would. He'd remember to ask her father for permission first. No one could ever deserve Callie, but if anyone had earned her, it was Brandon McLinn.

So why hadn't she signed the papers? Why?

He didn't know. He honestly didn't know. And it was like crossing a high-wire without a net.

Since Callie had left him in Marrakech, he hadn't checked up on her once. He'd fired Keith Johnson from her case. He'd even given his lawyers strict instructions not to give him news of her. They were to contact Eduardo when her lawyer had filed the signed paperwork for the divorce, and not before.

But he still hadn't got the call. Did that mean there was hope?

Closing his eyes, Eduardo turned his face toward the sun as he thought about how he'd isolated her during their marriage. No. No hope.

"Hey!"

Looking down, Eduardo saw a little girl of about eight or nine, standing apart from five other schoolgirls. She held up a picture. "You dropped this."

Reaching out, he took the photo of Callie and Marisol, taken at the Spanish villa at Christmas. Marisol was just three and a half months old then, giggling, flashing her single tooth. Callie was mischievously wearing the Santa hat she'd stolen from Eduardo, smiling as he took the picture. Her green eyes glowed with love. Grief choked him, so much his knees nearly went weak. "Thanks."

"I know how it feels to lose things," the little girl said. "Don't be careless."

He looked up, his eyes wide.

"See ya." With a skip, the girl turned away, racing back down the street with her friends, with the reckless joy of childhood freedom.

And a lightning bolt hit his heart.

Eduardo had told Callie to leave. He'd been the one who'd filed for divorce. He'd set her free, knowing she deserved better than a man who tried to control her, to spy on her, who wouldn't trust her.

But what if he could have just chosen to be a different man?

Eduardo stared at the flow of traffic on the busy street. What if his past didn't have to infect his future? What if he could choose a different life?

Hope rose like a wave inside his soul, no longer to be repressed. He'd set Callie free. But could he do the same for himself—be the man he wanted to be? The divorce wasn't final yet. Was there still time?

Could he ask her for a second chance?

Ask her to be his wife—not his prisoner, but his partner?

Gripping the photo, he whirled around, causing four construction workers to spit curses as he knocked past them on the sidewalk. Eduardo caught up with Sanchez just as his sedan was pulling from the curb. Yanking open the back door, Eduardo threw himself inside. "The airport!" he panted. "I need to see my wife—now!"

Sanchez gave him an enormous smile. "Yes, sir!"

He stomped on the gas, and Eduardo pulled out his phone to call Mrs. McAuliffe about the change in plans. Before he could, his phone rang in his hand. He saw Keith Johnson's number. Scowling, he turned the sound to Mute. But after he hung up with Mrs. McAuliffe, as the car crossed the George Washington Bridge, his phone buzzed again. Looking down, he saw his lawyer's number and a chill went down his spine.

His lawyer.

Did that mean...

Could it be...

Eduardo narrowed his eyes. No. As the phone stopped, then urgently started to vibrate a second time, Eduardo rolled down the window, and tossed it into the Hudson.

It wasn't too late for him to change. He wouldn't let it be.

He made it to the airport as his jet was warming up, and took his place on the jet bound for North Dakota. Refusing his surprised flight attendant's offer of his usual martini, Eduardo paced back and forth across the cabin for hours, planning what he would say to Callie. He tried to write down his feelings then finally gave up in disgust. He would pray that once he saw her, he'd know what to say.

Sitting restlessly in the white leather seat by the window, he felt like a jangle of nerves. Wishing the jet could go faster, he looked down through the wispy clouds and watched the green rolling hills of the East Coast slowly transform to the flat, brownish landscape of the northern prairies.

When they finally landed at the tiny airport outside of Fern, his legs were shaking as he went down the steps to the tarmac. The airport was just like he remembered when he'd visited so long ago, the day Callie had come to meet him as the local office liaison. But this time, he had no staff. He was alone.

Eduardo had forgotten what it was like to exist without layers of employees and servants insulating him from the real world. He felt clumsy, trying to remember how to do things himself, with no assistants. No bodyguards. On impulse, he stopped at the airport's single shop to buy Callie some flowers and an eight-dollar box of chocolates. The place was deserted, and it took five long minutes before the salesclerk even noticed he was there, and came out from the back to ring up his order.

But Eduardo didn't chew him out. He didn't try to throw his weight around. He no longer wanted to rule this town. He wanted to fit in. He was suddenly desperate to be part of Callie's world, if only she would let him.

He didn't go completely unnoticed. At the car rental counter, the female clerk looked at his face, then his credit card. Her jaw fell open, and her gum almost fell out of her mouth.

"Eduardo Cruz?" she said faintly. "*The* Eduardo Cruz? The owner of Cruz Oil?"

"Don't hold it against me." Impatient as he was to find Callie, he gave her his best attempt at a grin. "I, um, seem to have lost my phone. Do you happen to know the way to the Woodville farm? Walter and Jane Woodville's place?"

"Of course I know it." The young woman chewed her gum thoughtfully. "At the corner of Rural Route 12 and Old County Road. I went to school with their daughter." Her eyes darkened. "I saw her driving around in the Rolls-Royce yesterday...."

"Thank you. She's the one I came to see—"

"But she's not at home," she said. "I'm sorry to tell you this if you're a friend, but she was in an accident. A car accident."

Eduardo nearly staggered back. "What?"

"That car was smashed right up," she said sadly.

Car accident. Memories went through him of when he'd heard of his mother's death in a smash-up on a treacherous road on the Costa del Sol. An icicle of stark fear went down his spine. "You are mistaken," he said faintly. "That car is very safe...."

"Some kids were riding bicycles in the middle of the road. Her fiancé swerved, and the car smashed straight into a telephone pole. She's in critical condition at County General...."

Eduardo reached across the counter, his eyes wild. "Who's her fiancé? Who is he?"

"Brandon McLinn..."

He didn't wait to hear more. He grabbed a map off the counter.

"Mr. Cruz, I really am sorry—"

Running to his rental car, he drove for the hospital, racing down the highway at a hundred miles an hour. If he got pulled over by a policeman, he knew he'd go to jail. But he didn't give a damn.

He couldn't lose her. Not now...

Anguish gripped his throat. He could have been with her all this time. He could have been chasing her the last two months, trying to make her forgive him, trying to be the man she deserved. Instead he'd let her go. Why couldn't he have just treated her right from the beginning? Why had he wasted so much time trying to control their lives? Control was the illusion, not love. There was no such thing as perfect safety. No such thing as perfect control. You couldn't make someone love you. And even if you did, you couldn't make it last forever.

People left. People died.

But love endured. He could choose to love Callie with

all his heart and strength, love her with full knowledge of both her flaws and his own; love her with every ounce of his being until the day he died. That was his choice.

He'd once told her that love changed nothing. It was wrong. It changed everything.

Clutching the steering wheel, he prayed he'd reach her in time. Callie had to be all right. His daughter couldn't grow up without a mother. He couldn't live without his wife.

The afternoon sunlight cast the waving fields in a golden glow beneath the wide blue skies. He increased his speed to a hundred and twenty, as fast as the little rental car would go along the empty highway.

Don't leave me, Eduardo begged soundlessly. *Don't leave me.*

CHAPTER TWELVE

IT HAD been a horrible night. And a very long day.

Callie rose achingly from the chair by her sister's hospital bed. She needed coffee or fresh air. She was still wearing the same purple sweatpants and T-shirt from yesterday, with her hair pulled back in a ponytail. They'd all been awake through the night, and now, in late afternoon, everyone had collapsed with exhaustion. Brandon was curled up in a chair on the other side of Sami's bed, and Jane and Walter had fallen asleep on the couch, her mother's head on her father's shoulder, and baby Marisol snoring loudly against her grandpa's chest.

Callie quietly left the hospital room. Once she was safely in the hallway, she took a deep breath and sagged back against the door, covering her face with her hands. It was all her fault. If she hadn't given them the car they wouldn't have taken the detour through town. They wouldn't have been in the accident.

Tears burned Callie's eyes. But the crisis was past. Her sister would recover.

She was grateful beyond measure, but the tears weren't just out of gratitude. Callie had a good reason to feel an extra dose of anguish today. A private reason of her own...

She closed her eyes. She missed Eduardo so much. His handsome face. His glowing dark eyes. And his voice. She could almost hear it now, rough with an edge of Spanish accent.

"Where's my wife? Where is she, damn you?" The man's voice echoed down the hallways of the small hospital. "I want to see her *now*!"

She knew that voice. She still dreamed about it every night. Slowly Callie turned.

And saw Eduardo arguing at the nurses' station down the hall. His black hair was rumpled, and so was his suit. She'd never seen him so disheveled before, so completely out-of-place, so handsome and powerful and everything she'd ever wanted.

"Eduardo," she choked out.

At the end of the hall, he turned and saw her. With a sob, she started toward him at a run, in the same instant he started running for her.

They fell into each other's arms, and it was only when Callie actually felt him, strong and solid beneath her hands, that she knew for sure it wasn't a dream. She felt his protective, steadying arms around her and all the fear and shock of the last twenty-four hours fell away. She no longer had to be strong for her family. She burst into tears.

"Callie, Callie," he whispered fervently, kissing her forehead. "You're all right. Thank God, you're all right."

Pulling back, he looked down at her, his eyes glistening suspiciously in the hospital's fluorescent lights. Then he wrapped his powerful arms around her tightly, holding her as if he never wanted to let her go. Callie exhaled for the first time in two months, weeping with the joy of being again in his arms.

"You're safe," he breathed, stroking her hair as she pressed her face against his chest. "Safe."

Wiping her eyes, she looked at him in confusion. "But

what are you even doing here? I thought you were in New York?"

"Would you believe me if I said I was in the neighborhood?"

She smiled weakly.

"I, um, brought you some flowers and candy." Looking around, he cursed softly. "They are here somewhere…"

"Oh. Right." Her heart dropped. With all the worry about her sister's accident, she'd forgotten his week started today. She said dully, "You're here for Marisol."

Eduardo stared at her, his dark eyes infinite and deep as the ocean. "I'm here for you." He took her hands in his own. "Come back to me, Callie. Give me one more chance."

"What?" she breathed.

"Be my wife. Let me be your partner, by your side. Let me spend the rest of my life loving you. And striving to deserve your love in return."

Her voice caught in her throat. "I…"

He gave her an unsteady smile. "I'm too late, aren't I?"

"Too late?"

He looked past her ear. "You've moved on."

Turning around, she saw Brandon peeking out of her sister's door, his face questioning before he ducked back. Frowning, Callie turned back at Eduardo. "What are you talking about?"

"The girl at the car rental counter told me about your accident. She also told me that you're engaged. You and Brandon." His eyes were bleak as he tried to smile. "I guess I should offer my congratulations."

Callie nearly staggered back with shock.

"You don't know," she whispered. Sudden rising joy filled her heart, choking her with hope. "The engagement announcement was on my mom's web page days ago. It was even in the newspaper this morning. But *you don't know*."

Eduardo shook his head, his jaw tight, his eyes forlorn. "I fired my investigator two months ago. Told my lawyers not to talk about you. I even threw away my phone."

"Your *phone*?"

"I was mad at it." He gave her a small smile. "I still do some stupid things. But my therapist says there's hope…"

"Your therapist!" she cried, nearly falling over in shock.

"Talking about the past has helped me understand the choices I've made as an adult. And why I was so afraid to love you." He took a deep breath. "Because I do love you, Callie. So much." He looked down at the green cracked tiles of the floor. "Brandon is…he is a good man. I know he'll make you happy."

Moving closer, she reached up and lifted his chin. "Brandon and I aren't together. He's engaged to my sister."

Slowly Eduardo lifted his head. Shock filled his expression, followed by savage joy. "Your sister?"

"I gave them the car yesterday and she was hurt in the crash." She pressed her lips together. "We were worried. For a few hours last night the doctors weren't sure she'd make it. She lost a lot of blood. But she came out of surgery this morning and the doctors say she'll be fine. She just needs a lot of rest."

"Thank God." He hugged her close and whispered, "So she's engaged to Brandon. I always knew I liked her."

She pressed her cheek against his shirt, and her tears made the fabric wet as she sniffled. "Ever since it happened, all I could think about was that I wished you were here. So you could hold me and tell me that everything would be all right."

"Oh, *querida*." For a long moment, he held her tightly then he looked down at her. "I know I'm selfish and ruthless and occasionally a jerk. There will be times in the future you'll want to punch me. But give me one more chance to love you. Just say the word," he vowed, "and I will never again leave your side."

She started to speak, but he put his finger to her lips. "Before you give your answer," he whispered, "let me finish my argument...."

Lowering his mouth to hers, he kissed her in an embrace so pure and breathless and true that it left her in no doubt of his love for her, and so passionate it left her dizzy and swaying in his arms.

She looked up at him.

"Stay with me, Eduardo," she breathed, blinking back tears. "Don't ever go."

His dark eyes lit up with joy. "Callie—"

"I love you," she whispered, and he kissed her again, so long and hard that several members of the hospital staff cleared their throats and made loud comments suggesting they *get a room* before Eduardo finally pulled away.

"I wish I'd done things differently from the start," he said against her hair. "That I'd given you a real wedding, and asked your father for your hand..." He snorted, his eyes twinkling as he confessed, "Do you know I actually tried to write you a poem on the flight here?"

"You did?"

"A love poem."

"A love poem from the great Eduardo Cruz." Giggling, Callie shook her head. "Now that is something I really, really want to read."

"Not in this lifetime. You'd laugh yourself silly."

"I could do with a laugh." Callie put her hand on his hard, rough cheek, then slowly traced down his throat, to linger against his chest. "And we both know you'll give it to me sooner or later."

She felt him shiver beneath his touch. "Yes," he said huskily. "I will." He took a deep breath as he cupped her face. "I will give you everything. Everything I have. Everything I am. Both the good and bad."

"For better or for worse." Rising on her tiptoes, she kissed him again, in clear and complete defiance of the hospital staff. She felt the hard, satin strength of his lips, felt the heat of his tongue brush against her own. She wanted to kiss him forever. And she could. She was his wife....

Callie pulled back with a horrified gasp, her eyes wide.

"What is it, *querida*?"

"I signed the divorce papers yesterday!" she wailed. She gave a choked sob as she threw her arms around him. "Oh, Eduardo. We're divorced!"

He blinked then slow joy lifted his handsome features, like the rise of the first spring dawn after endless cold winter. He gave a low laugh. Lifting her chin, he stroked her tears away with the pads of his thumbs. "Oh, my love. That's the best news you could have given me."

She blinked in shock. "It—is?"

"Of course it is." He smiled down at her, then leaning forward, he whispered, "This time we're going to do it right."

It was a warm evening in late July as Callie stepped out of her parents' farmhouse to the porch, where her father was waiting in the twilight.

Walter Woodville turned then gasped as he saw his eldest daughter in her wedding gown. "You look beautiful, pumpkin."

Callie looked down shyly at the 1950s-style, tea-length gown in ivory lace. "Thanks to Mom. She did the alterations from Grandma's dress."

"Your Mama always makes everything beautiful. And so do you." Tears rose to his eyes as he whispered, "I'm so proud to be your father." His voice was suspiciously rough. Clearing his throat, he held out his arm. "Are you ready?"

She walked with him the short distance across the gravel driveway. The rising moon glowed across the wide ocean of her father's barley fields. The night was quiet and magical. Fireflies glowed through the sapphire night. As they went toward the barn, she could hear the cicadas at a distance, but even their eerie singing wasn't enough to drown the loud drumbeat of her heart.

Clutching her father's arm with one hand, and a bouquet of bright pink Gerbera daisies in the other, Callie looked back at the farmhouse. Her childhood home was a little careworn, with yellow paint peeling in spots. But it was snug and warm and full of good memories. She looked at the swing on the porch, at her mother's red flowers in pots. So many memories. So much love.

"I just hope we do everything right," she whispered.

Her father smiled. "You won't."

"Then I hope we do half as well as you and Mom."

He put his hand over hers, his craggy face sparkling with tears. "You will. You two were made for each other. He's a good one," he said gruffly.

Callie resisted the urge to laugh. Her father had a new appreciation for Eduardo since their three days up at the fishing cabin in Wisconsin. Any man who could face Callie's father, her four uncles and six male cousins, and Brandon, all with guns and hunting bows, was clearly man enough to be Walter's son-in-law. The way Eduardo had humbly asked permission for his daughter's hand in marriage hadn't hurt, either.

Somehow, even Brandon and Eduardo had managed to bury the hatchet. The story she heard afterward was a bit muddled, but apparently while they were at the cabin Brandon had nearly shot Eduardo in the foot with his hunting rifle. Callie was rather dubious about how this equaled friendship, but afterward the two men had drunk beer around the campfire. "Marrying you two Woodville sisters, we realized we needed to be allies," Eduardo said with a grin, and Callie wasn't sure whether she should be offended or not.

Eduardo had won Jane's approval even more easily, simply through his vigorous appreciation for her cooking and fruit pies. "Although," her mother had said coyly, "a few more grandchildren wouldn't hurt."

Eduardo had looked at Callie with a wicked grin, even as his voice said meekly, "Yes, ma'am."

At the thought, Callie's eyes welled up. She was finally sure about a question that had distracted her for days. She could hardly wait to tell Eduardo...

"Don't cry!" her father said, aghast. He pulled a handkerchief from his coat to dab at the corner of her eye. "Your mother would never forgive me if she thought I said something that smeared your makeup."

"I'm not crying," Callie wept. Blinking back tears of his own, he patted her hand and led her past the outdoor reception area, which had a temporary dance floor lit up by torches and surrounded by coolers full of beer and the finest champagne. They reached the barn, and Callie stood in the huge open doorway in her wedding gown beside her father, who was beaming with pride.

The music on the guitar changed to an acoustic version of the Bridal March. All at once, her friends and family rose from the benches used as makeshift pews, gasping as they stared at Callie.

But she had eyes only for Eduardo.

He stood at the end of the aisle, handsome in a vintage

suit. His dark eyes lit up when he saw her, and he looked dazzled. He was flanked by the best man and maid of honor, who themselves were planning to wed in just two months' time. Sami's leg still hadn't completely healed, and she used a crutch, but she glowed with happiness. So did Brandon, every time he looked at her. He'd cheered Sami throughout her hospital stay by talking about the small farm they would buy once they wed, using the insurance check from the wrecked Rolls-Royce. Callie felt a lump in her throat as she looked at two of the people she loved most in the world, who were both happy at last.

And so was she.

Today, she would marry her best friend. But Eduardo wasn't just her best friend. He was her soul mate, her lover, the man she trusted, the father of her child. The man she wanted to sleep with every night. The man she wanted to wake up to every morning. The man she wanted to fight with, to make love to. The man she wanted to yell at and laugh with. The man she wanted to love for the rest of her life. Her partner.

"Dearly beloved," the parson began, "we are gathered here today…"

As he spoke the magical words that would make them once again man and wife, Callie looked at her once and future husband. Swaying lanterns glowed above them in vivid colors as Eduardo looked down at her. Love illuminated his chiseled, angular face. His dark eyes were deep with devotion.

"Who gives this woman to be married to this man?"

"Her mother and I do," Walter said, and Callie heard the tremble beneath his rough voice, felt the shake of his burly arm as he handed her over to Eduardo's keeping. Kissing her father's cheek, Callie smiled down at her mother in the front row, who held baby Marisol in her lap.

As the parson spoke the wedding homily, Callie listened to the soft wind against the barley. She heard the creak of the old barn around them as Eduardo spoke his wedding vows, and the low timbre of his voice reverberated through her soul. She felt the strength of his powerful, gentle hand as he slid a plain gold band on her finger, simple and special and eternal. Just like their growing family.

Callie hid a smile. She could hardly wait to tell him that he wasn't just becoming her husband again, but a father again, too. Their baby was due in February. Perhaps she would whisper the news in his ear during their first dance, while they swayed together surrounded by flickering torches, beneath a sky so wide it stretched forever. Maybe they'd spend the summer here, autumn in New York, winter in Spain. Their love crossed oceans. But when it was time for her baby to be born, she knew there was only one place she wanted to be. Home.

And as she looked up at Eduardo, that's exactly where she was. In his arms, she was home. No matter where their lives took them.

"And do you, Calliope Marlena Woodville, take this man to be your lawfully wedded husband, for better or for worse, for richer or for poorer, to love and cherish from this day forward, until death do you part?"

In the breathless hush, Callie glanced back at her baby, at her family and friends in the old barn. It was exactly like she'd always imagined it would be. Closing her eyes, Callie took a deep breath, remembering all the impossible dreams she'd had as a girl.

Then, opening her eyes, Callie turned back to Eduardo, and spoke the two words that made all those dreams come true.

* * * * *

A Night of Living Dangerously

JENNIE LUCAS

CHAPTER ONE

"Is someone here?"

The man's voice was harsh, echoing down the dark halls. Clapping a hand over her mouth, Lilley Smith cut herself off mid sob and ducked back farther into the shadows. It was Saturday evening, and except for the security guards in the lobby downstairs, she'd thought she was alone in the twenty-floor building. Until five seconds ago, when she'd heard the elevator ding and she'd dashed into the nearest private office to hide, dragging her file cart willy-nilly behind her.

Stretching out her foot, Lilley silently nudged the door closed. She wiped her puffy, tearstained eyes, trying not to make a sound as she waited for the man in the hall to leave so she could cry in peace.

Her day had been so horrible it was almost funny. Coming home that morning from an unfortunate, one-time-only attempt at jogging, she'd found her boyfriend in bed with her roommate. Then she'd lost her fledgling dream business. Finally, calling home for comfort, she'd been disinherited by her father. An impressive day, even for her.

Normally it would have bothered Lilley that she'd had to catch up with work on the weekend *again*. Today it didn't even register. She'd worked as a file clerk for Caetani Worldwide for two months, but it still took her twice as long as Nadia, the other file-room clerk, to get her files sorted, delivered and returned.

Nadia. Her co-worker, roommate and, as of this morning, former best friend. Exhaling, Lilley leaned back against her cart as she remembered the stricken look in Nadia's face as she'd tumbled out of bed with Jeremy. Covering herself with a robe, Nadia had cried and asked Lilley for forgiveness as Jeremy tried to make their betrayal sound like Lilley's fault.

Lilley had fled the apartment and gone straight for the bus downtown. Lost, desperate for comfort, she'd called her father for the first time in three years. That hadn't gone too well either.

Thank heaven for work. This job was all she had now. But when would the stranger in the hallway leave? When? She couldn't let him—or anyone—see her like this—with red puffy eyes, working at a snail's pace as every single letter and number shimmered and moved back and forth on the files. Who was the man, and why wasn't he dancing and drinking champagne at the charity ball with everyone else?

Lilley shivered. She'd never been in this office before, but it was cavernous and cold, with stark, expensively appointed furnishings of dark wood, a gorgeous Turkish carpet and floor-to-ceiling windows that revealed twilight across downtown San Francisco and the bay beyond. Her head slowly tilted back to view the frescoed ceilings. It was an office fit for a king. Fit for...

Fit for a prince.

Lilley's lips parted. Panic ripped through her as she realized for the first time whose office this had to be. She gave a terrified little squeak.

The office door creaked open. Lilley reacted on pure instinct, throwing herself through the shadows into the nearest closet.

"Who's in here?" The man's voice was harsh and low.

Heart pounding, she peered through the gap in the door. She saw the hulking silhouette of the stranger's broad-shouldered body in the dim light of the hall, blocking her only avenue of escape.

She covered her mouth with her hands, realizing she'd left her file cart behind the black leather sofa. All the man had to do was turn on the light and he'd see it. Being caught sobbing in the hallway would have been humiliating. Being caught skulking in the CEO's office would be a career-destroying disaster!

"Come out." The man's footstep was heavy on the floor. "I know you're in here."

Her heart stopped in her chest as she recognized that husky, accented voice. It wasn't some random janitor or junior assistant who was about to catch her. It was the CEO himself.

Tall, dark and broad-shouldered, Prince Alessandro Caetani was a self-made billionaire, the CEO of a luxury conglomerate that reached to every corner of the globe. He was also a ruthless playboy. All the women who worked in his San Francisco regional headquarters, from the youngest secretary to the fifty-something female vice president, were madly in love with him.

And now he was about to catch Lilley alone in his office.

Trying not to breathe, she backed farther into his closet, pressing her body behind his jackets, against the back wall. His suits smelled of sandalwood and musk and power. She closed her eyes, praying the prince would turn and leave. For once in her life, she prayed her skill at being invisible to men would actually pay off.

The door was ripped open. The jackets were shoved aside

as a large hand ruthlessly grabbed her wrist. She gave a little shriek as he pulled her out of the closet.

"I've got you now," he growled. He switched on a lamp, and a circle of golden light filled the dark, cavernous office. "You little…"

Then he saw her, and his black eyes widened with surprise. Lilley sucked in her breath as, against her will, she looked straight into the face of her boss for the first time.

Prince Alessandro Caetani was the most handsome man she'd ever seen, from his muscular body beneath his black tuxedo to the cold expression in his dark eyes. His aristocratic Roman nose was offset by the slightly thuggish curve of his sharp, dark-shadowed jawline. He looked—and was, if the legends were true—half prince, half conqueror.

"I know you." Prince Alessandro frowned, looking puzzled in the soft glow of the lamplight. "What are you doing here, little mouse?"

Her wrist burned where he touched her, sending sparks up her arm and down the length of her body. "What—what did you call me?"

He abruptly dropped her wrist. "What is your name?"

It took her a minute to remember. "L-Lilley," she managed. "From the file room."

Prince Alessandro's eyes narrowed. He walked around her, slowly looking her up and down. Her cheeks went hot. Compared to his gorgeous perfection in his sleek, sophisticated tuxedo, she knew she was frumpy and frightful in her sweatshirt and gray baggy sweatpants. "And what are you doing here, Lilley from the file room? Alone in my office on a Saturday night?"

She licked her dry lips, trying to calm her shaking knees. "I was…was…" What had she been doing, anyway? Where was she? Who was she? "I was just…um…" Her eyes fell on the file cart. "Working?"

He followed her gaze, then lifted a dark eyebrow. "Why are you not at the Preziosi ball?"

"I...I lost my date," she whispered.

"Funny." His sensual mouth curved in a humorless smile. "That seems to be going around."

The sexy, deep, accented timbre of his voice moved over her like a spell. She couldn't move or look away from his masculine beauty as he towered over her, strong, powerful and wide-shouldered, with thighs like tree trunks.

Thighs? Who said anything about his *thighs*?

Ever since Jeremy had arranged her file-room job, Lilley had done her best to make sure her billionaire boss never noticed her. And now, beneath the prince's black, hypnotic gaze, she found herself suddenly wanting to blurt out why. She wasn't very good at telling lies, not even white ones. The hot, searing depths in Prince Alessandro's dark eyes whispered that she could tell him anything, anything at all, and he would understand. He would forgive and show mercy.

But she'd been around powerful men before. She recognized the intensity of his gaze for what it actually was: an emotional shakedown.

The ruthless playboy prince, show mercy? No way. If he knew about Lilley's father, about her *cousin,* he'd fire her. Or worse.

"Lilley," he mused aloud in the silent office. He tilted his head, and his eyes suddenly gleamed in the small circle of lamplight. "What is your last name?"

"Smith," she said honestly, then hid a smile. No help for him there.

"And what are you doing in my office, Miss Smith?"

The scent of him, sandalwood and musk and soap and something more—something uniquely *him*—washed over her. She gave an involuntary shiver. "Returning, um, files."

"You know my files go to Mrs. Rutherford."

"Yes," she admitted unhappily.

He moved closer. She could practically feel the warmth of his body through his crisp black tuxedo jacket. "Tell me why you're really here."

She swallowed, looking down at the expensive carpet beneath her old, scuffed jogging shoes. "I just wanted to work for a few hours in peace and quiet. Without anyone bothering me."

"On a Saturday night?" he said coldly. "You were searching my office. Going through my files."

She looked up. "No!"

Prince Alessandro folded his arms. His dark eyes were hard, his expression like chiseled stone.

"I was hiding," she said in a voice almost too soft to hear.

"Hiding?" His voice was silky. "Hiding from what?"

Against her will, the truth was ripped out of her. "From you."

His dark eyes sharpened. He leaned forward. "Tell me why."

Lilley could barely even breathe, much less think, with Prince Alessandro Caetani so close to her.

The soft golden glow of the lamp, the darkening twilight outside the windows filled the enormous, high-ceilinged office with deepening shadows. "I was crying," she whispered over the lump in her throat. "I couldn't stay at home, I'm days behind on my work, and I didn't want you to see me because I was crying!"

Struggling not to cry, Lilley looked away. If she wept in front of her powerful boss, her humiliation would be complete. He would fire her—whether for skulking in his office, for crying in such an unprofessional way, or for being so behind on her work, it hardly mattered. She would lose the last thing she valued. The perfect finale to the second-worst day of her life.

"Ah," he said softly, looking down at her. "At last, I understand."

Her shoulders sagged. He was going to tell her to gather her things and get out of his building.

The prince's gaze was full of darkness, an ocean at midnight, deep enough to drown in. "You were in love with him?"

"What?" Lilley blinked. "Who?"

The corners of his sensual mouth curved upward. "The man."

"What makes you think I was crying over a man?"

"Why else would a woman weep?"

She laughed, but the sound was almost like a sob. "Everything has gone wrong today. I thought I might be happier if I lost some weight. I tried to go for a jog. Big mistake." She looked down at her old running shoes, at her baggy sweatshirt and sweatpants. "My roommate thought I'd left for work. When I came back to the apartment I found her with my boyfriend. In bed."

Alessandro cupped her cheek. "I'm sorry."

Lilley looked up at him, shocked by his unexpected sympathy. Then her lips parted. Sparks spread from his touch, zinging from her earlobes to her scalp, down her neck and spine, causing heat to whirl like lightning across her skin. Her breasts felt strangely heavy, her nipples tightening beneath her workout bra.

His eyes narrowed in surprise. "But you're beautiful."

Beautiful? It was like a slap in the face. She ripped away. "Don't."

He frowned. "Don't what?"

His cruelty took her breath away. She blinked fast, glaring up at him. "I know I'm not beautiful. And it's fine. I know I'm not smart either, and I can live with that. But for you to stand there and taunt me like that…" She gripped her hands into fists. "It's not just *patronizing*, it's heartless!"

Alessandro looked down at her gravely, not saying a word. And Lilley sucked in her breath, realizing she'd just told off her boss.

She clasped her hands together. "I'm fired, right?" When he didn't reply, a shudder of grief went through her. Her hands shook as she picked up a file from the floor and reached for the metal cart. "I'll finish my work," she said miserably, "then collect my things."

He grabbed her arm, stopping her. "So a compliment is a taunt?" Staring down at her, he shook his head. "You're a strange girl, Lilley Smith."

The way Prince Alessandro was looking at her, for an instant she'd almost thought—but no. *Strange* was a code word for *helpless failure*. She said over the lump in her throat, "So my father has always told me."

"You're not fired."

She looked up at him with the first glimmer of hope. "I'm not?"

Leaning forward, he took the file from her hand and set it on top of the metal cart. "I have a different sort of penalty in mind."

"The guillotine?" she said weakly. "The electric chair?"

"You'll come with me to the ball tonight."

Her lips fell open. "W-what?"

His dark eyes were as warm as molten chocolate and hot as embers of fire. "I want you to be my date."

Lilley stared at him, her eyes wide, her heart pounding. Had she fallen into some strange dream? Prince Alessandro could have the most beautiful women on earth—and he'd already had quite a few of them, according to the celebrity tabloids. Frowning, she turned around to make sure

JENNIE LUCAS 15

he wasn't talking to some movie star or lingerie model behind her.

"Well, *cara?*" he said huskily. "What do you say?"

Lilley turned back. She felt dizzy from his attention, half-drunk beneath the intensity of his dark gaze. She said slowly, "I don't understand."

"What's to understand?"

Lilley cleared her throat. "I don't get the joke."

"I never joke."

"You don't? Too bad. I joke all the time," she said. "Usually by accident."

He didn't even smile. He just looked down at her, his face unmovable and oh, so handsome.

"You're serious?"

"Yes."

"But—it's the Preziosi di Caetani ball," she stammered. "The biggest charity event of the summer. The mayor will be there. The governor. The paparazzi."

"So?"

"So you could have any woman you want."

"And I want you."

His four simple words made Lilley's heart twist in her chest. She clasped her trembling hands together. "But you have a girlfriend. I've read—"

His expression hardened. "No."

"But Olivia Bianchi—"

"No," he said tersely.

Biting her lip, Lilley looked up at him. He wasn't telling her the whole truth. And the waves of danger emanating off his body nearly scorched her. If he found out who Lilley really was, she would lose her job—or possibly get dragged into court on charges of corporate espionage. Every instinct of self-preservation told her one thing: *Run.*

"Sorry," she said. "No."

His eyes widened. She'd clearly shocked him. "Why?"

She bit her lip. "My work—"

"Give me a real reason," he bit out.

A real reason? How about the fact that she was the daughter of a man he hated, and the cousin of another man he hated even more? Or the biggest reason of all: his strength, power and masculine beauty terrified her, making her heart pound and her body break out in a hot sweat? No man had ever had this effect on her, ever, and she didn't know what to do. Except run.

"My boyfriend…my ex-boyfriend," she stumbled, "will be at the ball tonight with my friend—Nadia. So you see I couldn't possibly go."

"He'll be at the ball?" Alessandro's eyes sharpened. "Do I know him—this man who made you weep?"

"He works in the Preziosi jewelry-design division."

His eyes gleamed. "All the more reason to go. When he sees you on my arm, he will remember your value and beg you to come back to him. You can accept his groveling or spurn him, as you choose. And the woman will suffer when she sees you as my date."

She stared up at him in amazement. "You don't have self-esteem issues, do you?"

He looked at her with an even gaze. "We both know it is true."

Lilley pressed her lips together, knowing he was right. If she went as his date, she would be the most envied woman in the city—possibly in all of California.

The thought of Nadia and Jeremy groveling at her feet and begging for forgiveness was a delicious one. All the times Lilley had worked late, all the times she'd asked Nadia to please explain to Jeremy and entertain him, and they'd betrayed her. She had no friends in this city now. None.

She lifted her eyes to Alessandro's. "I'm not a very good dancer."

He slowly looked her over. "I find that hard to believe."

"I took ballroom-dancing lessons as a kid, and my teacher asked me to quit. I was like one of those dancing elephants with tutus. All my boyfriends have complained about me stepping on their feet."

His expression changed, became softer. "Even if that were true," he murmured, "the fault would be your partner's, not yours. It is the man's responsibility to lead."

She swallowed. "Um. I...I never thought of that. I just assumed I was to blame."

"You assumed wrong," he said simply, then lifted his eyebrow. "But just out of curiosity, how many is all?"

"What?"

"*All* your boyfriends."

Oh heavens. She couldn't tell him her pathetic number. She lifted her chin and said with false bravado, "A few."

"Ten?" he persisted.

The heat in her cheeks deepened as her shoulders slumped. "Two," she confessed. "A boyfriend in high school, and..." A lump rose in her throat. "...and Jeremy."

"Jeremy. That is his name? The man who broke your heart?"

"He betrayed me." She looked at the floor. "But that's not what broke my heart."

He waited, but she did not explain. "So go out tonight. Your dancing skills are irrelevant, because we will not dance."

She looked up at him with a crooked grin. "Afraid of getting your toes stomped?"

"I do not dance."

Her eyes widened. "What—never?"

"No."

"But you're the sponsor of the Preziosi di Caetani ball!"

"It raises money for my favorite charity and gets good press for Caetani Worldwide," he said coldly. "That's what I care about. Dancing does not interest me."

"Oh," Lilley said uncertainly. She bit her lip. "I see."

But she didn't see at all. How could a man like Prince Alessandro, the heartthrob of women around the world, sponsor a ball and not dance? It didn't make sense.

He started to reach for her hand. "Come. We must hurry."

She backed away. She was afraid to let him touch her again, afraid of his strange power over her body. She gulped. "Why me?"

"Why *not* you?"

Setting her jaw, she folded her arms. "You're famous for many things, Prince Alessandro, but taking file clerks on charity dates isn't one of them."

He threw back his head and laughed. Turning, he went to the large modernist painting above his desk and swung it open to reveal a safe. Turning the combination to open the door, he pulled out two platinum and diamond cufflinks, then faced her with new intrigue. "You interest me, Lilley Smith. Not one woman in a thousand would have asked me why before saying yes."

"I guess I'm weird that way." She watched him put on his expensive cufflinks one at a time, saw the strength of his wrists and the sensual movement of his hands. He paused.

"My date for the ball fell through ten minutes ago."

"Miss Bianchi?"

"Yes."

She'd seen pictures of the Milanese heiress, who was blond, thin and beautiful—everything Lilley was not. She looked down. "I'm nothing like her."

"That makes you perfect," he said harshly. "Olivia will

learn how I respond to ultimatums. I need a date, and I found you in my office. It is fate."

"Fate," she whispered. He came back around his desk, his body a dark, powerful shadow. His eyes locked with hers.

"I need a date. You need revenge. This Jeremy will be on his knees for you before the night is through."

A low current went up her spine. No matter how much they'd hurt her, she knew revenge was wrong. And being close to Alessandro scared her. She wasn't just afraid for her job. He made her feel so...so strange.

"Why do you hesitate?" he demanded. "Are you in love with him?"

She shook her head. "It's just..."

"What?"

Swallowing, she turned away. "Nothing."

"I've watched you for weeks, little mouse, trying to avoid me."

Her lips parted in shock. "You saw me?"

He gave a single nod. "Scurrying the other way when you saw me in the halls. This type of behavior from a woman is very...singular. It puzzled me. But now I understand."

"You do?" she croaked.

He touched her cheek, forcing her to meet his eyes. "Most women I've met would have deserted their lovers in an instant to be with me. Loyalty is a rare quality. This man who betrayed you, he is a fool."

She couldn't argue with that. She stared up at him, mesmerized.

He dropped his hand. "But you have nothing to fear," he said simply. "Our romance will be only an illusion. I will not call you tomorrow. I will not call you ever. After tonight, you will again be just my employee, and I will be your boss, pretending not to notice as you avoid me in the shadows."

Lilley swallowed, still feeling his touch on her cheek. "You mean if I go with you to the ball tonight," she whispered, "you'll ignore me tomorrow? You'll ignore me forever?"

"Yes."

Lilley exhaled. She had to make him forget her existence. It was the only way to guarantee he wouldn't be curious enough to discover the omissions on her résumé. But in her heart of hearts, she knew that wasn't the only reason.

You're always running away, Lilley. Jeremy's stinging indictment rang in her ears. *You said you came to San Francisco to pursue your jewelry business and spend time with me. Instead you've avoided us both since the day you arrived here. Either you never really wanted me or the business, or you're the worst coward I've ever known.*

Lilley closed her eyes. That morning, she'd been too angry to listen to his words. Jeremy and Nadia had betrayed her, pure and simple. She'd done nothing wrong. Right?

Right?

But suddenly all she wanted to do was prove Jeremy wrong. To be one of the glamorous, carefree, fearless girls who wore sparkly clothes and danced, laughed and drank champagne. To be the girl courted by a knight in shining armor.

To be the girl who attended a ball with a prince.

She wasn't a coward. She wasn't. She could be as brave and ruthless as anyone. She could watch Prince Alessandro and learn!

Lilley opened her eyes. "I accept."

He looked down at her. "Do you understand, Lilley?" he said evenly. "It's not a real date. There will be nothing between us tomorrow. Absolutely nothing."

"Yeah, I get it," she said. "Monday I'll go back to the file room. You'll go back to Rome and probably Miss Bianchi, when you're done teaching her your little lesson. I'll continue to work for you and you'll never bother me again. Perfect."

He stared at her, then snorted a laugh, shaking his head. "You continue to surprise me, Lilley," he murmured, wrapping his hand around her waist. "Come. We haven't much time."

As he led her out of the office, she felt a rush of sensation from the heaviness of his arm around her. Trying to ignore the wobble of her knees, she glanced back at the file cart. "But I haven't finished my work—"

"It will be arranged."

"And I don't have a dress!"

His lips curved. "You will."

She looked up at him, annoyed. "Who am I, Cinderella? Are you supposed to be my fairy godmother? I'm not going to let you buy me a dress!"

In the hallway, he pushed the button to summon the elevator then took her hand in his own. "Of course you will." He gently pushed some strands of brown hair out of her eyes. "You will let me do exactly as I please, and I will give you an evening of pleasure. A beautiful gown, the envy of your coworkers and revenge against the people who betrayed you. It will be…an interesting night."

Lilley breathed in his scent of clean skin and sandalwood, of seduction and power. She felt his palm against her own, rough and hot, and her pulse quickened, sending shivers up and down her virgin body. "All right. Yes."

His dark eyes gleamed in the shadows of the hallway. "Yes?"

"Yes to the dress. To your help." She licked her lips and

gave him a trembling smile. "Yes to everything, your highness."

"Call me Alessandro." He lifted her hand to his mouth. She felt the press of his smooth, sensual lips and the heat of his breath against her skin, and gasped as fire raced up her arm and down the length of her body, igniting her like a match thrown into gasoline. "And women always do," he murmured.

She licked her lips, dazed. "What?"

He straightened. His dark eyes were hot as a smile curled his sensual lips.

"Say yes," he whispered. "To everything."

CHAPTER TWO

EVENING fog had rolled in, seeping beneath Alessandro's tuxedo as he stepped out of the limo onto the red carpet outside the hundred-year-old mansion on Nob Hill. It was August, but the fog was clammy and damp against his skin, a cold wet slap across the face.

Alessandro was grateful. A cold slap was exactly what he needed at the moment.

Flashbulbs of the waiting paparazzi popped around him as he heard Lilley's high heels clack against the concrete then step softly onto the red carpet behind him. Alessandro's body tightened. Overwhelming desire crackled through his blood, a shocking need that had begun the moment he'd gotten his first real look at her face in his office.

And now it was a hundred times worse. Just the drive in the limo had been almost unbearable, as he sat beside her. *He hadn't known she was so beautiful.*

He felt Lilley's graceful arm wrap around his, felt the light, gentle pressure of her hand against his forearm, felt the warmth of her touch through his tuxedo jacket.

With a shiver of desire, he looked down at her.

He'd noticed the mousy file clerk weeks ago. Rosy-cheeked and brown-haired, always wearing shapeless, unattractive dresses, she'd looked barely more than twenty and fresh from the country. After watching her veer away from him in a panic with her cart whenever their paths crossed, he'd been curious enough to have Mrs. Rutherford pull a copy of the girl's file. But he hadn't discovered anything very interesting there. She'd moved to San Francisco in June, and the file-room position was apparently her first job since working as a hotel housekeeper in Minneapolis a few years ago. Everything about her was forgettable, even her name.

Except that was no longer true.

Alessandro exhaled. He'd intended to teach Olivia she could be replaced with anyone, even an unfashionable, plump, plain file clerk, fresh from the farm. But the joke was on him, it seemed.

How come he'd never really seen Lilley Smith until today?

Unfashionable? A personal stylist at a luxury boutique had poured Lilley into a long, slinky red dress with spaghetti straps. Backless and daringly low-cut, the red knit gown seemed to cling to her breasts, teasing a man's gaze, threatening at any moment to reveal too much.

Plump? The dress showed off the curves her baggy clothes had hidden. Her breasts and hips were generous and wide, her waist small. She had the shockingly feminine figure that used to drive men wild...and still did. The classic 1950s Marilyn Monroe curves that made any man break out in a sweat. A droplet formed on Alessandro's forehead just looking at her.

And plain? That was the biggest laugh of all. Alessandro had seen the rare beauty of her naked face up close in his office—but now, after Sergio's makeup and hair team had done their work, her loveliness was shocking. Kohl and mascara darkened her deep-brown eyes, and red lipstick highlighted the seductive curve of her full, generous mouth.

Lilley's long, light-brown hair tumbled seductively down her bare shoulders and naked back.

Alessandro had watched her for weeks from a distance, but it was only today that he'd finally seen Lilley Smith for what she truly was.

A beauty.

A sex kitten.

A *bombshell*.

As they walked down the red carpet towards the sweeping steps of the hundred-year-old Harts Mansion, the paparazzi went crazy, shouting questions.

"Where's Olivia? Did you two break up?"

"Who's the new girl?"

"Yeah, who's the sexy brunette?"

Alessandro gave them a half smile and a brusque wave. He was accustomed to being followed and photographed wherever he went, from his palace in Rome to his yacht in Sardinia to his North American headquarters in San Francisco. It was the price he paid for being successful and a bachelor. But as he led Lilley down the red carpet, her feet dragged behind him. He glanced down at her, and realized she was shaking.

"What is it?" he said beneath his breath.

"They're staring at me," she said in a low voice.

"Of course they're staring." Alessandro turned to her, brushing hair away from her eyes. "So am I."

"Just get me through this," she whispered, her beautiful brown eyes looking big and scared. His heart twisted strangely. Tucking her hand more securely around his arm, Alessandro led her swiftly down the red carpet, using his body to block the more aggressive photographers leaning over the ropes. Alessandro usually stopped for photographs—an unfortunate necessity to maximize publicity for the children's charity that would benefit tonight—but he knew Lilley would never manage. Ignoring the shouted questions and frustrated groans, he kept walking, leading her up the sweeping stairs to the shadowy columns of the portico.

Once they were inside the mansion's double doors, past security and into the golden, glittering foyer, Lilley exhaled. Her luminous eyes looked up at him with gratitude. "Thanks." She swallowed. "That was…not fun."

"No?" he said lightly. "Most women think otherwise. Most see it as a perk of dating me."

"Well, I don't." Lilley shuddered. She licked her lips, fidgeting with the low neckline of her tight red gown. "I feel like a dork."

Heat flashed through Alessandro. He wanted to touch everywhere her fingers were tugging, to rip the fabric off her body and cover those amazing breasts with his hands, to nibble and stroke and lick every inch of her.

No, he told himself angrily. He had three rules. No employees, no wives, no virgins. There were too many women in the world, all too easily possessed, to break those cardinal rules. Lilley was an employee. She was also brokenhearted and on the rebound. Too many complications. Too many risks. Lilley was off limits.

But then again…

Alessandro looked at the red fabric barely clinging to her breasts. Looked at the graceful curve of her neck, at the roses in her cheeks and her pale skin beneath thick waves of soft brown hair. He felt a rush of forbidden desire.

Maybe it was a stupid rule, he thought. Maybe taking an employee as his mistress was a great idea. Wasn't his HR department always telling him to promote from within?

Lilley's beautiful eyes looked miserable and vulnerable. "I look like an idiot, don't I?"

Didn't she realize her beauty? Why did she hide it? Why

didn't she use it to gain attention in the workplace to get ahead, as other women would have done?

Was it possible that she really didn't know how lovely she was? He narrowed his eyes. "You are beautiful, Lilley."

Looking up at him, she suddenly scowled, her lovely expression peeved. "I told you never to call me that—"

"You are beautiful," he said harshly, cupping his hand against her soft cheek. He searched her gaze. "Listen to me. You know the kind of man I am. The kind, you said, who would never take a girl on a charity date. So why would I lie? You are beautiful."

The anger slid from her face. She suddenly looked bewildered and innocent and painfully shy. He could read her feelings in her face, something else he found shocking. It was an act—right? It had to be. She couldn't be that young.

He'd been open-hearted and reckless too, long ago. He remembered it like some long-forgotten dream. Perhaps that was why he felt strangely, unexpectedly protective.

He didn't like it.

"You really—" Lilley stopped herself, then bit her lip. "You really think I'm pretty?"

"Pretty?" he demanded, amazed. Lifting her chin, he tilted her head up towards the light shining from the foyer's glittering chandelier. "You are a *beauty,* little mouse."

She stared up at him, then her lips suddenly quirked. "You keep calling me that. Can't you just call me Lilley?"

"Sorry." His lips curved. "It's a habit. It was my name for you, when I was blind."

Lilley's brown eyes sparkled as a smile lit up her face. "So in one breath you tell me I'm beautiful, and in the next you tell me you're blind?"

Her smile was so breathtaking that it caught at his heart.

"Your beauty would make any man blind, *cara,*" he said huskily. "I told you that you'd be envied if you came with me to the ball. I was wrong. *I* will be the one envied to-night."

Her eyes grew big, her dark eyelashes sweeping wide against her pale skin. "Huh. You're not so bad at this complimenting stuff." Her smile lifted into a wicked grin. "Has anyone ever told you that?"

Against his will, Alessandro grinned back at her, and as their eyes locked a seismic tremble raced through his body. How was it possible that he'd ever thought of Lilley as an invisible brown sparrow?

From the instant he'd seen her pushing her little filing cart down the hall, why hadn't he immediately seen her beauty? Lilley's combination of sweetness and tartness, her innocent eyes and lush, sexy curves, caused a spasm of need deeper than his body, down to some fundamental part of his soul.

Soul? The word made his lip curl. *Soul.* What a ridiculous idea. Funny the tricks lust could play on a man's mind.

And he wanted her. Oh yes.

But he wouldn't let himself act on it. He was not a slave to lust. He was a grown man, the head of a worldwide company, and it was past time that he stopped chasing one-night stands and settled down. Olivia Bianchi would make a perfect princess, and when she inherited her father's designer-clothing business, Caetani Worldwide's reach would double in Europe. He did not love her, any more than Olivia loved him, but their union made sense. He'd nearly talked himself into proposing until she'd pulled that little stunt.

He should have expected Olivia's ultimatum. He'd been on the phone in his limo, en route to the office for his forgotten cufflinks, and he'd felt her simmering beside him in her black fur coat. The instant he'd ended the business call, Olivia had turned on him in angry, rapid-fire Italian.

"When are you going to propose, Alessandro? When?

I'm sick of waiting for you to decide. Make our engagement official, or find someone else to be your hostess at the charity ball!"

Five minutes later, he'd dropped Olivia off at her ritzy hotel. No woman, not even one as powerful and perfect as Olivia, would ever give him an ultimatum.

Now, as Alessandro led Lilley towards the ballroom of the Harts Mansion, he felt a rush of relief that he was still a free man. This was already proving to be the most enjoyable, surprising night he'd had in a long time.

Keeping Lilley close beside him, he paused at the landing on the top of the stairs, looking down into the ballroom. A hush fell beneath the soaring painted ceilings and enormous crystal chandeliers as hundreds of guests turned to stare up at them. Alessandro felt Lilley stiffen. She wasn't accustomed to being the center of attention, that was certain. She seemed to expect criticism, which he could not remotely understand.

"I can't tell you you're beautiful, because you'll hit me," he murmured. "But I know every man would kill to be in my place."

Her eyes flashed up at him, and he saw her lips quirk into a nervous smile. "Okay," she said in a low voice, bracing herself. "Let's go."

Alessandro led her down the stairs, where his board members, stockholders and friends waited. He spoke to each of them in turn, then moved across the ballroom, greeting the mayor, the governor, movie stars and visiting royalty by name. The men grinned and asked him for stock tips. The women flirted with him and tossed their hair. And they all gaped at Lilley beside him. None of the upper-level directors of Caetani Worldwide recognized her, he was positive, though they'd likely passed her many times in the hallways.

Insane to think he'd once been just as blind.

Speaking with each of his guests in turn, Alessandro thanked them for their donation to his favorite children's charity. He felt Lilley trembling beside him as if she wanted to take flight, and took her hand firmly in his own, pressing her forward with a gentle push against the naked skin of her lower back. Even that innocent, courteous touch was incredibly erotic. All he wanted to do was leave the gala ball and drag Lilley away to some quiet place. Perhaps his villa in Sonoma, which conveniently had ten bedrooms.

"Your highness," the head of the children's charity said breathlessly, looking up at him through her glasses with dazzled eyes, "won't you say a few words to start the bidding for the auction tonight?"

"Certainly," Alessandro said with a practiced smile. "I'll do it at once."

Gripping Lilley's hand, he crossed the ballroom towards the stage, and the crowds parted for them like magic. He felt her panic as he led her up the stairs, felt her small hand pulling desperately to be freed. It was only once they were behind the wings of the stage that he released her hand, looking down at her.

"Thanks for being my date tonight," he said huskily, and leaned forward to kiss her cheek. It was just an innocent, friendly kiss. Practically nothing. But when he pulled away, her eyes were huge.

His own lips burned where they'd touched her skin. For an instant, they just stared at each other. His blood roared in his ears, his heart pounding with the need to pull her into his arms and kiss her, really kiss her. He had to force himself to step back.

"Excuse me." Years of not showing feelings stood him in good stead. His voice was calm and even, betraying nothing of his tumult within. "This will take just a moment."

"Sure," she said faintly.

Leaving her in the wings, he walked to the microphone at the center of the stage. A hush fell across the ballroom, and Alessandro waited for the hearty cheer of the crowd which quickly followed. He was accustomed to being the center of attention, and far from being nervous, he was bored by it—all of it. There was only one thing that did not bore him right now, one thing that made his blood hum and his body come alive. One thing he wanted.

And he could not let himself have her.

Gripping the podium with his hands, he gave a speech, hardly knowing what he was saying. He could feel Lilley watching from the wings. His heartbeat was quick, his body hot with repressed desire.

"...and so I thank you, my friends," he finished. "Drink champagne, dance and bid high. Remember every penny raised tonight goes to help children in need!"

The cheer across the ballroom was even louder. With an absentminded wave, he left the podium and went straight back to Lilley, who looked as if she'd recovered her senses and was now staring at her watch, keeping time.

"Six minutes." She looked up at him with quirked lips. "I'm impressed. Usually speeches given by important men last for at least an hour. You're fast."

He gave her a lazy smile, then leaned forward to whisper, "I'm slow where it counts."

Alessandro had the satisfaction of seeing her shiver. That was some solace, at least—knowing she was as aware of him as he was of her. It amazed him, how Lilley hid nothing of her feelings. So young, he thought in wonder, so reckless and unrestrained. It reminded him of what he'd once been like himself, before he'd been betrayed. Like her, he'd once been young and hopeful, poor and driven to succeed...

Poor? The sparkle of Lilley's watch caught his eye, and he grabbed her wrist. "What's this?"

She tried to pull her wrist from his grasp. "Nothing."

In the background, he could hear the orchestra start a waltz. He was dimly aware of guests going out to the dance floor. "It's platinum. Diamonds. I don't recognize the brand."

"Hainsbury," she said in a small voice.

Hainsbury's. The damned discount jewelry chain that had recently tried—and failed—to execute a hostile take-over of Caetani Worldwide, solely in order to acquire the cachet of his luxury jewelry brand, Preziosi di Caetani. His eyes narrowed. "Who gave it to you?"

She swallowed. "My mother."

He told himself it was entirely reasonable that someone from the Midwest might own a Hainsbury watch. It was a coincidence, nothing more. His endless battles with the Count of Castelnau, his crafty, vicious French rival, were making him paranoid. He looked at Lilley's face. Clearly he was losing his mind to be suspicious of a girl like this.

"Nice," he said casually, dropping her wrist. "I wouldn't have recognized it. It looks nothing like their usual factory-made junk."

Looking away, she wrapped her hand around her wrist. Her voice was awkward. "My mother had it specially made."

He'd embarrassed her, Alessandro thought. Drawing attention to her Hainsbury-brand watch at a ball sponsored by the far more prestigious Preziosi di Caetani. "Whoever made it, your watch is truly exquisite." He smiled down at her and changed the subject. "Had enough of the ball? Ready to leave?"

"Leave?" Her lips parted. "We just got here!"

"So?" he said impatiently.

She glanced uneasily towards the dance floor. "People are waiting to talk to you."

"They already have my money."

"It's not just a question of money. They clearly want you. Your time and attention." She gave him a sudden crooked smile. "Though heaven knows why. I've yet to see your charm myself."

He gave her a sensual smile. "Do you want me to try harder?"

Her eyes widened and he heard her intake of breath. She muttered, "I'm no good at this."

"To the contrary."

She shook her head. "Forget it. Just don't try to charm me, all right? There's no point, and it might...I mean...we're just using each other tonight. Leave it at that."

Alessandro's gaze fell to her trembling lips. "Right. You're here for revenge. You haven't seen him yet, have you?"

"No." Her voice was quiet.

"He will fall on his knees when he sees you," Alessandro said roughly. "Come."

Grabbing her hand, he led her off the stage and across the dance floor, tracing through the crowds of swaying, laughing couples. Once, Alessandro would have been the first man on the dance floor. He would have pulled Lilley into his arms and moved her against his body in the music's seductive rhythm. But he hadn't danced for sixteen years now. Crossing the floor, he didn't even pause.

The charity director waited for him on the other edge of the dance floor. She beamed at him, gushing thanks and praise, and Alessandro accepted her gratitude with as much grace as he could manage. He was glad to help the charity, but the long line of guests that instantly formed, people waiting to thank him and shake his hand, seemed endless. Almost beyond endurance. He wanted to grab Lilley's hand and jump into his car, and not stop until they were completely alone, away from the crowds of reaching hands and yearning eyes.

But there were some duties from which neither royalty nor wealth excused a man. Standing on the edge of the dance floor like a king holding court, he endured the long queue of wealthy donors and powerful people as best as he could. As solace, he pulled Lilley to stand in front of him, wrapping his arms around her as if he were a child with a comforting blanket.

Except he was no longer a child, and Alessandro had a grown man's idea of comfort. Throughout the endless small talk he found himself distracted by the way her full breasts felt, pressed against his arms. He allowed himself one glance down, and saw that her low neckline barely covered the indecent swell of her breasts. He could see the shape of pebbled nipples though the red knit fabric. It was just as he'd suspected—she wasn't wearing a bra. And he wasn't the only man to notice. All the eyes of the male guests waiting to talk to him lingered long upon her, and Alessandro felt an urge to growl at them.

He was long past hard. He had the sudden bright idea of writing the charity a ten-million-dollar check, if it meant he could leave this ball and take her straight to bed.

He shouldn't. He couldn't. Sex with Lilley was a bad idea on every level. She was his employee, possibly in love with another man, and she was right—they were using each other tonight for mutual gain. He'd told her that straight out. A cheap one-night stand would only end in her recriminations, tears and perhaps a sexual-harassment lawsuit.

But with every passing moment, his self-restraint was growing frayed. Feeling her in his arms right now he felt oddly alive in a way he hadn't experienced in years. She made him feel…young again. As if he still had a beating heart.

And *that* was her biggest danger of all. He couldn't seduce her. He had to send her away. Had to—

Lilley glanced back at him, her lips parted. He saw the tip of her pink tongue dart out to the edge of her mouth and he nearly groaned. He wanted to taste those lips. Plunder her mouth with his. He wanted to rip the clingy red dress off her body, to spread her across his bed, to push himself inside her, to fill her hard and deep—

Basta. He broke out into a hot sweat. As the ambassador droned on to him about the fluidity of Asian exchange rates, all Alessandro could think was that it was a good thing Lilley was standing in front of him, blocking others' view of his trousers. Where was his self-control?

In front of him, Lilley stiffened. For a moment, Alessandro wondered if she'd felt his desire for her—how could she not? Then he saw she was looking over the crowd.

"Jeremy," she said in a low voice.

For a moment, Alessandro couldn't remember what she was talking about. Then his insides burned. He felt envious of this employee in his jewelry-design department, this man who'd had her at his command and let her go.

"Excuse us," he said to the people surrounding them. Ignoring their protests, he pulled Lilley to a quiet corner next to a window.

"Where is he?" he said, keeping his expression impassive.

"Over there."

He followed her gaze. His eyes narrowed in the desire to see this paragon but no one stood out to him at all. He felt irritated. *Irritated* wasn't a strong enough word. *Jealous?* No, impossible. Jealousy was for the weak, for sad, vulnerable men who served their hearts on platters to be shredded and devoured.

So he didn't feel jealous. He felt...annoyed. *Sì.* Annoyed.

He'd said he would help Lilley get the man back. Now he regretted his promise. Why should he help another, less-deserving man get what he himself wanted—Lilley in his bed?

But if Lilley truly loved this Jeremy, Alessandro would do the honorable thing. He would step aside with the noble self-sacrifice of a damned saint.

"Va bene," he ground out. "If you still want this idiot, this imbecile without a shred of sense or loyalty, I will help you win him."

Lilley flashed him a grin. "Um. You're too kind?"

"Just tell me one thing," he demanded.

"Only one?"

His fingers moved down her shoulders, stroking down the warm, bare skin of her back. He saw her eyes widen, felt her shiver and he fought back the urge to yank her body hot and hard against his own. "Why would you want him back, after he made you weep?"

Her smile fell. She took a deep breath, then lifted her left wrist. "Look at this."

A change of subject? He looked down at the bracelet on her wrist. He'd noticed it earlier, a pastiche of welded materials—colorful crystals on a brass chain, interspersed with rusty-looking numbers and held together with a tarnished buckle. "What about it?"

"I made it."

He grabbed her wrist, narrowing his eyes and tilting his head as he tried to make sense of the bracelet. He pointed to the metal number dangling off the chain. "What's that?"

"A room number from an eighteenth-century Parisian hotel."

It seemed strange to him, an artistic hodgepodge of junk. "How do you source the materials?"

"At flea markets and vintage shops, mostly. I create jewelry using old things I find." She swallowed. "I met Jeremy at San Francisco's trade show a few months ago, when my employer thought I was visiting my family. Jeremy loved my jewelry. We decided to be partners and open a boutique together. He was going to handle the financials. I would create the inventory." She blinked fast, and looked away. "When he chose my roommate over me, I lost that dream."

He could see her eyes were shiny with tears, and his insides gave a little twist. "The man's a damned fool," he said roughly. He tried to think of how to comfort her. "Perhaps it's for the best," he tried. "Running a business is a huge risk. You might have lost your investment. People don't want old trinkets. They want their jewelry shiny and new."

Her lips trembled, curving as she looked up. Her eyes were bleak. "I guess we'll never know, will we?"

His attempt at comfort was a clear failure. But Alessandro knew words weren't enough to make anyone forget the loss of a dream. He had no idea how to make Lilley forget her pain. He knew only one way, the same way he used to forget his own.

But he couldn't do it. He couldn't allow himself to make love to her.

The orchestra started a new song, and the notes of an exquisite classical waltz swirled around them like cherry blossoms tumbling from the sky. Lilley looked out at the crowded dance floor wistfully.

She'd told him she wasn't a good dancer, but he didn't believe that for an instant. He'd seen the sensual way she moved. Even walking, her body swayed like sunset against ocean waves.

But he couldn't dance with her. His hands tightened at his sides. He was helpless to offer comfort.

Unless he made love to her.

What could it hurt? His lust argued against his brain.

One night of pleasure. A few hours of comfort. One night wouldn't risk making her fall in love with him. It wasn't as if she were a virgin.

Although she was shockingly close. *Two boyfriends*. He still couldn't believe she'd only been with two men. She truly was innocent. And yet she'd seemed embarrassed of her number. He wondered what she would think if he told her how many women he'd slept with. Something he would never do, even if he knew the number.

"I'm sorry I don't dance," he said slowly.

She looked down. "It's all right."

The scent of her hair was like wild roses. He moved closer, fascinated by the swoop of her neck, by the snub edge of her chin. Her cheeks blushed a soft pink against creamy skin as her dark eyelashes fluttered. He asked suddenly, "How old are you, Lilley?"

"Twenty-three." She furrowed her brow. "Why? How old are you?"

"Ancient to you. Thirty-five."

"Thirty-five, and still not married?" She sounded as astonished as his shareholders. "Where I come from, most people are married by thirty."

"Advantageous for farm life, I assume."

Her brow furrowed. "I don't exactly come from a—"

"In my world," he interrupted, "a man marries to ensure his line, to make sure he has a son to inherit his title and estate when he's dead."

She flashed him a grin. "Gee, you make it all sound so romantic."

"It's not about *romance,* Lilley," he said sharply. "Marriage is an alliance. My wife will be a leader in society. An heiress with proper lineage, the future mother to my heir."

Her grin faded. "Like Olivia Bianchi."

Even hearing her name irritated him. "Yes."

Lilley's eyes were huge beneath the glittering light of the chandeliers. "So if she's the perfect bride for you, why am I here?"

"She threatened to leave if I didn't propose, so I told her to go."

Lilley blinked. "I feel sorry for her."

He barked a laugh. "Do not waste your sympathy on Olivia. She can take care of herself."

"She's in love with you!" She swallowed. "It was wrong of me to agree to this—this charade. When you're just trying to control her."

"I have no desire ever to see Olivia again," he bit out.

She frowned, clearly unconvinced. "When did you decide that?"

His eyes met hers. "I knew it from the moment I saw you in that dress."

Her lips parted in shock. It took her several moments to speak. "Um. Would you get me a drink?" she croaked. "And maybe some food? I haven't eaten all day."

"Certamente," he murmured. "What would you like? A martini? A merlot?"

"You choose."

"We'll start with champagne." Reaching out a hand, he cupped her cheek. "Wait here, if you please, *cara.*"

He felt her shiver beneath his touch, saw her lick her lips as she said with a trembling voice, "I'll wait."

He turned away, but after a few steps could not resist looking back at her. Lilley stood frozen on the edge of the dance floor, gloriously alluring in her red dress, watching him. She was surrounded by men who were already darting her greedy sideways glances.

Damned vultures. Alessandro scowled. He would hurry.

As he strode across the ballroom, he couldn't remember the last time he'd felt such need to possess any woman.

And he could have her. She was free and ripe for the taking. Yes, she was his employee, but he was the one who'd made that rule. He was the boss. He could break his own rules at will.

Alessandro thought again of the ten bedrooms at his villa. An image floated through his mind of Lilley spread naked on his bed, her full, generous mouth curved into a sensual smile, her deep-brown eyes looking up at him with a haze of longing and need. He nearly stumbled over his own feet.

And just like that, his decision was made. His body tightened as exhilaration raced through him. Employee or not, Lilley would be his.

Tonight. He would have her in his bed tonight.

CHAPTER THREE

LILLEY felt men in tuxedos jostle her on the edge of the dance floor, felt the annoyed glare of chic, half-starved women in black designer gowns around her. She took a deep breath, trying to steady her shaking hands. Alessandro's dark head towered above the crowds as he strode towards the bar, trailed by wide-eyed, adoring groupies.

And she was rapidly becoming one of them. Lilley exhaled. What in heaven's name was she doing? He'd told her outright that their date would only be an illusion. And yet, all night, Alessandro's eyes, his touch, had told her differently. Her body felt hot, her skin flushed and pink at the memory of his fingertips stroking her bare back. Of his fingers running lightly along her arm, his lips brushing her cheek.

Just being around him made her feel like a different woman. A bolder, braver one.

She didn't know why or how. Maybe it was the way he looked at her. The way his hard, muscular body felt against her own. Maybe it was his scent, like exotic lands and spice and sunshine. He made her feel tense and tingly and hot, and made her soul feel all jumbled and confused.

He made her feel a hunger she'd never known, and every moment she was near him, the hunger grew.

Lilley swallowed, rubbing her tense neck. She just had

to make it through the night. She'd keep her distance, keep her mouth shut, have some dinner and drink champagne for a couple of hours. Surely she could manage that? And tomorrow, it would all be nothing but a dream. On Monday she could go back to the file room, and Prince Alessandro Caetani would forget her existence.

She couldn't possibly believe his interest in her could be real. There was no way on the green earth that Alessandro would choose Lilley over Olivia Bianchi.

I have no desire ever to see Olivia again. She heard the echo of his husky voice. *I knew it from the moment I saw you in that dress.*

An electric current coursed through her body at the memory. She couldn't forget how he'd pulled her close, wrapping his arms around her as he spoke to politicians and football stars. She couldn't forget how his hot gaze had slowly perused the length of her body when they'd left the boutique, or the way he'd protected her past the paparazzi. A strange new tension had consumed her all night, causing her heart to beat too fast and her breasts to rise and fall in quick, shallow breaths against the snug bodice of her gown.

Maybe it was a good thing Alessandro didn't dance after all. If she felt his hard body swaying against hers, she might have hyperventilated and fallen like a stone on the dance floor. Every time their eyes met, every time he touched her, Lilley wanted things she could barely confess, even to herself.

"Lilley?"

Jeremy stood in front of her, his mouth agape at her tight red dress. He pushed up his black-framed glasses. "What are you doing here?"

"Oh. Hi Jeremy," Lilley said weakly. Licking her lips, she glanced at the black-haired woman behind him. "Hi, Nadia."

Her roommate's face was the picture of misery. She looked as if she were about to burst into tears. "I'm so sorry, Lilley," she choked out. "We never meant to hurt you. We never meant…"

"Stop apologizing," Jeremy told her. His Adam's apple bobbed over his bow tie as he glared at Lilley. "We would have told you days ago, if you'd let us. But you've avoided us. Avoided *me*."

Lilley's mouth had fallen open. "That's ridiculous!"

"I wish you'd just had the guts to tell me from the start you didn't want me, rather than pawning me off on Nadia. Is it any wonder we fell for each other? You were never there!"

Lilley shook her head fiercely. "You're just making excuses. You know I had to work! You're entirely to blame!"

His gaze met hers. "Am I?" His eyes traveled down her full, bouncy hair to the knit dress clinging to her breasts. "You sure never dressed like that for me. You're clearly here with someone you actually care about. Who is he, Lilley?"

It was time for her to lower the boom. Time to get revenge for their betrayal. As soon as she told them her date was Alessandro, they'd be shocked and jealous. Lilley opened her lips.

Then she saw Jeremy's hand on the small of Nadia's back.

It was a protective gesture, one Lilley had resisted every time Jeremy had tried to touch her. The truth was that, after one fun weekend at the trade show, their relationship had always been strained. She'd quit her job in France and moved to San Francisco to start this big new life, but she hadn't done anything to pursue her dreams. When Jeremy had tried to kiss her, she'd pulled away. She'd avoided being with him, coming up with excuses to stay at work a little longer. Looking back at their relationship, Lilley couldn't blame him for wanting to be with Nadia, a girl who actually had time for him, and who, as she'd seen to her shock that morning, actually seemed to relish his kisses.

She'd never loved him. The truth was, what hurt the most was losing her dream of the boutique. She couldn't start a business without Jeremy, she didn't have the remotest idea how to create a business plan or legally register her company or build a clientele. All she knew how to do was design jewelry that was funny and weird and definitely not for everyone.

She'd had such big dreams. And when he'd broken up with her, he'd ended them.

No. She'd done that herself, by never lifting a finger to pursue them.

"Who's your date, Lilley?" Nadia said hopefully through her tears. "Have you met someone?"

Maybe Jeremy had cheated on her, but she'd abandoned and rejected him for months. Maybe Nadia had taken her boyfriend behind her back—but hadn't Lilley begged her roommate to please, please make her excuses to Jeremy as she scurried off to work?

They'd been wrong. But Lilley had been a coward from start to finish.

Trembling, Lilley faced them. "I'm here with…with…" She swallowed, then lifted her chin. "A friend. I'm here with a new friend."

She turned to Jeremy.

"And you were right," she said. "I was never there. Not for you. And not for our business. I had all these dreams, but I was afraid even to try. I'm—I'm sorry."

Jeremy blinked, and the angry light in his eyes faded. "I'm sorry too," he said. "You're a nice person, Lilley, sweet and generous. You didn't deserve to find out about Nadia and me that way." He gave her an awkward smile. "I always liked you. But after you moved to San Francisco, you just…disappeared."

"I know." Her throat hurt. Every time Jeremy had made an appointment for them—at a bank, with a potential investor, with a real estate agent—she'd suddenly had somewhere else to be. She'd hidden behind her work. Her fear had won. "I'm sorry."

"Can you ever forgive me, Lilley?" Nadia whispered.

Lilley tried to smile. "Maybe if you do the dishes for the rest of the month."

"I will. Two months. Three!"

"And I'm sorry the boutique didn't work out." Jeremy rubbed the back of his sandy-blond head sheepishly. "I still think your jewelry is fantastic. You're just not ready to take the plunge. But maybe someday…"

"Right," she said over the lump in her throat, knowing it was a lie. "Someday."

Her roommate was openly crying as she leaned forward and hugged Lilley, whispering, "Thank you."

Lilley's throat hurt as she watched Jeremy and Nadia disappear into the crowd. Then she heard a dark, sardonic voice behind her.

"You didn't tell them about me."

She whirled around. "Alessandro."

"I was waiting to see you take your revenge." His tall, muscular body moved with a warrior's grace as he held out a flute of champagne. "Why didn't you tell them?"

"Because Jeremy was right. I never wanted him. Not really." She took the champagne flute from his hand and said softly, "If I don't have the guts to pursue my dreams, I shouldn't be angry if other people do."

"You could have made them suffer." His dark eyes were puzzled, almost bewildered. "I don't understand."

"That makes two of us," she whispered, and took a long

drink of champagne. The bubbles were a cold shock against her lips as she tilted back her head, gulping it all down. She closed her eyes, waiting for the alcohol to reach her brain and make her forget how she'd been so afraid to risk failure that she'd made it a self-fulfilling prophecy.

What was the point in her avoiding risk, if she ended up losing everything anyway?

"You're crying." Alessandro sounded aghast.

She exhaled, wiping her eyes. "No."

"I saw his face when he looked at you. He could still be yours for the taking, if you chose."

Lilley thought of the stricken expression on Nadia's face. Thought of the way Jeremy's hand had lingered protectively on her roommate's back. Thought of the way Lilley had never, not for one instant, felt a single spark of physical attraction for Jeremy—something she'd never even noticed until she'd experienced the lightning sizzle of electricity with Alessandro.

She shook her head. "I wish them all the best."

"God, you are so nice," he whispered, pushing back wavy tendrils of her hair. "How can you be so—merciful?"

An unexpected bolt of pain went through her. Another man calling her *nice*. Another word for *timid. Terrified. Coward.* No wonder Alessandro had called her little mouse.

Blinking fast, she looked down at her scandalous red dress and sexy high heels. "Do you think I'm a coward?" she whispered.

"What are you talking about?" Taking her empty flute, he pressed his own full glass into her hand. "Here. Drink this."

She looked up at him, her eyes full of unshed tears. "I shouldn't have said that aloud. You must think—"

"I think nothing." His dark gaze seared through her soul. "Never apologize for telling me what you're thinking. You can't hurt me. There is nothing between us, so you risk nothing."

She blinked at him, feeling quivery. "Now you're the one who is being nice."

He snorted, then shook his head, a small smile playing on his sensual mouth. "That is one accusation I've never heard before. Now drink."

Obediently, she took a sip. As she drank, she heard him muse aloud, "Delicious, isn't it? I just bought the winery from a Brazilian. Cost me a fortune." His lips curved. "But it gives me a great deal of pleasure, since I know it infuriates my worst enemy."

Lilley's eyes flew open as she pulled the flute from her lips. She said faintly, "Not the St. Raphaël vineyard."

"Ah, you recognize it?" He smiled in satisfaction. "It once belonged to the Count of Castelnau. Now it is mine."

"You don't say," Lilley said faintly, feeling sick. She'd heard Théo, her cousin and former employer, rage about losing that vineyard in a business deal to a Brazilian. It was only after he'd lost it that he'd realized its value. Typical, she thought. People were so much better at pursuing things they didn't need instead of enjoying what they already had.

But the two men had competed over acquisitions with growing ferocity for the last five years, ever since Théo had bought a small Italian luxury firm that Alessandro considered rightfully his by geography. If he ever found out she was Théo's cousin, he'd never believe Lilley wasn't a corporate spy. Especially after catching her in his office, all alone in the dark!

Her knees trembled. He caught her. "Are you all right?" he asked, looking concerned. "Did you drink the champagne too quickly?"

She looked up at him. She'd left her father's and cousin's names off her résumé because she'd known Caetani

Worldwide would have never hired her otherwise, in spite of Jeremy's recommendation, no matter how honest or hardworking she might be. But telling Alessandro the truth would gain her nothing, and would cost her her job—forcing her to go home to her father and perhaps even consider his demand that she marry his employee, a man twice her age.

"Lilley?"

"I just need something to eat," she managed. "I haven't eaten all day." She gave him a weak smile. "And I did jog a half mile."

"Of course." Taking the half-finished flute from her hands, he set both glasses on the silver tray of a passing waiter and gave her a sudden grin. "I've arranged for a private dinner of sorts. My driver has taken a selection from the buffet to the limo. We'll enjoy a little picnic on the way home."

"A picnic? In your limo?" she said faintly. She shook her head, feeling dizzy in a way that had nothing to do with champagne. With a wistful sigh, she looked back at the glamorous ballroom. "All right. I just—didn't expect it all to end so quickly."

"All good things come to an end," he said, holding out his hand.

Reluctantly, she took it. He led her across the ballroom, stopping many times to say farewell to his friends and admirers before they finally escaped up the stairs, through the foyer and out the double doors.

Outside, beneath the hundred-year-old mansion's shadowy portico, the August night was foggy and cold. "It must be midnight," she murmured.

"Almost. How did you know?"

"Because all night I've felt like Cinderella." She looked up at him, and gratitude, real gratitude, rose above her regret that the night was over. "Thank you for the best night of my life."

He blinked, then frowned. Abruptly, he pushed her against a white stone column. She shivered as she felt the cold, hard stone against the hot skin of her back.

"I don't think you understand," he said in a low voice. "I'm not taking you to *your* home." He paused. "I'm taking you to mine."

She stared at him in shock, hearing only her own hoarse breath and the rapid beat of her heart.

"You're my employee. There are rules." Alessandro's eyes were dark with heat, his dark hair dappled with streaks of silvery moonlight as he held her beneath the shadows of the portico. "But I'm going to break them," he whispered. "I'm going to kiss you."

Staring up at him, Lilley felt as though she was lost in a strange dream. Tendrils of hair whipped across her face; the fabric of her dress moved languorously against her thighs.

"All night I've thought of nothing but touching you." His hands moved down her shoulders to her naked back. He lowered his head to her ear, and she felt his lips brush her tender flesh. "If you want me to stop, tell me now."

She closed her eyes as she felt the warmth of his fingers stroke her bare skin, felt his powerful body, barely constrained by his civilized tuxedo, against her own. His fingertips stroked up her neck, and he tilted her head upwards, his face just inches away. She shivered, her lips parted. The two of them were alone in the foggy, moonlit world.

Then she heard paparazzi yapping like small dogs from the curb, barking out questions that were muffled by a sudden howl of cold wind. He twisted away from her sharply. Moonlight caressed the hard edges of his face, making him look like a dark avenging angel as he scowled behind them. He grabbed her wrist.

"Come on."

He pulled her down the stone steps, past the shouts and flashbulbs of the paparazzi and the reporters who screamed questions and lunged for Lilley as they passed. Alessandro knocked them aside with his powerful arm, gently pushing her into the waiting limousine before he slammed the door behind them.

"Drive," he ordered the chauffeur.

The uniformed driver gunned the engine, roaring away from the curb and plummeting down the steep San Francisco hill. Lilley exhaled as she looked through the window behind them. "Are they always like that?"

"Yes. Take the alleys," Alessandro said. "In case they follow."

"Of course, sir. The penthouse?"

"Sonoma." Alessandro replied, rolling up the privacy divider.

"Sonoma?" Lilley echoed.

He turned to her with a sensual, heavy-lidded smile. "I have a villa. It will give us complete privacy."

She swallowed. This was all happening so fast. "I don't know…"

He gave her a wicked half grin. "I swear I'll have you back in the city safe and sound before work on Monday."

Work! As if that was what she was worried about! Exhaling, Lilley noticed two plates of delicious food and white wine chilling in a bucket of ice. As the divider closed with a thunk, blocking off the driver's view of the back seat, she looked nervously at Alessandro. She'd been starving for hours, but suddenly dinner was the last thing on her mind.

Smiling, he put his hand on her cheek. She could see slivers of silvery light reflected in his fathomless black eyes as he whispered, "I thought a woman like you existed only in dreams."

Her shoulders stiffened. "You mean *nice?*" She felt a sudden lump in her throat. *"Sweet?"*

He gave a low laugh. "You have a way of turning my every compliment into an insult. But yes. You are those things." His hand slowly trailed down her neck, his fingertips stroking the sensitive corner of her shoulder, the hollow of her collarbone. "But that's not why I'm taking you home."

"It isn't?" she breathed.

"I want you in my bed." His gaze was hot. His thumb stroked her sensitive bottom lip, and sparks flashed up and down the length of her body. "I've never wanted any woman this much. I want to taste your mouth. Taste your breasts. To feel your body against mine and fill you until you weep with joy. I won't stop until I am satisfied." He stroked her jawline, tilting her face upward as he whispered, "Until *you* are satisfied."

She trembled, hardly able to breathe. His mouth was inches from hers, and her lower lip fell swollen, burning where he'd touched her. She could feel the warmth of his breath against her skin. Unconsciously, she tilted her head back, lifting her mouth a millimeter closer to his.

His hand slid down her neck, past her bare shoulder. "I offer you a night of pleasure. Nothing more." His palm caressed the length of her arm to the vulnerable pulse inside her wrist. "And nothing less."

Her heart pounded in her throat. She had to refuse him. *Had* to. She couldn't possibly toddle off to his villa in Sonoma and give her boss her virginity. There were a million reasons why this was a bad idea.

But her body refused to heed her brain. She felt as if she was spiraling out of control. She craved his darkness. Craved his fire. "A woman would have to be a fool," she breathed, "to get involved with a man like you."

The ghost of a smile haunted Alessandro's cruel, sensual mouth. He cupped her face with both hands.

"We all must choose in this life," he said, searching her gaze. "The safety of a prison, or the terrible joy that comes with freedom."

She stared up at him, stricken. He seemed to know the secret desires and fears of her innermost heart.

As if in slow motion, he lowered his mouth to hers, whispering, "Live dangerously."

She closed her eyes.

His kiss was electric, like sensual fire. She felt the smooth hot satin of his lips, felt the roughness of his chin, the powerful strength of his arms around her. The heat of his tongue was like liquid silk softly stroking inside her mouth. Sparks of pleasure spiraled down her body, making her breasts taut and heavy, tightening a coil of tension low and deep in her belly. Her nerve endings sizzled from her fingertips to her toes.

She felt as if she were exploding into pure light.

When he pulled away, she heard the low, hoarse gasp of his breath—or was it her own?

She stared up at him, knowing she'd remember that first kiss until the day she died.

Streaks of light moved across their skin as the limousine traveled through the city. They stared at each other, and Lilley's cheeks burned like the rest of her. She'd never known a dream could feel so real. So warm. So hot. She felt as if she were floating—flying. She blinked, feeling dizzy. She could almost see a trail of scattered diamonds sparkling against her skin where he'd touched her, like synesthesia.

Prince Alessandro Caetani could have had any woman he wanted. And he wanted *her*. He moved towards her, gently pushing her back against the leather seat, and she felt the hard weight of his body over her own. She felt his hands on her skin, and suddenly, she no longer felt like a timid, cowardly mouse.

She felt beautiful.

Powerful.

Reckless.

In his arms, she wasn't afraid. Of anything.

She closed her eyes, tossing back her head as he kissed down her throat with his hot, sensual mouth. "No one's ever made me feel like this," she breathed. "Touched me like this."

"I..." Suddenly his hands stilled against her skin. His head lifted. "But you've had other lovers," he said. "At least two."

Her eyes opened. She swallowed. "Not...exactly."

"How many have you had?"

"Technically, well...none."

He sat up, looking at her with wide, shocked eyes. "Are you trying to tell me you're a *virgin?*"

She sat up beside him, her mouth suddenly dry. "Is that a problem?"

He glared at her, his jaw hard. Turning, he pressed the button to lower the privacy shield.

"Sir?" the driver said courteously, not turning his head.

"Change of plans," Alessandro said. "We're taking Miss Smith home."

"What?" Lilley gasped. Her cheeks burned. "Why? That..." she glanced uneasily at the driver in the front seat, "that thing I just told you doesn't matter!"

Alessandro turned to Lilley with cold eyes. "Give Abbott your address."

Folding her arms, Lilley muttered out the address of her apartment building. The driver nodded and smoothly turned left at the next streetlight. Lilley waited for Alessandro to roll the limo's dividing window back up so they could have privacy. But he didn't, and she realized he intended to leave it open, keeping the driver as their de facto chaperone.

Setting her jaw, Lilley turned to stare out the window at the passing lights of the city. Her body felt suddenly cold. She felt bereft. Alone.

As they drove into the increasing traffic of the city, Alessandro wouldn't even look at her. Sulkily, Lilley picked up a plate of food. The dinner was delicious, but cold, and epicurean pleasures suddenly seemed small. The plate was empty by the time they reached her working-class neighborhood, when she realized that Alessandro really, truly did not intend to kiss her again.

Kiss her? He wasn't even going to *look* at her. Her night of magic, her time of feeling reckless and beautiful, was definitely over. But she couldn't accept it. After the brief, explosive joy she'd experienced so briefly in his arms, she couldn't just shrug off her loss and go quietly back to her empty apartment!

Her heart hammered in her throat. "You're making a fuss over nothing. It's not a big deal."

Alessandro looked at her. The lights and shadows of the city swept over the hard, angular lines of his cheekbones and jaw. "It is to me."

Glancing uneasily at the driver, she leaned towards Alessandro. "Just because I am slightly less experienced than your other lovers—"

"Do you not understand what I was offering?" he bit out. "A night. Perhaps two. Nothing more!"

"I wasn't asking for more!" she said, affronted.

"I will never go home to meet your parents, Lilley. I will not marry you." His dark eyes were furious. "I will not *love* you."

A pang went through her at his cold words, but she lifted her chin in defiance. "Who said I wanted love?"

"Virgins always do." He looked her up and down. "Do not be stupid, Lilley."

Stupid. Her cheeks felt suddenly cold as echoes of childhood taunts from school went through her. *Fri-lly, Li-lley, stupid and si-lly!*

Alessandro stared out the window, his jaw like stone. His body language informed her that he was done talking, his decision made.

The limo pulled to a stop at her building. The driver got out and opened her door. The night air rushed in, cool and clammy against her burning skin.

"Good night," Alessandro said coldly, not turning his head.

"This is really how you're going to end our date?" she whispered. "Kissing me—then kicking me to the curb?"

He turned, and his black eyes glowed like dying embers as a hard smile lifted his lips. "Now, *cara,* at last you understand what it means to be my lover."

Lilley stared at him. "I understand, all right," she choked out. Tears filled her eyes as she turned away. "You don't want me."

"Not want you?" he demanded.

She looked back, miserable and bewildered. "Yes, you just said—"

"I am saving you from a mistake," he said harshly. "Be grateful."

She swallowed. "Okay," she said. "Good-bye."

She stepped out onto the curb in front of her 1960s-era apartment building. She took a deep breath of the cool night air and looked down her dark, empty street, littered with parked cars. An old newspaper blew down the black asphalt like a tumbleweed. She'd only lived here two months, but she'd been in this same place for far too long. In France. In Minnesota.

Her apartment building towered over her, seeming almost malevolent in the darkness. She knew what waited for her there, too. Nadia would be out dancing with Jeremy all night, and Lilley would be alone. She'd curl up on the couch beneath her mother's old handmade quilt and watch television shows about other people's lives. Maybe she'd take a long bath, then lights out.

Was that doomed to be her whole life's fate?

She would never have left her cushy job as a housekeeper in France if her cousin hadn't been mean to the mother of his child, causing Lilley to quit her job in solidarity in an instinctive, emotional reaction that would have made her mother proud. But that had been the end of Lilley's courage. From the instant she'd set foot in San Francisco, she'd done nothing but hide.

We all must choose in this life, Alessandro had said. *The safety of a prison. Or the terrible joy that comes with freedom.*

"Lilley." His voice was hoarse in the limo behind her. "Damn you. Just go."

With an intake of breath, she turned back to face him. Without a word, without letting herself think, she climbed back into the limo. She felt his shocked stare, heard his intake of breath as she slammed the door behind her.

"Do you know the choice you're making?" he demanded harshly.

Her body trembled as she looked at him. "I used to dream of my first lover," she whispered. "I dreamed of a knight in shining armor who would adore me forever."

"And now?" he bit out.

"I'm just tired of being afraid." She swallowed, blinking back tears. "Tired of hiding from my own life."

He stared at her for a long moment. Then, pressing the

button to close the divider, he spoke a single word to the driver. "Sonoma."

Lilley watched the divider lift higher, higher. It finally closed with a thunk, the noise reverberating like a door slamming behind her.

Then Alessandro moved. She had a single image of the dark heat of his eyes, the curve of his cruel, sensual mouth, as he pushed her back against the leather seat. Then his powerful body covered hers in a rough, ruthless embrace. His lips seared hers in a hot, hard kiss of sweetly poisonous honey.

Opening her mouth to his plunging tongue, she gave him—everything.

CHAPTER FOUR

AN HOUR later, as Alessandro carried her from the limo, Lilley blinked up at him in the moonlight, feeling drunk on his kisses. She felt hot, so hot. As he held her against his chest, she swayed with every step. The night was clear and the moon glowed in the velvet-black sky.

His Spanish-style villa was surrounded by rolling vineyards frosted with silvery light. In the distance, she could hear night birds calling.

The drive from the city had passed in seconds, it seemed, drenched with kisses. When the limo had arrived at the villa, she'd been so light-headed and breathless that she'd opened the door and fallen into a sprawl on the gravel driveway. Alessandro had picked her up in his strong arms, his gaze full of heat for what was to come.

Now, as the limo disappeared down the driveway, Lilley looked up at him in wonder. The stars seemed to move over his dark head, twinkling magically in the night sky.

She felt intoxicated, and she'd had only a glass and a half of champagne at the ball. There could be no doubt what—who—was drugging her senses.

At the door, he held her with one arm and punched in a security code. Around the villa, she briefly saw a pool and tennis courts and vast vineyards beyond. Then he opened the door with his shoulder and carried her inside, kicking the heavy door closed behind him.

Inside, the villa was dark and silent as he carried her up the 1920s-era wrought-iron stairs. He didn't have to say a word. She saw the whole sensual world in his dark eyes.

Upstairs, he pushed open a door at the end of the hall. She saw an enormous bed lit by a flood of moonlight from the windows. Reverently, he put her down on it. She shivered beneath the pool of silvery light as, never looking away from her, Alessandro pulled off his tuxedo tie and jacket and dropped them to the floor. He kicked off his shoes then climbed into bed beside her.

His hands were everywhere as he kissed her swollen lips. His embrace deepened, became hungrier and harder as his mouth pressed against hers, so hot and wet. His tongue twined with her own, and his hands cupped her breasts over the thin fabric of her gown, causing a gasp at the back of her throat. He stroked down to her waist, caressing her bare, shaking arms. Finally, he cradled her face and kissed her again with deepening fervor. She kissed him back with all the reckless passion of twenty-three lonely years.

There is nothing but now, she thought, dazed. *Nothing but this.*

She gasped as his hands moved beneath the clinging fabric of her bodice to her naked breasts. Her nipples tightened to hard points, sharpening in exquisite pleasure as he squeezed each of them gently between his fingers. Suddenly, he yanked the dress down, causing the spaghetti straps to snap as the fabric surrendered.

He showed rough brutality to her dress. But he caressed her body as if she were a precious, fragile treasure. His lips were hot against her skin as he moved down, nibbling her chin, licking her throat. She gasped as his large hands covered her full, naked breasts, squeezing each nipple, holding up each as a delicacy for the pleasure of his mouth. When he lowered his head, she felt the moist heat of his breath against her nipple and gripped the white bedspread beneath her. She held her breath as his entire mouth enfolded her nipple, suckling gently, his tongue swirling against her tight, swollen peak. She inhaled in tiny, desperate gasps as his hot, wet mouth moved to suckle the other breast in turn.

His hand stroked up her bare leg, dragging up the hemline of her long dress. The heavy weight of his hard, muscular body pressed her down into the softness of the bed, and she felt his fingertips languidly explore up her bare calf to caress the hollow behind her knee. As he suckled her breast, his hand continued to move upwards.

Stroking her outer thigh.

Her inner thigh.

She gripped the mattress, holding her breath. Alessandro lifted his mouth from her wet, hard nipple. Straddling her, he slowly unbuttoned his shirt. He tossed his platinum and diamond cufflinks carelessly to the floor. Wearing only his black tuxedo trousers, he moved down, between her legs, and she had her first look at the hard ripples and shadows of his bare chest in the moonlight. She bit down hard on her lip to stifle a gasp. His shoulders were broad, his muscles strong and powerful as an athlete's. The edges of his flat nipples were dusted lightly with dark hair that made a trail down his taut, defined belly before disappearing beneath his waistband. There wasn't an inch of fat anywhere on his body. She could hardly comprehend so much masculine beauty; he was like a dark angel.

At the end of the bed, Alessandro slid the dress off her unresisting body. Looking down, she realized she'd lost her high heels. Where? She couldn't remember. In the limo? Outside the villa? On the stairs…? It was all a sensual blur, and she was lost, utterly lost in sensation.

He pulled off his trousers and silk boxers, and Lilley's lips parted as she got a full look at the first wholly naked man she'd ever seen. And what a man. Her eyes traced over his powerful thighs, the strength of his body. And in the middle. She swallowed as her own breath suddenly choked her. Alessandro was huge. He would never fit inside her. Would he? Could he? How? Someone had made a mistake!

His dark eyes glowed in the shadows as he approached. She felt hypnotized, unable to move, unable even to cover her naked breasts or her lacy panties with her hands. He lay down beside her, turning her body to face him, and ran two fingertips down her side, from her shoulder to the swell of her breast to the valley of her waist and curve of her hip. She trembled, overwhelmed, helpless with desire.

Taking her hand, he gently suckled two of her fingers. Pulling her fingers from his mouth, he held her hand against his naked chest, looking at her. He seemed to be waiting. For what? What could he want…what could he expect from her…?

Taking her courage in her hands, shivering with her own daring, she leaned up and kissed him. His lips were hot and hard against hers, and as he let her set the rhythm, her confidence grew. A sigh of pleasure escaped her as he pushed her back against the soft pillows with a low growl, and covered her body with his own.

He was naked on top of her. Only the thin cotton of her panties separated them. She felt his hardness strain between her thighs, and the ache low in her belly increased. Closing her eyes, she gripped his shoulders as he kissed her, pulling him down harder.

Her head fell back with abandon as he kissed down her throat, kissing the valley between her breasts to the soft curve of her belly. She felt the swift flick of his tongue inside her belly button, but before she could be shocked, his teeth were gently pulling down the top edge of her panties.

He pushed her legs apart and she felt his breath against her thighs. She shivered as he kissed up her legs. He gave a teasing lick beneath the bottom edge of her panties, and her fingernails gripped into his shoulders. She held her breath, eyes still squeezed shut, as his hand cupped the mound between her legs. He sucked her most sensitive spot through the lacy fabric, and she cried out.

He ripped off her panties, tossing them on the floor in a mangled heap of lace. Her eyes flew open and she took a single deep gulp of air before she felt his mouth on her. Right on her. Licking her, spreading her wide with his fingers so he could taste every slick fold. She felt wet, so wet. His tongue played with her, teasing her, one moment lapping her with its full width, then moving to flick her sensitive nub with the tip. The feeling of his mouth on her was like nothing she'd imagined, pleasure so intense it was almost agony. She was being sucked into a maelstrom of ecstasy, drowning in the waves. Her hips lifted of their own accord to meet his mouth as the tension in her deepest core built higher and higher.

She couldn't endure this sweet torture, this agony of pleasure, for much longer. She writhed beneath him, her body twisting as she tried to pull away from the insistent, ruthless pleasure of his tongue. But he held her hips firmly, spreading her wider still, as he suckled between her legs. He thrust one thick finger inside her to the first knuckle. Then two fingers. Then three, going deeper, stretching her wide, giving her a small shock of pain to season and salt the sweet, wide, wet slide of his tongue.

Her body arched off the bed as she tried to move away from his fingers inside her, but he would not let her escape the exquisite agony of her pleasure. She gripped the bedspread as the storm inside her exploded. As if from a distance, she heard the cry from her lips lift to a scream of joy.

Sheathing himself in a condom, Alessandro lifted his powerful body over hers, as she still arched in ecstasy on the bed. Positioning himself, he whispered in her ear, "I'm sorry."

He pushed inside her in a single stroke, shoving himself to the hilt. The sudden pain made her gasp. As he filled her so deeply, ripping the invisible barrier inside her, Lilley's scream of joy changed to a choked gasp. He held perfectly still, letting her get used to the stretch of him inside her.

"I'm sorry," he murmured again. Lowering his head, he kissed her face, her cheeks, her lips. "The only way over it is through it." Her answer was a muffled sob as she turned her face into the pillow.

Then slowly, very slowly, he began to move inside her, and a miracle happened. The ocean of pleasure, which had receded beneath her like a wave, sucking sand beneath her feet, began to rush in like the tide. Having him inside her started to feel…good. She'd thought she was satiated, but to her shock a new need built within her. With each slow, deep thrust, he filled a place deep inside her that made her body tighten with new desire.

As her body accepted him fully, Alessandro moved with increasing roughness, riding her harder and deeper, holding her hips with his hands. Her breasts swayed with the increasing force of his thrusts, the headboard slapping against the wall. The pleasure—the pain—made her writhe, her back arching off the bed as she panted for breath, her body desperate with the need for new release. He held her down as he pushed inside her, and he was so huge, so deep, and it felt good, so good. She held her breath, closing her eyes. Her head tilted back and the tension inside her coiled—and coiled—then sprang.

She gave a silent, mindless scream as explosions ripped through her, shaking her whole body as at, the same moment, she heard his growl rise to a shout and he slammed into her with one final, cataclysmic thrust.

When Lilley opened her eyes, she found Alessandro lying on top of her, holding her protectively. She closed her eyes. For no reason she could explain, she suddenly felt like crying. Except he'd taken her to a whole new world.

Why had she ever been so afraid of something so magical?

"I hurt you. I'm sorry."

At the sound of his low voice, she looked up at his face. The shadowed mystery of his dark eyes held regret and barely satiated desire and something more.

"You didn't," she lied.

He gave her a skeptical look.

"A little," she admitted, then, tossing her arms above her head against the soft pillow, she sighed happily. "But would it be cheesy to say it hurt so good?"

He tenderly kissed her forehead. "Horribly cheesy."

Then he kissed her mouth with something more than tenderness. His kiss deepened, his tongue twining with her own as his hands cupped her cheeks. She sighed with pleasure, then gave an involuntary wince as he crushed her bruised lips.

"I'm hurting you." He started to roll over, but she stopped him.

"You're not."

"You're lying."

"So let me," she whispered.

A sensual smile curved his lips. He kissed her again, his mouth hot and hard against hers. She felt him move against her, and sighed with bliss.

He suddenly rolled her over on the bed, pulling her on

top of his naked body. She gave a little squeak of surprise as he looked up at her with dark, wicked eyes. "Your turn."

Lilley stared at him. He expected her to lead in bed? To ride him? Her heart pounded in her throat. She was so clumsy. She'd make a fool of herself. "I...I don't think I can do this. I don't know how."

"You will." Looking straight into her eyes, he put his hand on her cheek. "I can teach you."

Alessandro leaned up to kiss her, and she forgot to be afraid. Holding on to him, letting him guide her to find her own rhythm, she allowed him to teach her to follow her own pleasure, and lead him to his. She rode him, and joy and freedom filled her soul. For the first time in her life, Lilley was the fearless woman she'd always wanted to be.

Alessandro had never known sex could be like this. Lilley was an intoxicating combination of innocence and fire.

He'd never been so insatiable before. He knew that for the rest of his life he'd remember how he'd had the honor of being her first lover. He'd remember teaching her to control the rhythm and pace as she rode him, timidly at first, then with rising reckless confidence.

Afterward, sweaty and sticky from lovemaking, they'd showered in the enormous, gleaming marble bathroom. Alessandro had watched her as she'd tipped her head back beneath the water. The sight of her arching body as water poured over her breasts and streamed off her tight, pink nipples had been too much for him. She'd flicked him a teasing glance, and he'd suddenly realized she was playing with him. With a growl, he'd pushed her against the cool marble of the shower and made love to her against the wall as hot water sprayed all over them both.

Lilley was a very apt student. No wonder each sexual encounter between them was more explosive than the last.

His innocent virgin was transforming into a wanton sex goddess in front of his eyes.

Rosy-skinned and exhausted, they'd fallen into bed a few hours before dawn and woken up starving a few hours later. They'd made love a fourth time, fast and hot, then ventured downstairs for breakfast.

Alessandro found himself wanting to impress her. He'd given his staff the weekend off, so he made her his signature breakfast dish, a sausage frittata. As he cooked, she scooted around the kitchen wearing an oversized robe, gathering ingredients for her French toast, a delicious confection of nutmeg and cinnamon sugar. They sat together at his kitchen table, basking in the morning light, drinking freshly squeezed orange juice and feeding each other bites of food.

For the first time in Alessandro's adult life, he had no desire to check in with work, or catch up on the morning news. All he wanted to do was look at her, touch her, be with her. He couldn't get enough of her exquisite skin and her curvaceous, soft body.

But it was more than just her body.

Being around Lilley made him feel…different. Made him *feel* his own heart beating. After so many years of being empty and bored, playing the game, making money to keep score, sleeping with women he barely knew and dodging the constant onslaught of people begging for his attention, he could let down his guard. Lilley asked for nothing. She would never hurt him or lie to him. Her openness and honesty reminded him of the person he'd been long ago, before everyone he loved had betrayed him.

For some reason, Lilley liked him. Not his money or his title or even just his body. She liked *him*. The man inside. And looking at her in the morning light, Alessandro realized that whatever he'd promised her yesterday, he had no intention of giving her up. He didn't care if it was selfish.

He wanted more than a one-night stand.

"This is delicious," Lilley murmured, leaning forward at the breakfast table. Her oversized robe fell open to reveal her delectable breasts as she took another bite of frittata. She gave him an impish smile. "To be honest, I didn't expect cooking to be one of your talents."

A moment before, he'd been finishing his last piece of French toast, licking the crumbs off his plate. But looking at her state of undress instantly made him want her again, made him want to sweep their dishes to the floor and make love to her on the table. He swallowed. "I usually don't cook. You inspired me."

She smiled at him, her trusting warm eyes the color of deep, dark caramel, her beautiful face suffused in the soft glow of morning light as she whispered, "Not half as much as you inspire me."

Alessandro stared at her, lost in her gaze. He could no more stop himself from wanting her than he could stop breathing.

But keeping her would be wrong. Very wrong.

I have no reason to feel guilty, he told himself fiercely. He'd tried to let her go once already. She'd made her own choice. He'd told her up front he could never marry her or love her. She could protect her own heart.

Reaching his hand out to her cheek, he slowly stroked down her neck to her swelling breasts half revealed by the gape of her robe. Her lips parted in surprise and he could not resist the invitation. Leaning over the table, he kissed her. He felt her soft lips move against his, matching his passion, and nearly groaned. Selfish or not, nothing on earth could make him give her up. Not now. Not yet.

Rising to his feet, Alessandro pulled her from her chair.

Untying her sash, he dropped her robe to the floor, leaving her naked skin glowing in a pool of morning light. He gave a shuddering intake of breath. "Walk ahead of me," he said hoarsely. "So I can see you."

Her eyebrow quirked. In a quick movement, she jerked open his own robe, dropping it to the floor beside hers.

"You first," she suggested sweetly.

Thirty seconds later, Lilley was giggling with little screams of laughter as he chased her, both of them naked, back upstairs. They didn't even make it to his bedroom, but ended up on the priceless heirloom rug in the upstairs hall.

They spent the rest of Sunday making love in every room of his villa. In the garden, in the library, in the study, and finally, long past midnight, back in his bed. They fell asleep wrapped in each other's arms.

But now, just a few hours before Monday's dawn, Alessandro was wide awake as Lilley slept beside him. He'd lost count of the number of times they'd made love in the last thirty hours. More than ten. He paused, then shook his head, amazed. Less than twenty?

Each time he possessed her, instead of being satiated, he only wanted her more. His passion for her consumed him, and his hunger only grew.

But their weekend was over. He looked down at her, kissing her forehead softly as she slept in his arms. He listened to her breath. She clung to him, naked, sighing sweetly in her sleep as she whispered something that sounded like his name.

Guilt, a very unfamiliar emotion, blew through Alessandro like an icy breeze. Virgins fell in love. He knew that too well. They were not experienced enough in the ways of the world to separate their bodies from their hearts. And a girl like Lilley, so warm, vivid, brilliant and kind, deserved a man who could give her a future. A man who could actually love her.

Unlike his usual sort of mistress, Lilley Smith was not a ruthless coquette who used her body as a weapon for power and gain. He wondered if he could ever again be fully satisfied by a cold-hearted woman like Olivia Bianchi. How could that ever compare to Lilley's intoxicating warmth and joy as she gave all of herself, body and soul?

Already Alessandro wanted her again.

Angrily, he clawed back his hair, which was still damp from the sweat of their passionate night. Careful not to wake her, he rose to his feet and walked naked through the balcony doors, out into the warm, clear August night. Moonlight stretched over his vineyards, frosting the hills with silver as he looked out at his land, trying to calm his unquiet heart.

He closed his eyes, feeling every bit of his thirty-five years. His soul felt old and dark compared to hers. Was that his intention—to suck up her youth and optimism like a vampire, feeding on her innocence until his own darkness consumed her?

"Alessandro?" he heard her murmur sleepily.

Gripping his hands, he went back into the bedroom. He found her lying in bed, her gorgeous curves covered only by a sheet. She sat up in surprise when she realized he'd been standing naked on the balcony. "What's wrong?"

"Nothing," he said.

She swallowed, biting her lip. "Do you regret our time together?" she whispered. "Are you thinking about—Olivia?"

"No!" Shaking his head, he said the first thing that came to mind. "I'm thinking about the Mexico City deal. Wondering how our design team in San Francisco will update the Joyería designs once they take over."

Alessandro closed his mouth with a snap, shocked at his

own stupidity. He'd been so concerned about not hurting Lilley, he'd blurted out something he should never have revealed to anyone except his board of directors. If it became public, it would ruin everything. He'd given Joyería's current owner, Miguel Rodriguez, some legally vague reassurances that he would keep the Mexican designers on staff and the studio in Mexico City separate from Caetani Worldwide's offices in San Francisco, Shanghai and Rome. If Rodriguez heard about his plans to economize, the man could well cancel the deal and sell the company to a competitor.

Alessandro looked at Lilley sharply, but she seemed completely unaware of the import of the information he'd unthinkingly shared. She smiled, shaking her head.

"You always work, don't you?" she said softly. "That's why you're so successful." Her gaze grew troubled as she hugged a pillow over her breasts. "Maybe if I were more like you, I wouldn't be such a screw-up."

He frowned. "A screw-up?" he demanded. "Who said that?"

Her smile became sad. "No one has to say it. I came to San Francisco to start my jewelry business, then chickened out." She looked down at the bed. "I'm not brave like you."

He sat down beside her. "There are all kinds of bravery in the world, *cara*." Reaching over, he lifted her chin, forcing her to meet his gaze. "You have an open heart. You trust people in a way I could not. And your jewelry is unique and beautiful. Like you," he said huskily. Setting his jaw, he gave her a decisive nod. "You will start your business when the time is right. I know it."

Her large brown eyes looked up at him with almost painful hope. "You do?"

"Yes." He dropped his hand. "I failed many times, in

many different businesses, before I made my first fortune. Selling children's plastic bracelets, of all things."

She gave an amazed laugh. "You? Selling plastic bracelets? I don't believe it."

He gave her a sudden grin. "It's true. The trend exploded across America and I made my first million. I was determined to succeed. No matter how many times I failed, I wouldn't give up." He stroked her hair. "You are the same. You just don't know it yet."

"You think so?" she breathed, her eyes huge.

He nodded. "If it's important to you, you'll make it happen. Whatever it costs."

"What made you so driven to succeed?"

His lips flattened. "When my father died, he left debts I had to repay. I dropped out of college and worked twenty hours a day." He looked away. "I will never feel powerless again."

"Powerless? But you're a prince!"

"Prince of nothing," he said harshly. "An empty title I inherited from a fifteenth-century warlord. The men of my family have always been corrupt and weak."

"But not you." Her clear eyes met his. "You are the leader of Caetani Worldwide. You built a billion-dollar company from nothing. Everyone loves you," she whispered.

He felt uncomfortable with the adoration he saw in her eyes. "I'm nothing special," he said gruffly. "If I can start a business, so can you. Start a business plan, work through the numbers."

"That might be hard, since I read letters and numbers in the wrong order."

"Dyslexia?"

She nodded.

"What is it like?"

"It's different for different people. In my case the letters and numbers won't stay put."

He barked a laugh. "And you're working in my file room?"

She gave him a sudden cheeky grin. "Now you understand why I was working late." Her voice became wistful. "I've never been really successful at anything except making jewelry. Maybe that's why my father thinks I'm hopeless at taking care of myself. He threatened to disinherit me if I don't come back to Minnesota and marry one of his managers."

"Disinherit you!" Alessandro pictured a hard-working farmer with a small plot of land in the bleak northern plains. "He wanted you to marry a manager on his farm?"

Lilley blinked, frowning at him. "My father's not a farmer. He's a businessman."

"Ah," Alessandro said. "He owns a restaurant? Perhaps a laundromat?"

Her eyes slid away evasively. "Um. Something like that. My parents got divorced a few years ago, when my mother was sick. The day she died was the worst day of my life. I had to get away, so I found...a job...with a distant relative. My cousin."

She stumbled strangely over the words, looking at him with an anxiety he couldn't understand.

"I'm sorry," Alessandro said in a low voice. "My mother died a few years ago, and my own relationship with my father was always complicated." *Complicated* was an understatement. His father, Prince Luca Caetani, had married Alessandro's mother for her money, then spent it on his mistresses. He'd died when Alessandro was nineteen, leaving debts and an unknown number of bastards around the world. Alessandro was his father's only legitimate child, the heir to the Caetani title and name, but every year some stranger came out of the woodwork, claiming blood ties and asking for a handout from the company Alessandro had built with his own two hands.

Just wait till you're older, son, his father had gasped on his deathbed. *You'll be just like me. You'll see.*

Alessandro had vowed he would never be anything like his father. He was selfish, but not a monster.

Right?

"I actually thought about going back." Lilley's trusting eyes shone at him. "But now I know I won't. You make me feel…brave. Like I can do anything. Risk anything."

Alessandro's heart gave a sickening lurch. He gripped his fists so tightly the knuckles turned white.

Lilley was half in love with him already. He could see it in her face, even if she herself wasn't aware of it yet. If he kept her as his mistress, how long would it be before he obliterated her light completely? Until she, too, had a heart as dark and empty as night?

He'd crossed a line. He'd violated her innocence in a way he could never take back.

If that wasn't the work of a monster, what was?

With an intake of breath, he turned away. In just an hour or two, dawn would break across the purple hills. But there could be no sunrise for Alessandro. He felt cold to the bone.

There was only one way to cut her loss. One way to leave her heart bruised, but not shattered. He exhaled, closing his eyes.

He had to let her go.

"It's almost morning," she said, sounding sad. She splayed her small hand against his chest. "In a few hours, I'll go back to the file room. What about you?"

He opened his eyes. "Mexico City."

Lilley took a deep breath. "Alessandro," she whispered, "I want you to know that I—"

Turning to her almost violently, he put his finger against her lips. "Let's not talk." Pulling her down on the mattress beside him, he breathed in the scent of her, the intoxicating smell of sunshine and flowers. He gloried in her warmth and beauty for the last time.

"This has been the happiest day of my life," she whispered. "I'm just sad to see it end." She gave him a crooked smile. "In a few hours, you'll forget I ever existed."

He looked down at her. "I'll never forget you, Lilley," he said, and it was the truth.

"Oh," she breathed. Relief and gratitude filled her eyes. She thought his words meant they might have a future. She didn't know they were the death knell for any relationship they might have had.

She put her hand on his rough, unshaven cheek. "Then give me a kiss I'll never forget."

He looked at her full, rosy lips, and his whole body shuddered with need.

One last time, he told his conscience savagely. He would give her up at dawn. Set her free before he did any further damage to her soul.

Cupping her face, Alessandro kissed her, as if trying to burn the memory of her lips against his for all time. Tasting the sweetness of her mouth, he spread her lips wide, plundering her with his tongue. Pulling the pillow away from her body, he rolled her beneath him on the bed, covering her naked body with his own.

Alessandro looked down at Lilley's beautiful face. He knew the bitter memory of the joy shining now in her sweet, joyful eyes, her strange trust and belief in his goodness would haunt him for all time. An ache like regret pierced his soul.

Then, closing his eyes, he pushed himself inside her.

CHAPTER FIVE

A MONTH later, Lilley felt sick as she sat in a hard office chair in the basement office of the human resources department. The fluorescent lights above the desk flickered and hummed as Lilley licked her dry lips, praying she'd heard wrong.

"What?" she croaked.

"I'm sorry, Miss Smith, but we must let you go." The kindly older man on the other side of the desk shifted uncomfortably in his chair. "I'm afraid Caetani Worldwide isn't the right place for your skills."

Fighting nausea, Lilley took a deep breath as grief and pain washed over her. She'd known this would happen, known she'd lose her job no matter how hard she tried. Effort couldn't compensate for her slowness in filing numbers and letters that danced in front of her eyes.

Maybe she really was incapable of taking care of herself, just as her father said. Case in point: she'd slept with her boss, and then was surprised when Alessandro disappeared before she woke up on Monday morning and never bothered to contact her again. Exactly as he'd told her he'd do. Her throat suddenly hurt. She really wasn't smart.

"I can assure you," the HR director continued, "there's a very generous compensation package."

"I was too slow, right?" she whispered, blinking back tears. "I took too long to finish my work."

The man shook his head, his ponderous jowls wobbling. He didn't look as if he wanted to fire her. He looked as if he wished the earth would swallow him up beneath his desk. "You did a good job, Miss Smith. You were popular with the rest of the staff. Yes, you took longer than the other file clerk, but your work ethic—" He took a deep breath, tapping a file on his desk. "That's neither here nor there." His voice was clipped. "We will give you an excellent recommendation and I can assure you that you'll find a job soon. Very, *very* soon."

He started to explain the details of her severance package, but Lilley barely listened. The sick feeling was starting to win, so she focused on her breathing, staring hard at the little gray trash can on the floor by his desk. Fighting the desire to throw up into it.

"I'm sorry it turned out this way," he said finally. "But someday you'll be glad that..." He saw that she wasn't listening and was clutching her stomach with one hand while covering her mouth with her other. He sighed. "Please sign this." He pushed a paper towards her on the desk. Grabbing the pen he offered, Lilley skimmed the document—her father had drummed that much into her, at any rate—and saw she was basically promising not to sue the company for sexual harassment. Harassment?

She sucked in her breath. That meant it wasn't her work that was at fault, but she was being fired by—

She cut off the thought, unable to bear his name. Scribbling her signature, she rose to her feet. The HR director shook her hand.

"Best of luck, Miss Smith."

"Thanks," she choked out. Grabbing the file he held out,

she fled to the women's bathroom, where she could be sick in privacy.

Afterward, Lilley splashed cold water on her face. She looked at her wan, green expression in the mirror. She tried to force a grin, to put the cheerful mask back in place that she'd worn for the last month while enduring teasing and innuendo about Prince Alessandro. But today, she couldn't even smile.

Fired. She was fired.

Numbly, she walked to the elevator. She exited on the third floor and went to her desk in the corner of the windowless file room. Other employees had pictures of family or friends or pets hanging at their desks. Lilley had a lonely pink geranium and a postcard that her cousin's wife, Carrie, had sent from Provence a few weeks ago. On the tidy surface of her desk, she saw someone had left a gossip magazine for her to find. Again.

Her body felt cold as she looked down at the latest issue of *Celebrity Weekly*. The cover had a picture of Alessandro in Mexico City, where he'd been living for the last month in his attempt to keep the Joyería deal from falling apart. But last week, Lilley's cousin Théo had made a successful counterbid. It should have made her feel glad, but it didn't. Her heart ached to think of how Alessandro would feel after failing—at anything.

At least she was used to it.

Her eyes moved to a smaller picture at the bottom of the magazine's cover that had been taken at the Cannes film festival months before. Alessandro wore a tuxedo, looking darkly handsome, holding the hand of a beautiful blonde dressed in black. Olivia Bianchi.

Playboy Prince to Wed at Last, the cover blared. Someone had underlined the words with a thick black pen.

Ever since she'd been Alessandro's date at the ball, she'd

been paying for it. Some of her coworkers had worried Lilley might think too well of herself for briefly being their boss's mistress. Well, she thought bitterly, no chance of that.

Lilley jumped as she heard a man clear his throat behind her. Turning, she saw Larry, a security guard she knew. Just yesterday, Lilley had given him advice about how to get ink stains out of fabric, something she'd dealt with fairly often as her cousin's housekeeper. But today, his face was regretful and resigned.

"Sorry, Lilley. I'm supposed to escort you out."

She nodded over the lump in her throat. She gathered up her geranium, the magazine, the postcard from Provence, her nubby old cardigan and the large bag of toffees she kept at the bottom of her desk for emergencies. She packed up her life in a cardboard box and followed the security guard from the file room, trying to ignore all the employees staring at her as she was escorted from the building in a walk of shame.

In the lobby, Larry checked her cardboard box for contraband—what did he think she might take? Pens? Copy paper?—and then took her employee pass card. "Sorry," he mumbled again.

"I'll be fine," she whispered, and was proud she managed to leave the building without either crying or throwing up.

Numbly, Lilley took the bus home. As she reached her apartment, her cell phone rang. She glanced at the number. Nadia had missed all the action, so Jeremy must have told her the news. But Lilley couldn't face her roommate's sympathy right now. Or the suspicions Nadia had voiced lately, which Lilley was desperately trying not to think about: the reason for her frequent nausea over the last week.

Turning her phone to Mute, she threw it on the counter. She gulped down some dry crackers and water to help her stomach calm down, then changed into flannel pajamas and a pink fleece robe. Wrapping herself in her mother's quilt, she lay down on the couch and closed her eyes, even though she knew she was far too upset to sleep.

She was woken by the rattle of her cell phone on the kitchen counter. Sitting up, she saw the deepening shadows and realized she'd slept for hours. Pulling a pillow over her head, she tried to ignore the rattle. The phone finally stopped buzzing, then after a brief pause, it rudely started again. Muttering to herself, Lilley got up and grabbed it. She blinked when she saw the out-of-state number. *Alessandro,* she thought, still half confused by her dream, the dream she'd had over and over all month. She could still feel the heat of his lips against her skin. She swallowed.

"Hello?" she said almost timidly.

"Lilley Smith?" a jovial voice boomed at the other end. "You don't know me, but your résumé has come to our attention, and we'd like to offer you a paid internship with our company in New York."

By the time Lilley hung up the phone, her dreams about Alessandro were gone. She finally understood. He wasn't just ridding her from his company. He was completely erasing her from his life.

Her eyes fell on the magazine, visible from the cardboard box on the kitchen counter. Snatching it up, she stared with narrowed eyes at the picture of Alessandro with Olivia Bianchi. The blond Italian socialite looked like a smug, satisfied Persian cat who'd just licked up a whole bowl of cream.

Another huge wave of nausea overwhelmed her. Tossing the magazine to the floor, she covered her mouth and ran down the hall. Afterward, her eyes fell on the brown paper bag that sat ominously on the sink, like a loaded gun. Nadia had bought it for her days ago at the drugstore, and Lilley had scrupulously ignored it.

She couldn't possibly be pregnant. They'd gone through boxes of condoms! They'd used protection *every single time,* all weekend long.

Except...

She froze. Except that one time. In the shower.

Wide-eyed, she stared at herself in the bathroom mirror.

She exhaled. How could their affair have ended so badly? She'd fallen asleep so happily in Alessandro's arms, foolishly believing they might have a future. Then she'd woken up alone. Wrapping herself in a bedsheet, she'd called his name teasingly as she went downstairs. Instead, she'd discovered only his housekeeper. "The prince has been called away," the woman said stiffly. "Abbott will drive you back to the city." She'd handed Lilley the red gown, mended and pressed, and served her eggs, coffee and toast at the same table where Lilley had enjoyed that joyful, sensual breakfast with Alessandro just the day before. The chauffeur had driven her back home without a word. Lilley's cheeks still burned to remember.

But in spite of everything, she couldn't regret their time together. How could she, when she'd finally discovered what it felt like to take risks? To be truly alive? She'd discovered passion that had been like a fire consuming her body, making her soul blaze like a beacon in the night.

All right, so she'd never see him again. She could accept that, since she had no choice. She could even be grateful for the experience. For the memory.

But what if she was pregnant?

Lilley squeezed her eyes shut, her heart pounding. She would take the test and find out for sure. It would prove once and for all that she'd just eaten some bad Chinese takeout or something.

Her hands shook as she took the test, then waited. She told herself she wasn't worried. Hummed a cheerful little lullaby she'd sung to her cousin's baby in France. Looked at her watch. Two minutes. It was probably too soon to check, but it wouldn't hurt just to—

Pregnant.

Pregnantpregnantpregnant.

Her shaking hands dropped the stick in the trash as she staggered down the hall and into the kitchen. She found herself with a kettle in her hand and realized she was making tea, just as her mother had always done in times of crisis.

"Sweetheart, there are very few problems in the world that can't be made better by a hug, a plate of cookies and a cup of tea," her mother had said, smiling. It had worked like a charm when Lilley was nine and had failed a spelling test, and when she was a teenager and the other kids mocked, "Guess your father can't buy you a new brain." It had even worked when her father had asked her sick mother for a divorce, abandoning their family home in Minneapolis to build a huge mansion for his mistress on the shores of Lake Minnetonka.

She swallowed, trembling as tears filled her eyes. The difference was that her mother had been there. Lilley missed her so much. Paula Smith would have hugged her daughter, told her everything was going to be all right. And Lilley would have believed her.

The kettle screamed. Numbly, Lilley poured boiling water over the fragrant peppermint tea. Holding her steaming, oversized mug in her shaking hands, Lilley went to the couch.

A baby.

She was going to have Alessandro's baby.

Raw, jagged emotion washed over her. He'd arranged for her to be fired and had offered a job that was three thousand miles away. There was no other explanation for her to be spontaneously head-hunted for a fantastic internship with a New York jewelry company at double her current salary. He wanted Lilley out of San Francisco, so he wouldn't have to see her *scurrying in the halls* and could settle down, mouse-free, with his beautiful, sleek bride.

Setting her mug on the end table, she picked up the magazine from the floor. Opening it, she skimmed through the article. Alessandro was holding his annual wine-harvest celebration at his villa in Sonoma. Rumor was that it was going to be an engagement party.

Friday. That was tonight.

Lilley's fingertips stroked the image of Alessandro's handsome, cold face. She'd been so sure he would want to see her again. For the last month, she'd jumped every time her cell phone rang. She'd had such naive faith. She'd expected him to call, send flowers, a card, *something*. He hadn't.

But it turned out he had given her something, the greatest gift any woman could receive. A baby. She placed her hand on her soft belly. She'd always disliked her plump figure, wishing she could be thin and athletic. But now she realized her extra pounds didn't matter. Her amazing body was creating a baby. How could she be anything but grateful to it?

How would Alessandro react when she told him?

The memory of his harsh voice came floating back to her. *I will not marry you. I will not love you.*

She'd known from the beginning that Alessandro only considered her a fling. He'd been honest from the start. If Lilley had a broken heart, she was the only one to blame, because she'd allowed herself to hope for more.

Setting down the magazine, Lilley rose to her feet and walked to the tiny window in her pink fleece robe. Opening the gingham curtains, she looked out into the quiet street, remembering the night she'd made the choice that had changed her life so completely, the night she'd decided to give her virginity to Alessandro.

She would regret leaving San Francisco. She'd come to love the city, and had even become friends again with Jeremy and Nadia. Perhaps she would come to appreciate New York. But she would be going alone.

Then she remembered: she'd never be alone again.

She placed her hand on her belly as a wave of joy, sudden and unexpected as a child's laugh, washed over her. How could she be sad about how her time with Alessandro had ended, when he'd given her such a gift?

And the grip around her heart loosened. She would leave, as he wanted. But there was one thing she had to do first. She couldn't exactly make an appointment to see him via Mrs. Rutherford, who was highly skilled at blocking former lovers from contacting him. And this wasn't the sort of news she wished to convey via his business email address. He'd deliberately never given her his private phone number. So as unpalatable as it was, that left only one option.

Picking up the magazine, she looked down at his hard, handsome face, and at the image of the villa in Sonoma where they'd first made love. Where he'd taken her virginity. Where he'd filled her with his child.

Before she left him forever, she had to tell Alessandro he was going to be a father.

"Alessandro, at last." Olivia's sultry voice immediately set Alessandro's nerves on edge. "Did you miss me, darling?"

Forcing his lips into a smile, Alessandro turned to face her, his shoulders tight. He'd seen her arrive through the window of his study. His first party guest to arrive tonight.

It was unlike Olivia to be early to anything, so that meant she'd heard the rumors. And unfortunately the rumors were true.

The five-carat diamond ring in his jacket pocket felt like an anchor, heavy enough to drag him down through the floors of his villa, through his wine cellar and continuing straight to hell.

"I've missed you." Olivia gave him a smile that showed her white teeth. She was impeccably dressed as always, in a black one-shoulder cocktail dress that showed off her tanned body, muscular and slender from hours of running and self-denial. As she came towards him, her diamond bangles jangled noisily on her skinny wrist. She'd be the perfect Caetani bride, he told himself firmly.

And he needed to settle down before he became every bit as reckless and corrupt as his father. His night with Lilley had shown that all too clearly.

Alessandro pushed away the memory of Lilley's big trusting eyes and soft, sensual body that always hovered on the edge of his consciousness. He never should have allowed himself to touch her. Never.

Olivia came forward to kiss his mouth, but at the last moment, his head twisted away, causing her lips to land squarely on his cheek. His body's abrupt reaction surprised them both. Surely his body, at least, should have been pleased to see her? He hadn't had sex for a month. And what a hellish month it had been.

She drew back, her eyes offended. "What is it?"

"Nothing." What could he say? That he'd missed her while he was in Mexico City? That he'd thought of her when he'd lost his bid on Joyería to his most hated rival, that French bastard Théo St. Raphaël?

The truth was that it hadn't been Olivia's face he'd yearned to see the night he'd suffered that bitter disappointment. He'd hungered for a different woman's face. Her soft body. Her kind heart.

Alessandro took a deep breath. Lilley was likely already packing for New York. She almost certainly hated him now. He could only imagine how she'd felt this past month since he'd abandoned her without even the bare courtesy of a farewell. Usually his one-night stands at least got flowers.

But his coldness was deliberate. He was being cruel to be kind.

Olivia's red lips lifted into a determined smile. "I was so glad when you called me," she murmured. "I was almost starting to think you'd broken up with me."

"I did." He stared down at her. "I do not care for ultimatums."

"Lesson learned," she said, still smiling, though it did not meet her eyes. She tucked her hand into his own. Her skin felt cool. She had no softness, either of body or soul. "I'm glad we're back together. We're perfect for each other, aren't we?"

Alessandro looked down at her beautiful face, her big green eyes and sharp, hollow cheekbones. Physically, she didn't have a single flaw. She would fit well into his world. No one would ever be able to hurt her or criticize her performance as his *principessa*. *"Sì,"* he said tightly. *"Perfetto."*

They walked down the hall towards the two-story foyer. From the landing, he saw many new guests had already arrived. This party had been planned in celebration of the early wine harvest, just for a few friends. But six weeks ago, feeling arrogantly certain of impending success with the Joyería deal, he'd invited business associates, thinking it would be the perfect victory lap.

Instead, the grape harvest was turning weak and the Mexico City deal was a failure. And he was going to propose to Olivia. It wasn't a celebration. It was a wake.

With every step, he felt the dead weight of the diamond ring grow heavier in his pocket. He wondered who'd leaked the story about him purchasing it in Mexico City. Some underpaid store clerk, most likely. He'd carried it for over a week now, but he'd called Olivia only two days ago.

He'd been dragging his heels, but now he'd made his decision and wouldn't go back. He was thirty-five and had defiled one virgin too many. He'd selfishly and ruthlessly possessed Lilley, when he'd known it would ultimately bring her pain. He'd sworn he'd never be like his selfish, callous father. And yet, seducing his innocent, brokenhearted file-room girl, he'd come perilously close.

Olivia's cool, bony arm twisted hard around his as they walked down the stairs. The weather forecast was calling for thunderstorms, so the party had been moved indoors from the pool, although many guests had remained outside. He could hear a jazz trio playing in the ballroom, and he saw friends and business acquaintances from Silicon Valley. The men wore suits similar to Alessandro's, and their wives wore shiny cocktail dresses, and everyone was drinking his wine. He should be enjoying this…shouldn't he?

He heard Bronson arguing loudly at the door. His normally staid butler seemed to be struggling with an unwanted guest. "Service entrance is at the back," Bronson insisted, trying to close the door.

"I'm not here for a delivery!" a woman said, pushing at the door. "I'm here to see Alessandro!"

The butler sucked in his breath as if she'd just insulted his mother. *"Alessandro?"* he repeated in disbelief. "You mean His Serene Highness, Prince Alessandro Caetani?"

"Yes!"

"The prince is currently hosting a party," Bronson said coldly, his tone clearly adding *and is unavailable to the likes of you.* "Make an appointment though his secretary. Good evening."

But as he started to slam the door, the woman blocked him with a foot. "I'm sorry to be rude," she begged, "but I'm leaving in the morning and have to see him. Tonight."

Prickles went down Alessandro's neck.

He knew that sweet voice. It was clear as a freshwater lake to a man dying of thirst. Dropping Olivia's hand, he went down the stairs to where white-haired, dignified Bronson was struggling with the door like an American bouncer at a bar. The butler panted, "Unhand the door this instant—"

Grabbing the door over his head, Alessandro wrenched it open. The butler turned. "Your highness," he gasped. "I'm sorry for this interruption. This *woman* has been trying to force her way into your party. I don't know how she talked her way past security at the gate, but..."

"It's all right," Alessandro said, hardly knowing what he was saying, staring at the woman from his dreams on the doorstep.

Lilley looked even more beautiful than she had a month ago. Her long brown hair was swept back in a ponytail, her face was bare of makeup. Unlike all the other women squeezed into tight girdles and barely able to move in sequined dresses, Lilley wore a simple tank top and a flowery cotton skirt, a casual summery outfit that effortlessly showed off her stunning curves. She shone like an angel standing in front of the distant dark storm clouds over the horizon.

"Alessandro," Lilley whispered, looking at him. The pupils of her large, limpid eyes seemed to dilate, and the honey-brown gaze pulled him into their endless sweet depths. Hearing her speak his name, he felt electrified.

"Security!" his butler cried, motioning to a body-

guard on the other side of the room. Alessandro grabbed
Bronson's arm.

"I will handle this," he growled. "Thank you."

Mollified, the butler nodded and backed away. "Of
course, sir."

Taking Lilley gently by the arm, Alessandro pulled her
inside the foyer. She looked up at him, her lips parted.

His hand involuntarily tightened, his fingers trembling
at the point of contact against her soft skin. Waves of sensual memories washed over his unwilling body. The last
time they'd been together, they'd made love in every room
here, including this foyer. He looked at the wall behind her.
There.

Suddenly choking with need, he felt an overwhelming
drive to carry her up to his bed—to claim her body as his
own. He'd thought being away from Lilley would make him
forget. It had only made him want her more.

Blood roared in his ears as he reached around her and
closed the heavy oak door. Dropping Lilley's arm, he
folded his hands to keep himself from touching her. He
said hoarsely, "You shouldn't have come."

She took a deep breath. "I had no choice."

"What is she doing here?" Olivia demanded peevishly
in English behind him. "Did you invite her, Alessandro?"

Oh yes, Olivia. He'd forgotten her completely. He glanced
back at her, irritated. "No, I did not invite her." He turned
back to Lilley. "Why are you here?"

Lilley moved closer to him, a soft smile on her lips. Her
brown eyes were luminous, catching at his soul. She seemed
like a creature from another world, a kinder one filled with
magic and innocence. Her pretty face was suffused with a
strange glow. "I came to see you."

He stared at her, bewildered. *I came to see you.* No
pretense? No games? No story about *just being in the*

neighborhood? He hardly knew how to deal with such straightforward, vulnerable honesty. He'd had so little experience with it.

"You weren't invited," Olivia said coldly. "You need to leave."

It was clear by her scowl that she'd recognized Lilley as the woman Alessandro had taken to the Preziosi di Caetani ball. Olivia glared at her as if she hoped the hot laser beam of her eyes might cause the younger woman to burst into flame.

But looking back at Olivia, Lilley's gaze didn't have a shred of anger or even fear. Instead, she looked at the Italian heiress with something almost like…sympathy.

"I'm not here to cause a scene," Lilley said quietly. "I just need to speak to Alessandro, alone. Please. It will only take a moment."

"Alessandro doesn't want to talk to you." When he remained silent, Olivia tossed her head, giving Lilley a nasty glare. "Get out before I throw you out, you cheap little— file clerk."

But her attempted insult seemed to roll right off Lilley like water off a duck's back. She turned back to Alessandro with a soft smile. "May I please speak to you? Alone?"

Being alone with Lilley, mere minutes before he planned to propose to Olivia, was a bad idea. A *very* bad idea. He opened his mouth to tell Lilley firmly that she must go. Instead, his body twisted and he heard himself saying in Italian, "Will you please excuse us?"

Olivia drew back with a hiss between her teeth, visibly furious. "Certainly," she said coldly. "I'll go greet the mayor and my good friend Bill Hocking," she said, referring to a well-known Silicon Valley billionaire. Her warning couldn't have been clearer. But suddenly he didn't give a damn.

"Grazie," he answered mildly, as if utterly oblivious of her affronted fury.

With a scowl, Olivia turned on her heel and stomped away, her bare back looking almost skeletal in the black one-shouldered gown.

Alessandro looked back down at Lilley, who, with her soft body and simple cotton clothes seemed even more impossibly alluring than he remembered.

Amidst all the noise around them, the jazz music, the soft clink of wineglasses and laughter of guests, he felt as if they were alone. "I never expected to see you again," he murmured. "I can't believe you crashed my party."

She smiled. "Really brave of me, right? Or really stupid."

"Brave and stupid are often the same thing."

Lilley shook her head, and he saw unshed tears in her eyes as she laughed. "I'm glad to see you, Alessandro. I've missed you."

Hearing her leave herself so vulnerable, he felt it again—that odd twisting in the vicinity of his heart. "But you shouldn't have come here tonight."

Her eyes met his. "Because this is an engagement party."

Alessandro tried to keep his face blank. "You read gossip magazines."

"Unfortunately."

Bracing himself, he waited for the inevitable scene, for her tears and recriminations. Instead, she just gave him a wistful smile.

"I want you to be happy." She lifted her chin. "If Olivia is truly the one, I wish you all the happiness in the world."

Alessandro's jaw fell open. It was the last thing he'd expected her to say. He took a deep breath, suddenly uncertain how to proceed.

"You—aren't upset?" he said finally. His cheeks became

hot as he heard how foolish the words sounded to his own ears.

"There's no point to being upset over something I cannot change." She stared down at the marble floor. "And I truly didn't come to cause a scene."

"Then why did you?"

She looked up, her eyes luminous and wide. Beneath the darkening light of the upper windows, her eyes were the color of a mountain stream. Not just brown, he realized. Her eyes were a thousand shades, depths of green and blue and amber like a deep, ancient river.

"I have something to tell you before I can leave San Francisco."

Leave? Why on earth would she leave? Then Alessandro remembered he'd convinced a friend to offer her a job in New York. When he'd been in Mexico City, enduring night after night of hot dreams, he'd thought sending her three thousand miles away from San Francisco was the only sane thing to do. Now, he thought it the stupidest idea he'd ever conceived. His shoulders tightened. "Lilley—"

The doorbell rang, and as Bronson hesitantly came towards the door Alessandro grabbed Lilley's hand. He pulled her out of the foyer, away from the hubbub of the party, leading her down a side hall.

"Where are we going?" she asked, not resisting him.

His hand tightened around hers. "Where we can be alone."

Turning down a second hallway towards a quiet wing, Alessandro tried to ignore how right her hand felt in his own, tried not to feel the enticing warmth of her soft skin. But as he pulled her into the music room where he often hosted concerts and parties, the large room suddenly felt small, the temperature hot and stifling. As he walked around the grand piano and past the Picasso on the wall, his tie felt tight around his neck. He just kept walking through the music room. Opening the sliding glass doors, he pulled her into a small private garden.

Outside, the air was cool. The garden was green and stark, just a lawn, really, surrounded on three sides by a ten-foot privet hedge that separated them from the poolside terrace. On the other side of the hedge, he could hear muffled conversation and the clink of wineglasses as guests milled around the Olympic-size pool and terrace.

Alessandro realized he was still holding Lilley's hand. He looked down at their intertwined fingers. She followed his gaze and he heard her intake of breath, felt her tremble.

Their eyes met in the rapidly deepening twilight. The sky above the villa was dark with threatening clouds, and he heard a distant rumble of thunder. He heard the wind howl through the trees. Lilley's full cotton skirt swirled around her legs.

Electricity filled the air as the temperature seemed to drop five degrees around them. But Alessandro still felt hot, burning from the storm inside him. Desire arced though him, and with an intake of breath, he dropped her hand.

Lilley deserved better than a series of cheap one-night stands. For her sake, he couldn't risk her loving him. And for his own sake…he couldn't risk caring for her. He'd learned long ago to trust no one. Sex and money were real. Love was a lie.

He knew this, but his body shook with the effort of not touching her, from not putting his arms around her and sinking into her softness and warmth. He tightened his hands into fists.

"Why did you come?" he ground out.

Colorful fairy lights high in the trees swayed violently in the rising wind. A flash of lightning illuminated Lilley's stricken face.

"You're in love with Miss Bianchi, aren't you?"

He set his jaw. "I told you. Marriage is a mutually beneficial alliance. Love has nothing to do with it."

"But surely you wouldn't want to spend the rest of your life without love." Long tendrils of soft brown hair blew across her face as she searched his gaze. Her expression faltered. "Would you?"

Thunder crackled in the sky above. Alessandro heard gasps from the other side of the hedge as the first raindrops fell, and guests ran back inside the villa.

"Just tell me what you have to say, then leave," he said tightly.

Lilley blinked, then looked down at the grass beneath her feet. "This is hard. Harder than I ever thought it would be."

Rain began to fall more heavily. He watched a fat raindrop slide down her rounded cheek to her full, generous mouth. Her pink tongue unconsciously darted out to lick the thick drop of rain against her full, sweetly sensual lips, and he nearly groaned.

He had to get her out of here before he did something they'd both regret forever. Why had he ever allowed himself to take a single forbidden taste of what did not belong to him by right?

"It was a mistake for me to seduce you," he said in a low voice. "I'm sorry I ever touched you."

She looked up, her eyes bright with grief. "Was it so awful?"

Awful? A new ache filled his throat. He hated that for the first time in nineteen years, he'd found a heart he did not want to break, and here he was breaking it. "Your first time should have been special, with a man who loved you, who might someday marry you. Not a one-night stand with a man like me."

"Don't be so hard on yourself." She tried to give him a smile. "It was two nights."

He nearly shuddered with the memory of how good it had been between them. How she'd tasted. How she'd felt beneath him. He forced himself to say, "You will find someone else."

She stared at him. "That's why you're sending me to New York."

Thunder boomed over them. "You knew it was me?"

"Of course I knew." She looked at him with a tremulous smile. She swallowed, then squared her shoulders. Rain was starting to soak her long brown hair, causing her tank top and cotton skirt to cling to her skin. "Thank you for arranging the internship. It was—very kind."

Her generous spirit only made Alessandro feel more like a brute. His head was throbbing with pain. He tightened his hands into fists. "I wasn't being kind, damn you. I was sending you away because I'm getting married. Not for love. Her father's company will be an asset." His hands tightened. "But when I speak vows, I will be faithful to them."

Lilley searched his gaze. "And if I were an heiress like her?" she whispered. "Would you choose me as your bride instead?"

Looking at her, he held his breath. Then slowly, he shook his head. "You would never fit into my world." His hand lifted. "It would destroy everything about you that I admire most. Everything that is cheerful and bright."

He barely caught himself before he touched her cheek. Thunder cracked again above their heads, as loud and metallic as a baseball bat against the earth, and he dropped his hand. "Olivia will be my perfect bride."

"I can't let you marry her. Not without knowing what I, what I…" She licked her lips. "What I have to tell you."

Alessandro's suit was now completely wet. The two of them were alone in the emerald garden, below the black sky. The scent of rain washed over the leaves, over the earth, over the distant vineyards and the pink bougainvillea twisting up the stucco of his villa.

And looking at her beautiful, stricken brown eyes, he suddenly knew what she was going to say.

"Don't," he ground out. "Don't say it."

She hesitated, her lovely round face looking scared. Her hair and clothes were now stuck to her skin. He could see the full outline of her breasts and hard jut of her nipples beneath her thin cotton tank top. He could see the shape of her curvaceous legs beneath her skirt as lightning flashed above them. "Alessandro—"

"No, *cara*." He put his hand to her lips, stroking the rain off her face with the pads of his thumbs. "Please," he whispered. "Do not speak the words. Leave us that, at least. I can see your feelings on your face. I already know what is in your heart."

Lilley looked up at him, her expression breathless. The rain began to fall more heavily and he realized he'd cupped her face in his hands. Her wet, full, pink lips were inches from his own, and he suddenly couldn't breathe. He was hard and aching, his lips pulsing with the drive to kiss her. His body clamored for him to push her roughly against the hedge and claim her as his own.

Using every drop of willpower he possessed, Alessandro dropped his hands, stepping away. He said harshly, "Go to New York, Lilley."

"Wait," she choked out as he turned away. "You can't go. Not until I tell you—"

He whirled to face her, his expression cold. "Do not fight

me. We must never see each other again. There is nothing you can say to make me change my decision."

She took a deep breath.

"I'm pregnant with your baby," she whispered.

CHAPTER SIX

THUNDER pounded the dark sky, shaking the earth beneath her feet. Lilley held her breath, waiting for his reaction.

The violently swinging fairy lights above the hedge caused shadows to move across the sharp planes of Alessandro's handsome face as he said hoarsely, "Pregnant."

"Yes."

A sharp flash of lightning illuminated his grim black eyes as he took a single step towards her. "You can't be."

"I am."

"We used protection."

She spread her arms helplessly. "That one time, in the shower…"

He sucked in his breath. "No."

"But—"

"No." Clawing back his wet black hair, he paced three steps across the lawn. Lilley watched him with a building sense of despair. Her body felt ice-cold, soaked to the bone. But that was nothing compared to her heart. She'd known he didn't want her, and that he wouldn't want their baby. But knowing it in her head and hearing him say it out loud were two different things.

She wrapped her arms around her shivering body, trying to comfort herself and the baby inside her. *It's all right,* she told herself, using the words her mother had often said to her when she was young and sad. *It'll be all right, sweetheart.*

It worked. She felt the anguish give way a fraction inside her. Lifting her head, she looked at Alessandro. She whispered, "It's all right."

He stopped pacing. "What?"

Love was a gift, Lilley realized. Love was always a gift. Even if the person you loved chose not to love you back.

She looked at Alessandro, so handsome and impossibly sexy even with his expensive suit soaked with rain. His dark hair was plastered to his forehead and tousled. Compassion for him, for this man she'd almost loved, filled her heart, crowding out her grief for the husband and father he could never be. She took a deep breath. "Nothing has to change for you."

The expression on his face was suddenly as dark and ominous as the storm. "What?"

"You told me from the start that our affair would only be a fling." She shook her head. "I don't expect you to help me raise our baby. I just thought you should know."

Alessandro's eyes were black. The muscles of his powerful body tightened. "If you don't expect me to raise your child, exactly what do you want from me?"

She blinked. "Want?"

"What are your demands? A house? Money?"

His words were hard, but she saw the tremble of his body beneath the sheeting rain. And Lilley suddenly wondered what sort of people he'd lived with, that his first thought upon hearing she was pregnant was to expect her to demand money.

"I don't need anything," she said quietly. *Except a father for my baby,* came the painful thought. *Except for a man who can love me.* But she would have to be brave, to be both mother and father to her sweet baby, who would need everything she could give. "Thank you for giving me two nights I'll never forget. Thank you for believing in me. And most of all," she whispered over the ache in her throat, "thank you for giving me a baby."

Blinking fast, she looked up at his face for the last time, trying to memorize his features into her memory. The aquiline silhouette of his nose. The hard angle of his jaw. His eyes like dark embers, blazing fire. "I hope your life is full of joy. I'll never forget you." She turned away. "Good-bye."

Lilley started walking back towards the villa, her sandals squishing in the wet grass, her heart breaking.

His hand grabbed her shoulder, whirling her around. He looked down at her as the rain continued to pound them both. His eyes burned with fury. "You think you can tell me you're pregnant—and just *leave?*"

Lilley sucked in her breath, almost frightened at the darkness in his eyes. "There is no reason for me to stay—"

"No reason?" His voice was nearly a shout. He visibly controlled himself. His jaw twitched as he loosened his grip on her upper arms. "If you truly are pregnant with my child," he ground out, "how can you just turn and leave? How can you be so cold?"

"Cold?" she gasped, ripping away. "What do you want from me? You want me to fall to the ground and cling to your knees, begging for you to love me and this baby, begging for you never to let me go?"

"That at least I would understand!"

"I can't change your nature!" she cried, then took a deep gulping breath. "You made your feelings clear. You want a wife you can be proud of. You want Olivia. And you want me three thousand miles away!"

His eyes narrowed as he said in a low voice, "That was before."

"Nothing has changed."

"Everything has changed, if the baby is really mine."

It took several seconds for the meaning of his words to sink in. Then her eyes went wide. "You think I would sleep with another man, then lie to you about it?"

Alessandro's posture was so taut, he seemed like a statue. Like a stone. She could barely hear his voice as he said, "It happens." His expression looked strange. "You might have gone back to the jewelry designer. Accidentally gotten pregnant, than decided to cash in."

"Cash in?" she said incredulously. "Cash in how?"

He searched her gaze. "Do you swear you're telling me the truth? The child is mine?"

"Of course the baby is yours! You're the only man I've ever slept with in my whole life!"

"I want a paternity test."

She stiffened. "What?"

"You heard me."

The insult was almost too much to bear. "Forget it," she whispered. "I'm not doing some stupid paternity test. If you trust me so little, if you believe I'd lie to you about something like this, then just forget it."

Lilley's body shook as she turned and walked away. Tears streamed down her face, blending with the rain. She was halfway across the empty lawn before he stopped her, and this time, the expression on his face had changed.

"I'm sorry, Lilley," he said quietly. "I do know you. And you wouldn't lie."

Their eyes locked. She exhaled as the knots in her shoulders loosened. Then he spoke.

"Marry me."

She heard the roar of her own heartbeat above the splatter of rain. "Is that a joke?"

His sensual lips curved upward. "I never joke, remember?"

Her head was spinning. She'd never expected him to propose, not in a million years, not in her most delusional dreams. "You…want to marry me?"

"Is that so surprising? What did you expect—that I'd kick you and our unborn child to the curb and merrily go and propose to another woman?"

Biting her lip, she looked up at the ruthless lines of his face. "Well…yes."

"Then you don't know me at all."

"No," she whispered. "I guess I don't." She felt dizzy and still a bit sick. She'd barely made it to Sonoma in Nadia's old car without being sick, she'd been so nervous. And now he wanted to marry her? She licked her lips, feeling as though she might cry. "You want to help raise our baby?"

Alessandro's jaw was tight. "I will protect you both. I will give the baby my name. It is my duty."

Her heart, which had been soaring in blind hope, crashed to the ground. His *duty?* She exhaled. "You don't need to marry me to be involved in our baby's life."

"Yes. I do."

"Why?"

"Because it is necessary."

"You're old-fashioned."

"Yes."

"But you don't love me!"

He folded his arms. "Irrelevant."

"Not to me, it isn't!" She exhaled, clenching her hands. "Listen, Alessandro, I'll never try to keep you from seeing your child—"

"I know that you will not, once we are wed."

"I'm not going to marry you!"

"Of course you will," he said coldly.

She shook her head, causing wet tendrils to slap against

her cheeks. "Be in a loveless marriage for the rest of my life? No thanks!"

"I understand. You still want your knight in shining armor." He set his jaw. "But whatever either of us might have once planned for our lives is over. We are expecting a child. We will wed."

"No—we would be miserable!"

"Miserable?" he said incredulously. "Don't you understand? You will be my bride. A princess. Rich beyond your wildest dreams!"

"I don't care—I don't want it! Not when I know you don't love me and never will!"

He grabbed her by the shoulders, his hands sliding against her wet skin. "You would deny our child a name out of some childish yearning for fairytale dreams?"

"It's not childish." She closed her eyes, which suddenly burned with tears that he'd used his knowledge of her heart against her. "You are cruel."

"I am *right,*" he said grimly. "You have no reason to refuse me." He paused. "I will even be faithful to you, Lilley."

He spoke the words as if being faithful to her would require a huge sacrifice, practically more than any billionaire prince could bear. And it was probably true. "Gee, thanks," she said sarcastically, glaring at him. "But I have no interest in being your duty bride."

"Your objection is to the word *duty?*" He narrowed his eyes. "What do you think marriage is?"

"Love. Friendship. Having each other's backs. A poetic union of souls—"

His grip on her tightened. "And passion?" His voice became husky beneath the rain. "What of passion?"

Her heart fell to her sandals and back again. She felt his strength, his warmth, the irresistible pull of his power. Against her will, she craved him.

"It was good between us." He ran his fingers lightly along her jawline, his thumb along her sensitive lower lip. His soft stroke caused a spark down her body that made her suck in her breath. "You know how it was."

Memories shuddered through her of how it had felt when he'd made love to her. Her breasts felt heavy, her nipples aching and tight. She swallowed. "It was a fling," she breathed. "You said so yourself. I'm not the right woman to be your bride."

"My assessment has changed." He cupped her face. His eyes were dark with heat. "For the last month," he whispered, "I've thought of nothing but having you in my bed."

She licked her lips. "You—you have?"

"I told myself you deserved a man who could love you. But everything has changed. Only our child matters now." His gaze fell to her lips. "But that's a lie," he said in a low voice. "That's not the only reason I want you as my bride. I want you to be mine. I want to possess you completely. Every night. For the rest of our lives."

Lilley could barely breathe. "But Olivia—"

"I would have married her out of duty. Not desire." He looked into her eyes. "You are the one I want, Lilley." His mouth lowered to hers with agonizing slowness as he whispered, "Don't you know that by now? I want you. And now I will have you—forever."

As he kissed her, she closed her eyes, her body shaking as his lips took ruthless possession of her own. His lips were hard and hungry as the rain poured over their skin and thunder pounded across the lowering black sky.

She heard his low growl as in a sudden movement he pushed her back against the hedge. She felt the rough, wet branches of the shrubbery against her back as he held her tight against his wet, muscled body. He moved his hands through her hair, tilting her head to deepen the kiss. In the force of their embrace, their wet clothes slid and clung to their skin. His hands roamed everywhere, over her cotton tank top, over her hips. She felt his hand reach beneath the hemline of her skirt, dragging it slowly up her thighs. His hand slid upwards, and she gasped, placing her hand over his. "No."

"Don't refuse me," he said in a low voice. "It's what we both want."

"I do want you," she panted, then choked out a sob. "But I can't marry you. I'd have to give up everything I believe in. I'm afraid it would destroy me to love you."

"So don't love me." He caressed her hair, looking down at her with serious dark eyes. "It's too late for our own dreams, Lilley," he said quietly. "All that matters now are our baby's."

She sucked in her breath. He was right, she realized. All that mattered now was their child. She closed her eyes. "Will you love our baby? Will you be a good father?"

"Yes," he said simply.

Her heart twisted as she took a deep breath, then another. For an instant, she held her breath. Then she let her dreams for love go.

She opened her eyes.

"I can accept...a marriage without love," she whispered, then shook her head. "But not without trust. Not without respect. I won't be humiliated by a paternity test. Either believe that the baby is yours...or let us go."

Staring at her, Alessandro slowly nodded. "All right, *cara,*" he said in a low voice. "All right."

Swallowing back the ache in her throat, she whispered, "Then I'll marry you."

Alessandro drew back. "You will?" The rain had lifted, and a beam of twilight sun burst from behind the clouds, illuminating his hard features with gold. "You'll be my wife?"

Wordlessly, she nodded.

His eyes lit up, and the edges of his lips curved up into a bright smile that made him look younger, almost boyish. She'd never seen him look that way before. As Lilley stared up at him, the noise of the storm faded, and thunder became a distant memory.

Maybe it would be all right, she thought, dazed. Maybe passion and a baby would be enough to start a marriage.

She prayed it would be. Because that was all they had.

CHAPTER SEVEN

LILLEY'S hair flew around her, tangling in the cold night wind as Alessandro drove his yellow Ferrari convertible across the vast, lonely Nevada desert. She couldn't stop looking over at him at the wheel. Moonlight frosted his dark hair with silver.

The party had ended in scandal, when Alessandro had privately informed Olivia that she'd been misled by the gossip columns and he intended to take Lilley as his bride. Olivia had stomped out of the villa, but not before she'd grabbed Lilley's arm in the foyer.

"You'll regret this," the beautiful Milanese heiress had hissed, pressing her fingernails into Lilley's flesh. "You might be pregnant with his child, you piece of trash, but you're not worthy to be his wife. You think you've beaten me. But I will find a way to destroy you."

Turning, the gorgeous blonde had departed, her skinny shoulders straight as she'd stormed out of the villa. In the next room Alessandro was already announcing their engagement to all of his friends, introducing them to Lilley at his side. They'd applauded and murmured congratulations, but she'd felt their bewildered eyes on her, as if they were wondering why on earth someone like Alessandro would choose her for his bride. Something she kept wondering herself. Then he'd announced with a wicked smile, "We're eloping to Las Vegas. Tonight."

Lilley had gasped along with everyone else. They would drive to Las Vegas, he insisted, as his private jet was en route to San Francisco after delivering supplies to a desperate community decimated by a hurricane. "We'll be married by morning," Alessandro had told her after he'd gotten rid of the guests. He paused. "Unless you wish to wait until your father can attend the ceremony…"

She'd felt a prickle at the back of her neck, knowing she had to tell Alessandro the truth about her family before they could possibly marry. She shook her head. "No. I don't want my father at the ceremony, and you wouldn't either. We're not exactly friends. I'm not even sure he loves me." She took a deep breath. "Speaking of which," she said in a small voice, "there's something I need to tell you. Before I can marry you."

"No need." His expression had suddenly become cold, closed off. "I already know what you're going to say."

Alessandro knew about her family? Her jaw dropped. "You—you do?"

He nodded, his eyes hard. "There's no point in talking about it, because there's nothing I can do to change it."

She bit her lip. "So you—you forgive me?" she whispered.

"Yes," he said grimly, then shook his head. "But I will never be able to love you."

Lilley wasn't worried about him loving her at that moment. She'd just been praying he wouldn't utterly despise her. Relief washed through her. He knew her secret. Of course he did, she thought, suddenly so giddy she was almost light-headed. He'd probably known it all along! Alessandro Caetani was a brilliant competitor, which is why her cousin found him to be such an infuriating foe. He knew stuff. With a tearful, joyful sob, she threw her arms around him.

Surprised, he'd put his arms around her. "I'll have my people pack up your things and meet us in Las Vegas. No need to pack clothes," he'd said gruffly. "I'll provide you with those."

"I need my jewelry materials and tools, and the quilt my mother made me."

"You have a passport, yes?"

"Yes." With a whole bunch of stamps in and out of French airports she wouldn't have to hide. "Why a passport?"

"I have a little place in Sardinia." He'd smiled, his eyes hot. "A honeymoon cottage."

They drove all night in his convertible, across the dark, vast Nevada desert. Sometime during the night, she'd fallen asleep against his shoulder. When they arrived in Las Vegas, Alessandro woke her with a kiss to her forehead.

"Welcome to your wedding day, *cara,*" he whispered, and she opened her eyes blearily to see the white light of dawn breaking over the distant craggy mountains.

Alessandro took her to the luxury Hermitage Hotel and Resort, where he ordered a lavish private buffet for two brought up to their penthouse suite. Five waiters with over-flowing carts brought up fifty different items for Lilley to sample—waffles, omelets, pecan-stuffed French toast, slabs of bacon, watermelon, fruit salad and chicken-fried steak. Afterward, Alessandro escorted her to an overpriced bridal boutique downstairs in the hotel. Selecting a tuxedo for himself, he casually bought the first wedding dress she admired.

"You can't!" Lilley cried when she saw the twenty-thousand-dollar price tag, even as her eyes traced the beaded white fabric longingly.

Lifting his eyebrow, he gave her a grin. "I can."

They collected their marriage license downtown, then returned to their suite at the Hermitage where a bridal bouquet and boutonniere waited for them beside the grand piano. It was intoxicating. Dreamy. They made love on the huge bed overlooking the Las Vegas Strip, then made love again in the shower before changing their clothes. Then, when Alessandro first saw Lilley in her wedding dress, he pulled her straight back into bed.

Lilley sat astride his lap, riding him as he leaned against the headboard, her necklace bouncing softly against her swollen breasts with every thrust. After their third lust-fueled explosion of the afternoon, he kissed the necklace's pink-heart crystal and brass chain. "Any man on earth would pay a fortune to have such a necklace for his wife." His expression changed. "It's just too bad that..."

"What?"

He exhaled. "Nothing." Taking her hand, he pulled her from the bed. "Let's get to the ceremony before we get distracted."

Two hours after their appointed time, they finally married, surrounded by white candles at the hotel's private wedding chapel. An acquaintance of Alessandro's who owned the hotel, Nikos Stavrakis, was the only witness as they breathlessly spoke their vows.

And just like that, Lilley was a princess. Wearing a white suit he'd purchased for her, she boarded her husband's waiting jet, bound for the Mediterranean.

On board, Lilley found the possessions his staff had packed for her. The box of her life was small indeed—just her mother's homemade quilt, her jewelry tools and an excited, gushing note from Nadia wishing her luck and all the joy in the world. "Jeremy will be moving in with me now—I know you won't mind because you're a happily married princess! I can't believe you *married* Prince Alessandro! You'll be famous now!"

As the jet flew the long miles east across the country and towards the Atlantic, Lilley fell asleep on a couch, holding her mother's quilt to her chest. When she woke up, Alessandro was watching her from a nearby white leather chair.

"I will always protect you," he whispered, leaning forward. His eyes were dark. "I want you to know that. And I will protect our child."

She sat up, clutching the quilt. "Protect us. But not too much." She gave him a weak smile. "My father tried to protect me from the world he didn't think I was strong enough to handle. If not for my mother, I would never have been allowed out of the house."

"Which is why he wanted you to marry one of his employees." His lips lifted in a humorless smile. "When will you tell him about our marriage?"

Her eyes slid away. "I don't know. It's—complicated."

"I understand." He looked down at his folded hands. "My father married my mother for her money, then spent it all on his mistresses, whom he flaunted to her face. He thought condoms were for the weak. He scattered bastards carelessly all over the world."

She sucked in her breath. "Oh, Alessandro—"

He looked up, his handsome face stoic. "He died when I was nineteen, and left us only debts in his memory. My mother would have starved in the street, if I hadn't started work to support her. When she died five years ago, she was living in a palace in Rome. As I vowed she someday would." He exhaled. "I'm trying to tell you that you never need to worry now, about anything. I will always take care of you."

She blinked back tears, giving him a smile as she reached

across the aisle to stroke his face. "We will take care of each other."

He turned his rough cheek into her caress, then placed his hand over her own. "You won't regret giving up your dreams to marry me. I'm no shining knight, but I will treat you well. You won't have a business of your own, but I will work hard for you and the baby. I'll give you all the precious jewelry you could possibly desire."

Frowning, she drew back her hand. "What do you mean—giving up my dream of having a business?"

He stared down at her. "You have no time for a career. Not anymore. Your place is to be my wife, and raise our child."

"You don't tell me this until *now*—after we're already married?"

"I thought it would be obvious," he said stiffly, looking uncomfortable.

"No," she whispered. "You knew I would be upset. Which is why you waited till now." She forced her voice to be calm. "I never agreed to give up my business."

He looked at her. "If that dream had ever meant anything to you, you would have done something about it long ago."

Lilley's eyes widened, then she sucked in her breath. He was right. She could have built her business for years, but instead, she'd squandered her time being paralyzed by fear.

"Money will never be an issue for you again," he tried. "I will provide you with everything you desire." He gave her a smile. "And if you want to make jewelry as a little hobby to entertain yourself, I have no objection to it."

"Generous of you," she muttered.

He stared down at her, then set his jaw. "Once you have properly settled in as my bride, as the mother of our child, well then—we will see," he said grudgingly. His eyes softened as he stroked her cheek. "I want you to be happy, Lilley. I will do everything I can to make that happen."

Feeling his hand upon her skin, seeing the tenderness in his eyes, she exhaled. It would be fine. Somehow, it would all work out. "I want to do the same for you."

His eyes were hot and dark as he gave her a wicked grin. "Ah, but you've made me so happy already. You make me happy on an hourly basis," he breathed, leaning forward to kiss her. He stopped, his face inches from hers. "Just promise you'll never lie to me."

"I'll never lie to you," Lilley promised, and she meant it, with all her heart.

"Io bacio."

"Io bacio," Lilley repeated, balancing a book on her head.

Standing by the window overlooking the bright-blue water of the Costa Smeralda, her Italian tutor smiled. *"Tu baci."*

"Tu baci," Lilley repeated rather breathlessly, walking across the marble floor in four-inch high heels.

"Lui bacia."

As Lilley repeated all the conjugations of *baciare,* she found herself smiling. Her tutor had clearly chosen the verb *to kiss* in honor of her standing as a newlywed. And though her feet ached from the expensive shoes and her body ached from standing up straight in the designer skirt suit for hours, she felt strangely happy. Yes, her head ached from a full schedule of etiquette and deportment lessons, mixed with Italian classes in which she not only learned the word for fork, *la forchetta,* but she was taught which one to use for salad and which for dessert. But she was...happy.

This wasn't the same world she'd left behind in Minnesota, that was for sure. Her father had come from nothing. He'd never given a hoot about etiquette. Now, after a week in Sardinia, Lilley felt exhausted, but it was the best kind of tired. She felt sore, too, but there was a very delicious reason for that as well. A hot blush filled her cheeks as she remembered what Alessandro had done to her in bed last night, and what she'd done to him. The braver she got, the more she acted on her own needs and fantasies, the more he liked it.

"Molto bene," the Italian tutor finally said with satisfaction.

"You arc a quick learner, *Principessa,"* said the Swiss woman who'd come from a famous boarding school in the Alps to teach her deportment.

"Grazie," Lilley said with a laugh. A quick learner? She'd certainly never heard *that* one before. But it helped that she didn't have to read, just listen, repeat and practice. Her husband had given the instructors precise instructions.

Her husband.

After a week in Alessandro's white wedding-cake villa in Sardinia, seven blissful days of life as his wife, Lilley still adored the word *husband.* She held the word close to her heart, cuddled it like a child. She had a *husband.* And—she glanced discreetly at her watch, almost causing the book to slide off her head—it was almost five o'clock. Her favorite time of day.

The Italian tutor followed her gaze and nodded. "We are done." He turned to gather his briefcase. *"Buona sera, Principessa."*

Madame Renaud pulled the leatherbound book off Lilley's head. *"Bonsoir, Principessa,"* she said, *"et merci."* Madame followed her tutor out of the door.

Principessa. Another word that still seemed exotic and foreign—nothing to do with her at all.

The instant her instructors were gone, Lilley raced upstairs towards the master bedroom as fast as her tight beige pencil skirt would allow her. She rushed down the hall, past priceless works of modern art that to her looked like a pre-schooler's squiggles, past expensive white furniture that was mostly just hard and uncomfortable in her opinion.

But there was one thing about this villa that she loved: their bedroom. Her high heels clicked loudly as she hurried down the hall. Passing a window, her eyes fell on the view of the turquoise Mediterranean and white sand beach. All right—two things she loved about this house.

A week ago she would have had difficulty placing the Italian island of Sardinia on a map, but now she was in love, because the Costa Smeralda, the island's green coast, was the most joyful and beautiful place she'd ever seen. The open windows lured in a warm, sweet wind to blow against her hair, and the bright golden sun warmed her body and heart. As if those needed any warming.

Running her hand along the curving handrail of the villa's white staircase, she snorted as she remembered Alessandro's description of this vacation home. Some *cottage!* It had eight bedrooms and a full staff, though they always disappeared at five o'clock each night, as Alessandro had ordered, so the two of them could be alone.

Lilley smiled to herself. She enjoyed her lessons during the day, but at night...She shivered. At night, she and her husband set the world on fire.

At the end of the hallway, Lilley pushed open their bedroom door, half expecting to find Alessandro on the bed, wearing only a strategically placed jewelry box. Yesterday, he'd worn only a large black velvet box which held a priceless diamond and emerald necklace. He seemed to enjoy giving her such expensive trinkets, so Lilley always tried to accept them graciously, even though the impersonal, sterile new jewelry was the last thing she cared about.

Spending time in bed with him, on the other hand...well. She'd take all of that she could get.

But today, their bedroom was empty. So was the study where Alessandro had had business meetings all day with high-level board members from his headquarters in Rome. Peeking through the window, she saw him pacing by the pool, talking on the phone. Lilley's eyes devoured his strong physique in a snug white T-shirt, old jeans and bare feet as he paced from the white cabana to the poolhouse. Behind him, palm trees waved against the sparkling blue sea.

The pool! Perfect! She'd get him splashing in there yet!

Squelching a mischievous laugh, Lilley raced back to their bedroom and changed into a tiny bikini, one of the six he'd bought for her in Porto Cervo. Tying the strings at her hips and back, she glanced at herself in the mirror. Funny how she'd once felt so embarrassed about her plump body. She'd worn baggy clothes that didn't fit, trying to hide her shape. But Alessandro loved her body so much, what could possibly be wrong with it? How could she not love her overlarge breasts, her curvy belly, her wide hips, with their child growing inside her?

For the first time in her life, she felt comfortable in her own skin. Even the morning sickness had all but disappeared since she'd become Alessandro's wife. A coincidence? Or were her body and unborn baby in agreement with her, all of them deliriously happy about their new lives?

Lilley looked at the brilliant ten-carat canary diamond ring on her finger. He'd bought it for her at the Caetani boutique in Las Vegas, as if the million-dollar price tag were nothing at all. It was pretty, though it weighed down her hand. As she went outside, the facets sparkled. She saw her husband sitting in a chair by the pool with a computer in his lap, and he was more seductive to her than any diamond.

His dark form shone brighter than the white sun, which on Sardinia was really saying something.

Palm trees waved in the warm breeze, giving a hint of moving shade over Alessandro as she walked around the pool, swaying her hips.

He didn't look up, but continued to stare intently at the screen. She went around to the back of his chair, then bent to rub his shoulders. "Hi."

"Buon pomeriggio, cara," he said absently, typing.

"Buon pomeriggio?" Smiling, she shook her head. *"Buona sera."*

His expression still distracted, Alessandro glanced up at her. Then he got a good look at her bikini, and his eyes widened. He snapped his computer shut. *"Buona sera,"* he replied with interest. "Your Italian is coming along."

"I've always been interested in your native tongue," she said with a suggestive smile. When she saw his gaze linger upon her breasts, she glanced innocently at his computer. "I'm sorry to interrupt, were you done?"

"I am now," he growled. Pushing the computer to a side table, he pulled her into his lap and thoroughly kissed her. As she felt his sun-warmed lips against hers, melting her from the inside, she closed her eyes and breathed in his scent. With his body against hers in the sunlight, she felt intoxicated with pleasure.

There was only one thing that bothered her.

For the last week, they'd made love constantly, eaten delicious meals, slept in each other's arms. Last night, he'd taken her into the village for dinner, and afterward he'd held her hand as they walked through the winding streets. She'd thought she might die of happiness. Then they'd strolled past an outdoor nightclub. She'd eagerly tried to pull him towards the music, towards the dancing couples spilling out onto the street. But he'd shaken his head. "I don't dance. You know that."

"Oh, please," she'd cajoled. "Just this once!"

But he'd refused. Except when they were in bed, Alessandro didn't allow himself to do anything that might make him appear vulnerable or foolish. He didn't dance. He didn't *play.* He didn't splash in the pool.

But that was about to change. It was time he learned to let himself go.

Playfully, Lilley pulled away from his embrace. "I need some cooling off."

She walked over to the pool's steps, swaying her hips as she waded slowly into the pool, relishing the shock of cool water against her skin. She went deeper, until the water level bobbed at her breasts. Then she glanced at Alessandro out of the corner of her eye. Oh yeah. He was watching, all right. With a soft, innocent sigh, she sank all the way into the water, swimming with long, sensual strokes. She bobbed up to the edge of the pool, at the foot of Alessandro's chair.

"Join me," she suggested, smiling up at him.

Looking down at her, Alessandro slowly shook his head. "Not my thing."

Languorously, she dipped her hair back in the pool. She felt his burning gaze as she lifted her head from the water. Droplets trickled down her skin, down her neck and breasts. She stretched her arms over her head, moving her body in a lazy sway against the translucent water.

"Join me," she sighed.

He looked as if he were having trouble breathing. Licking his lips, he shook his head.

Lilley sank fully beneath the water and was down there for several seconds. When she finally resurfaced, he'd half risen from his chair as if alarmed. She swam to the edge of the pool, a sensual smile curving her lips. Leaning against the edge, she threw something at his feet. He looked down at it.

It was her bikini.

"Join me," she whispered.

Alessandro looked at her, his lips slightly parted. She heard the hoarse intake of his breath.

Then he moved. She'd never known any man could move that fast. Still dressed in his T-shirt and jeans, he did a cannonball right into the pool beside her. The water swayed wildly, splashing Lilley's head and face as he rose to the surface, throwing back his dark head like a god of the sea. His wet, translucent white T-shirt clung to his shoulders, pecs and tight abs.

Swimming over to her, he grabbed the edge of the pool with one hand, and with the other, he pulled her against him without a word. Lowering his head, he kissed her in a hot, hungry embrace. As his lips seared hers, his tongue teased inside her mouth, and she blindly reached out to the side of the pool to steady herself. Treading water with his powerful legs, he cupped her face with both his hands, deepening the kiss. A sigh of pleasure escaped her. Lost in the moment, Lilley flung both her arms around his shoulders, letting go of the edge.

She had an instant of weightlessness, of swirling pleasure with no beginning or end, as they sank together into the water. Falling, falling, they held tight together in the intensity of their embrace before his legs suddenly kicked beneath them, bringing them back to the surface.

Gripping the edge of the pool, they coughed water out of their lungs. When they could breathe again, they stared at each other, both of them bobbing in the cool water. The white sun beat down on them, reflecting glittering light against the sky and their tanned skin.

Leaning forward, Alessandro pushed her against the

edge of the pool, splaying his large hands over hers. He kissed her deeply, plundering her mouth. Tilting back her head, Lilley closed her eyes, feeling the heat of his mouth and the sun on her skin. Cool ripples of water moved against her naked breasts as he kissed her throat, nipping her shoulder, suckling the tender flesh of her ear.

"Mi piace stare con te," he whispered. *I like being with you.*

"Baciami," she whispered. *Kiss me.*

With a muttered groan, Alessandro turned around in the water. Pulling her arms around his shoulders, he lifted her onto his back and swam towards the steps of the pool. Her naked breasts pressed against his shoulder blades, her body rubbing against his clingy white T-shirt. As he climbed up the steps of the pool, water poured from his shirt and jeans that clung to his powerful body. He pulled her into his arms and looked down at her. There was a strange expression in his dark, handsome face. One she'd never seen before.

"Mia moglie," he whispered. "My sweet wife."

He carried her across the terrace and into the white villa, trailing water with every step. From a distance, she heard seagulls crying and the honking horns of boats. She breathed in the scent of lemon and orange groves mixed with chlorine from the pool and the salt of the sea. She placed her hand on his wet cotton shirt. It revealed every hard muscle of his torso, and she could feel the beat of his heart.

Inside the villa, it was cool, dark and quiet. The housekeeper and other staff had already left for the evening, going back to their homes in nearby villages. She and Alessandro were alone as he carried her up the stairs to their bedroom, to the enormous bed with the sleek white duvet.

The verandah doors were wide open. The wind blew in from the sea, causing the curtains to oscillate slowly in the breeze as Alessandro set her down on their marriage bed, where she'd already had endless revelations of pleasure and joy.

Never looking away from her face, he slowly pulled off his T-shirt, revealing his muscular, tanned chest and broad arms. His jeans and silk boxers were next, as he stripped the wet fabric off his body and left them on the cool marble floor in a crumpled heap. Naked, he moved beside her on the bed.

His kiss was hot and hard, like the rest of him. Then his embrace grew tender, his lips gentling as he whispered words of adoration in Italian that she only half understood, but that caused her to tremble. He pulled away, looking down at her in the shadowy bedroom, and she could hear their breath mingling in the silence. An inexplicable ache of emotion rose to the back of Lilley's throat.

Reaching up, she put her hand on his rough, scratchy cheek.

I love you.

But she couldn't speak the words. She couldn't be that reckless, or that brave.

Alessandro made love to her slowly, taking his time as he caressed and licked and worshipped every inch of her body, until she exploded in the same instant that he groaned and filled her with his seed. Afterward, they held each other. For several minutes, he slept, and she watched him, looking at the contented smile tracing his sensual mouth. She turned towards the open verandah and the translucent curtains swaying peacefully in the breeze. She could see the distant glint of sunlight sparkling like diamonds against the blue water. And she could no longer deny it, not even to herself.

She'd fallen in love with Alessandro. Fallen? The truth was she'd been in love with Alessandro Caetani from the night he'd found her alone and crying in his office that Saturday night.

Lilley's fingertips stroked the dark hair of his chest. He'd brought her pleasure that she never even knew existed. But was she doomed to love a man who would forever give her expensive jewels instead of his heart? Was there anything she could do to win Alessandro's love?

She thought of the etiquette lessons, the Italian lessons, the designer clothes he'd chosen for her. He was changing her completely, and if she were honest with herself, she didn't like all the changes. Her jewelry tools were collecting dust, and except for her wedding gown, he hadn't allowed her to choose a single item of clothing on her own. Other than the jewelry she had made, nothing she wore was truly hers. He dressed her like a doll. He didn't trust her taste, or her ability to fit into his world.

Lilley took a deep breath. She could live with that, she told herself. She'd be the wife he wanted. She'd keep her mouth shut and focus on being elegant and restrained. She'd try harder at her lessons and wear the clothes he wanted her to wear. She would be whomever he wanted her to be, if it would win his love.

Then it would all be worth it—wouldn't it?

Suddenly shivering, she nestled closer into Alessandro's warmth. In a moment, his eyes would open, and he'd lazily suggest dinner, or perhaps he'd want to make love to her again.

Whatever it took. She would convince him to give her the tiniest fraction of his heart, as she'd recklessly given him all of hers. And it would be enough. She would make it be enough. With a deep breath, Lilley squeezed her eyes shut.

Somehow, she would make him love her.

CHAPTER EIGHT

"Stop him. I don't care how, just stop him!"

Sitting at his desk, Alessandro nearly shouted with fury before he hung up on his company's chief financial officer. Clawing back his hair with a silent snarl, he lifted his hand to throw his phone across his study. Then he stopped himself, clutching the cold metal tightly in his hand.

Exhaling, he set the phone carefully on his desk. Rising to his feet, he paced in front of the window, swearing at Théo St. Raphaël in English and Italian and tossing in a few profanities in French, too, for good measure. Damned vulture. Their rivalry had begun years ago when the Frenchman had bought the Italian firm next door to Caetani Worldwide's headquarters in Rome. The insult had deepened when St. Raphaël had stolen the Joyería deal a month ago. But this was the final straw. The man was brazenly making a play for the takeover of a Japanese company that Alessandro needed to deepen his reach in Asia.

Alessandro growled. He'd spent years building up contacts in Tokyo, in hopes of someday gaining control of the firm. And St. Raphaël had no reason to buy the company. It was pure retaliation for Alessandro's purchase of the French vineyard. It was a taunt, pure and simple.

He must be imagining he smelled Alessandro's blood in the water after the humiliation in Mexico City.

And why wouldn't he? *Someone had betrayed him.* Alessandro's chief financial officer had discovered why Miguel Rodriguez had sold Joyería to St. Raphaël instead of Caetani Worldwide. The Frenchman had learned of his plan to close the Mexico City studio and move it to San Francisco. Rodriguez had sold Joyería to the Frenchman to protect his employees' jobs.

But how had St. Raphaël possibly known?

Sitting heavily at his desk, Alessandro stared at his computer. He'd been working with his team remotely as best he could, but the Tokyo deal was spinning out of control, and that was causing problems. He needed to end his honeymoon early and return to Rome.

Alessandro glanced out of the window, instinctively looking for Lilley. It was past five o'clock. She'd come into his study an hour ago, but he'd sent her away—something he'd had to do too often in the last two days. He'd spent a few hours in bed with her last night, then he'd returned to his study to discuss strategy with his Hong Kong office. Last night he'd fallen asleep over his keyboard.

Alessandro exhaled. He should have gone back to Rome two days ago. By remaining in Sardinia, away from his team, he'd put a woman ahead of his business. Something he'd never done before.

But this wasn't just any woman, it was his wife.

There. He spied Lilley on the beach far below. A smile curved his lips and his shoulders unconsciously relaxed as he watched her frolic in the surf, dressed in one of the bikinis he'd bought her in Porto Cervo. Today the color was violet. He saw her pause and look up towards the sprawling white villa, as if she felt him watching her. Visibly squaring her shoulders, she went to talk to some children playing a distance down the beach. He squinted. He vaguely recognized a dark-haired young boy and small girl, the children of live-in servants from the next villa down the coastline. Lilley flopped down on the sand beside them and started enthusiastically to help build their sand castle.

He watched her as she played on the beach. She was so happy, so natural, so free, so good with children. He'd seen the sweet, tender look in her eyes whenever she spoke to him of dreams for their unborn child. Lilley was everything a man would want in a wife. Everything he'd want the mother of his children to be.

She had only one flaw. She loved him.

She'd very nearly confessed her love before their wedding, but he'd seen on her face what she was going to say and stopped her. He exhaled. As long as the words were never said, they had a chance. They could be lovers, even friends. Once the child was born, Lilley would channel her love into their baby. She would raise their child with a mother's tenderness, while Alessandro would protect them and provide for them, ensuring his children would inherit a vast empire.

His wife and children would never be poor. Never be ashamed of their father. His behavior would be above reproach.

He regretted the shabby wedding he'd given Lilley, in the chapel of a Las Vegas casino, with no family and friends. It had been shabby indeed, but expedient and quiet. He had to give Lilley time to complete her lessons, to be fully polished like a hard-edged gemstone before he exposed her to the cutting, subtle mockery of his friends, or the people who passed for his friends. It was the only way to protect her, helping her become strong enough to protect herself.

No man he knew in Rome would have married a pregnant mistress. He would have simply paid her off with a generous check and perhaps a few gifts at the child's birth.

But Alessandro had always vowed his children would

know who their father was. After his own father's selfish, callous example, and even more after his mother's sickening revelation after his death, Alessandro had known the risk of sex, and so he'd waited until he was truly in love. When he'd fallen hard for a twenty-five-year-old waitress in his freshman year at Stanford, he'd taken his time, wooing her for months like a perfect gentleman. Until Heather had dragged him to her apartment and begged him to make love to her. She'd told him he didn't need a condom, because she was on the Pill.

"You trust me, don't you?" she'd asked with big eyes. After so many years of waiting, sex had been a revelation. He'd been rapturous with joy. When she'd gotten pregnant, it had seemed like a miracle.

Until his father died, leaving a shocking amount of debt and creditors all suddenly clamoring to be paid. Alessandro had dropped out of Stanford, planning to get a job to support his mother, and to propose immediately to Heather, so she'd know he intended to take care of her and the baby. He'd rehearsed his speech the night he planned to propose. They'd be poor at first, he would say, but he would work full-time by day and invest every penny he could. Someday, he would promise, he'd give her the life of a princess.

He bought a cheap ring he could ill afford and made her a picnic, preparing bologna sandwiches and fruit salad to eat in the park. But things didn't go according to plan. As he gave her the speech, Heather was silent, setting down her sandwich barely tasted. Afterward, he took her out dancing, his favorite thing to do. He was trying to show her how romantic their lives could be, even without money.

But in the middle of the first song, Heather had stopped on the dance floor. She'd looked up at him, her eyes full of tears.

"I like you, Alessandro," she'd whispered. "I really do.

You're lots of fun and an amazing, generous lover." She exhaled. "But the baby's not yours. I lied."

"Not…" He staggered back. It felt like a physical blow. "Not mine?"

She flushed. "You kept saying you wanted us to wait for true love and all that. But I'm sorry, I couldn't go for two long months without sex!" At his expression, her cheeks colored and she looked away. "The first night we slept together, I already knew I was pregnant."

The loud dance music roared in his ears. His throat closed. "But why?"

"I thought you would make a good husband. A good father." She bit her lip. "The other guy's married. He'll never marry me or help raise the baby. But he owns a tech firm in Cupertino. If I tell him, I know he'll give me money." She'd looked at Alessandro beneath the flashing lights and pulsing music. "I don't want my baby to be poor," she'd whispered. "I'm sorry."

And just like that, she'd left him on the dance floor.

It was the last time Alessandro had ever gone dancing or made a fool of himself over anyone. The last time he'd fully trusted a woman.

Until Lilley.

He could have chosen not to marry her. She'd gone out of her way to make it easy for him to abandon her. She'd apparently had zero expectations of his moral character. It had astonished and angered him. Of course he wished to marry the mother of his unborn baby.

Although he hadn't insisted on that paternity test.

A cold trickle went down his spine. He didn't have any actual proof the baby was his. His hand felt clammy as he forked his fingers through his hair. Lilley wouldn't lie to him, he told himself. He didn't need a paternity test, and he wouldn't insult her by asking for one. Lilley had been a virgin before he'd seduced her, and if she said he was the father, he was. End of story.

"Alessandro? Are you still in here?"

He turned in his swivel chair to see Lilley leaning against the door frame. Her hip was jutted out, her plump breasts overflowing the violet bikini top. His mouth felt dry as he surveyed her full, bare thighs and the hourglass curves of her body. His gaze traced down her long, curvy legs and back up to her swelling, pregnant breasts. He was hard in a millisecond.

"Still working, after all this time?" she murmured, smiling as if she had no idea what the sway of her hips did to him as she walked towards him. "Haven't you heard the adage—all work and no play?"

His little wife had become remarkably adept at the art of seduction in the nine days they'd been married. Still smiling, she put her hand on his shoulder, rubbing his neck. "You said you'd join me on the beach an hour ago."

He looked back at her. "I said no such thing."

"You could be building sandcastles with me."

"Running around, kicking the waves? Not interested."

She shook her head, tutting her tongue. "How can you own a villa in Sardinia, and never want to play on the beach?"

"I'll play here," he said huskily, pulling her into his lap. "With you."

Her eyes widened, and Alessandro felt her instant surrender, her body's full attention. It was always like this between them. How many times had they made love since they'd wed? And yet he was still not satiated. He could not get enough of her.

Cupping her face, he pulled her mouth against his. Her lips felt so soft, so warm, and the stroke of her tongue felt like liquid fire. Her legs straddled his on the office chair, with her soft backside barely covered by the tiny bikini. The warmth between her legs pressed against the erection now straining beneath his trousers.

Kissing down her neck, he pressed his face between her large breasts, barely contained in the tiny triangles of fabric. She moaned as she moved against him, unconsciously grinding her body against him. He looked at her beautiful face. Her eyes were closed, her lips parted, her expression rapt. Even a lifetime wouldn't be enough to satisfy his endless desire for this incredible woman.

Twining a hand in her hair, he pulled down her head and gave her a hard, deep kiss as his other hand pulled the strings on her hips. Yanking off the bottom of her bikini, he tossed it to the floor and unzipped his fly, letting himself spring free. Lilley's eyes flew open as she realized what he intended, but it was too late.

Lifting her up, he brought her body down hard over him, impaling her in a single thrust. He groaned as he filled her so hard and deep that her body stiffened, even as she choked out a gasp of shock and pleasure.

He was deep inside her. Stretching her to the hilt. And it was good, so good. And wet. Oh God. Waves of sweet ecstasy washed over him and he closed his eyes. Lifting her a second time, he thrust again and a second, louder groan burst from his lips. But he didn't get the chance to do it again. She picked up the pace, her breasts swaying against his face as she controlled the rhythm. He leaned forward, breathing in the scent of sunshine and salt. Pushing aside a triangle of her bikini top, he suckled a swollen, taut nipple as his other hand gripped her thigh. She let out a little cry as she arched her body, tossing back her head as she rode him hard in his office chair, going faster, faster, deeper, deeper.

The pleasure was too intense. He hadn't taken her since

last night, which seemed like forever ago. His stamina wouldn't last. A low moan came from the back of her throat and he felt her soft breasts bounce against his mouth, felt her deep wet core sucking him further and further into ecstasy. He tried to restrain himself—to hold back the wave that threatened to burst. But he couldn't—hold back—for much longer—

Like a miracle, he heard a soft cry from her lips, which became louder as she clutched his shoulders with her hands, her fingernails gripping into his flesh. She gave a final sharp scream and he felt her convulse and tighten all around him. Just in time. In a rush, he surrendered to the pleasure and exploded into her. Lights danced behind his eyelids as he gave a ragged gasp, groaning as he pulsed and poured himself into her.

He held her for long moments in his office chair. When she finally rose unsteadily to her feet, he stood and zipped up his fly, still feeling disoriented. She was just wearing her bikini top and only half of that, really, since she had one breast exposed. He saw her shiver with cold and pulled off his long-sleeved, button-down shirt, wrapping it tenderly around her nearly naked body.

"Thanks," she murmured. She gave him a mischievous smile. "I love visiting you at work."

He laughed, then looked down at her. His tailored shirt hung down to her mid-thigh. "You look...cute."

"So do you." She ran her hand down his bare chest. "Because now you are far more suitably dressed..." She gave a sudden impish grin. "For the beach!"

He blinked at her.

"Woman!" he thundered. "When will you stop?"

"When you do what I want!"

"Not going to happen." He hesitated. "There's been a complication, Lilley. I need to leave for Rome."

"What's happened?"

He scowled. "Théo St. Raphaël happened."

She sucked in her breath. To his surprise, she seemed to understand the gravity of the situation even before he explained. "What—what about him?"

"It wasn't enough he stole the Joyería deal," he ground out. "Now he's after my expansion in Asia as well. Almost as if it's—personal."

"Maybe it is," she said in a small voice. "I don't get how you guys fight over things you don't even need. You have his winery. Call him. Offer an exchange. A truce—"

"Is that a joke?" he said in amazement. "I'd burn down my palazzo before I'd ask Théo St. Raphaël for a truce." He looked at her, and his voice gentled. "I am just sorry our honeymoon must end."

She licked her lips, then shrugged. "It's all right. I love Sardinia, but I'm sure I'll love Rome as well. I'm excited to see the palazzo. Meet your friends."

"Lilley." His good humor fled. "We've talked about this."

"*You've* talked about it," she said sulkily, her fingertips curling against the dark hair on his chest.

"You're my wife. You promised to obey me."

Indignant, she stared up at him. "I did no such—"

"Your place is at home," he interrupted.

"My home is with you." She looked down at her bare feet. "Unless you're ashamed of me."

Taking both her hands in his own, he pressed them to his lips. "My friends aren't the warmest, friendliest sort of people. I doubt you'd like them."

The cuffs of his long-sleeved shirt hung over her hands, making her look very young as she looked away. "You mean they won't like *me*."

"I'll send for you soon," he said softly, pulling her into his arms. "I promise." And to seal that vow, he lowered his mouth to hers in the gentlest, tenderest kiss he'd ever given her.

To his shock, she pulled away, her brown eyes flinty. "No."

His eyebrows lowered. "Don't you understand? I'm trying to protect you."

"I don't want to be protected, I want to be your wife!"

He exhaled, tried to keep his voice light. "If you're weary of Sardinia, I could leave you at our country estate in Tuscany. You could see the famous paintings of Florence, decorate the nursery, learn how to make bread—"

"No!" She stamped her foot against the marble floor, a gesture marred by the fact that she was barefoot and it caused a grimace of pain across her face. Rubbing the sole of her foot, she scowled at him. "I'm going with you to Rome!"

"Lilley," he tried, "please."

"I'm not afraid of your friends." When he didn't answer, she tossed her head. "What do you think they'll do? Fight me with their bare hands? Wrestle me into the mud?"

"No," he said quietly. "They'll be more subtle. They'll attack any weakness they can find. Your manners, your clothes, even your dyslexia—"

"Are you telling me," she said scornfully, "there'll be some kind of *reading test* before they let me in their little club?"

Trying to keep his patience, he set his jaw. "I am just trying to keep you happy and safe."

"By keeping me a prisoner?"

He folded his arms. "You're not exactly suffering here, Lilley. Most people would call this place heaven, not a prison." At her glare, he amended, "And it's just until your lessons are done. Until you're ready."

"So you *are* ashamed of me."

"Don't be ridiculous!"

"I won't embarrass you," she whispered. She looked up at him with pleading eyes, pressing her fingertips against his bare chest. "Please. Don't leave me here without you. I can't...I can't bear us to be apart."

He felt helpless against that gaze. Setting his jaw, he looked down at the floor. "They will hurt you."

"I'm stronger than you think."

"Olivia is there."

For a second, Lilley fell silent. Then she lifted her chin. "We'll have her to tea."

He snorted in disbelief. "That might be overdoing it."

"I'm serious," she insisted in a small voice. "I feel guilty. She was in love with you, she thought you were going to propose to her, and we eloped. We hurt her."

"*You* didn't do anything," he said sharply. "And if I treated her badly, she can handle it, believe me. She'll find someone else to marry, someone twice as rich and better-looking in the bargain."

"No one's better-looking than you," Lilley said, then her smile faded. She looked away, chewing on her bottom lip. "Do you think she was in love with you? Really and truly?"

Mesmerized, Alessandro watched her white teeth sinking into pink flesh that was full and swollen from days of lovemaking. Then he came back to himself. "Absolutely not," he said sharply. "She just knew as I did, that on paper, we were perfect for each other."

Lilley's expression fell, and it occurred to him that such an honest statement might hurt her feelings. "But now I have you," he said reassuringly. She blinked up at him. "The mother of my precious child," he added. Her lower lip wobbled. He wrapped his arm around her waist and said hopefully, "The woman who's given me the best sex of my life?"

A laugh finally escaped her. Then she shook her head, squaring her shoulders. "And I'm coming with you to Rome."

Alessandro's instincts screamed *No.* But he saw the yearning in her eyes and could not deny her what she wanted. What they both wanted. He didn't want to be apart from her, either.

"Very well, *cara,*" he said quietly. "Rome."

She sucked in her breath.

"Thank you!" she cried, flinging her arms around his shoulders. "You won't be sorry. You'll see. I can handle them. I'm not scared!"

As Lilley kissed his cheeks over and over, murmuring her appreciation, Alessandro almost believed he'd done the right thing. He would protect her, he told himself. And Lilley was strong. She'd gained a great deal of confidence in the days of their marriage. What had caused such a rapid change in her? The Italian lessons? The etiquette classes?

Whatever it was, she would be fine. He was worrying over nothing. After all, they were married now, and expecting a child. What on earth in Rome could possibly break them apart?

CHAPTER NINE

Rome. *Roma.* The Eternal City.

What was the Italian word for *disaster*?

Another fabulous, sophisticated dinner at an elegant restaurant with Alessandro's friends, and once again, Lilley was hiding in a bathroom stall. She was becoming a connoisseur of fancy Roman bathrooms.

Since they'd arrived in Rome three weeks ago, Alessandro had worked endless hours at the office. The only time she saw him—aside from the middle of the night when he made love to her—was at dinner, and that almost always included his friends, who were thrilled to see him.

They were not quite as thrilled about her.

For the last two hours, she'd sat at the table with a frozen smile on her face while Alessandro and his friends talked and laughed in rapid-fire Italian. And it was her own fault. But their first night in Rome, Alessandro had taken her to an elegant restaurant with an English menu. A kind gesture, but Lilley was so nervous, trying to make his glamorous friends like her, that the letters on the menus had refused to stay still. In the end, she'd tried to laugh it off, and her husband had taken over and gallantly ordered for her. But ever since, she'd insisted on only Italian menus. At least then she had an excuse for why she couldn't read them.

And she'd insisted to Alessandro that she preferred that

he speak to his friends in their native Italian. "I'll learn the language more quickly that way," she'd said.

What she'd mostly learned was that his friends made her uncomfortable and she wished that she and her husband could stay home. Home in the bedroom of their palazzo, where Alessandro made her so happy, or creating jewelry in her makeshift studio in the mews, or decorating the large sitting room she was turning into a nursery suite. Heck. Even going for another OB visit, with her chauffeur on one side and her bodyguard on the other, would be more fun than this.

Hiding in the bathroom stall, Lilley stared down at her beige Prada shoes. She'd lasted two hours before she fled to the bathroom. A new record, she tried to comfort herself. It was helpful to be pregnant, because no one questioned long disappearances. Lilley's beige designer suit skirt strained at the seams, feeling too tight around her waist, and she wished she hadn't eaten so much bread. None of the other women ate bread.

No. They seemed to survive on gossip and malice.

It's your imagination, she tried to tell herself. Her Italian was still pretty bad. Alessandro's friends could be saying anything, and she'd likely misread the women's sidelong glances. As soon as her language skills improved, she would no doubt discover his friends were actually quite nice....

The bathroom door banged open.

"Can you believe Alessandro is married to that fat pudding-faced creature who can barely read and has nothing to say for herself?"

Lilley froze, recognizing the voice.

"A tragedy," another woman agreed. "I can hardly believe a fine specimen like Alessandro was trapped by a stupid little nobody."

"Well. I wouldn't say she's *little*," the first woman replied slyly.

Trembling, Lilley peeked through the crack in the stall door and saw Giulia and Lucretia standing at the wall of sleek sinks, refreshing their lipstick in the mirrors. Both of them wealthy heiresses married to still richer men. And they were both so thin they looked like clotheshangers in their designer clothes from Milan.

"Such a shame," Giulia sighed, giving her nose a pat of powder as she stared at herself in the mirror. "Olivia should be with us tonight, like always."

"She will be again," Lucretia said comfortingly. Smacking her lips together, she tucked her lipstick back into a tiny crystal clutch. "The fat little gold digger will realize she doesn't belong here. Once the brat is born, Alessandro will tire of her and send her back to America. Then he will be with Olivia again. As they were meant to be." She glanced at the other woman. "Are we done?"

"I think so," Giulia replied. Smiling at each other, they left the bathroom.

The bang of the door reverberated behind them. Lilley clasped her hands together, her heart pounding. Her skin felt clammy, her body flashing hot and cold. It was her own fault for remaining hidden, she told herself. If she'd come immediately out of the stall, Giulia and Lucretia would never have been so rude. They would not have been so cruel if they'd known she was there, listening.

Then Lilley realized—

The women had spoken in *English*.

"Oh," she breathed aloud, a soft gasp, falling back against the wall as if she'd been punched. Slowly, she swung open the stall door. She saw herself in the mirror, saw how little the stark, minimalist dress suited her taste or her figure. She was wearing the same style as Giulia and Lucretia, but instead of making her blend in with the fashionable set, it only emphasized the rounder shape of her body, and made her normally rosy skin seem washed-out and pale.

Or maybe their words had done that. Alessandro had said his friends could be mean, but she hadn't believed him. She'd never imagined anyone could be so deliberately cruel to a virtual stranger, a new bride far from her home country.

Lilley wondered what Giulia and Lucretia would say if they knew her father was Walton Hainsbury, if that would make her more palatable. But somehow she doubted it. They would simply find new reasons to mock her.

Staring at her own pale, miserable, and yes—a little pie-faced—expression, Lilley swallowed. The ache in her throat felt like a razor blade, but she wasn't going to show them they'd hurt her. No way. Straightening her shoulders, she went down the hall.

Her high-heeled shoes clicked against the floor as she walked across the elegant restaurant, past all the wealthy, gorgeous patrons who actually looked as if they fitted in here. She saw Alessandro sitting beside Giulia and Lucretia and their husbands, tossing his head back in laughter as the women regarded him with sharp, sly smiles. And suddenly, Lilley's courage failed her. Turning, she veered towards the bar.

A handsome young bartender in a white jacket, drying glasses with a white towel, turned to her. *"Sì, signorina?"*

Lilley looked at the wall of liquor bottles behind the bar. If ever a moment called for liquid courage, this was it. But she was pregnant, and anyway she'd never had much experience with alcohol. Except for the night of the Preziosi di Caetani ball, when she'd drunk a glass and a half of champagne. Alessandro had made her feel so precious and beautiful... Her eyes filled with tears.

"Signorina?" the bartender said. *"Prende qualcosa?"*

She wiped her eyes. *"Acqua frizzante, per favore."*

A large hand grabbed her shoulder. With an intake of breath, she turned, but it wasn't Alessandro. Instead, she saw a dark man with ice-blue eyes, an acquaintance of her husband's that she'd met at a cocktail party a few nights before. The Russian tycoon who owned gold mines across the Yukon…what was his name? "Prince Vladimir. Hello."

The man looked down at her with interest. "What are you doing here, little one?" He looked around. "Where is your husband? You do not look well."

"I'm fine. Great in fact." Blinking back tears, she turned back to the bartender as he held out her sparkling water. "Oh no—I forgot my purse!"

"Please. Allow me," Prince Vladimir said, pulling out his wallet. He blinked with surprise when the bartender told him the amount. "So little?"

"It's water," Lilley said. "I'm pregnant."

"Ah," Prince Vladimir said. "Congratulations."

"Thank you. Not everyone knows yet." Lilley glanced back at the table across the room. "Believe me, if I could drink something stronger, I would."

Vladimir followed her glance, and understanding filled his eyes. "Ah. But you have nothing to fear, *Principessa,*" he said quietly. "Your husband is smitten. I've seen the way he looks at you."

Holding the cold glass against the hot skin of her cheek, she whispered, "You mean the way he doesn't look at me."

"Then he is a fool." He put his finger on her bulky crystal necklace. "This is beautiful. Where did you buy it?"

Startled by his touch, Lilley nearly jumped. "I made it."

"You did!"

She shook her head. "Alessandro doesn't want me to wear it in Rome. He said it might make his friends laugh at me, but I don't care. They're going to laugh anyway," she said in a low voice. She straightened. "I have to wear one thing that feels like mine."

"It's beautiful." His finger ran along the bottom edge of her necklace, just below her collarbone. "It's art."

His touch made her uncomfortable. Innocent as it was, the situation might be misconstrued. Even now, Alessandro might be watching them, growing wild with jealousy...

She glanced back at their table, and saw he was busy laughing, having the time of his life with his cold-hearted friends, saying things she couldn't remotely understand.

Clearly, Lilley's plan to make Alessandro fall wildly in love with her was going perfectly.

Tears filled her eyes. How she wished they were still in Sardinia, with nothing but warm sunlight, cool blue water and swaying palm trees around them, far from the rest of the world!

Instead, she was here with him in Rome. As she'd insisted. And as he'd warned her, she was miserable.

Vladimir followed her gaze. "Come, *Principessa,*" he said quietly. "I will take you back to him."

As he led her across the elegant restaurant, the tension in Lilley's throat ratcheted up with every step. They reached the table, and the laughter of the group abruptly fell silent.

"Cara." Alessandro turned with a smile. "I was starting to wonder..." Then he saw Vladimir behind her, and the tenderness in his eyes evaporated. He said shortly, "Hello."

"Your wife isn't feeling well," Prince Vladimir said. "I suggest you take her home."

"Yes," Alessandro said grimly, rising to his feet. Throwing money on the table, he said to his friends, *"Mi scusi. Buona notte."*

Placing his hand against the small of Lilley's back, Alessandro escorted her out of the restaurant. Collecting his Ferrari from the valet, he helped her into the car. He didn't speak. He didn't even look at her.

He drove swiftly and silently through the streets of Rome, and Lilley glanced at him out of the corner of her eye. His face was dark, his expression hard. Miserably, she looked away.

The harder she tried to please him, she thought in despair, the worse it seemed to get.

"I'm sorry," she whispered. "I didn't mean for you to have to leave your friends early."

Alessandro changed the gears on the Ferrari with more force than necessary. His jaw was tense as he said in a low voice, "I'm sorry you felt it necessary to tell Vladimir Xendzov you wished to leave, rather than coming to me."

She blinked at him. "I was just trying to—"

"Save it," he cut her off. He pulled past the guardhouse outside their palazzo, driving through the gate.

Parking his car haphazardly in the small courtyard, he stomped into the sixteenth-century palace. Hurt and furious, Lilley followed him. He was far ahead of her, already halfway up the dark, sweeping stairs, when she stopped, clenching her hands.

"You're not being fair!" she bit out.

Alessandro stopped on the stairs, pulling off his tie. He looked down at her, his jaw set. "Are you coming to bed?"

Lilley blinked, taken aback. He stood above her, his button-down shirt tight across his muscular chest, his black trousers fitted low on his hips. Yes. She wanted to go to bed with Alessandro, damn him. Angry as she was, her nipples were hard, her breasts heavy and she felt a spiraling need low and deep in her belly. Her body was instantly at his command.

But—make love with a cold heart? When they both were angry?

She straightened, tightening her hands, and vehemently shook her head.

"I *said*," his voice was deceptively cold as he came down the steps towards her, "are you coming to bed?"

"No," she ground out.

His black eyes glittered.

"Then," he said, "I will bring bed to you."

She saw the intent in his eyes the instant before he grabbed her. Cupping the back of her head, he lowered his mouth to hers in a punishing kiss. As she tried to push him away, his hands gripped her hair, and he deepened the kiss, wrenching her lips apart with his own. He used his tongue like a sensual weapon, plundering her mouth, and, against her will, her body responded. As her sensitive nipples brushed against him, her breasts were crushed against his hard chest, and she melted into his arms.

Leaning her back against the stairs, he kissed her with such brutal ferocity that she surrendered, allowing him to push her down onto the carpet. With a low growl, he yanked her skirt up to her hips. Without a word, he started to unzip his fly.

That woke her up.

"No," she said, grabbing his wrist as she looked straight into his eyes. "No."

His eyes widened. He exhaled, then pulled away. Rising to his feet, he zipped up his trousers, not looking at her.

"I never want to see you with Vladimir Xendzov again," he said coldly. Then, without a look, he walked up the stairs.

Lilley sat up, feeling disheveled and dizzy, her skirt at her waist. He'd nearly made love to her—and she'd nearly let him do it! Then, when she'd refused him, he'd just left her! Her fury returned, redoubled. Standing up, she readjusted her ugly, expensive beige skirt. Her eyes narrowed as she followed him up the stairs to their bedroom, where she heard the shower running in the en suite bathroom. She pushed open the door, and saw him in the shower, standing naked beneath the running water.

Yanking open the glass door, she leaned into the shower and slammed on the handle, shutting off his water.

"What the hell?" he exploded.

Hot steam floated between them, water dripping noisily off the travertine wall. She glared at him, folding her arms. "How dare you treat me like that, you big—jerk!"

"What did you expect?" he ground out. "That I'd kiss your toes with adoration after you spent the whole night flirting with another man?"

"I wasn't flirting! He was comforting me! After—"

Alessandro's eyes narrowed. "After what?"

She swallowed, fighting tears. "It doesn't matter."

He stepped out of the shower, his body naked and dripping wet. His voice was dangerous as he said, "Tell me."

In the mirror, she saw the reflection of his magnificent, naked body, and next to him, she saw herself, fat and dowdy in the unflattering beige suit that made her look like a lump. "I can't."

"Tell me!" he thundered.

She flinched, and her lips turned down. "They were mean to me."

He gripped the door of the shower. "Who? Who was mean to you?"

"You were right," Lilley whispered. "I never should have come to Rome." She blinked back tears. "I don't belong here."

Moving forward, Alessandro grabbed her shoulders. His eyes were dark as he said in a low voice, "Just tell me who."

She tried to laugh it off. "Nothing, really. They followed me into the bathroom where I was hiding at the restaurant—"

"You were hiding?"

"—and spoke to each other. In English, to be sure I'd understand. They called me fat and stupid, and said you'd divorce me. They couldn't wait for you to be back with Olivia."

He stared at her, his mouth a grim line. Then he abruptly released her, turning away. Lilley stared at his muscular backside as he headed for the door.

He was walking away from her without a word. Again.

"Don't you care?" she choked out. "Don't you care at all?"

Alessandro whirled around, and his expression was so full of fury that she gasped.

"I care," he said. "They will regret hurting you."

"What are you going to do?" she whispered, afraid of the strange darkness she saw in his eyes.

"They are women. I cannot physically hurt them. But," he stretched his intertwined hands, "I can take what they care about the most. Their money."

"How?"

He looked past her ear. "A few well-placed calls to the banks…to the businesses that employ their husbands in well-paid sinecures." He gave a smile as cold as death. "They'll be penniless."

She stared at him, her mouth agape. "I thought they were rich."

"It's a front. They're deeply in debt."

"I thought they were your friends!"

His lip twisted. "Friends?"

"You seemed to be having such a good time…"

"I grew up with them," he said tersely. "But we're not close. We share a past. We share a history. But no. They are not my friends."

Staring up at him, Lilley thought of the friends she'd had

in Minnesota growing up, playing marbles with the housekeeper's daughter Lisa, going for long bike rides with Katie from school, ice skating on the pond with her friends and drinking hot chocolate.

Alessandro hadn't had that. His friends weren't real. Pity and grief for him welled up inside her. And suddenly she couldn't hide her feelings. Not any more.

"I don't need revenge." Blinking back tears, she took a step towards him. "There's only one thing I want. One thing I need."

His jaw twitched. "What?"

"You," she whispered. "I love you, Alessandro."

She heard the catch of his breath. Then his eyes became wistful.

"I know," he said quietly. "I've known since before our wedding, when you almost blurted it out, and I stopped you."

"What?" She didn't remember anything like that. "What are you talking about?"

"Don't you remember? You said you had something to tell me before we could marry. I stopped you because I already knew. You were in love with me. I could see your feelings on your face."

Lilley's lips parted as she remembered the moment in Las Vegas when she'd tried to tell him the truth about her family. "That was what you thought I was going to say?" she said slowly. "That I was in love with you?"

He shook his head. "I couldn't let you speak the words. I thought it would ruin things between us, that it would make a good marriage impossible."

He didn't know. Lilley's head was spinning. Alessandro didn't know about her family. All these weeks they'd been married, she'd thought he was so kind not to reproach her, so generous to forgive and forget. But he hadn't known. He still didn't know!

"But now," Alessandro said in a low voice, "I don't know what to think. I don't know if I can love anyone, Lilley." Clenching his jaw, he looked away. "When I was nineteen, I was betrayed by everyone who loved me. The woman I thought I loved told me she was pregnant by another man. My father died after ignoring me most of his life. And then my mother," he took a deep breath, "informed me that I was not his son."

"What?" Lilley gasped.

"By their second year of marriage, she'd already grown to hate him. She had a brief affair, and got pregnant with me. My father never knew. He died thinking I was his son, and still left me nothing but debts and an unknown number of half-brothers and half-sisters around the world."

Grief was shining in his black eyes. She'd never seen him so open with his feelings before. "I'm sorry," she choked out, wrapping her arms around him. "Who is your real father?"

He looked away. "Not someone I ever wanted to know."

"I'm sorry," she breathed again, but it seemed woefully inadequate. Reaching up, she kissed his cheeks, his lips, his chin, his shoulders. She offered comfort by kissing every part of him she could reach. "I'm so sorry." Tears streamed unchecked down her face as their eyes met. "But I'm your family now."

He exhaled as he looked down at her. "I don't know if I can love you, Lilley," he said in a low voice. His dark eyes shimmered. "But if I could ever love any woman on earth… it would be you."

Lilley's heart stopped beating, then suddenly raced at a gallop. "It would?"

"You're the first woman I've trusted in a long, long time,"

he said softly, stroking her cheek. "Because I know you'd never lie to me—about anything."

A tremble went through her. How could she ever tell him about her family now? How could she possibly explain what had started as a fib of omission to help her get a job, but had turned into months of lying straight to his face?

Honey, she could say casually over waffles some Sunday, *a funny thing about how you thought my father owned a shop. He does own a store, but a few more than one!* Maybe they'd have a good laugh. Maybe he'd forgive her.

But then she'd have to tell him about Théo.

She had to tell him. Before he found out some other way. And she would, she promised herself. Once their marriage was on stronger footing. Once his friends didn't hate her. Then she would tell him everything. She *would.* Even though it would make him hate her.

She trembled just to think of it....

"I'm sorry I never gave you the wedding you deserved," Alessandro said, stroking her cheek.

She gasped. "I loved our wedding!"

He shook his head ruefully. "You should have had friends at the ceremony. Family." He looked at her. "Have you told your father about me yet?"

Her father. She swallowed. "Um. No. Not yet." Squaring her shoulders, she forced herself to add, "But I will take you to Minnesota to meet him. Anytime you like."

"How about Christmas?" Holding her in his arms, he smiled down at her, the expression on his handsome face tender and bright. "We'll have a wedding reception in Rome first. Then plan one there."

"A reception?"

"Two. One on each continent. I want to properly celebrate." He stroked her hair. "With our family and friends."

"Oh," she breathed.

"It'll give your father a chance to know me." He gave her a sudden wink. "I'll win him over."

His charm and thoughtfulness just made her feel more guilty. "Of course you will," she said over the lump in her throat. "No one could help loving you."

His expression grew serious. "But I don't need anyone to love me." He pulled her against his naked body, stroking her back over her beige jacket. "I only need you."

Lilley suddenly felt like crying. She felt his naked body stir, and her own immediate response flooded her with need. She shivered as his hands gently caressed her breasts over the fabric, squeezing her plump flesh with his fingers, rubbing her swollen nipples until they were hard and aching beneath her jacket.

Her gaze fell on the bathroom mirrors and she saw their image, his naked body and muscular backside, as his lips lowered to her neck. The image caused a wave of immediate pleasure as he unbuttoned her jacket.

"You're mine," he murmured against her skin. She felt him hard between her legs, felt the gentle, insistent stroke of his fingertips as he pulled off her silk camisole and bra, running his palm down the valley between her pregnant breasts to her small waist and softly rounded belly. "Say it."

She opened her eyes. "I'm yours."

"Forever," he demanded.

She swallowed. "Forever."

Alessandro fell to his knees in front of her. Lifting her skirt to her hips, he yanked her panties to the floor. Moving his head between her thighs, he lifted one of her legs over his shoulder.

Her hands gripped his naked, hard-muscled shoulders as she felt his hot breath between her thighs. Then, the last moment before he kissed her, he lifted his head to look at her face.

"Never lie to me, Lilley," he whispered. "And we'll last forever. No one will ever be able to break us apart."

He lowered his mouth between her legs, and as waves of pleasure exploded inside her, Lilley tilted back her head with a gasp, closing her eyes. Her heart pounded as she realized what she'd done. She should have told him the truth from the beginning. From the very first day. She'd thought it would be better to wait until he had a reason to care. But when he discovered she'd lied to him for months, after he'd allowed himself to be so vulnerable and care for her—trust her—it would be the beginning of the end.

No. She felt his wet, slick tongue between her legs and shuddered with need, closing her eyes with anguish. She couldn't lose him. Not now. Not ever.

She would find a way to tell him the truth. And pray it wasn't the end…of everything.

CHAPTER TEN

ALESSANDRO'S jaw dropped when he first saw his wife at the top of the stairs.

After five weeks of planning, he'd known she was choosing her gown with care for their wedding reception at their palazzo tonight. She'd insisted on picking her dress herself, in utmost secrecy. Now he saw why. Lilley was wearing a ball gown of watered silk in blending swirls of purple and fuchsia, with a snug corset tight beneath her breasts and loose over her swelling belly. Pink flowers adorned her long, flowing brown hair which tumbled over her shoulders.

She paused at the top of the landing, waiting for his reaction. "Well?" she asked with a deep breath. "What do you think?"

Alessandro opened his lips to tell her she must change, to tell her she couldn't wear such an outrageous gown, not when they'd be surrounded by the critical eyes of the most stylish citizens of the most stylish city in the world. He opened his mouth to tell her that fitting in was the only way to survive.

Then Alessandro saw the hope in Lilley's vulnerable brown eyes. He realized what a risk she'd taken, choosing a dress like this for the night of the reception she'd spent weeks planning.

She was, quite deliberately, taking a risk.

And the truth was she looked beautiful. Looking at her face, Alessandro suddenly didn't give a damn what anyone else thought. He didn't care about anyone but her.

He held up his hand with a smile. "You look beautiful."

Relief and gratitude rushed across Lilley's beautiful face before she gave him a mischievous grin. *"Grazie,"* she said, swishing her skirt as she came down the stairs. She adjusted his tie with a dimpled smile. "You don't look so bad in that tuxedo yourself."

Then, standing on her tiptoes, she reached up and kissed him so long and hard that if guests for the reception hadn't already started to arrive, he would have taken her straight upstairs and ripped the colorful ball gown right off her.

As they went to the ballroom to greet their guests, Alessandro marveled at the changes Lilley had made in the palazzo. In the two months they'd been in Rome, Lilley had tossed out all his elegant, creaky antiques and replaced them with furniture that was both comfortable and warm. His palazzo had once been a showplace. Now it was a home.

And it had never looked better than it did tonight. It was early December, and there was a fire in every fireplace, white twinkling lights on the trees outside and holly and pine boughs on all the mantels, to celebrate the upcoming season.

Looking across the ballroom, Lilley gave a sudden intake of breath. "Uh-oh. The ambassador is hitting on Monica Valenti." He followed her gaze to see the gray-haired ambassador clearly invading the personal space of the nineteen-year-old starlet. Lilley threw him an apologetic glance. *"Mi scusi."*

As he took a flute of champagne from a passing waiter, Alessandro watched his wife with admiration. Their ballroom was packed. Lilley had invited everyone: aristocracy, government officials and entrepreneurs, from the highest circles of Roman society. She'd even invited Lucretia and Giulia.

His wife had a forgiving soul. He did not.

Alessandro had called both women and disinvited them in no uncertain terms. Now they were missing this reception, which somehow—he wasn't sure quite how—had turned into the social event of the year. The humiliation would teach the two women to show his wife a little more respect. His lips curled. The next time Lilley saw them, he suspected they would be in a far friendlier mood.

Finishing the glass of St. Raphaël champagne, he placed his empty flute on a silver tray and watched as his beautiful wife disengaged Monica Valenti from the ambassador with such friendly, warm charm, that instead of taking offense, the gray-haired man smiled at her, clearly enchanted.

And who wouldn't be enchanted? Surrounded by skinny women who wore drab designer gowns of beige and black, Lilley stood out like a bird of paradise. Guests followed her, waiting to speak with her, and Alessandro suddenly remembered how shy and terrified Lilley had been when he'd taken her to the Preziosi di Caetani ball. That was just a few months ago. So much had changed since then.

Lilley's eyes met his across the crowded ballroom, and he gave her a wicked half smile, thinking of what he intended to do to her later. Her brown eyes widened, and her cheeks turned a charming shade of pink. Ah, she was so adorable, his wife. So innocent and easy to read.

She looked away, their eye contact broken as a man came to speak with her, blocking Alessandro's view of her face.

He scowled as he recognized Vladimir Xendzov talking to Lilley, touching the bulky necklace around her neck. It was her newest strange concoction, created from gold and sapphire gem clusters she'd found in an antique shop in Venice. He wondered what they were talking about. He trusted his wife, but he didn't trust Xendzov. Setting his jaw, he grabbed a glass of bubbly pink champagne, then gaped at the raspberry in the bottom. He'd look like a fool drinking *that*. Setting the flute back on the tray, he barked at the waiter, "Get me a Scotch."

The man bowed and backed away, and Alessandro looked slowly around the crowded ballroom. Lilley had thrown herself into planning this reception as if her life depended on it, finding caterers and musicians and florists. The end result was as unique and offbeat as Lilley's jewelry. No one was dancing yet, but the mood was lively with a brash, lilting Irish rock band Lilley had hired from Dublin, just for fun. Dinner was being served buffet-style, with exotic dishes representing every country where Caetani Worldwide owned a subsidiary. The hodgepodge of cultures should have been a disaster. Instead… He looked around and saw powerful men laughing, saw their beige-clad wives giggling like schoolchildren. It was a hit.

Lilley was a hit.

Emotion rose in Alessandro's heart.

Why had he never realized it before? Lilley was perfect as she was. She didn't need to change. She didn't need to fit in. She was born to stand out.

The feeling in his heart expanded to his throat, choking him, and suddenly he had to tell her. He had to take her in his arms and tell her how proud he was of her, how much he cared about her, how much he…that he…

His feet moved across the marble floor, beneath the twinkling lights of the multicolored, sparkling glass chandeliers she'd bought in Venice. Alessandro moved faster, pushing through the crowds. His view of Lilley's face was still blocked by the people clustered around her, by the Russian who called himself a *prince*. Alessandro needed his wife in his arms. Now.

"Darling." Olivia suddenly stood in front of him, blocking his way. Skinny and pale, dressed in a black sheath that showed her complete lack of décolletage, she looked like an angel of death.

"What are you doing here?" he demanded.

"I was invited." Her lips curled up on the edges, reminding him of a cat, although that seemed disrespectful to cats. "By your *wife*."

She spoke the word as if it left her mouth with a foul taste. He set his jaw, glaring at her. "Lilley is too generous."

"Of course she is generous," Olivia's smile widened. "She can afford to be."

"What are you talking about?"

"She's rich."

Alessandro snorted. "Lilley doesn't come from money. That's one of the things that makes her so trustworthy. So different from you," he said pointedly.

She gave a tinkling little laugh. "Oh, this is delicious. Do you truly not know?" She walked slowly around him, running one red-painted fingertip along the shoulder of his tuxedo jacket. Her thin face was smug as she leaned forward to whisper, "She's Walton Hainsbury's daughter."

Alessandro stared at her. As if from a distance, he heard the lilting rock music, heard the laughter and low conversation of the Italian guests around him, the crème de la crème of Roman society. Then the marble floor seemed to move beneath his feet.

Walton Hainsbury's daughter. The man who owned the huge discount jewelry chain that had tried to seize control of Caetani Worldwide in a hostile takeover last spring. He shook his head fiercely.

"You're insane," Alessandro said. "Lilley comes from a little town in the midwest."

Olivia threw back her head and laughed. "You mean

Minneapolis? Oh, darling." She made a show of wiping her eyes. "It's a large city. The headquarters of many international corporations." She lifted a perfectly groomed eyebrow. "Including..."

Including Hainsbury Corporation, he remembered with a sickening twist of his gut. And Walton Hainsbury lived nearby. An icy chill went down his spine. He lifted his chin. "Lilley is not his daughter."

"Not just a daughter, but his only child. His heir."

My father threatened to disinherit me, her voice whirled through Alessandro's brain, *if I didn't come back to Minnesota and marry one of his managers.*

She'd had that platinum Hainsbury watch, which her mother had had especially made. How? How had she done that?

My father's a businessman.

He owns a restaurant? Perhaps a laundromat?

Um. Something like that.

Alessandro ignored the sudden pounding of his heart. He wouldn't believe it. He couldn't. "When we met, Lilley was working in my file room. My *file room,* Olivia."

She looked down at her finely sharpened red fingernails. "What better place for a corporate spy?"

A strangled noise escaped Alessandro's throat. He remembered finding Lilley alone in his private office that first night. *I just wanted to work for a few hours in peace and quiet. Without anyone bothering me,* she'd said.

His throat closed. And most damning of all. She'd known. She'd known about his plans for the Joyería deal. She could have given that information to Théo St. Raphaël.

Impossible, he told himself harshly. Lilley had no connection to the French count. Perhaps she'd had a motive to hate Alessandro back then, after he'd seduced and abandoned her in Sonoma. But she'd had no opportunity to...

"I'm surprised your company even hired her," Olivia said thoughtfully. "Considering her last employer."

Alessandro tried to remember the job Lilley had mentioned, the most recent one, which for some reason she'd left off her résumé. It all seemed like a million years ago. "She worked as a maid. In Minneapolis. And she worked for a relative..."

She looked at him in disbelief. "I've never seen you so stupid and slow. Until six months ago, she was Théo St. Raphaël's housekeeper in the South of France. He's her cousin, you know. She left his employ just days before she started working for you."

It felt like getting hit in the face. Alessandro staggered back. "Théo St. Raphaël?" he said faintly. "The Count of Castelnau is Lilley's cousin?"

"She's lied to you all along." Olivia regarded him. "But you expected that, didn't you? You always expect women to lie to you. Surely you had her background checked before you married her?"

His heart hammered in his chest, so hard and fast he thought it might break through his ribs. "No."

"Prenup?"

The ballroom, the noise of the guests, seemed to be spinning around him. The crowds parted, and he saw Lilley's face. She smiled at him across the room, her face shining, as honest and bright and beautiful as ever. He turned his head away, feeling sick. "No."

"Clever girl," Olivia murmured. "I wonder what else she's lied to you about." She gave him a sideways glance. "How well do you really know her?"

His jaw was tight. "I know she's pregnant with my child."

"Do you?" Her eyes were steady and cold. "Do you really?"

It felt like an ice pick through Alessandro's brain. He

heard the echo of Heather's voice from long ago. *The baby's not yours. I lied.*

He tightened his hands to fists. "Of course the baby is mine," he ground out. "Lilley wouldn't lie about that."

"You know how conniving and ruthless people can be."

"I know how conniving *you* can be," he said harshly.

"Me? I'm an amateur." Olivia laughed, covering her mouth with her hand. "All this time you believed her to be some small-town innocent, didn't you? And she probably planned this from the start. Perhaps her goal is full control of Caetani Worldwide, split equally between her father and her cousin."

He stared at her. "I don't believe you," he choked out.

But that was a lie. He did believe her. That was the problem.

Olivia's eyes met his. "So ask her."

With a low curse, Alessandro pushed past her. Shoving through the crowd, Alessandro stalked towards his wife. Just moments before, he'd felt such reckless joy, a strange breathless certainty about Lilley. Now, that feeling had evaporated as if it had never existed. All that was left was cold despair.

And fury. As he walked towards her, blood started to pound through his body, boiling hot, thawing him out limb by limb. He welcomed the anger. Stoked it.

He'd given Lilley everything, and she'd made a fool out of him. She'd lied to him from the beginning. Faked her name. Her résumé. And perhaps even—

No. He cut off the thought savagely, his hands clenching at his sides. Guests saw his face and backed away, the crowd parting for him like magic.

Lilley was laughing as she talked to Vladimir Xendzov, and the man's eyes caressed her face with admiration. Was

Lilley flirting with him? Toying with him? Using him, as she'd used Alessandro?

Lilley looked over Xendzov's shoulder and blanched when she saw Alessandro. "What's happened?" she breathed. "What's wrong?"

"Tell me your name," Alessandro said in a low voice.

The other guests clustered around Lilley glanced between them, suddenly uneasy at his tone of voice. Looking bewildered, she answered, "Lilley Caetani."

"No." He set his jaw, hating her soft, deceptive beauty that had lured him into trusting her. And more. "Tell me your *name*."

More guests fell silent, turning to look. The Irish rock music abruptly stopped. Suddenly, amid hundreds of people, it was quiet.

His wife swallowed, looking to the right and left. Then with a deep breath, she whispered, "Lilley Smith."

"Tell me!" He thundered. "Your *name!*"

She suddenly looked as if she was going to cry. "Alessandro, I was going to tell you."

"When?" he bit out. "After you'd stolen my company for Hainsbury and your cousin to pick through?"

"No!" she gasped. "I tried to tell you before our wedding. You said you already knew. You always know so much. I believed you!"

"You believed I would actually marry you, knowing that? You lied from the start, even about your name!"

She flinched. He saw the tremble of her eyelashes. "I changed my name three years ago, when my father divorced my mother while she was dying. I didn't want to be a Hainsbury anymore. So I took her maiden name—"

"You knew Caetani Worldwide would never hire you with either Hainsbury or Théo St. Raphaël's name on your résumé."

"Yes," she admitted in a small voice.

"You came as a spy."

"No! I was just desperate for a job while I tried to start my business!" She shook her head tearfully. "I went to San Francisco to follow my dream—"

"Bull," he said brutally. "You went to San Francisco to seduce Jeremy Wakefield into giving you information about Preziosi designs, so your father could have them copied in China in advance. Until I took you to the Preziosi ball and you realized a greater prize was possible for you." He gave a hard laugh. "You decided to become my mistress, so you could funnel information to your family."

"I would never betray you!" she said with a sob. "I was going to tell you everything! I swore it to myself, when I finally realized you didn't know about my family. All this time, I thought you did, until the day I first told you I loved you."

Her voice trembled, but her tears weren't going to work on him, not this time. "That was weeks ago." He grabbed her by the shoulders, looking fiercely into her weepy eyes. "All this time, I thought I could trust you. And you were waiting to stab me in the back. What was your goal? How are they going to work against me? Are your father and cousin planning a hostile takeover of my company?"

"You know me better than that!" She hiccupped, and her eyes became huge as she looked up at him. Unchecked tears streaked her rosy cheeks as she whispered, "Don't you?"

"I wish to God I'd never met you." Alessandro's pulse hammered in his ears, and he couldn't breathe. Couldn't even think. "There's just one last thing I need to know."

"What?"

He gently touched her full bottom lip, the lip he'd once thought could only speak the truth. "How deep do your lies go?"

Her lips parted beneath his touch. His hand slowly traced down her neck, skimming over the breasts and corset to the bright pink-and-purple skirts that covered her swollen belly. "Is the baby mine?"

Her eyes widened as she gasped.

"Tell me the truth, Lilley," he said in a low, dangerous voice. "Did you sleep with another man?"

A sob came from the back of her throat. As he stared down at Lilley's beautiful, tortured face, Alessandro suddenly forgot about the crowded ballroom, forgot Caetani Worldwide, forgot Olivia behind him. All he could think was that he'd loved Lilley. That had been the feeling swelling in his heart moments before. That had been what he'd wanted to tell her. *He loved her.*

But now he knew the woman he'd loved was a lie. Lilley had deceived him from the beginning. He'd asked for a paternity test, and she'd talked him out of it. She'd lured him into loving her, so she could rip out his heart. Just like all the rest.

Unwilling memories rushed through him. Lilley's teasing smile as she tried to get him to play. Lilley naked in the pool in Sardinia. Lilley defending everyone, even people who didn't deserve it. Lilley clinging to him for comfort and strength. Lilley's deep, loving eyes that promised eternity. All a lie.

She stood in front of him now, swaying on her feet, looking as if she might faint. "You really think I would do that?" she whispered. "That I'd sleep with another man, then marry you and spend the rest of my life lying to you? How can you think that? I love you!"

"Nice," he murmured. Touching her cheek, he tilted her face towards the light of the chandelier. "The tears in your eyes, the catch in your voice." He dropped his hand and said acidly, "You'd almost have me believe that you cared."

"I do care!" she choked out. "I love you—"

"Stop saying that," he said harshly, then set his jaw, glaring at her with hatred. "Fine. Don't tell me. I wouldn't believe a word you said anyway."

Lilley clasped her hands together, looking pale and small in her vivid ball gown, flowers tumbling from her long brown hair. Then she glanced at Olivia behind him.

"She did this, didn't she? She took my white lie and twisted it into evidence of a black heart." A tremble filled her voice as she looked back at him. Tears were streaking her face. "And you believed her. You never thought I was good enough to be your wife. You never wanted to love me. And this is your easy way out."

"I despise you," he said coldly.

She gave a sob, and Vladimir Xendzov placed a hand on his shoulder. "Enough. You've made your point."

Alessandro twisted out of the man's grasp, barely restraining himself from punching his face. "Stay out of this." He suddenly hated Xendzov, Olivia and every other vulture in his colorful, festive ballroom. Setting his jaw, he looked around the ballroom and shouted, "All of you—get the hell out!"

"No," Lilley said behind him. "Stop it, Alessandro."

Her voice was harder and colder than he'd ever heard from her lips before. Surprised, he turned back to face her.

Lilley's eyes were still grief-stricken but her shoulders were straight, her body rigid. "Our guests haven't done anything to deserve your abuse. And neither have I." She squared her shoulders and said, "Either tell me, *right now,* that you know this baby is yours, or I will leave you. And never come back."

An ultimatum. He stiffened. "I'm just supposed to trust your word, am I?"

Lilley's face turned pale, almost gray. "I'm not going to

stay in a marriage you don't know how to fight for." She glanced back at Olivia bitterly. "She's the one you always wanted. A woman as perfect and heartless as you."

In a swirl of purple-and-pink skirts, Lilley turned away.

Alessandro grabbed her shoulder. "You can't leave," he ground out. "Not without a paternity test."

She looked at him, and he could have drowned in the deep grief of her brown eyes. "I'm done trying to make you love me," she whispered. "Done."

Alessandro couldn't show weakness. Couldn't let her know how close she'd come to breaking him entirely. "You'll stay in Rome," he said harshly. "Until I allow you to leave."

Her eyes glittered.

"No," she said. "I won't."

Her face looked strange, her eyes half-wild as she took a deep breath.

"I slept with a different man, just like you said." Blinking back tears as she looked up at him, she choked out with a sob, "And I loved him."

Her words were like a serrated blade across Alessandro's heart. He staggered back, stricken. "And the baby," he breathed, searching her eyes. "What about the baby?"

Lilley's brown eyes were dark as a winter storm. Tears streamed down her face like rain. For answer, she pulled her canary-yellow diamond ring off her left hand and wordlessly held it out to him.

Numbly, he reached for it. Lilley turned away, pushing through the crowds, not looking back.

And this time, he didn't try to stop her. Gripping the ten-carat diamond ring tightly against his palm, Alessandro closed his eyes, leaning his head against his fist as he felt the first spasms of grief course through his body.

CHAPTER ELEVEN

A WEEK later, Alessandro sat in his study staring at divorce papers, feeling numb.

He hadn't seen Lilley since she'd fled the reception, running out into the streets of Rome with only her passport and wallet, still dressed in the fuchsia ball gown. He had no idea where she was, and didn't care. Let the lawyers find her.

He looked down wearily at the documents spread across his desk. He didn't need Lilley, he told himself. He didn't need their baby.

Except a hard lump rose in his throat every time he passed the room that would have been the nursery. The walls were soft yellow, and Lilley's painting of baby elephants, monkeys and giraffes was propped against the wall. Alessandro's car still held the stuffed elephant he'd bought the day before the reception, and it was in his trunk right now, wrapped in festive paper decorated with baby animals, tied with a bright yellow bow.

The ache in his throat increased. Alessandro clenched his jaw. He'd burn the toy, he thought savagely. Then he'd repaint the nursery's walls with a color that wouldn't remind him of either Lilley or the baby. No blue. No pink. He couldn't use brown, either, the color of her eyes. Nor red, the color of her lips. So what was left?

Black. Just black.

He leaned his forehead into his hands. He was better off without them. Better off without Lilley constantly pestering him to jump in the pool or dance or play. Without hearing her soft voice speak dreamily of their future children, of a happy marriage that would last fifty years. Without seeing the sensual, breathless expression in her face as she looked up at him in bed, the moment before he pushed inside her.

Va bene. He didn't need them. He'd go back to the life he'd had before, working all day to earn money he didn't need, having meaningless affairs that were forgotten by morning. Trusting no one. Forever alone. *Perfetto.*

He covered his face with his hands.

His phone rang. "*Buon giorno,* darling," Olivia said cheerfully. "Now you're rid of your mistake, I want to ask you to lunch. To celebrate."

"I'm not divorced yet," he said in a low voice.

"Come to lunch anyway. I don't mind."

Her low, smug voice jarred him. Swiveling in his chair, he turned towards the window, towards the view of the city and hazy blue sky. Where was Lilley? Was she with another man? He remembered the way Vladimir Xendzov had looked at her. Remembered Jeremy Wakefield's awed face when he saw her in the red dress.

Who was the father of her baby?

I slept with a different man, just like you said. And I loved him.

His lips twisted. That meant she'd lied when she'd told Alessandro she loved *him.* Another lie to add to the pile.

Through the window, he saw a limo park at the gate of his palazzo. A driver got out of the limo, opening the door for a well-dressed, dark-haired man, who went to talk to the security guard. Frowning, Alessandro sat up straight, narrowing his eyes, trying to see the man's face.

Then he did. And he rose to his feet with a half-strangled curse.

"Darling, what's wrong?" Olivia asked. "What is it?"

"Someone's here," he said curtly. "I have to go."

"Who could possibly pull you off the phone with me?"

"Théo St. Raphaël."

"What?" Olivia's voice was suddenly sharp. "You don't need to see him. Wait at your house, I'll pick you up and take you for lunch—"

"Sorry," he said shortly, and he hung up, tossing his phone on his desk. As he ran down the stairs, his blood was pounding for battle. His hands were clenched into fists, ready for a fight, any fight. Brushing past his bewildered housekeeper, he went into the courtyard.

"Let him in," Alessandro ordered his guard in Italian. Théo St. Raphaël came through the gate, looking polished and powerful in a suit and yellow tie, holding a leather briefcase. He looked calm, cool and under control, all things Alessandro hadn't felt for a week. The hot Italian sun shone down on his scrubby T-shirt and jeans as Alessandro stalked through the dusty courtyard to finally meet his rival.

"What the hell do you want?" he demanded. "Come to gloat?"

Théo St. Raphaël stared at him as if he were insane. "Gloat?"

"I bet you and—" he still couldn't say her name out loud "—your cousin had a good laugh after she helped you steal the Mexico City deal. It was clever for her to lure me into giving information in bed!"

In a swift movement, St. Raphaël leapt five steps across the courtyard in a flutter of dust and punched Alessandro solidly across the jaw.

"That's for Lilley," he said, panting as he rubbed his wrist. "Damn you."

It would have knocked a lesser man to the ground. As it was, Alessandro felt the impact of the blow all the way to his knees.

His own fist flew back on instinct. Then he straightened, rubbing his jaw. "At least you have the decency to attack me to my face, St. Raphaël," he said. "Rather than stabbing me in the back."

"Lilley kept one small secret from you. *One.*"

"Small?" Alessandro said incredulously. "She told you my plans for the Mexico City deal! Convinced me to marry her when she was in love with another man! And worst of all…" He cut himself off, and his voice hardened. "Why are you here? What more could she possibly want?"

The Frenchman glared at him. "In your office."

Alessandro stiffened, then realized his security guard was watching with interest, as were the paparazzi who'd been parked across the street ever since the scandalous night of their reception. He set his jaw. "Fine."

Turning on his heel, he led the count silently into the palazzo.

"I'm here to collect Lilley's things," St. Raphaël informed him once they reached his study. "Her tools. Her mother's quilt."

"And the clothes I bought her?"

"She doesn't want them."

Alessandro sank into his office chair, feeling weary. He swiveled towards the window. He'd nearly thrown her most precious belongings away in his rage after she'd disappeared, but he hadn't been able to do it. The tools and quilt were too much a part of what he'd loved about her. "It's boxed up by the front door. Help yourself." He glared at the other man. "I'll be glad to get it all out of here."

St. Raphaël stared at him coldly, then set his briefcase

on the desk. Opening it, he pulled out a file and held it to Alessandro.

"What's this?" he asked, not touching it.

"The Mexico City deal," St. Raphaël said scornfully. "If you still want it."

Alessandro opened the file. Skimming through it, he realized it was a contract to exchange Joyería for the St. Raphaël vineyard. He looked for a catch. He couldn't find one.

"I will step away from the Tokyo deal as well."

Alessandro looked up in bewilderment. "I don't understand."

"Lilley's idea."

"But why would she arrange this, when she's the one who betrayed me?"

"Lilley didn't betray you," St. Raphaël bit out. "Someone else gave me that information. She said she wanted payback for the way you replaced her with some cheap file-room girl." He paused. "I had no idea she was talking about Lilley."

"Olivia?" Alessandro said in a strangled voice. "Olivia Bianchi?"

St. Raphaël's eyes settled on his. "The two of you deserve each other."

Was it possible he was telling the truth? Had Olivia betrayed him? Alessandro suddenly remembered all the times he'd done business on the phone in the back of the limo, with Olivia sitting bored beside him. She'd certainly known about his rivalry with St. Raphaël.

She'd had motive, means and opportunity.

The Frenchman leaned forward, his knuckles white against the desk. "But you must promise, in writing, that you will keep the design studio in Mexico City. I gave

Rodriguez my word that none of his people would lose their jobs. And, unlike you, I do not wish to be a liar."

Alessandro's eyes narrowed. "I didn't lie. I might have *implied*—"

"You lied. Worse than Lilley ever did. All she was trying to do was get a job. You were trying to enrich your own pockets at the expense of someone else's honor. You lied to Rodriguez. Just as you lied to Lilley when you didn't mention until after you were wed that you wouldn't allow her to work."

Alessandro's cheeks grew hot. Then his chin lifted coldly. "Lilley slept with another man, then tried to pass off her unborn child as mine."

With a snort, St. Raphaël stared at him, then shook his head. "If you believe that, you're even more stupid than I thought." He pulled out one last paper. "Here. Give that to your lawyers."

I slept with a different man, just like you said. Alessandro remembered Lilley's wide, stricken eyes as she stood in her pink ballgown amid the holly and ivy. He remembered the strange way her voice had trembled. *And I loved him.*

Alessandro's heart gave a sickening lurch.

What if Alessandro was the man she'd loved—before he'd turned on her so brutally, in public, with his ex-mistress egging him on, practically chortling with glee?

He'd vowed to honor and protect his wife. Why hadn't he cared for her enough to speak with her privately? To ask, to listen, to give her the chance to explain? Instead, he'd turned on her like a rabid dog. He'd attacked her, his beautiful wife who had never done anything but love him with all of her gentle, loyal heart.

"Where is she?" he whispered.

"She left France a few hours ago." The other man's lips

pressed together in a thin line. "She wanted to visit her father, then scout out locations for her jewelry line."

"She's doing it?" Alessandro said faintly. "Really doing
it?"

St. Raphaël glared at him. "My wife says Lilley's jewelry is a sure thing. And she should know." He drummed
his fingers on the desk. "You know, I should thank you. For
doing the right thing by my cousin."

Alessandro's lips lifted humorlessly. "You mean marrying her?"

"Divorcing her," he replied coldly. "Lilley is the kindest
person I know. She doesn't have a mean bone in her body.
She and her baby deserve better than you." He closed his
briefcase with a snap. "But business is business. I have
wanted these vineyards back for some time. Have your
lawyers review the documents. There is no need for us to
meet again. *Adieu.*"

Without another word, Théo St. Raphaël left. Numbly,
Alessandro stared down at the file, and at the divorce papers still spread across his desk beneath. Picking up a page,
he tried to read it, but the words seemed to move and jump
across the pages. It was as if he were suddenly seeing the
world from Lilley's point of view.

Pushing the papers aside, he rose to his feet. From the
window, he saw St. Raphaël carry a large box out through
the gate. His limousine soon disappeared back into the
streets of Rome.

Alessandro looked up. The bright-blue sky seemed
smeared violet. As if the world were going dark.

I love you, Alessandro.

I'm yours. Forever.

He closed his eyes, pressing his hot forehead against the
cold glass of the window. But even with his eyes closed,
even if he covered his ears with his hands, he could still

hear Lilley's shaking voice, still see the grief in her eyes. *I'm done trying to make you love me. Done.*

And the truth hit Alessandro like a blow.

Lilley hadn't betrayed him.

He had betrayed her.

His eyes flew open. He'd told her she wasn't good enough to be his wife, or good enough to be liked by his friends. He'd insisted on buying her clothes. He'd told her why her jewelry would never sell, then insisted that she give up her own dreams in order to sit alone in their palazzo, waiting for him to come home.

He'd let her love him without offering her anything in return, except coldly expensive jewels, which he should have realized long ago, she would never, ever want.

No wonder when he'd turned on her so viciously at their reception, Lilley had finally given up. For months, she'd bent over backwards trying to please him. She'd convinced herself he was worthy of her love. That night, even her romantic, loyal heart had been forced to see the truth.

He'd finally proven that he wasn't her knight in shining armor, and never could be.

She was right. He'd been afraid to love her, terrified to let himself be vulnerable again. For sixteen years, he'd kept his heart locked up. When Olivia had given him an escape, his cowardly heart had taken the first chance at the exit door.

Lilley was right. Cold rage filled him. Rage at himself.

Alessandro turned back to the window, staring at the early twilight of December. The blue sky was streaked with pink and orange, like a brilliant fire on the horizon.

We all must choose in this life, he'd told her once. *The safety of a prison. Or the terrible joy that comes with freedom.*

He'd thought of her as a timid little mouse. But all along,

she was the one with the courageous heart. He was the one
who'd been hiding.

But not anymore. *Not anymore.*

Whirling around, he grabbed the phone off his desk so
fast he nearly it knocked to the floor.

He would bring the laughter and trust back to her eyes,
even if it made him look like the biggest fool on the face
of the earth. If he couldn't even do that...then that bastard
St. Raphaël was right. Lilley and his child really would be
better off without him.

Alessandro would find her. Win her.

Squaring his shoulders, he set his jaw.

He would deserve her.

After six hours, Lilley's backside was well and truly sore.

She shifted on the hard cushion of her father's repro-
duction Louis XIV couch as she sat in his fancy parlor. She
looked down at her watch. Six hours he'd made her wait
now. *Six.* It was her first visit in three years, and he'd just
left her here, alone and unwelcome in the sprawling house
he'd built for his mistress, a forty-thousand-square-foot
mansion on a sprawling estate near Minneapolis.

Clearly this was her punishment for not coming home
in June to marry his employee, as he'd demanded.

Her lower back gave a sudden stab of pain, and she rose
to her feet. The parlor had beautiful views of snowy Lake
Minnetonka through the black, bare trees, but it still felt
like an office, not a home. There were no personal photographs, just posters from various Hainsbury's advertising campaigns. The closest framed poster showed a happy
young couple embracing on a park bench with the image of
an engagement ring superimposed around them. Beneath
it in big letters was the tagline, Hainsbury Jewelers. When
Only Perfection Will Do.

Perfection. Engagement rings. Love in general. Lilley hated them all right now. But most of all, she hated her knack for loving men who did not have the capacity or desire to love her back.

Her father's abandonment had left a hole in her heart. But Alessandro had done far worse. He'd cut through that hole with a machete, leaving one side of her heart drenched in acid, the other smashed with a meat mallet.

She'd given her husband everything, and it still hadn't been enough. Alessandro hadn't even tried to hear her side. He'd just taken Olivia's every word as gospel—even believing it was possible Lilley might have slept with another man!

Well, she *had* slept with another man. Without thinking, she reached up and touched the brass-and-pink-rock-crystal necklace hanging around her throat, a gesture she'd repeated many times over the last week. A tragedy that the man she'd loved, the man she'd been so sure Alessandro could be, had been entirely a figment of her imagination.

She swallowed, blinking fast. But work would see her through. After all she'd endured, she was no longer afraid of failure.

She just hadn't been thinking big enough. Instead of opening a boutique, she was starting her own line of handmade, unique jewelry art, as Vladimir Xendzov had called it. After Alessandro had effectively ended their marriage, Lilley had spent days weeping in her old housekeeper's suite in her cousin's castle before she'd resurfaced to play with her cousin's baby. Théo's wife had demanded, "Where did you get that fabulous necklace?"

"I made it myself," Lilley had replied, turning away. Then something inside her made her pause. Made her turn back around. With a deep breath, she'd added, "I've decided to start my own business. I'm going to sell handcrafted jewelry to luxury boutiques and exclusive department stores across the world. I'm going back to the States to try for a business loan."

Carrie had shaken her head vehemently. "No!" she'd cried, and for a moment Lilley was taken aback. Then her friend smiled. "Don't take out a loan with some banker, please. Let me do it! This is just the investment I was looking for."

Closing her eyes, Lilley took a deep breath. Her dream was coming true in a way she'd never imagined. She had her financing now and was dependent on no one, not even Carrie. She'd finally been brave enough to take a risk. Alessandro had helped her do that, she admitted quietly to herself. He'd taught her how to have the confidence to follow her dreams. Her business might succeed or fail, but either way, it was all up to her.

She'd finally become strong enough to stand up for what was right, even if it terrified her. And she would rather be alone than be with a husband who didn't love or trust her.

Lilley was no man's housekeeper. No man's helpless wife. And apparently, no man's daughter.

As the sun started to set, scattering pink light over the snow beneath a black lattice of trees, Lilley finally gave up and turned for the door.

"What do you want?" Her father's voice was low and hard. Lilley saw him in the doorway, and her mouth fell open with shock.

Walton Hainsbury seemed to have aged decades in the three years since her mother's funeral. His beady eyes glared at her through his wire-rimmed glasses, but his face looked pale as he took a long suck of his cigar.

Her nose wrinkled at the smell. Cigars had become her least favorite smell in the world. He'd been smoking the day he'd left Lilley and her mother, when he'd announced he would go and build a mansion on Lake Minnetonka for his far younger mistress. Eighteen-year-old Lilley had cared for her mother at their family home in Minneapolis for two years, until she died.

"What are you doing here?" Walton rasped, looking contemptuously at the powder-blue coat and dark, fitted jeans. "Have you come crawling here to try to worm your way back into my will? It's too late, missy! I've left everything to charity!"

Lilley stiffened. "I didn't come for money."

"Likely story."

The accusation stung. "I've never asked you for money. Not once. You know I haven't." Lifting her chin, she looked at him. "I just came to tell you you're going to be a grandfather."

He stared at her. She noticed that the color of his skin was ashy, his jowls flabby, as if he'd lost weight. He took several puffs of his cigar before he said in a low voice, "You're pregnant?"

She nodded.

His eyes narrowed at her bare left hand. "And no husband." He glared at her. "You couldn't marry the man I chose for you. Had to throw yourself away!"

"The man you chose for me was twice my age."

"If you'd married him, I could have left him my company. I would have known you'd always have someone to take care of you. But you wouldn't see sense, as usual. And now it's too late."

She heard a wistfulness in his voice. A lump rose in her throat. "I'll be all right. I can take care of myself."

"You can't," he barked. "You've just come back with another mouth to feed, expecting me to solve things for you as I always do."

The accusation was so unjust, she sucked in her breath.

"You've never solved anything for me! You just made me feel helpless and stupid as a kid. The instant you knew about my dyslexia, you treated me differently. Same as you did when Mom got sick!"

"I loved your mother," he said harshly. "As I loved you. I tried to take care of you both—"

"By divorcing her when she was dying? By deserting us both so you could build—" She looked around the gilded parlor. "—*this* for your mistress? Where is Tiffany, by the way?"

Walton looked away. "She left me a few months ago."

"Oh." Lilley blinked at him, not knowing what to say. *Good riddance* seemed rude.

"I never wanted to leave your mother," he added gruffly. "Paula's the one who told me to go."

Lilley's brow furrowed. "What?"

He exhaled. "I've never dealt well with illness, I'll give you that. But when I told your mother about Tiffany, I was trying to wipe the slate clean. I vowed to her that if she could forgive me, I'd be a better husband, a better man." His lips trembled in a smile. "But she told me to get the hell out of our house. She refused to see me again. And so I didn't." He clawed back his wispy hair. "Not until the funeral, when she couldn't stop me."

"I never knew. I just assumed—"

"Your mother didn't want to drag you into our quarrel. I respected her wishes."

"And took all the blame," she whispered.

He looked at her. "I reckon I deserved it." He looked away. "So who's your baby's father? Some penniless musician? An artist? Any chance the man has a shred of honor or decency?"

"If you're asking if he's married me, the answer is yes. We were married in September in Las Vegas."

His face grew more ashen. His long eyebrows shook as he said, "You got married! Without telling me!"

"You disinherited me. I didn't think you'd care."

"Tell me you got a prenup."

"No."

His hand trembled as he stabbed the cigar towards her. "I haven't worked hard all my life to let some greedy fortune hunter steal it all now!"

"He doesn't want your money," she whispered. She looked away. "And anyway, he's about to divorce me."

"After such a short marriage? Who will take care of you and the child?"

"I will." She took a shallow breath, trying not to inhale his smoke which was making her feel sick. "Théo offered me a spot at his headquarters in Paris, in his mergers and acquisitions department. He said I have a fresh take on things, an original mind. But his wife Carrie and I had already decided—"

"Original mind?" her father interrupted derisively. "You can't survive on your own, and take care of my grandchild alone. You will come home," he ordered. "You'll move in with me."

Lilley sucked in her breath. "Why can't you believe in me, Dad? Just once?" she whispered. "Why can't you forget my dyslexia and tell me you believe in me, tell me I can do anything I put my mind to?"

Walton scowled. "Lilley—"

"Forget it." She turned away. "Good-bye."

Leaving the parlor, she fled the mansion. Outside, the frigid Minnesota air hit her skin with a vengeance, making her shiver in her warm jacket. Cold December light gleamed off Lake Minnetonka, and she could see a white cloud of fog rising up from the ice as she climbed back into her rental car. Starting the engine, she drove down the gravel driveway, her back tires sliding over the packed snow.

But when she reached the gate, the security guard ignored her. She waved at him furiously, but he turned the other way, a phone to his ear. Finally, she got out of the car and stomped to the guardhouse. "Open it," she demanded. "Right now!"

The guard pushed the button to open the gate, but leaned out of his window. "Mr. Hainsbury wants you to wait."

Lilley muttered under her breath. She was done waiting for anyone, especially men who'd proven over and over in every possible way that they didn't love her. Climbing into her car, she gunned the engine. "Let him wait."

But as she pulled out of the long driveway and out onto the quiet country road, she saw her father run through the gate, waving his arms as he shouted after her. For a moment, she stared towards the inviting open road. Then, cursing herself aloud, she slammed on the brake.

Lilley closed her eyes, heart pounding as she leaned her head against the steering wheel. Then, slowly, she turned off the engine.

She climbed out of the car, turning back towards her father. He was wheezing loudly and his run slowed to a walk. But she didn't take a single step. She let him walk all the way.

"You don't know, do you?" he said in a low voice. "Before I found out about the baby, I thought that was the only reason you turned up here. Because you found out."

"Found out what?"

He looked at her. "I'm dying, Lilley."

She stared at him, not moving. "What?"

He gave her a wan smile. "That's why Tiffany left." He held up the lit cigar between his fingers and stared down at it. "Doctors give me a few months, maybe a year. I wanted you to marry Gerald because…then I'd have known," he whispered. "That you'd always be all right."

Trembling, Lilley looked at her father in the gray December light. She'd had a happy childhood, back when her parents had loved each other. Her father had taught her to ride a bike. Taught her how to weld. He'd taught her how to evaluate uncut gems, and the different names for the stones. He'd shown her, through his example, the value of hard work and big dreams. She exhaled.

"There's no hope?"

He dropped the cigar, crushing it beneath his feet. "Nope." His lips creased. "I've made a lot of mistakes, Lilley. First with your mother—then with you. But even I couldn't be stupid enough to make this last one, and let you leave, knowing I might never see you again." He lifted his head. "I do love you, Lilley," he whispered. "And I've always been proud of you. I know I wasn't always a good father, and I'm sorry. But before I die, I need…I'm asking—" His voice cracked. "—for you to forgive me."

Lilley stared at him, her heart squeezing in her chest. Even her mother had forgiven Walton at the last. He'd treated them both badly. But she suddenly knew she wasn't going to let him die alone.

Narrowing her eyes, she shook her head decisively. "Not going to happen."

Her father's face fell. Then she added with an unsteady smile, "There's no way you're going to die. I know you, Dad. Death itself wouldn't be able to talk you into a deal you didn't like."

He exhaled. He looked up, and his eyes were filled with tears. "I told you that you needed me. That was a lie. The truth is—I'm the one who needs you." He swallowed. "I swear to you, if I live long enough, I'll be a better grandfather than I was a father."

She felt a lump in her throat. "You weren't so bad. Really."

"No?"

"Well." She gave him a crooked smile. "You did teach me how to ride a bike." He smiled back at her. But as she started to reach out to him, the road suddenly rumbled and shook beneath her feet. She heard a loud honking behind her.

Turning in surprise, she saw a delivery van barreling down the country road, followed by a semitruck so huge it hung over the edges of the asphalt. The delivery van drove by, honking.

"What the devil?" her father sputtered, coughing.

"Abbott," she whispered in shock. What was Alessandro's chauffeur doing in Minnesota, driving a delivery van on this small country road?

The semi parked behind her car, blocking her on one side as the delivery van blocked the other. Confused, she started walking towards Abbott, who'd leapt out of the driver's seat and was swiftly walking around to the back of the van.

"Abbott, what are you doing here?"

She stopped as he opened the van's back doors. Looking inside, Lilley sucked in her breath, her hand over her mouth.

There was a knight in the back of the van. A medieval knight in full armor.

The knight pushed up his visor, and she saw Alessandro's dark, handsome face. His warm black eyes were glowing with such adoration that her heart caught in her throat.

She exhaled, tilting her head to look up at him in the back of the van. She'd slipped on the ice and fallen into some kind of coma. She was dreaming. That was the only explanation for Alessandro wearing armor in Minnesota, standing in the back of a van, in front of a snowy white lake.

"What are you doing here?" she breathed.

"I've come for you," Alessandro said, his eyes looking straight into hers. "I was a coward and a fool. Come back to me, Lilley," he whispered. "Let me show you I can be the husband you always dreamed of."

Tears filled her eyes as she went towards the van. With a scrape of metal, he hopped off the van's edge. But the heavy weight of his armor seemed to take him off guard. His visor snapped shut with a loud clang as he fell heavily on the snowy road.

Lilley was beside him in an instant, kneeling as she gathered him in her arms. "Are you all right?" she said anxiously. "Are you hurt?"

Sprawled out across the road, Alessandro didn't move. Dear God, what if a sharp blow in that tin-can suit had knocked him out? Lilley's hands shook as she pulled up his visor.

But she saw he was silently laughing. She fell back on her haunches in wonder.

"Oh my God. You've totally made a fool of yourself," she breathed in awe. She shook her head, suddenly smiling. "Dressing up in armor? What were you thinking?"

"I've never seen any angel half as beautiful as you." He lifted his armored hand to touch her cheek. "I would battle far more than armor to be in the arms of the woman I love. I would slay dragons for you," he whispered.

What had he said? *What had he just said?* That he loved her? She felt her heart expand and bend and swell until it was big enough to swallow the whole world. She looked down, her lashes brushing shyly against her cheek. "Come on," she murmured. "I'll help you up."

But the armor was even heavier than she'd thought. First Abbott, then her father, had to come and help him to stand up.

"Hello, sir," Alessandro said to her father, smiling.

"I don't think we've ever met in person. I'm Alessandro Caetani."

Walton blinked, his eyes wide. He looked at Lilley. "This is your husband?" he asked faintly.

Unable to speak, she nodded, then turned back to Alessandro.

Behind her, she heard her father give a low whistle. "What a merger this will make." But as she turned with a scowl, Walton quickly said to Abbott, "Care for a drink at the gatehouse? Something to warm your blood?"

"You bet."

Lilley and Alessandro stood alone on the snowy, empty road. A wind blew off the lake, whipping through her hair, but she no longer felt the cold. She felt warm all over, filled with light.

"What possessed you to do this?" she whispered, putting her hand on the side of his shiny helmet. "This crazy thing?"

He moved his metal glove over her hand. "I wanted to show you I'm sorry," he said in a low voice. "I never should have asked if the baby was mine."

She swallowed, looking down.

"I shouldn't have let a single white lie keep me from trusting you for thousands of reasons," he said. "One most of all." He lifted her chin with his finger. "I love you, Lilley."

The winter sun burst through the gray winter clouds. A beam of light caught his armor, making him sparkle like diamonds.

"It took losing you in Rome to make me realize you were right. I was afraid. Now, the only thing that scares me is losing you. I'll do anything to win you back, Lilley," he whispered. His dark eyes met hers. "Absolutely anything."

The white, gray and black of winter suddenly filled with

the beautiful pinks and greens of spring in Lilley's eyes. He loved her. And their lives together were only beginning.

"I love you, Alessandro," she whispered, throwing her arms around his hard, cold armor.

For a long moment, they held each other on the quiet road. Then Lilley pulled back, her forehead furrowed as she glanced back at the huge semitruck, still parked behind her car. "But why did you bring that?"

"Oh." Alessandro gave her a sudden grin. "I was afraid I'd kill us both if I actually tried to sit on a horse, so I made other plans." Looking at the truck's driver, he motioned with his hand. The driver hopped out and went to the back of the truck. She heard the distant roar of an engine, and then a vintage Cadillac De Ville—in hot pink—rolled off the ramp to park beside them.

As the driver disappeared for his drink at the gatehouse, Lilley walked slowly around the Cadillac, her mouth open.

It was a classic convertible from the 1960s, the exact same fuchsia as the ball gown she'd worn to their reception in Rome. "What is that?"

He grinned at her. "Our getaway vehicle, *cara*. To ride off into the sunset."

She looked back at him. "And what if you hadn't found me? What if I'd already been gone?"

"Then I would have sold my business and driven all over the country, looking for you," he said gravely behind her. "Everywhere. Until you were in my arms."

She gasped a laugh. "Dressed as a knight? Driving a hot-pink Cadillac? The paparazzi would have had a field day! They'd have said you'd lost your mind!"

"I have," he said softly. "Along with my heart. All I want to do, for the rest of my life, is make a fool of myself. Over you."

Tears fell from Lilley's lashes. Standing on her tiptoes,

she held up his cold visor with her fingertips and kissed him. Her husband kissed her back fervently, reverently, passionately. They had been standing in the snowy road for hours, or perhaps minutes, when she finally pulled away for air. His black eyes glimmered down at her. She had no idea if the tears on his cheeks were hers or his. But what did it matter? They were one.

"Thank you for being a fool," she said, her heart welling with joy. "Thank you for making all my childhood dreams come true."

He looked down at her, his handsome face glowing with love and shining with the strength of steel. "And thank you," he whispered, stroking her cheek, "for making me want to dance."

They danced at their first anniversary party the following September. As Alessandro led Lilley to the dance floor in their Sonoma ballroom, he whirled her in a circle, making her colorful skirts twirl. She heard a soft *"awww"* from their fifty or so guests, just family and friends, including a deep sigh from her father, who was holding his baby grandson, Teo.

Alessandro pulled her close on the dance floor. Lilley looked up at him breathlessly as he swayed against her.

"My, oh my," she murmured, fluttering her eyelashes. "You're quite the dancer. Have you been taking lessons?"

"You know I have. You've been taking them with me." He twirled her, then gave a mischievous grin. "No broken toes in sight."

"Because you're leading me."

"No," he whispered, pulling her close. "We lead each other."

Lilley looked up at him, dazed with happiness. Their lives over the past ten months had been filled with one joy after the next. They now split their time evenly between Rome and San Francisco, where Lilley had started her fledgling jewelry company, Lilley Caetani Limited. Her first collection had already been a great success at the international jewelry trade show in San Francisco.

So much had changed in the last year. Lilley was still awed to think how, just fifteen months before, she'd attended the trade show as a guest with a dream. Now she was an exhibitor. With Carrie's financial backing, her fledgling company had already made a splash in the trade dailies and orders had started to flood in from around the world. She would have to hire more employees soon. Lilley often traveled with her husband and their baby to Singapore or Norway or Namibia, getting inspiration for her designs. She happily traveled wherever the continuing expansion of Caetani Worldwide took them.

There was only one of Alessandro's potential acquisitions that she absolutely wouldn't allow. Alessandro had made multiple offers to buy her company and merge it with Caetani-Hainsbury Worldwide, which she'd refused in no uncertain terms.

"Sorry, my company is not for sale," she'd said breezily. "I'm not interested in being part of some soulless, heartless conglomerate—"

"Hey!"

She'd grinned. "Sorry. But my company is small and I like it that way."

He'd tilted his head thoughtfully. "We could double your growth projections, especially in Europe. And there might be other fringe benefits as well," he'd murmured. "Think about it."

"Not for sale at any price," she said primly.

He'd lifted a wicked eyebrow. "Oh? Are you sure?" And he'd pulled her into bed. Lilley sighed at the memory. Of course, she would never sell him her company, but it was sure fun to let him try.

Tonight's anniversary party in Sonoma had been Alessandro's idea. He'd planned the whole thing from start to finish. The wine harvest looked to be excellent this year, and all their friends and family beamed as they held up glasses, toasting Alessandro and Lilley on the occasion of their one-year anniversary.

Olivia Bianchi, alas, was not in attendance. Lilley hadn't even tried to invite her. She'd learned she couldn't please everyone, and she didn't need to impress anyone. The only people she cared about were right here: her friends Nadia and Jeremy, who were now engaged. And her family. Her cousin had come all the way from France, along with Carrie and their baby. Alessandro and Théo might never be friends, but they'd managed to achieve a sort of détente. They'd moved their rivalry to the realms of basketball and extreme sports like skydiving. Great, Lilley thought with an inward groan. Just what she needed. A husband and a cousin who were fighting to jump out of a perfectly good plane.

Even her father was doing better, now that he'd retired and given up day-to-day management of Hainsbury's to Alessandro. The company was on track to merge with Caetani Worldwide, and all of it would be left in trust to Walton's grandchildren. Her father had moved to San Francisco to be closer to them, and to focus on getting healthier. And, like a miracle, he seemed stronger every day. Especially on the days he played with his grandson.

Friends and family were all that mattered, Lilley thought. Not fame. Not the glitter of wealth. The only diamonds that mattered were the ones in the bright smiles of the people she loved. As her dance with Alessandro ended and their friends applauded wildly around them, her father brought the baby to the dance floor.

"I think the kid wants to dance," Walton said gruffly.

A new song began, and Alessandro took baby Teo in his arms. Nuzzling his chubby cheeks and downy head, he looked down at his son tenderly. "I can teach him."

Lilley's heart swelled as Alessandro held their cooing baby against his tuxedo jacket, and wrapped his other arm around her. Smiling, she leaned her head against her husband's strong shoulders as they swayed together in time to the music. Listening to Teo's baby giggle and Alessandro's joyful baritone laugh, Lilley suddenly knew their lives together would always be happy like this. Their days would shine with endless brilliant facets, in a hodgepodge of sparkling gemstones and tarnished brass, rough rock crystals and gleaming platinum, that when welded together...formed a family.

* * * * *

Special Offers

Every month we put together collections and longer reads written by your favourite authors.

Here are some of next month's highlights—and don't miss our fabulous discount online!

On sale 6th June

On sale 6th June

On sale 6th June

Save 20%
on all Special Releases

Hot reads!

These 3-in-1s will certainly get you feeling
hot under the collar with their desert
locations, billionaire tycoons and
playboy princes.

**Now available at
www.millsandboon.co.uk/offers**

THE
CHATSFIELD®

Join our *EXCLUSIVE* eBook club

FROM JUST £1.99 A MONTH!

Never miss a book again with our hassle-free eBook subscription.

★ Pick how many titles you want from each series with our flexible subscription

★ Your titles are delivered to your device on the first of every month

★ Zero risk, zero obligation!

There really is nothing standing in the way of you and your favourite books!

Start your eBook subscription today at www.millsandboon.co.uk/subscribe

The World of Mills & Boon

There's a Mills & Boon® series that's perfect for you. There are ten different series to choose from and new titles every month, so whether you're looking for glamorous seduction, Regency rakes, homespun heroes or sizzling erotica, we'll give you plenty of inspiration for your next read.

By Request

Back by popular demand!
12 stories every month

Cherish™

Experience the ultimate rush of falling in love.
12 new stories every month

INTRIGUE...

A seductive combination of danger and desire...
7 new stories every month

Desire™

Passionate and dramatic love stories
6 new stories every month

nocturne™

An exhilarating underworld of dark desires
3 new stories every month

For exclusive member offers go to
millsandboon.co.uk/subscribe

Which series will you try next?